Experience the grand dame of ~~...~~

(*New York Daily News*)

No Choice But Seduction
A MALORY NOVEL

"[Lindsey's] signature blend of witty writing, charmingly unique characters, and a sexy love story continues to be irresistible."

—*Booklist*

"In typical Lindsey fashion, untold secrets, hidden relationships, fascinating family interaction, steamy passion, and an intricate plot add to the mix."

—*Library Journal*

"A delightfully fun and engaging story guaranteed to leave readers smiling . . . Even if you've never read a Malory book, you'll enjoy this one."

—*The Columbia (SC) State*

Temptation's Darling

"A fun, light romance . . . full of witty banter, drama, action, mystery, humor, and unexpected twists."

—*Harlequin Junkie*

Marry Me by Sundown

"With humor, a lively pace, appealing characters, a dash of danger, and solid historical detail, Lindsey's latest provides a compelling picture of the Old West, in the author's inimitable style."

—*Library Journal*

Beautiful Tempest
A MALORY NOVEL

"With its lively, bantering dialogue and sharp-edged repartee between hero and heroine, along with the rising sexual tension, readers know they are in for a fast-paced treat."

—*RT Book Reviews* (Top Pick, 4½ stars)

Make Me Love You

"[Lindsey] never disappoints, writing love stories that get to the heart of what love can and should be. . . . Compassionate, powerful, and filled with surprises."

—*RT Book Reviews* (Top Pick, 4½ stars)

Wildfire in His Arms

"If readers need to remember why they are Lindsey fans, she delivers. . . . She incorporates sassy dialogue, plenty of verbal sparring, lots of heat, and a bit of humor, all in perfect proportions."

—*RT Book Reviews* (4½ stars)

Stormy Persuasion
A MALORY NOVEL

"This is the story Malory pirate fans have been waiting for. . . . There's adventure, sensuality, battles, storms, family high jinks, and rapier wit. . . . Lindsey delivers!"

—*RT Book Reviews*

One Heart to Win

"A character-rich, action-packed Western . . . Simmered in vengeance and shot through with humor."

—*Library Journal*

Let Love Find You

"Filled with Lindsey's trademark humor, sensuality, and emotional intensity . . . Lindsey knows what readers want and makes us believe in love."

—*RT Book Reviews* (Top Pick, 4½ stars)

When Passion Rules

"A whimsical, magical tale . . . perfect for a lazy summer afternoon."

—*Library Journal*

That Perfect Someone
A MALORY NOVEL

"A bit of heaven . . . love, laughter, adventure, and passion collide."

—*RT Book Reviews* (Top Pick, 4½ stars)

A Rogue of My Own

"Filled with sexual tension . . . Engagingly satisfying from start to finish."

—*Single Titles*

The Devil Who Tamed Her

"Simply riveting . . . Excellent."

—*The Charleston Gazette*

Captive of My Desires
A MALORY NOVEL

"It's pretty fabulous when Johanna Lindsey's new romance hits the shelves each summer. And when it's a book about the Malory clan, it's fantastic."

—*Detroit Free Press*

Marriage Most Scandalous

"Johanna Lindsey . . . once again gives her fans a hero to fall in love with."

—*Duluth News Tribune*

A Loving Scoundrel

"Lindsey stirs it up with so much energy and spirit that it's hard not to find it delicious."

—*Publishers Weekly*

A Man to Call My Own

"Twists and turns galore and a Wild West setting make for a delightful romp by veteran romance writer Lindsey."

—*Booklist*

MORE THAN SIXTY MILLION COPIES OF JOHANNA LINDSEY'S BOOKS IN PRINT!

MORE THAN FIFTY NOVELS FROM THE "IRRESISTIBLE" (*BOOKLIST*) JOHANNA LINDSEY!

ALSO BY JOHANNA LINDSEY
AND POCKET BOOKS

Temptation's Darling

Marry Me by Sundown

Make Me Love You

Wildfire in His Arms

One Heart to Win

Let Love Find You

When Passion Rules

A Rogue of My Own

The Devil Who Tamed Her

Marriage Most Scandalous

A Man to Call My Own

MALORY-ANDERSON FAMILY SERIES

Beautiful Tempest

Stormy Persuasion

That Perfect Someone

No Choice But Seduction

Captive of My Desires

A Loving Scoundrel

JOHANNA LINDSEY

A Malory Novel

No Choice But Seduction

POCKET BOOKS

NEW YORK LONDON TORONTO SYDNEY NEW DELHI

The sale of this book without its cover is unauthorized. If you purchased this book without a cover, you should be aware that it was reported to the publisher as "unsold and destroyed." Neither the author nor the publisher has received payment for the sale of this "stripped book."

Pocket Books
An Imprint of Simon & Schuster, LLC
1230 Avenue of the Americas
New York, NY 10020

This book is a work of fiction. Any references to historical events, real people, or real places are used fictitiously. Other names, characters, places, and events are products of the author's imagination, and any resemblance to actual events or places or persons, living or dead, is entirely coincidental.

Copyright © 2008 by Johanna Lindsey

All rights reserved, including the right to reproduce this book or portions thereof in any form whatsoever. For information, address Pocket Books Subsidiary Rights Department, 1230 Avenue of the Americas, New York, NY 10020.

This Pocket Books paperback edition April 2024

POCKET and colophon are registered trademarks of Simon & Schuster, LLC

Simon & Schuster: Celebrating 100 Years of Publishing in 2024

For information about special discounts for bulk purchases, please contact Simon & Schuster Special Sales at 1-866-506-1949 or business@simonandschuster.com.

The Simon & Schuster Speakers Bureau can bring authors to your live event. For more information or to book an event, contact the Simon & Schuster Speakers Bureau at 1-866-248-3049 or visit our website at www.simonspeakers.com.

Interior design by Erika R. Genova

Manufactured in the United States of America

10 9 8 7 6 5 4 3 2 1

ISBN 978-1-6680-5004-0
ISBN 978-1-4165-7968-7 (ebook)

For the new angel in the family,
Angelina Jo-Helen Haunani Lindsey

No Choice
But Seduction

prologue

LEAVING HOME TO visit his family.

Boyd Anderson found something distinctly annoying about that phrase. Yet it was true. In the last eight years, every time he sailed to Bridgeport, Connecticut, in the hopes of catching one of his four older brothers at home for a visit, too, not one of them had ever been there. He'd had to sail elsewhere to find them.

Captains all of them, Boyd's brothers sailed around the world, but they all used to come home eagerly because their only sister, Georgina, would be there waiting for them. But Georgina had married an Englishman, Lord James Malory, and now she lived across the ocean from Connecticut, and that's where Boyd had to sail if he wanted to see her. Which was one good reason why Boyd had been thinking about settling down in London himself.

He hadn't made a firm decision yet, but he was definitely leaning toward it for a number of reasons, but mainly because the Anderson clan now went to London where their sister lived more often than they returned home. And Georgina wasn't the only Anderson who had married into the Malory clan. Boyd's older brother Warren had amazed the family by doing the same thing when he married Lady Amy Malory. While Warren still sailed for at least half of each year, taking his family with him, he spent the other half in London so his children could get to know their many, *many* cousins, aunts and uncles, great-aunts and great-uncles, and their grandparents.

Putting down roots would be a major change in Boyd's life. It would mean giving up the sea for good after having sailed since he was eighteen. Thirty-four now, he'd made his home on his ship, *The Oceanus,* for fifteen years! No one knew better than he did how much he'd prefer a home that didn't rock.

He'd been considering leaving the sea for other reasons also. Seeing Georgina and his brother Warren both happily married to members of the Malory clan, Boyd had more and more been craving that kind of happiness for himself. That was not to say he wanted to settle down with a Malory woman, even if there were any left of a marriageable age. Hell no. That would mean facing a solid wall of Malory opposition, which he'd rather not do. But he wanted a wife. He was ready. If his association with the Malory clan had taught him anything, it was that marriage could be a wonderful thing. He just hadn't found the right woman yet.

He was also heartily tired of short, unmemorable relationships with women. His brother Drew might be happy to have a sweetheart in every port, but Drew was a carefree charmer who easily formed those little attachments and thus had women to return to—all over the world!

It wasn't that easy for Boyd. He didn't like making promises he wouldn't keep, nor did he make decisions quickly, at least not important ones such as picking the future Mrs. Boyd Anderson. And he didn't like spreading his affections among many women. Was he simply a romantic? He didn't know, he just knew that romancing a variety of women didn't satisfy him the way it seemed to satisfy Drew. What Boyd really wanted was to have just one woman by his side for the rest of his life.

He knew why he hadn't even come close to finding her yet. Traveling as much as he did, he had to keep his dalliances short and fairly impersonal. He needed to spend more time with a woman he was attracted to, really get to know her. But when did a sailor ever get to spend more than a few days in any one port? If he settled in London, he'd have all the time he needed to find that one special woman meant just for him. She was out there. He knew she was. He just needed to be in one place long enough to find her and woo her.

Boyd looked out over the busy docks and the town of Bridgeport beyond and felt a pang of sadness. This might be the last time he was ever here. The big house the Andersons had grown up in had been empty since Georgina had left. There were friends and neighbors here whom he'd known all his life and would miss, but family was where the heart was, and Georgina had been the heart of his family since their parents had died.

Boyd's captain, Tyrus Reynolds, joined him at the rail. Boyd didn't captain his own ship and never had. His family thought he was too free-spirited to want to take on that sort of command, even though he'd always sailed with his ship. He'd never disabused them of that notion, even though it was not correct.

"If you weren't in such a hurry to get to England," Tyrus grumbled, "we could have at least detoured a bit to one of the Southern ports for a cargo of cotton instead of taking on passengers here."

Boyd grinned down at the older man he called a friend as well as captain. Boyd was a bit under six feet himself, but Tyrus was much shorter and had a crusty temperament.

"You don't consider a load of passengers a good cargo?" Boyd asked.

Tyrus snorted. "When I have to entertain them for the whole trip? *And* deal with their complaints! Rum and cotton don't complain."

"But we're looking at about the same profit, if all of the cabins are filled. And it's certainly not the first time we've taken on passengers. You're just out of sorts because you're remembering the last time when that hefty grandmother kept trying to seduce you."

Tyrus groaned. "Don't remind me. I never mentioned it to you, but she actually snuck into my cabin and right into my bed. Scared the bejesus out of me, waking up to her snuggled to my side."

Boyd burst out laughing. "I hope you didn't take advantage of her."

Tyrus's snort was much more meaningful this time. Boyd glanced away so Tyrus wouldn't see his grin. Damn, he wished he could have seen that, but just imagining it made him want to laugh again.

Boyd's eyes, caught by the bright lavender and pink colors on the dock below, stayed on the tall woman wearing a lavender skirt and a pink blouse. The sleeves of the blouse were rolled up. It was midsummer and definitely a warm day. With the back of one arm, the woman wiped her brow, knocking her bonnet off her head. She had black hair, but he'd already seen that in the long braid she wore down her back. He wished she would turn around instead of just giving him a view of her back, not that that side of her was unattractive. The bonnet merely fell to her shoulder, caught by the bonnet ribbons tied around her neck, but she didn't bother to lift it back to her head because she was engrossed in what she was doing.

He was amazed. She was feeding the seagulls and every other bird in the area that noticed her tossing out food from the basket on her arm. There was nothing wrong with that. He fed birds and other wild animals himself on occasion. But she was doing it on a busy dock!

A flock of birds was surrounding her, and more kept coming. She was becoming a nuisance. People were having to walk far around her flock. Some stopped briefly to watch her, fortunately, without blocking his own view. One dockhand tried to shoo off the birds to clear his path, but they merely moved closer to their benefactor. The dockhand said something to her. She turned and smiled at him. And Boyd was dumbstruck by the front view of her.

She wasn't just pretty. To his eyes she was exquisite. Young, probably in her early twenties. Skin lightly tanned from the summer sun, black bangs curved toward her temples, a narrow, beautiful face, and dimples when she smiled. And she was buxom. God, curves like that usually only showed up in his more pleasant dreams!

"Close your mouth, lad, you're drooling," Tyrus said.

"We may have to delay our departure."

Tyrus had followed his gaze. "The devil we will, and besides, I do believe she's one of our passengers. At least I saw her on deck earlier. I'll go check with Johnson if you like. He signed on the passengers for this trip."

"Please do," Boyd said without taking his eyes off her. "If he says yes, I may have to kiss him."

"I'll make sure I don't mention that to him," Tyrus said, laughing as he moved off.

Boyd continued to watch the young woman, savoring the view. How ironic that he'd just been thinking about finding a wife and there stood a perfect candidate. Was it fate? And damn, she had some remarkably luscious curves.

He was going to meet her. If she wasn't a passenger, then he'd just stay behind and let *The Oceanus* sail without him. If she was a passenger, he had a feeling it was going to be the most pleasant journey of his life. But he didn't go down to the dock just yet. Along with the excitement he was feeling came a little nervousness. What if she was only sweet on the eyes? What if she had a bad temperament? God, that would be too cruel. But it couldn't be. Anyone who would take the time to feed wild birds had to have some compassion in her. And compassion usually went hand in hand with kindness and a pleasant disposition. Of course it did, he assured himself. Damn, this better not be the one time it didn't!

She stopped tossing food to the birds. He, too, heard the sound that had drawn her attention elsewhere. From his position on the ship, he could see an injured bird lying on top of a high stack of crates. He'd noticed it there earlier, but hadn't realized it was injured or he would have gone down to collect it and see if Philips, the ship's doctor, could help it before they sailed.

Boyd liked animals, too, and always tried to help those in need. As a child, he'd brought home every stray animal he found, much to his mother's exasperation. Apparently this young woman was of a like mind, since she was now searching for the bird that was making the plaintive noises. Boyd figured the bird was making a racket because it was trying to get down to the food she was spreading around and couldn't. He doubted the young woman could see the bird from where she was on the dock, but she was circling the crates, looking for it, and finally she glanced up.

Boyd hurried down to the docks. He knew she was going to try to climb up those crates to reach the bird, which would be dangerous. The crates were stacked five high, which was at least twice her height, and instead of being tied down as they should have been, they were stacked in a pyramid, with the larger ones at the bottom so the stack would be less likely to topple over.

Boyd arrived too late. She'd already climbed up to the third crate, her toes perched on the edge, and had reached the bird. She was trying now to coax it into the basket.

Boyd held his tongue, afraid that if he said anything, it would distract her and she'd fall. For the same reason, he didn't try to climb up and yank her down. But he wasn't about to let her get hurt. He wasn't leaving until she was safely on the ground again.

The bird, lured by the food in the basket, finally toppled into it. The young woman had managed to get up there with the basket hooked to her arm, but now that the basket had a live occupant, it wasn't going to be as easy getting down. She must have realized that as she glanced down at her feet.

"Don't move," Boyd called out. "Give me a moment and I'll take that basket for you, then help you down."

She turned her head and looked down at him. "Thank you!" she called back, dazzling him with her smile. "I had no idea this was going to be much more difficult than it first appeared."

He used a small, empty barrel as a stepping-stone to reach the top of the first crate. He didn't need to go any higher to take the basket from her, and he merely jumped back down to set it aside. But she didn't wait for his assistance. She was lowering herself to the second crate when her hold slipped and she tumbled backward. Boyd moved quickly and caught her in his arms.

Her eyes were wide with shock. So were his. What an unexpected boon. He couldn't seem to move. He looked down into her dark emerald-green eyes, and her face. . . . God, his eyes had deceived him. She was much prettier up close. And holding her cradled in his arms like that, with the fingers of one hand touching one of her breasts and his arm wrapped around her derriere, his body responded, and all he could think about was kissing her.

Unnerved that he could desire a woman so intensely and so quickly, he set her down instantly. Away from him.

She straightened her lavender skirt before she glanced back at him. "Thank you so much. That was—alarming."

"You are most welcome."

With a friendly nod she introduced herself. "I'm Katey Tyler."

"Boyd Anderson. I own *The Oceanus*."

"Do you? Well, I own one of the cabins on it, at least until we reach England." She grinned.

God, there were those adorable dimples again. His body wouldn't calm down. He was surprised he was even capable of conversation—if he could call it that. What the devil had induced him to mention that he owned the ship? He never did that! It smacked of bragging—or trying too hard to impress.

"Is Katey short for Catherine?" he got out.

"No, my mother liked to keep things simple. She knew she was going to call me Katey, so she figured why not just skip the Catherine part and name me that."

He smiled. She looked like a Katey somehow. Sleeves rolled up, hair braided instead of tightly bound in a severe coiffure, climbing dockside crates! Boyd had a very, very strong feeling that he'd found his future wife.

"I'll take the bird," Boyd offered. "Our doctor can tend to it."

"What a perfect idea! I think it's broken its right wing. I was going to look for an older child who would like to care for it."

Boyd's smile deepened. She was beautiful *and* she had

a kind heart. "I can't tell you how delighted I am, Katey Tyler, that you're going to be sailing with us."

She blinked at him uncertainly. "Well—thank you. You can't imagine how much I've been looking forward to this—oh!"

All of a sudden she ran off. Boyd turned around and saw her running toward a child who had wandered over to the edge of the dock. Only a few years old, the child was precariously leaning over, looking down at the water, and was in danger of falling in. Child in hand now, Katey was looking all around her, probably for the child's parents, then she marched off into the crowd.

Boyd started to follow her, but decided against it. She might think he was being too forward. She'd seemed startled when he'd expressed his pleasure at sailing with her. Had he been too direct, perhaps even improper? Well, he wasn't exactly used to the ways of courting. But he was sure he could be as charming as his brother Drew if he put his mind to it.

After taking a thorough ribbing from Philips about his having to waste his doctoring skills on a tasty snack, Boyd returned to the deck. The gangplank hadn't been lifted yet; the last few supplies were still being loaded. And Katey Tyler was on board.

His eyes, then his feet, went right to her. She was standing at the rail near the plank, gazing at the town as he had earlier done. He stopped right behind her.

"We meet again."

He'd startled her, possibly with the husky tone of his voice. She turned around so swiftly, she brushed against him. No, he'd been standing too close, smelling the lilac scent of her hair, so she couldn't have avoided the collision. But she was blushing now as she tried to move away and couldn't with the rail behind her. Loath to lose the contact,

Boyd was a bit slow in stepping back to give her room.

"You don't hail from Bridgeport, do you?" he said.

"How did you know?"

"Because I'm from Bridgeport. Believe me, if you had lived here, I would have been coming home much more often."

His words and his smile might have been a bit too bold because she was obviously flustered. She glanced down, then started to turn back toward the dock, but something else caught her attention.

"Who would have thought they'd be so troublesome," a carrot-haired young woman said as she came up to them, holding a toddler in each hand. "We're going to have to hover over them if we bring them up to the deck again."

Katey bent down and picked up one of the children and set it on her hip, ruffling its hair. Boyd couldn't tell if the tot was a boy or a girl.

"That's not a bad idea, Grace. They are a bit too inquisitive at this age," Katey said.

"Well, here, give her back. I'll get them settled below-decks before we sail."

"Yours?" Boyd asked as soon as the other woman walked off with the two children.

He was joking, but Katey glanced at him with a frown on her pretty face. Then her eyes widened and she said, "Yes! Actually, I didn't think to mention it, but I'm married and on my way to join my husband in England. I should go and help my maid. Those two darlings can be a handful."

She rushed off. Boyd was left standing there poleaxed, no doubt about it.

Tyrus came up to him, clapping a hand on his shoulder. "Ain't that always the way? The good ones are already taken."

Boyd shook his head and groaned. It was going to be a long voyage.

one

THE NOTE WAS delivered by a scruffy child who didn't know he had the wrong house. The mistake wasn't his fault. He hadn't been told there were many different Malory houses in London. He'd come to the first one he'd been directed to, pleased that it hadn't taken long to earn the few coppers in his pocket. And just as he'd been told to do, he'd run off before Henry could question him.

Henry and Artie, two crusty old sea dogs, had shared the job of butler at James Malory's house ever since James had retired from his life at sea and they'd both retired with him. But recently James had gone back to sea, briefly, to rescue his brother-in-law Drew Anderson, who'd got himself into a coil when according to one of his crewmen who'd managed to escape, pirates had stolen his ship right out of London harbor! With him on it! Henry and Artie had tossed a coin to see who would sail with James for the rescue. Henry had lost.

Henry tossed the note without reading it onto the mountainous pile of calling cards and invitations that had come in from people who didn't know the Malorys of this particular household weren't in residence. A normal butler would never have let the tray on the hall table overflow with invitations and letters. But in the eight years since

Henry and Artie had begun sharing the job, neither of them had learned how to be a proper butler.

That afternoon when Boyd Anderson returned to the Malory house in Berkeley Square, he found the note on his tray, along with a few other cards that had slid off the larger pile next to it. He didn't usually have a tray of his own in his sister Georgina's house, but then he usually only visited for a week or two, never as long as several months as this visit had turned out to be. Nor was it the first time Georgina's mail had got mixed up with his.

Despite having given it a lot more thought, Boyd still hadn't made up his mind yet about settling in England. But that wasn't why he was still here. He hadn't returned to sea yet because he was doing his sister a favor. Although Georgina had married into the large Malory family and any one of her numerous in-laws would have been delighted to take care of her children while she was gone, Georgina's seven-year-old daughter, Jacqueline, balked at joining her young twin siblings at the country home of their cousin Lady Regina Eden, because she didn't want to be that far away from her best friend and cousin, Judith. Other Malorys in London could have taken her, but since Boyd was staying at her London house, Georgina had asked him to keep an eye on Jacqueline until he sailed again.

He would have preferred to go along for the rescue. That would have been a fine bit of work to tease his brother Drew about. But he had, in fact, done Georgina another good turn by not insisting on going, since her husband didn't get along well with any of her brothers, himself included. The man didn't even get along with his *own* brothers. And there was no way he and James Malory wouldn't come to blows if they ended up on a ship together. Besides, the look on James's face when Boyd had suggested accompanying him, well, it had made Boyd glad he had an excuse to stay behind after all.

"We all know where she'd rather stay," Georgina had remarked. "But Roslynn mentioned in passing that she *might* be enceinte again, so she needs peace and quiet in her household just now, which won't be the case with Judy and Jack in residence. When you're ready to sail will be soon enough to deposit her there."

Roslynn Malory turned out not to be pregnant. Boyd ended up not sailing as expected. And Jack, as her father had named her at birth, was happy enough where she was, since she still got to visit with her cousin Judith as often as she liked.

Boyd wasn't exactly worried about Drew, anyway. Georgina did enough worrying for all of them. But Boyd knew his brother well and had no doubt that he'd extricate himself from whatever trouble he'd gotten into long before Georgina and her husband arrived to help. Hell, considering how long they'd been gone, he was beginning to suspect they hadn't even caught up to Drew's ship yet!

Georgina hadn't expected Boyd to stay in London this long. No one had, himself included. But when his ship, *The Oceanus*, returned from the short run he'd sent her on, instead of leaving with her, he sent her off again. And gave more thought to giving up the sea for good.

The Andersons' family business, Skylark Shipping, also had an office in London now. While the family had avoided England for many years due to the old war and the hard feelings that had ensued from that, they were once again firmly entrenched in trading with the English. In fact, now that England was central to all of their newly acquired routes, the London office had grown considerably in the last eight years. Boyd wouldn't half mind taking over the running of it.

Become landlocked? God, why didn't he just do it already? Because oddly enough, he loved the sea. He just hated what it did to him.

Georgina had introduced him to London society more than once on his visits here. He even kept a wardrobe at her house specifically for his London stays that was more appropriate for a gentleman, since the English dressed quite a bit more fancily than sailors did! He didn't go excessive in frilly cravats or lacy cuffs as some of them did. In fact, he took a cue from his brother-in-law, James—well-tailored, but subdued and even open-collared. And he had a few velvet jackets that spruced him up for evening social events.

On this extended visit he'd been receiving invitations to balls and soirées from Georgina's acquaintances that knew he was still in town, and he'd occasionally accepted. He wasn't actively looking for a wife, but if the right woman showed up, that would be incentive to settle down. He'd thought he'd found her. Katey Tyler would have been the perfect woman for him—if she wasn't already taken!

God, how did he let *her* sneak into his mind again? Once she did, it took days and a good bout of drinking to get her out again. But only briefly. She was somewhere in his thoughts more often than not. It seemed that knowing he couldn't have her because she already had a husband made him want her even more! He'd never been able to figure out what exactly it was about Katey Tyler that had twisted him inside out on that voyage. She wasn't even the kind of woman that usually caught his eye.

She was too tall for one thing, only a few inches shorter than he was. He preferred to feel tall where his women were concerned, and Mrs. Tyler didn't give him that feeling when she stood eye to eye with him. But it didn't matter. One look at her lushly abundant curves and nothing else mattered.

She could talk a lot—about nothing. That was a remarkable feat. Even more remarkable, he'd never found that annoying! Her dimples often made her seem like she was smiling when she wasn't. And she contradicted herself a lot, which could be quite confusing, but he actually found that endearing. It made her seem charmingly absentminded. Her nose was slim, almost patrician, her brows rather thin, her mouth—he could never think about her mouth without becoming aroused.

No woman had ever affected him like that before, or stayed in his thoughts this long.

Gabrielle Brooks had caught his interest though. What a relief that had been, assuring him that he wasn't a lost cause! She could have banished Katey from his mind—well, that had been his original hope. Gabby had arrived in London at about the same time he did and had become Georgina and James's houseguest because her father, an old friend of James's, had asked James to sponsor her for the Season.

A pretty thing, Gabby could have turned his thoughts toward marriage if Drew hadn't been taken with her, too. Not that his carefree brother ever intended to get leg-shackled, as the English put it. But Gabby seemed to be fascinated with Drew, too, so Boyd had stopped thinking about her as a possible wife. Besides, she was the daughter of a pirate, as it turned out, and Boyd would have had a hard time getting past that simple fact. Pirates were the nemesis of honest sailors.

He glanced at the two invitations on his tray that were actually for him and carefully put back the four that were addressed to his sister. He opened the folded note since he couldn't tell whom that was for. He had to read it twice before the meaning sank in. And then he was bolting up the stairs shouting his niece's name.

When he found Jacqueline in her room, the color returned to his cheeks and his heart slowly returned to its normal beat. He read the note once more.

> I have your daughter. Start gathering a fortune
> if you want her back. You'll be told where to
> bring it.

Boyd shoved the note in his pocket, deciding it had obviously been delivered to the wrong house. He wondered if any of Georgina's neighbors had daughters. He didn't know, but he'd have to take that note to the authorities.

"What's wrong, Uncle?"

Glancing at Jack's woebegone expression, Boyd replied, "I could ask you the same thing."

She started to shrug, but then she sighed and said, "Judy's riding her first horse today in Hyde Park. Not a pony, a real horse Uncle Tony bought her."

"And you weren't invited to watch?" he guessed.

"I was, but—I think only Uncle Tony should share that with her. He's so been looking forward to it."

Boyd managed to stifle a grin. His niece was only seven years old, but sometimes she amazed him with her insight and consideration for others. She obviously wanted to be in the park watching her best friend ride her first real horse, but she'd taken the girl's father's feelings into account instead.

Boyd had known about the outing and had been afraid that Jack would feel left out. He'd actually considered buying her a horse as well, but then he realized his sister might have a fit if he did. Actually, it was James's likely reaction that had decided him against it. If Sir Anthony had been looking forward to seeing his daughter's excitement upon riding her first real horse, James was probably looking forward to the same.

"Besides," Jacqueline added. "Judy's coming over tonight to spend the weekend, so I'll be hearing—"

She didn't finish because Henry burst in completely out of breath, as if he'd run up the stairs just as Boyd had done. Without saying what had brought him upstairs in such a hurry, he glanced at the daughter of the house then motioned for Boyd to come out into the corridor. Henry knew that small children had big ears, and this was one thing he was going to make absolutely sure Jack didn't overhear.

"A messenger just came from Sir Anthony," Henry whispered urgently in Boyd's ear. "'E's asked for every man in the 'ouse to come and 'elp 'im search for 'is daughter. She's gone missing in the park."

"Damn," Boyd said, and pulled Henry downstairs with him before he showed the old salt the note.

It made sense now. The note hadn't been delivered to the wrong house on the street, just the wrong *Malory* house, which mistake happened frequently with eight separate Malory households in the city.

"A search isn't going to be necessary," Boyd said grimly. "But I need to get this note to Sir Anthony immediately."

"Bleedin' 'ell, the cap'n is going to be furious 'e ain't 'ere to 'elp."

Boyd didn't doubt that the captain Henry referred to was James Malory. The two younger Malory brothers were quite close, just as Boyd was close to Drew and Georgina, they being the three youngest in their family.

"Then I'll just have to represent him," Boyd said as he rushed out of the house.

two

THE COACH RIDE was terrifying. It was an old coach. The seats didn't even have padding on them. They might have had padding when the coach was new, but how many centuries ago was that? Both windows were open to the elements. Any glass that might have been there had long since been broken and removed.

Mere cloth had been tacked over each opening to at least keep the wind from blowing in, but it kept out most of the daylight as well. At least there was no chance of freezing when it was merely the middle of October. Judith was grateful for one less thing to fear.

She hadn't cried yet. She kept telling herself she was a Malory and Malorys were made of sterner stuff. And besides, her eyes would sting if she cried. She knew they would. And her hands were tied so she couldn't wipe her eyes. But it was hard to keep those tears from falling.

What had started as a thrilling day had turned into a nightmare the likes of which she'd never before experienced. She'd been showing off in the park. She didn't want her father to worry that the horse he'd bought her was too big for her, or that she couldn't handle it properly.

It was a beautiful mare, a slender horse only a few

hands taller than her pony. And she was well balanced in the seat. Her father had bought her a normal saddle, not a sidesaddle, and had told her she had a few more years to go before she needed to learn how to ride like a lady. She'd just wanted to see how fast the mare would go and prove that he didn't need to worry about her.

But her short gallop had taken her around a bend in the path, far away from where her father had been standing watching her and out of his sight. She'd already been slowing the mare down to turn around and go back when she'd been yanked off her. The mare had been slapped and raced away, and Judith had been dragged through the thick foliage beside the path with a hand over her mouth to keep her from screaming.

Still a voice had threatened, "Make any noise and I'll cut yer throat and toss yer dead body in the bushes."

She didn't make any noise. She fainted instead.

When she woke, her hands were tied, her feet were tied, and her mouth was gagged. Falling off the cushionless bench to the floor of the coach had woken her.

She didn't try to get back up on the bench, didn't think she could manage it. And the fear took over. She knew that the coach was speeding recklessly. Her small body was bounced all over the dirty floor. Wherever she was being taken, she was sure she'd never get there. The old coach was going to wreck and crumple around her.

But eventually it did stop in a normal manner and the door was opened. Something was immediately thrown over her, a cloak or a blanket, giving her no time to turn to see who was there. She was rolled in the cloak so that it covered every inch of her before she was dragged across the floor by her feet and then had the wind knocked out of her as she was dropped over a bony shoulder to be carted somewhere.

She still hadn't gotten a look at who had stolen her, but the voice that had threatened her, while gruff, had sounded like a woman's. But that didn't lessen Judith's fear.

She heard sounds now, lots of them, and voices, even a bit of laughter. And the smell of food was strong, making her realize how hungry she was. But Judith no sooner took all that in than it faded away, as if they'd merely passed by an open doorway or a kitchen or a dining room and were now leaving it far behind. She could see nothing from under that cloak, but she could tell that she was being carried upstairs. The person toting her began to breathe more heavily from the exertion.

A door was opened. It creaked. And then she was dumped on something soft. A bed?

The cloak wasn't removed from her. She tried to wiggle out of it so she could see again.

"Stop that," a voice growled at her. "Be still, be quiet, and ye willna be getting hurt."

She went still. She'd already been quiet. And the door opened again, but she wasn't being left alone. Someone else had arrived.

"I thought that was ye I saw slinking past the door tae the tavern room," a man said in an accusing tone. "Where the devil ha' ye been, womon? When ye dragged me down here tae visit yer aunt, ye didna say ye'd be disappearing for an entire day. I wake tae find ye gone this morning. What was I tae think, eh?"

He'd approached the bed as he spoke, but he backed away from it now with a gasp and turned around to snarl at the woman. "What is that?"

"That's yer fortune," she said with a chuckle.

The cloak was snatched off her. The lamplight in the room blinded her for a moment, but as soon as her eyes adjusted, Judith stared wide-eyed at a tall man with bright carrot-red hair and light blue eyes. He wasn't ugly or mean-looking. He was dressed decently, too, like most gentry. And she watched his face grow pale as he stared down at her. She was frightened, but for some reason the man seemed to be even more frightened of her.

He turned his horrified expression on the woman. "Her hair? *His* eyes?" he choked out. "D'ye think I didna ken who she belongs tae?"

"Did ye think I'd be trying tae hide it?"

"Ye've lost yer mind, there's nae other excuse!" he exclaimed. "Look at this crooked nose. Did ye think I was born wi' it? Look at these scars on my face! D'ye know how many bones of mine that mon broke? I'm lucky tae be alive after the beating he gave me, and ye steal his daughter? How could ye do this? Why?"

"Every time ye put a few drinks in ye I've had tae listen tae ye whine aboot the fortune that should've been yers. Well, ye should be glad I've finally agreed wi' ye. Aye, it should've been yers, it ne'er should've gone tae some silly chit who didna need it then and certainly doesna need it now, after marrying intae a rich family. So it's coming home where it belongs, tae us."

Geordie Cameron shook his head incredulously. He'd never really regretted marrying this woman—until now. He'd hired her to run his first shop in Edinburgh, since he knew nothing about owning a shop. He'd ended up succumbing to her flirtations and asked her to marry him. She was from the lower classes, but at that point in his life, he didn't care. He might have done something like this himself back then. In fact, he had tried to force this child's mother to marry him. In the end, Roslynn had changed his mind with her generosity.

"What a mon says when he's foxed isna usually what he thinks when he's sober. I gave up on that fortune years ago. My great-uncle had every right tae give it tae whom he pleased, and my cousin was his closer relative, so he gave it tae her. He would ne'er ha' give any part of it tae me, hating me as he did."

"Ye still should ha'—"

"Shut up, womon, and listen tae me. I'm telling ye why ye've lost yer mind. My cousin Roslynn gave me the means tae open our shops. Ten thousand pounds she gave me, slipped it in my valise wi'oout my knowing, wi'oout wanting a thank ye for it. It was enough tae open all three of our shops, and they've supported us well enough. We're no' rich, but we're no' lacking, either. And this is how we repay her?"

"And ye think I've lost my mind when ye just told the lass who we are?"

"Ye did that the moment ye mentioned that bloody fortune in relation tae her mother."

She tsked, then grumbled, "And I took such precautions tae hide who we were. I even stole an old coach this morning afore I set oout tae London Town, just in case I might be noticed hying off. But nae one saw me. It was all tae easy. I had a plan tae get intae their house, but while I was watching it, oout comes the bonny lass here wi' her father. Sae I followed them instead tae a big park, a much better place for a nabbing, I was thinking, until I realized the mon wasna letting her oout of his sight. I was aboot tae leave when the lass rode right intae my hands."

"I dinna care how ye did this, I want tae be hearing how ye're going tae *un*do it. Ye're taking her back."

"Nae," she replied flatly. "And it's tae late for that. Afore I left London, I arranged for the note to be delivered tonight, telling them where tae bring the fortune to.

They've received it by now." But then she smiled at him. "Ye're the best thing that ever happened tae me, mon, there's nae denying that. And now I'm paying ye back in making us richer than a few shops ever could. Sae what if we may ha' tae leave the country because of this," she added with a shrug. "That's a small price tae pay for a fortune. Sleep on it. Ye'll see I'm right in the morning."

She then scooped up the child and set her down on the floor in the corner of the room so they could have their bed back. Geordie immediately grabbed both pillows from the bed as well as the top blanket and put them around the child to make her more comfortable. His wife laughed at him. He gritted his teeth, hoping a night's sleep would make *her* see the error in what she'd foolishly done. He didn't like thinking that he'd have to put his own wife in prison just to save her life. But he had no doubt at all that what she'd started was going to get them both killed by Anthony Malory if the lass wasn't returned to him posthaste.

"Please, *please* tell yer father I had nothing tae do wi' this," he whispered to the child as he gently covered her. "It wasna my idea, I swear."

"What are ye mumbling aboot?" his wife demanded.

"Nothing, m'dear."

three

THE MEWLING WOKE Katey Tyler for the second time that night. A cat? A baby? It was hard to tell exactly what was making that noise, but it was very irritating, and it seemed to be coming from the room directly next to hers. Her bed abutted the wall that divided the rooms, and while she had briefly considered trying to move the bed to get farther away from the noise, it was a big bed and she didn't think she could manage it without waking everyone else on the floor.

They had arrived at this inn on the outskirts of Northampton quite late last night. It wasn't fully occupied so Katey had been able to get her maid, Grace, a room, too. She wished that hadn't been the case, because if Grace were here, they could probably have moved the bed together.

The adventurous thing to do would be to get up and go investigate the sound. After all, hadn't Katey come to England to have adventures? Well, not England exactly, it was merely the first stepping-stone on her trip around the world. But the whole point of her trip was to see and do new things and to put some excitement into her life. Adventure, excitement, maybe even a little romance if she was lucky.

She'd gotten more of the latter than she'd bargained for on the Atlantic crossing from America to England, or she would have if she hadn't panicked and set herself up with an identity that wasn't really hers to avoid being bothered by men. But it was just as well that she'd presented herself as a married woman. She was just starting her grand tour and didn't want it to end immediately by her falling in love with the first handsome man she came across.

That had been a definite possibility when she'd met Boyd Anderson. When he'd held her in his arms there on the dock in Bridgeport, Connecticut, saving her from a nasty fall off the crates she'd climbed up on, she'd been quite flustered. But when he smiled at her! Good grief, what that had made her feel inside was so strange it frightened her, so she'd been glad of an excuse to run off.

And she hadn't really calmed down from that encounter by the time he approached her on the deck of his ship a short while later. What did she know about men, after all? Having three marriage proposals from old men in her village hadn't prepared her for someone like Boyd Anderson. Even having a sixteen-year-old lad chasing after her carriage when she was riding out of Danbury with her mother had engendered no feelings but amusement. The boy had followed them about during their brief shopping trip to the bigger town, but hadn't said a word until they left. Then he'd shouted after her that he'd make her a fine husband! She'd been twelve at the time. She'd done no more than giggle while her mother rolled her eyes.

But Boyd Anderson with his curly, golden brown hair and those dark brown eyes that so easily mesmerized her was the most handsome man she'd ever seen. And if he hadn't approached her again there on the deck, so soon after their first meeting, how differently that trip might have turned out. But he did. He even brushed against her, overwhelming her with his masculinity. And then that new smile, so sensual it stole her breath and produced a wealth of new sensations that unsettled her enough to bring the panic back. It was no wonder she had jumped on the idea that *he* gave her, when her maid had approached with the two children they were escorting to England, and he'd teasingly asked if they were hers.

He hadn't approached her again, so pretending to be married had served her purposes. It had kept him from making any more overtures. But, oh, how exciting that had been! Knowing he was attracted to her, seeing it in his eyes, in his expression, every time he got near her. His restraint had been especially admirable because he had seemed like a powder keg of passions!

Thinking about him was keeping her from getting back to sleep immediately, but that wasn't unusual. She regretted having panicked when a man as handsome and masculine as Boyd had expressed interest in her, but that's why she'd come on this trip—for adventure and experience. The next time she encountered the attentions of a handsome man, she'd know how to handle the situation.

The annoying mewling noise started up again. If she were in her own home, she would immediately have investigated. She couldn't bear to think of animals in pain, hungry, or being abused. She'd chased farmer Cantry about the village square once with his own stick, having grabbed it from his hand when she caught him using it on his horse. Deer ate apples from her hand, they had such trust in her. And two of her neighbor's cats left field mice on *her* porch regularly as gifts.

Again the sound grated on Katey's ears and heart. Finally she threw off her covers, grabbed the robe she'd left at the foot of the bed, and was out the door before she'd even belted the robe. She was about to pound on the door to the other room when she arrested her fist just in time.

She didn't *really* want to wake anyone else just because her sleep was being disturbed.

She pulled her long black hair out from under the robe as she debated what to do. It was probably just a cat trapped in an empty room. This would be the second time she'd come across that situation in her travels, if that was what this was. It had been late summer when she'd arrived in England, it was now early fall, and innkeepers left windows open, even windows in their vacant rooms, to keep them fresh-smelling as long as they could before the weather turned too cold. Stray cats found their way in through those open windows looking for food, then forgot how to get out and made a racket about it.

Trying the door would tell her immediately if the room was occupied. If it was locked, she'd have to consider going downstairs to complain to the innkeeper. If it opened, the noisy cat would likely scurry out into the corridor and run off, and her problem would be solved.

The door opened when she turned the knob. She pushed it wide enough for the cat to run out, but no cat appeared. There was an orange glow in the room as if a fire was dying out, or a lamp was turned down low, which indicated the room was occupied by people rather than stray cats.

She closed the door quietly, embarrassed now that she'd opened the door to someone's room. She didn't move, though. What had caused the mewling sound? A baby? That had been her other thought. The parents might be so used to the sound that it wouldn't wake them. But there it was again, that mewling, and oddly, it sounded more desperate now.

She was just going to have a little peek, she told herself as she opened the door again and stuck her head around its edge to see into the room. A lamp was turned so low it was probably going to extinguish itself at any moment.

There was the bed, occupied by a couple of people under the sheets, one softly snoring.

She looked quickly for a basket on the floor that might contain a baby, and if she found it, she was going to wake its parents to take care of it. But she found a pair of wide eyes staring at her instead, eyes that seemed to be pleading with her, belonging to a child who was gagged and sitting on the floor in the corner. Boy or girl she couldn't tell, nor could she see if the child's hands were tied, too. A blanket concealed that, but she guessed that they were, since no effort had been made to remove the gag.

The sensible thing to do would be to close the door and run downstairs for help. But Katey didn't care about being sensible. She had to get that child out of there. She'd worry later about whether she had any right to interfere. A visit to the local magistrate would clear that up, and if the child had to be returned to its parents, maybe the magistrate could instill enough fear in them to keep them from mistreating their child again.

That mistreatment infuriated her and carried her straight across the room without a thought for the two people sleeping in the bed. But when she reached the child and removed the blanket, which revealed the long copper hair of a female child, Katey saw that the mistreatment was much worse than she'd thought. Not only was the girl tied hand and foot, but a long strip of cloth also secured her in place, one end tied around her ankle, the other tied around one of the legs of the bed. That's why she hadn't tried to wiggle or roll her way out of there.

Katey quickly untied the long strip of cloth and picked up the girl. Now she was more mindful that the people in the bed could wake up at any moment. Whispering "Shh" to the child just in case she didn't realize she was being

rescued and started making noise again, Katey furtively
tiptoed out of the room and managed to close the door
behind them without having to set the girl down. She then
rushed to her own room, placed the girl in the room's single
chair, quickly locked her own door, and lit a lamp so she
could see what she was doing before she tackled the ropes.

The ropes turned out to be thin strips of rough cloth,
with knots that were much too tight to work loose, since
the child had apparently strained against them. But Katey
traveled prepared for minor mishaps and emergencies.

While she usually left her main clothes trunks tied to
their coach if they were only briefly staying in a place,
with their driver sleeping in the coach to guard them, she
carried a valise with an assortment of underclothes, an
extra traveling dress, and a small sewing kit.

She fetched the little pair of scissors from the sewing kit
now and quickly snipped through the girl's bindings. But
no sooner was the child released than she made a mad dash
for the chamber pot in the corner of the room, stumbling
and tripping on the way no doubt because her limbs were
numb from having been constrained for so long. The poor
child! No wonder she had been making such pitiful noises.

Katey turned aside to give the girl a moment of pri-
vacy. She opened the food basket she and Grace had taken
to carrying ever since they'd gone to bed hungry one night
because they'd arrived at an inn too late to get a meal.

"Are you hungry?" she asked as she pulled out some
bread and broke open the round of cheese.

"I'm famished."

"Well, come sit down here. It's not a feast by any means
and a bit stale, but—"

"Thank you so much," the girl cut in, and snatched the
bread from Katey's hand.

"If you wait a moment, I'll make you a plate."

"I can't wait," the girl said around a mouthful. "This is fine, really."

Katey frowned. "When did you last eat?"

"This morning. Or was it yesterday morning? I don't know what time it is."

Neither did Katey. It could be nearing dawn for all she knew. With the curtain in the room closed, she couldn't tell. But she was staring appalled at the girl now.

"How could your parents do this to you? Did you misbehave so horribly?"

"My parents would never treat me this way," the girl said, her tone almost offended. But she paused when she saw a pastry in the basket and grabbed that before she continued, "If you mean the man and woman in that other room, I've never seen either of them before in my life."

Katey found that highly doubtful and started to say so, but held her tongue. The child *was* desperately hungry, eating everything in sight. She *had* been tied and left on the cold floor to sleep. If those *were* her parents next door, then they ought to be shot.

"So how did you come to be there?"

The girl sat down in the chair at the table and ate more slowly. Katey now saw that she was exceptionally beautiful. Her sun-gold hair was streaked with copper, and although it was mussed up, it was still clean and shiny. And her eyes were such a dark, lovely shade of blue. She had a scratch on one cheek. And while the pink velvet riding habit she was wearing was dirty with dust and what even looked like a cobweb clinging to the skirt, it wasn't an old garment. The material had the sheen of being quite new, and it fit the girl perfectly. It must have been made for her, which meant she must come from wealth.

And then the girl's little voice broke into her thoughts. "The woman pulled me off of my new horse and said she'd cut my throat and leave my body in the bushes if I made any noise. I don't know why I don't remember what happened after that, but when I woke, I was tied up on the floor of an old coach. And then I was carried into that room."

"They stole you!?" Katey gasped.

"The woman did. The man, it sounded like he's a cousin to my mother, and I remember her talking once about a cousin who gave her a lot of trouble before I was born. It wasn't his idea to bring me here, though. He wanted to take me straight back to London. He seemed to be very afraid of my father and what he would do to him. But the woman refused to let me go. She wants the fortune she thinks she'll get for me. And she seemed to have the final word."

Katey was starting to have a few misgivings now that she knew a relative was involved. He wouldn't have allowed the girl to be seriously hurt, would he? Then again, he'd kept her tied up and hadn't even fed her!

She glanced at the child again, still stuffing food in her mouth, and her misgivings went away. How dare they mistreat this child!

"I'll see that you get home," Katey said with a reassuring smile. "I'm traveling to London myself. We'll leave first thing in the morn—"

"Please, could we leave now?" the girl interrupted, her expression turning frightened. "I don't want them to find me again. I heard them say that the lock on the door was broken, when they tied me to the bed, so they'll know someone helped me out of there, that I couldn't do it myself."

"And they'll look close by," Katey concluded with a nod. "Very well, we'll leave now."

four

KATEY'S MAID, GRACE Harford, grumbled about setting off down the road before dawn. Well aware of Katey's habit of embellishing ordinary events into dramatic stories, she didn't believe a word of Katey's explanation of why they were leaving the inn so early accompanied by a little girl. Hadn't they escorted Katey's neighbor's nieces all the way to England? Didn't an innkeeper in Scotland ask Katey to escort his young son to the boy's mother in Aberdeen when he heard she was heading that way? People took one look at Katey Tyler with her big green eyes, dimpled cheeks, and winsome smile and instantly trusted her, even with their children. Judith Malory, as the girl had introduced herself, was just another child who had been entrusted to Katey's care for a journey, and that was that, as far as Grace was concerned.

People *did* take a liking to Katey as soon as they met her, but Katey wasn't sure why. Not once did she think it was because she was pretty. Her mother had been beautiful with her coal black hair and emerald green eyes. But while Katey had taken after her, no one had made much of her looks when she was growing up, so she didn't either. In her opinion, her maid with her wealth of freckles and curly red hair was more interesting-looking than she was.

Katey was quite tall at five feet nine inches. When her father had died, when she was ten years old, she'd already been as tall as he was, and she'd kept growing after that. She'd turned out to be five inches taller than her mother. Adeline had claimed Katey got her height from her side of the family, because her own father had been rather tall.

Now Katey rarely thought about her height and only felt self-conscious when she got near a man who was shorter than her, but that didn't happen often. What bothered her more than her height were her curves. She'd heard men describe her as a fine, strapping wench. Too many times she'd caught men staring at her ample bosom, even the old men in the village!

But aside from that, Katey had felt comfortable in the tiny village of Gardener, and she'd been outgoing and always willing to lend a helping hand if someone needed it. Even strangers had been drawn to her. She could be standing in a group of people, and a passing stranger would ask *her* for directions and ignore everyone else, not that many strangers had passed through that tiny village.

But the same thing could be said of her neighbors in Gardener. They often came to her because she was accessible, friendly, and if she couldn't help with something, she usually knew someone who could. And she added a little excitement to their lives in the tales she told.

Katey wasn't a bit surprised that Grace had concluded this was just another of Katey's tales. Five years older than Katey, who had just turned twenty-two, Grace had come to live with the Tylers ten years ago and had made herself invaluable as a housekeeper and a friend. But she was stubborn in her opinions, so Katey didn't try to convince her maid otherwise. She just sat back in their coach on the way to London and smiled to herself, savoring that for once the exciting tale she'd told was actually true.

Judith was surprised, though, and as soon as the maid curled up on the seat opposite them and went back to sleep, the girl whispered to Katey, "Why didn't she believe you?"

"You don't have to whisper," Katey replied. "She's a very sound sleeper. Shaking her is about the only way to get her to wake up. Shouting doesn't even do it. But as to why she doubted me, well, that's a bit of a story in itself."

"I'm not tired," Judith said as if encouraging her to tell the story.

Katey grinned at the girl. "Very well, where to start? I grew up in the most boring town you can imagine. It wasn't even a town, just a small village. There were no shops other than the general store my family owned. There was no inn, no tavern. We had one seamstress, who worked out of her house, and one farmer who dabbled at carpentry and sold furniture out of his barn. Oh, and we had a butcher, though he wasn't really a butcher, just a local hunter who kept the wildlife from roaming through the village."

Judith, wide-eyed with interest now, said, "Animals roamed your streets?"

"Oh, yes. Nothing too dangerous, mind you, though a moose did tear down Mrs. Pellum's fence one year. It probably would have left peaceably if she hadn't tried to chase it off with her broom. But a village can't be much smaller than Gardener. If someone needed a doctor, or a lawyer, they headed down the road to the town of Danbury twenty miles away. No new families ever moved to our village, and children left as soon as they were old enough to do so."

"Is that what you did?" Judith asked. "Left like the other children?"

"Not as soon as I would have liked to. My mother was there, you see, and it never occurred to me to leave without her. She had no one but me after my father died. Well, she did, but her family had disowned her, so they didn't count as family anymore."

"Why'd they do that?"

Katey shrugged. "To hear her tell it, they were wealthy aristocrats and very concerned with social classes. They refused to let her marry my father simply because he was an American. Well, possibly because he was a merchant, too. 'In trade' was how my mother put it. They apparently objected to that as well."

Judith wasn't surprised. "It's a kind of snobbery that's common among the gentry. Many of them look down on anyone in trade."

"Do they? Well, that sounds awfully narrow-minded to me. If my father hadn't been a store owner, he never would have gone to England in the first place, wouldn't have met my mother, and can you imagine, I never would have been born!"

Judith gave her a look that said clearly, *Please don't talk to me like I'm a child.* Katey almost burst out laughing. The little girl did really seem years beyond her age.

"He came here to open a shop?" Judith asked next.

"No, I doubt that ever occurred to him. You see, at home he had all the suppliers he needed for his store from the nearby town of Danbury, but he didn't really sell anything interesting, just necessities and produce from the local farmers. He came here to England to see if he could find something more exotic to sell and found my mother instead. So she eloped with him, burned her bridges you could say, and she never saw her English family again."

"I thought I recognized your accent." Judith grinned.

"I have American relatives now m'self. But why didn't your mother come home to England after your father died?"

Katey sighed to herself. It's what she had wanted her mother to do, and she'd broached the subject at least once a year for the last twelve years since her father had died, but Adeline Tyler despised her family for turning their backs on her, and she flatly refused to ever set foot in England again. Besides, she had taken over the running of the store and actually enjoyed the work. It was like a further slap in the face to the Millards, her English relatives, that she was now in trade herself. Not that her family ever knew that, since she didn't communicate with any of them, but she seemed to silently gloat about it.

To the curious child sitting next to her, Katey said, "When my mother's family disowned her, she more or less disowned them, too. And I think she despised England because of it."

Judith nodded. "But what's all that got to do with your maid doubting what you told her?"

Katey chuckled. She'd thought the girl had forgotten about that, but since she hadn't, Katey asked her, "Have you ever been so bored because one day runs into the next, giving you no memories worth recalling?"

"Never," Judith replied instantly.

"Then you've been very lucky, because that's what my life was like growing up in Gardener. And I wasn't the only one who woke up each day with nothing to look forward to. The villagers who were left were all old, and they all led uneventful lives. They didn't seem to mind, but if something exciting happened, they certainly enjoyed hearing about it. So every once in a while I gave them something exciting to hear about."

"You lied to them?"

Katey blinked. The child wasn't only beautiful, she was intelligent and too perceptive by half. And while Katey would never dream of discussing such things about herself with a stranger, she felt an unusual kinship with the girl, probably because they had shared Katey's first real adventure on her grand tour.

"Goodness, I never thought of it as lying. I merely created minor fabrications, embellishments, really, about things I happened to witness. For instance, when I noticed Mrs. Cartley's cat on top of her roof next door, it had seemed like the cat was stuck up there, afraid to come down. Now I love animals, and I wasn't about to leave it up there. And I knew the Cartleys weren't home because they'd left to visit their daughter in Danbury that morning and wouldn't be back for several more hours. So I went over and climbed Mrs. Cartley's rose trellis to get up on their roof, but by the time I actually got up there, the cat was gone!"

"It got up the nerve to jump down?"

"No." Katey chuckled. "It got down the same way it climbed up, with a ladder! I forgot that Mr. Cartley had been repairing his roof earlier that week. He'd left his ladder leaning against the back of their house. The excitement was over, and very bland excitement at that. So instead of mentioning that to Mrs. Cartley later, I told her that her cat had got up on our roof, which was much higher, our house being two stories, and that my maid risked life and limb to climb up the old oak tree next to our house to save it. Grace ended up being the heroine for the month, which she didn't mind one bit, and it gave everyone something to talk about instead of the weather."

"That sounds like my cousin Derek claiming the fish he caught this summer was two feet long, but his wife told us later it was only six inches. It was more interesting hearing that it was a big fish, but it was certainly funny when we found out it wasn't even big enough to keep. So that's the kind of tales you tell?"

"Similar—but not exactly. You see, I was about your age when I started getting 'creative' sometimes in describing what I saw and did. I'd had a bad disappointment that year. I thought I'd be going to school in Danbury, where I could finally meet some other children my age, even if it did mean two long rides each day on my pony, there and back. But an old professor retired to Gardener the year before, and my mother managed to talk him into tutoring me instead. So when I saw a stranger stealing tomatoes from my mother's garden out back while I was helping her roll out biscuits for dinner, I merely watched, figuring if he was hungry enough to steal them he was welcome to them. But when she came back in the kitchen, I thought she might blame me for the missing tomatoes, since she knew I was upset with her for keeping me at home, so I told her I chased off a thief with the rolling pin I'd been using."

"You got to help in the kitchen?" Judith said. "I wish I could do that, but our cook just feeds me a sweet and tells me to run along."

Katey was amused that the child was more interested in the cooking than the thief. "We only had one maid, Grace," Katey said, nodding toward their sleeping companion. "So we all shared in the chores."

"Would your mother really have noticed a few missing tomatoes?" Judith asked.

"Oh, yes, she knew exactly how many tomatoes were on her plants and exactly how many were ready for picking. She loved her garden. I did, too, come to think of it. I spent many an hour with her in our backyard."

The child didn't notice the melancholy that had snuck up on Katey with those memories. God, she missed her mother. It was such a stupid accident that had taken her life last winter, a mere slip on a bit of ice.

Judith sighed next to her. "That's another thing we don't have, vegetable gardens. My uncle Jason has lots of buildings at Haverston, his estate in the country, just for growing things indoors year-round. The gardens in our square in the city, though, just have flowers. Cook buys all our food from the market."

It was odd how one child might look at chores with envy, another might see them as a bother, and yet another could see them as merely a break from monotony.

"So you lied to your mother?" the child asked baldly.

Katey blushed, hearing it put that way. "I had to tell her about the thief. He was very real. I just didn't want her to know that I stood there and did nothing to try to stop him. But it caused such a to-do in the village that the men were out hunting for that thief for days. It gave them something to talk about for nearly half the year. You should have seen how it put the 'life' back into them, if you know what I mean. So although my mother gave me a terrible scolding for risking my life and warned me never to do anything so foolish again, I learned something else from that incident. I learned how to remove the boredom from all our lives, if only briefly."

"So you often embellished events you witnessed?" Judith asked.

"Yes, she got in the habit of creating excitement out of thin air," Grace said as she sat up across from them with a yawn.

"Not often," Katey told her maid.

"Often enough to make me the heroine of the village," Grace grumbled.

"You've enjoyed being the heroine. Why, the entire village cried when you left. They merely waved good-bye to me."

Grace chuckled. "Very well, so I did enjoy that part of it."

"I can't imagine what it must have been like, not having something exciting going on all the time," Judith remarked. "With my family, there is always something interesting happening. Why, my uncle James and aunt George went off just last month to chase pirates. And at the end of summer my cousin Jeremy married a thief who turned out to be the missing daughter of a baroness."

Katey blinked. Even Grace looked doubtful, then rolled her eyes at Katey as if to say, *The chit has picked up your bad habits this quickly?* And it did sound as if the child was doing some embellishing of her own.

Katey was about to laugh, but then Judith added, "Did you come here to meet your English relatives?"

Katey went still. That was one subject she didn't want to discuss. She'd had every intention of doing so on the voyage over and had been looking forward to it. And after they arrived in England, she'd gone straight to Havers Town, which, according to her mother, was the closest town to the Millard family estate in Gloucestershire. But once there, she'd abruptly changed her mind.

"She did," Grace answered the girl. "She just didn't have the guts to knock on their door and took us off to Scotland instead."

"That's not why we came here," Katey said, annoyed with her outspoken maid. "It was just something to do while we were here, and now it's something that can be done some other time—or perhaps never. They probably don't even know I exist. Besides, we were already planning on touring Scotland."

"How can you not want to meet your family?" Judith asked, amazed.

"They disowned my mother. I never understood how they could want nothing more to do with their own child. It was a mean thing to do, and I'm not sure I want to acknowledge a relationship to people like that."

Judith nodded, but Grace, glancing out the window, suddenly said, "You might want to brace yourselves. There's a reckless driver coming down the road, and if Mr. Davis hasn't noticed, he might not move us out of the way in time to avoid a collision."

Judith peeked out the window and paled. "It's her! The woman who stole me is driving that coach."

"Katey's story was true then?" Grace demanded, glancing between Katey and Judith.

"Yes, all of it," Katey replied.

"Well, it looks like she's slowing down," Grace said, still watching the approaching coach. "I'm guessing she'd like a word with us."

Katey's mouth tightened. "I'd like a word with her, too, but I'll have to forgo giving her a piece of my mind. It's more important that we get the girl home to her family." And then Katey told the child, "Duck down so she can't see you if she tries to look in the window. And don't worry. We won't be letting her anywhere near you again."

five

Boyd had never seen Sir Anthony Malory as upset as he was yesterday in Hyde Park. When Boyd found him, the man was half out of his mind with worry. But he'd expected that because several of Anthony's servants whom he'd passed had told him just how terrified the man was. They had found his daughter's horse on the other side of the park and they feared she was lying in the bushes somewhere bruised, broken—or dead.

Malory didn't even give Boyd a chance to tell him he had news. He'd practically dragged Boyd off his mount when he rode up to him and lifted him off his feet by his lapels to shake him. Malory was nearly six inches taller than Boyd, so he was quite capable of doing that.

"Where's the army you were supposed to bring?" Anthony had shouted at Boyd. "I know bloody well my brother has got at least a half dozen male servants in his employ."

Usually Boyd wouldn't stand for being manhandled like that and would already be throwing punches. It was a bad habit he'd developed as the youngest of five brothers who rarely got the upper hand with any of them—unless he was using his fists. But he felt for this man and knew what it was like to be frantic with worry over a family member. That Anthony's brother James had been responsible for Boyd's worry about Georgina had long ago been forgiven. Mostly.

But because he understood what the man was going through, Boyd hadn't tried to explain to Anthony, he'd simply shoved the note in his face. He managed not to fall to the ground when Anthony abruptly released him. And he watched warily as Anthony read the note.

Suddenly Anthony stopped shouting, and an odd calmness descended on him. Well, not so odd. While most of the Andersons got loud when they were angry, the Malorys tended to react in the opposite way. It was when they were quiet that you needed to worry.

"Money?" Anthony had said, looking up from the note. "They frighten my daughter and drive me half-mad for money? They can have all the bloody money they want, but I'll have their hides in exchange for it."

That had been Anthony's first reaction to the note. But that had been yesterday. It had taken him the rest of the day to get his wife to stop crying with assurances that Judith would be fine, now that they knew she hadn't fallen off her horse or been seriously injured. But it was nerve-racking, waiting for the next communication from the abductors to arrive, and Boyd elected to wait it out at Anthony's house.

Boyd had explained, "I'd just as soon my niece, Jacqueline, not know about this until your daughter is safely back at home, and rather than lie to her, I'd prefer to avoid her. So if you wouldn't mind putting me up for the night?"

Anthony was on his way to being quite foxed by then, which was his way of dealing with waiting. He'd skipped dinner as he didn't have food on his mind. Neither did Boyd for that matter, and when several more bottles were delivered to the parlor, he'd grabbed one for himself.

He never did find his way upstairs to a bed. He passed out

on one of several sofas in Sir Anthony's parlor. Voices woke him the next morning from a pleasant dream—about her.

Dreaming was the only time his thoughts about Katey Tyler were pleasant, and this dream was soothing rather than passionate. He was in a field of daisies near his home in Connecticut. He'd found a wounded deer there once. It was a seagull he found in his dream, a bird he would always associate with Katey now. And he was bending to examine it when he saw her slowly approaching him, dressed in pink and lavender, the sun sparkling all around her.

She had a small bunny in the crook of one arm and a squirrel perched on her shoulder. Squirrels could be vicious, but he knew this one wouldn't hurt her. Her compassion for animals was the first thing about her that had touched his heart.

His dreams flitted from one scene to another without rhyme or reason, and now they were lying in that field side by side, holding hands. A profound peace filled him because she was his, no matter how briefly. She leaned up. With the sun behind her, he could barely see her face, but he felt her lips soft on his cheek.

The dream might have turned sensual if it had continued. His dreams usually were hot and passionate when she was in them, and she was in them too often. When he was awake, his thoughts about her frustrated him because she was off-limits—a married woman. And he wished to hell she would stay out of his mind and his dreams.

She'd put him through two lusting weeks of hell on that voyage a month and a half ago. She had no idea how much he'd wanted her. But because she was already married and happily on her way to meet her husband, he'd backed off. That had been one of the hardest things he'd ever done, and he'd done his best to avoid her. No easy feat aboard a ship. But while he didn't expect to see her again, he simply couldn't forget about her. He'd been that strongly attracted to her—her personality, her beautiful face, her smile, her luscious body . . .

It was Jeremy Malory's voice that dispelled the dream and woke him. James's oldest son, Jeremy had the black hair and cobalt blue eyes that only a few Malorys possessed. He looked nothing like his father, who was blond and green-eyed, and everything like his uncle Anthony—which was a source of amusement to most of the family.

The lad was explaining, "Danny and I arrived home from our wedding trip this morning. You can imagine my surprise when my butler immediately pulled me aside—he didn't want to fret m'wife—and told me that you commandeered my entire household last night. Then he handed me this. It had been anchored down with a large rock on our front steps."

"This" was a note that Jeremy handed to Anthony. Apparently, the wait was over.

"Delivered to another wrong house?" Boyd guessed as he sat up and stretched the sleep from his limbs. "These people obviously don't know your family very well."

"Morning, Yank," Jeremy greeted him, adding, "If they knew our family well, they never would have done this."

"Good point," Boyd agreed.

The Malory family wasn't just very large, very rich, and very titled. The two younger brothers, James and Anthony, had been such rakehells in their day, never losing a duel whether with fists or pistols, that they were also well known for being quite deadly. Bottom line, you didn't cross a Malory without ending up very sorry for it.

Anthony wasn't paying attention to the two younger men as he glanced over the note, then tossed it on the table in front of Boyd. "Tomorrow!? Do they really think I can't get my hands on a fortune today? I'd drag my banker from his bed if need be."

Boyd picked up the note. It was much more detailed than the first note had been. It mentioned the place, the time, the date, and, lastly, that the fortune was to be delivered by someone other than a family member, and that Anthony wasn't to be involved or to come anywhere near the place of the exchange. That was stressed twice. They might not know the family well, but it sounded as if they *did* know Anthony Malory. There were also a number of misspellings, though that wasn't necessarily pertinent.

"Do you even know how much money they want?" Jeremy asked his uncle.

"A fortune is a fortune. I'm not putting a price on my daughter's life."

"Quite right." Jeremy nodded. "Who are you going to send to make the exchange?"

"I'll go," Boyd offered immediately.

He was ignored, or perhaps just not heard. He was clearing his throat to say it louder when Anthony said, "I'd send Derek, but he's visiting his father at Haverston this week."

"What about Uncle Edward?" Jeremy suggested.

"No, my brother's up north on business."

"There's no reason why—," Boyd tried again, but he was again ignored.

"I suppose I could send for Derek. There's time enough for him to get back to London before tonight."

"No need for that," Jeremy said. "I'll go."

Anthony snorted at his nephew. "From a distance, you look just like me. You ain't going."

Jeremy grinned, but then said, "Well, damn, where's m'father when he's—"

Boyd stood up in annoyance, interrupting loudly this time, "Have either of you heard a word I've said? I'm perfectly capable of handling this."

Anthony stared at him for a moment, then shook his head. "No offense, Yank, but I've heard you're a bit of a hothead."

"Since I've been provoked a number of times in the last few minutes and haven't lost my temper, that speaks for itself, doesn't it? Besides, I've grown very fond of your daughter since Jack has been in my care."

"Did you just call my sister Jack?" Jeremy said with a raised brow. "Thought you and all your brothers hated the name m'father gave her."

"No, we just hate your father," Boyd said with a tight-lipped smile.

Jeremy chuckled. Boyd wasn't amused. "Look, I might be the youngest of the Anderson brothers, Anthony, but I'm thirty-four years of age and even your own brother trusted me with the care of his daughter. That note says you can't personally make the exchange, and I'm sure you're not going to let your wife go or trust this to a servant or someone you don't know personally. And the rest of your family appears to be out of town. So I'm volunteering. Much as I'd like to put my fist into whoever did this, and believe me, I'll be glad to help you track them down afterwards, I think getting Judith safely home first is more important."

Jeremy pointed at the note Boyd had returned to the table. "The meeting place is the first crossroads south of the town of Northampton. Do you even know where Northampton is?"

"No, but even us Yanks know how to follow directions," Boyd replied drily.

six

Katey stopped for the woman once Judith was huddled under a blanket on the floor. It wasn't a matter of choice. The woman's coach nearly ran them off the road in her effort to get them to pull over. Then she climbed down from the driver's perch of her coach and stood next to theirs, windswept and wild-looking, belligerently demanding to search it.

"I think not," Katey indignantly told the woman through the window they'd opened. "You nearly caused us an accident! If you're trying to rob us, be warned, I have a pistol in my hand at this very moment."

She didn't really have a pistol, but she should have had one, and she was now determined to buy one in the next town they came to.

She gripped the handle of the door, though, just in case the wild woman tried to yank it open. But the woman appeared to believe her about the pistol and quickly lost her belligerence. She began to whine instead about an ungrateful, willful, lying daughter with copper hair and the bluest eyes who had run away from home.

And just so they'd be sure to doubt the child if they *were* helping her escape, she added, "She makes up fantastic tales, she does. I ne'er know when tae believe her m'self. Hae ye seen her?"

Katey had just come from Scotland so she recognized the woman's accent easily enough. And later she was going to laugh about the likelihood that her own mother might have said the same thing about her many a time.

Grace even whispered at her back, "Sounds like you, doesn't it?"

Katey, still too angry to be amused, ignored her maid. Obviously, it hadn't occurred to the woman that if they had the child, they'd know that the woman was lying about being the girl's mother, simply because the child's accent wasn't the least bit Scottish.

In an attempt to get them out of there sooner rather than later, Grace stuck her nose out the window and told the woman, "We haven't seen any children, but good luck in your search." Then she shouted up at their driver, "Mr. Davis, continue on."

But a few miles down the road, Grace looked out the window again and said, "I should have stayed out of it. She recognized me."

"From where?"

"The inn. We passed each other in the corridor last night. I went downstairs to see if I could find something to eat in their kitchen. I didn't want to disturb you for our food basket, in case you were sleeping already. I could see a bit of suspicion in her eyes back there on the road when I spoke to her. She realized I was in the same inn as she was last night. And she's not going away."

Katey frowned and leaned over to glance out the window, then gasped, "Good grief, she's following us now? This is getting out of hand, isn't it?"

Grace shrugged, then grinned. "I'm not worried about it. She's alone. If that man you said she was traveling with was with her, he was doing a good job of hiding in their coach. And we do have Mr. Davis with us. You pay him enough that he can move his arse to take care of any trouble of that sort. What can she do?"

"I wouldn't count on Mr. Davis helping," Katey said as she sat back against the seat again. "He warned me when I hired him and his coach that if I wanted guards, I should hire some. He isn't a brave sort. He hasn't minded sleeping with the trunks, but I've wondered more than once if he'd actually try to stop anyone from taking them."

"That he's slept near them has been deterrent enough to keep anyone from nosing around."

"I suppose, but I'll make sure we have a real guard before we travel across the Continent. For that matter, I think I'll buy our own coach before we set sail for France."

Grace chuckled. "I'm glad you're getting used to being rich."

Katey blushed slightly. It had taken her some time to get used to being wealthy. Her family had lived comfortably enough, but owning the only store in a small village certainly hadn't made them rich. Her mother had never mentioned the inheritance she'd received from her father, who had died soon after she'd left England, before he'd had a chance to strike her from his will. She hadn't expected his money and didn't want it, so she'd never touched it.

Katey only found out about the inheritance after her mother died. She'd still been in shock over Adeline's death when the Danbury lawyer came to tell her about the large sum of money that had been sitting unused for all those years. Deep in mourning, Katey simply hadn't cared. But then her neighbor Mrs. Pellum had taken in two young nieces when their parents died, and she started desperately looking for someone to escort them to England, claiming she was too old to raise small children again, but her youngest sister in England would be glad to have them.

And that's when Katey realized she didn't have to live in Gardener anymore. She agreed to escort Mrs. Pellum's three- and four-year-old nieces to England. And since Katey didn't plan to ever return to Gardener, she gave away most of her possessions, including the store and the house. Besides her clothes, all she'd packed were a few small mementos of her mother's to take with her.

She said all her good-byes. And while she was fond of many of her neighbors in Gardener, she wasn't especially close to any of them. If Grace, her maid, hadn't agreed to go abroad with her, she would have been the only person in Gardener whom Katey would have missed dreadfully.

Judith hadn't interrupted as she'd listened to them, but as children will do, she'd latched on to one remark and asked, "You're not staying in England?"

"Goodness, no, this was just the beginning of a grand tour for us. We'll be sailing for France next, and come to think of it, I should probably wait until we get there to buy a couch, so we don't have to ship it over."

"Don't do that," Judith said. "French coaches are pretty, but they aren't comfortable. If you're going to be traveling a long way, you'll want an English coach."

"And how would you be knowing things like that, child?" Grace asked with a chuckle.

"My mother ordered one and within a week found it so uncomfortable she sent it to my uncle Jason to use as a decoration in one of his gardens. M'father laughed and laughed about that, which had my mother quite annoyed with him. It's a bone of contention with her, that she has nothing to spend her money on, because he buys her everything she could ever want."

"But why was he amused that she didn't keep the coach?" Katey asked.

"It was that it ended up being such an expensive garden piece that he found so funny!"

Katey smiled at the girl. "Well, I'm sure not all French coaches are as uncomfortable as your mother's was, but thank you for the warning."

The mention of the word *warning* had the child offering up a warning of her own. "That woman could have a weapon."

Katey's expression turned serious again. "I know. But I'll have one myself shortly, just as soon as we reach the next town. You're probably getting hungry again, too. Let's hope our 'follower' heads down a different road so we can stop for breakfast."

They did stop at the next town, and when Katey returned to the coach with a small pistol tucked into her reticule, she already knew they were still being watched.

"She thinks she's being clever, that we don't know she's there," Grace said when Katey rejoined them. "But she's definitely keeping an eye on us."

Katey took her seat before she peered across the street at the old coach with the woman standing behind it, trying to be unobtrusive as she peeked around it. "We should just confront her."

"Don't do that!" Judith said in alarm. "I couldn't bear it if you got hurt because of me."

Katey gave it a moment's thought, then said, "I'm concerned that she might stop us again on a deserted stretch of the highway and do something more reckless." Katey didn't really want to have to actually use her new pistol. "I'm also picturing a mad, dangerous dash through the streets of London when we get close to your house and she gets desperate to stop us."

"You *would* imagine something like that," Grace mumbled in disgust.

Katey ignored the maid and continued, "The fool woman obviously didn't believe us and is sure we have you and are taking you back to your family. So the easiest way for us to convince her that she's on the wrong track is for us to not travel immediately to London."

"You want to rent a room at the inn here and wait her out?" Grace guessed.

"That would be ideal, but how are we going to get Judith inside when the woman is watching us this closely? We need to lose her first, and the only way to do that is to convince her she's wrong. This town isn't far enough off the highway for her to think we aren't still heading to London. But if it appears that we're retracing our steps—"

"North?" Grace cut in.

"Yes, maybe even back to Northampton, since it's not that far from here. I know that's going out of our way, but she's more likely to think she's wasting her time and take her search elsewhere if she sees us riding in the opposite direction of London."

"That's not a bad idea," Grace admitted.

"I know," Katey said, pleased with herself. "We can even get a room in a different inn and have a nice lunch sent up while we pass a few hours, just to make sure she's no longer in the area. I'd like to give her time to get off the highway so we don't run into her again later. And we'll still have plenty of time to get Judith home before nightfall."

"That's assuming she doesn't follow directly behind us all the way back to Northampton."

"Well, let's find out."

They implemented the new plan, heading back the way they'd come. Grace still kept a close eye on the road behind them. It was disappointing to see that the Scotswoman hadn't given up yet. She was still back there, though at a greater distance. And then it was a relief to see her stop a rider heading in their same direction.

Grace closed the curtain over the window and sat back in her seat with a smile. "Doubt is taking hold of her. It looks like she's starting to stop others to ask if they've seen the girl. Before long we might even lose sight of her."

seven

"ALL RIGHT, YANK," Anthony said, "I'm going to trust you to carry out the switch. But I'm not going to be far away in case anything goes wrong."

Boyd was inordinately pleased that Anthony Malory was expressing confidence in him. Perhaps it was because his family still viewed him as the "baby brother," a hothead who was quick to engage in fisticuffs. While his brothers grew older, they failed to notice that he did, too. Yes, he admired pugilists greatly and welcomed any chance to test his own skills, but he was far less impulsive than he'd once been. He was gratified that a Malory, and one he actually admired, recognized that he was capable of handling such a tense, important situation.

Anthony wasn't about to wait until tomorrow for the exchange to take place when he could try to find his daughter today. Northampton was only a few hours' hard ride away, after all. They could be there and search the entire town before nightfall. Not that they were going to do anything so obvious. They didn't know how many people were involved in the blackmail scheme and couldn't take the chance that the criminals would be watching for a search like that, or even watching the roads. Which was why Anthony, Jeremy, and Boyd left London in a coach.

Three horses were tied to the back of it in case they needed to move more quickly. But the coach would conceal Anthony, who would, they assumed, be recognized, and Jeremy, who closely resembled Anthony. Boyd merely rode along with them while they figured out their separate plans of action.

"They'd be stupid to set up a meeting place near their own town," Anthony speculated. "So I seriously doubt they live anywhere near Northampton, which eliminates a door-to-door search. But they might be holding Judy in an abandoned house or barn, someplace where they can keep Judith without drawing notice to her."

"You think they'd sneak her into an inn?" Boyd asked.

"Maybe," Jeremy said. "She's small. It could be done, so we probably shouldn't discount it."

"If we're discussing all possibilities, they could take her anywhere without sneaking about if they've threatened her into being quiet," Boyd pointed out. "Would she do as she's told? Or is she brave enough to yell for help?"

Anthony slammed his fist sideways into the wall of the coach. "She's probably too terrified to do anything!"

Jeremy tried to ignore the outburst from his distraught uncle and told Boyd, "She's as gusty as my sister Jack is, and too smart to do anything foolish. Why don't you check the inns. I really can't see them being stupid enough to use an inn where other people might notice, but we have to cover all possibilities. My uncle and I will drive around and look out for abandoned buildings."

"You keep supposing they aren't stupid, but I have to disagree," Boyd said. "They did this. They're damn stupid. But I know what I need to do and where to meet you two later to report my progress, so I'll take off now and get started on the search. Hopefully I'll have some news by the time you roll into town."

They stopped long enough for Boyd to get his horse and ride off. As much as they'd like to, they couldn't all race toward Northampton. That would attract attention. The coach was going to progress in a normal manner, while Boyd would reach the town an hour or two sooner.

Grimly thinking about what he was going to do if he got his hands on the people who did this, Boyd almost didn't see the wild woman turning her coach around in the middle of the road. On horseback, he merely moved around the ancient vehicle, thinking the woman shouldn't be driving if she didn't know how to turn around without blocking the entire road.

"Wait up, mon," the wild-haired woman shouted at him. "I'm looking for my daughter. The lass has run away from home again. Ha' ye seen—"

Boyd didn't stop, but shouted back, "I've seen no women today other than you."

"I'm no' that auld, mon, tae be having a grown child yet," she called back in an offended tone.

Boyd was running out of patience. He'd already been stopped twice for directions that he couldn't give. He was following directions himself!

So he said simply, "I've seen no females of any sort. Good day." And he rode on.

He made good time after that, galloping past other vehicles going his way, avoiding those heading south. But about twenty minutes later, a red-haired gent racing down the road on a horse pulled up to hail him.

"Ha' ye seen a Scotswomon heading this way?"

Boyd didn't answer, he just pointed his thumb behind him and rode on. Busy road, but if anyone else tried to stop him, he might just speak with the pistol in his pocket.

eight

GEORDIE CAMERON WAS terrified. He should just go home and leave his wife, Maisie, to her own devices. If she ever returned to Scotland, she'd find a divorce waiting for her, or a jail cell.

Sleep on it, she'd said? He'd wanted *her* to sleep on it so they could agree in the morning to take the child home and never do anything so stupid again. That was the only outcome that would allow him to forgive Maisie. But he'd woken to an empty room and a scrawled note that the child had escaped.

Well, good for her, had been his first thought, although he couldn't imagine how she'd done it after Maisie had tied her to the bed, but he'd hoped that was the end of it.

He'd packed his bag, found that his driver and coach were waiting where they should be, and asked the innkeeper where his wife was. The man hadn't seen her, but in a gossiping mood, mentioned that someone had come looking for an old coach that had been stolen. And that's when the fear came back.

He was afraid his wife had gone looking for the girl again, and if she found her, that she'd continue with her extortion plans. Then Anthony Malory would find

Geordie and kill him. He could envision no other outcome—unless he could find Maisie first.

He borrowed a saddle for one of his coach horses, thinking he could catch up to Maisie much quicker that way.
Having to pass through Northampton slowed him down a
little, since the inn they'd stayed at was on the north road
out of town. But the city wasn't as big as it might have been
after a fire had destroyed most of it in 1675, and the streets
had actually been widened during the rebuilding.

South was the only direction he could think to go.
The child would travel in that direction to get back to
London. Hopefully she hadn't just set off down the road
on foot. Maisie would find her too easily that way. But
she could have gotten a ride if she was smart enough to
ask someone. It was a well-traveled road, especially in the
morning when produce was being brought in to market.
She might even already be home. He could hope . . .

It was Maisie he had to find and drag home. Not that
he wouldn't take Roslynn's daughter home if he happened
to find her instead. But he'd just as soon not go anywhere
near the Malorys. And a lot of travelers were on the road.
He didn't ask them all, but the few he did stop kept pointing him south. Maisie was making a nuisance of herself,
apparently, according to one farmer.

But then the traffic slowed down. He'd passed several
roads that went off in other directions. He was beginning
to wonder if he was going the right way still. Did this road
go all the way to London? He couldn't remember from his
one other time in England. And there'd been no one to
ask for the last half hour. But then he saw another coach
heading his way and rode quickly toward it.

Anthony Malory's driver had been told to stop for no one, and he'd had to get nasty a couple times, to keep from slowing down. But this new traveler was persistent and rode alongside the coach for a moment to ask, "Ha' ye seen a Scotswoman? She'd be driving a coach, I'm guessing, unless she stole a horse," and then in a shout as the coach kept rolling by him, "Ye could ha' just said nae, mon!"

Anthony yanked aside the coach curtain, vaguely recognizing that voice. He just caught sight of the carrot-red hair as the petitioner continued on his way down the road. That was enough for him to pound on the roof to get the driver to stop. Geordie Cameron in the same vicinity as the people who'd taken his daughter? The same man who'd gone to extremes to steal Roslynn's fortune from her eight years ago? Coincidental? Not bloody likely.

He leapt out of the coach before it fully stopped. Geordie was still close enough that Anthony didn't even bother grabbing his horse tied to the back of the coach. He simply raced after him and almost reached him, too. But Geordie had heard something to make him glance back. And seeing the one man he'd hoped to never see again bearing down on him . . .

Geordie shrieked, slammed his heels into his mount, and tore off into the woods alongside the road. Disgusted to have missed grabbing him by mere inches, Anthony ran back for his own mount.

Jeremy was out of the coach by then and even handed Anthony the reins to his horse, having witnessed the chase. He merely asked, "Who is it?"

"A dead man," Anthony said as he mounted up and turned around to give chase. "He just doesn't know it yet," he added before he, too, disappeared into the woods.

His mount was a Thoroughbred. Geordie was riding a coach horse. It didn't take long to catch up to him, yank him off his horse, and drop him on the ground.

Anthony dismounted slowly, now that he had his man. Geordie was staring up at him terrified, while trying to scoot backward.

"Wait!" Geordie shouted. "Ye mun hear me oout! It wasna me!"

It was the wrong thing to say, because it smacked of culpability. Anthony bent over to lift Geordie's face up to his fist.

"Och, God, no' my teeth again. Wait!"

Geordie covered his face with both arms. Anthony kicked him in the side. The arms fell away with a groan. He didn't usually kick a man when he was down, but this pathetic worm didn't deserve gentleman's rules.

Anthony bent to one knee to grab a fistful of red hair before he asked, "Where is she?"

"I dinna know. I swear!"

His fist slammed into Geordie's face for the second time. "Wrong answer, Cameron."

"My nose!" Geordie screamed as he tried to stem the blood pouring from it. "Ye broke it again!"

"Did you think you were walking away from here?" Anthony asked. His voice was calm, even when he added, "I'm going to need a shovel by the time I'm done with you."

"Ye can ask her! She'll tell ye it wasna me!"

"Ask who?"

"Yer daughter—nae, dinna hit me again! It was m'wife who took her. She brought me down here tae visit her aunt, she said. Then she disappeared for the whole day and came back wi' yer daughter. She's oout of her mind and I tauld her sae. The lass knows I had nae part of this."

"Then where is she?"

"I would ha' brought her home tae ye this morn, but she escaped on her own! I'm no' oout here looking for her, I'm looking for m'wife tae make sure *she* doesn't find her again."

"And what gave your wife the idea to do this?"

Geordie blanched again.

nine

"I'M EXPECTING MY niece and her servants. Have they arrived yet?" Boyd described Judith for the innkeeper, adding, "She's a remarkably beautiful child. If you saw her, you'd never forget her."

This was only the second inn Boyd had come to, and he still had a lot of ground to cover.

He'd already paid for a room just to get on the man's good side. And he had a few more questions ready for the innkeeper as soon as the man responded negatively to his niece story. Boyd had suggested that Judith might have been walked through the front door of an inn, but he didn't *really* think that would be the case.

So he wasn't expecting to hear, "Yes, sir, second door at the top of the stairs. Right next to yours."

After Boyd recovered from his surprise, he asked, "How many servants does she have with her this time?" He made it sound as if he was expecting an extravagant amount, but he was really hoping to find out how many people he was going to be up against when he rescued Judith.

"Only two women came in with her, sir. If there were other servants, she didn't require rooms for them."

Boyd gave the man a nod of thanks. Good fortune of

this sort didn't usually land in his lap. And now he had a decision to make. Wait the hour or so until Anthony got to town to tell him that he'd found where Judith was being kept, or get her out of there himself? He favored the latter and was halfway up the stairs when Jeremy hailed him.

Boyd waited for the lad to reach him before he asked, "What are you doing here?"

"Getting lucky. First inn I check and here you are." And then Jeremy chuckled. "Actually, I recognized your horse out front."

"I thought we'd agreed you wouldn't show your face around here because you resemble your uncle too much?"

"Relax, Yank. It's over—or mostly so. My cousin managed to get herself out of this mess on her own." Jeremy explained what Geordie Cameron had confessed to. "So Uncle Tony is searching along the highway south of where we ran into Cameron. He sent me north to do the same."

"Is that why your voice sounds hoarse?"

Jeremy nodded. "Considering how smart my cousin is, if she had no luck catching a ride with someone and is trekking it instead, she's more'n likely ducking into the woods whenever she sees someone coming toward her on the road. But I got no response to my shouts, so she's probably further south by now. Uncle Tony would like you to remain here for the day—just in case. He'll send word."

Boyd frowned. "I'd say we're in the middle of 'just in case.' She's here."

"Who?"

"Who do you think?"

"Now don't get testy," Jeremy said. "I just told you she escaped."

"And I just described Judith to the innkeeper. He said she's up here."

"Hell's bells, the Scot lied?"

"Why would he tell the truth?" Boyd countered.

"Because my uncle was going to tear his limbs off."

"A much better reason to lie, if you ask me."

"Bloody hell." But then Jeremy rolled his eyes. "Wait a minute. Just because she *was* here doesn't mean she still is. So this is where they were keeping her—and where she escaped from."

Boyd nodded, accepting that possibility. "Easy enough to confirm, since I was told which room she's in. Come on, let's see if anyone is still in it."

They stood outside the room. Boyd was about to try the door when they both heard from the other side of it, "I'm famished again."

Jeremy immediately yanked Boyd down the corridor. "Bloody hell," he hissed. "That *was* my cousin's voice."

"I heard," Boyd replied, his pistol now in hand. "We do this with the least danger to Judy."

"Then put that away. You're good with your fists. You don't need to be brandishing a weapon that might get them firing some of their own."

Boyd agreed, "My thought was to frighten them enough to prevent any actions on their part, but you're right. According to the innkeeper, it's just two women with Judy, so a weapon shouldn't be necessary."

"Cameron's wife? It's sounding like the Scot did lie after all."

"Either way, we just have two women to deal with at the moment, so here's the plan," Boyd said in a whisper. "I'll kick the door in. You grab your cousin and take her to her father. Don't stop for anything. There was a lot of money involved in this, so we don't know how many thugs they might have hired to help and where they might be stationed around town. I'll take care of whoever is left in the room and turn them over to the constable before I catch up with you."

"Shh," Jeremy said as the door they were planning to break down started to open.

They turned their backs on the door. As Boyd tried to appear inconspicuous by unlocking the door to his room, he heard a woman say, "I won't be long fetching some food. Lock this door behind me."

A woman's chuckle came from inside the room. "You worry too much, Grace."

The woman who was going to get food didn't even glance down the corridor in their direction. She simply marched toward the stairs, then disappeared from view.

"Now would be a good time to get Judy, while there's one less person for me to deal with," Boyd said.

He didn't have to kick the door in. They got to it before it was locked from the inside and burst into the room together. The element of surprise worked well.

Jeremy went straight to his cousin. She started to say his name excitedly, but he put a hand over her mouth as he cautioned her to be silent, and within seconds he'd swept her up in his arms and was gone.

Which left Boyd staring incredulously at the remaining occupant of the room. Likewise, she was staring back at him. The woman of his passionate dreams, supposedly a mother with children of her own—or other children she'd stolen?—had abducted Anthony Malory's daughter. He grabbed her and, putting a hand over her mouth, pulled her out of there and into the room next door.

ten

"NOT ONE WORD," Boyd told the woman in his arms. "If I even hear you breathe, I'll gag you."

He hadn't removed his hand from her mouth yet! When he realized that, he knew he was in trouble. He ought to set her down and put some distance between them. His mind might clear then. It certainly wasn't clear now. But he couldn't bear to take his hands off her yet.

Mrs. Tyler in the flesh, not a dream this time. Whether he was sleeping or awake, she'd filled his mind to the point of becoming a nuisance ever since he'd clapped eyes on her. But this was real. And she wasn't the spirited, kind-hearted young woman he'd thought she was.

"Those children you sailed with, they weren't yours, were they? You stole them, too, didn't you?"

He wasn't letting her answer. He didn't think he could withstand a barrage of excuses from her. He'd end up believing whatever she chose to tell him, and he'd let her go with an apology and a smile. But she was starting to squirm against him. Oh, God . . .

He walked across the room, dragging her with him, and kicked an armless chair toward the center of the room. He thrust her into it, then leaned down, putting his face close to hers.

"You can't imagine how close I am to ravishing you. Get up from that chair and I'll consider it an invitation."

"You're making a *really* big—!"

He quickly put his finger to her lips. There was enough warning in his eyes that she didn't try to finish what she had started to say, despite how angry she'd sounded.

"Do I need to be more explicit in how close you are to ending up in my bed?" he asked as he removed his finger. "Or was that an invitation?"

She shook her head at him without breaking the virulent glare she had pinned on his face. She had big, beautiful eyes, dark emerald, furious—did she think he cared?

He straightened up and looked down at her. "Not going to try to get up?"

She shook her head again.

"I'm disappointed. If I were thinking clearly, I wouldn't have warned you, and then we might be bouncing around on that bed over there instead. That's still an option. Go ahead and stand up. Please."

She didn't move a muscle. He gritted his teeth. He wasn't sure whom he was more angry at, himself, or her. The rules of decency might be suspended—she was a criminal, after all. But he still couldn't bring himself to take advantage of that fact, despite how beautiful she was, despite how much he still wanted her.

She was dressed in a simple light blue frock. With long sleeves and a high collar, there was nothing sexy about it—except it hugged the luscious curves of her body. Her long black hair was in a thick braid down her back. It was how she'd worn it on the ship. She'd even hooked the end of it on her belt to contain it. He'd thought she'd done that because of the fierce wind out on the ocean, but she'd laughed at one of the dinners she'd shared with him and his captain and told them it was to keep her from sitting on it. So why didn't she just put it up in some fancy coiffure the way other women did? Because she wasn't like other women!

He moved around behind her to try to end the visual temptation she was putting him through. It didn't help at all. Why the devil did he bring her in here? He still couldn't think straight. He should have carted her straight to jail. He should at least have sent for the local constable. He didn't move to do either. The idea of Katey Tyler in jail turned him cold.

He could hie off with her, get her out of England. He owned a ship. It would be easy enough to do. But then what? Enjoy her for a week or two, then let her go at a port on some other continent? So she could get back to her business of child stealing, just somewhere else? When he thought of Roslynn Malory crying all day over the well-being of her daughter, he knew he couldn't do it.

Then what the hell was he going to do with her? He knew he was just avoiding the inevitable.

He hadn't moved far enough behind her. He caught a whiff of her scent, uniquely hers, a little floral, a little spicy like hot apple pie, a little earthy. He closed his eyes, fighting the urge to touch her again. He lost.

eleven

KATEY WASN'T FRIGHTENED—YET. She'd noticed that Judith had recognized and been glad to see the young man who'd carted her off, so she wasn't worried about the child. And she'd instantly recognized the man who'd dragged her into this other room. Boyd Anderson, the owner of *The Oceanus*. How could she ever forget *him*? He was the first handsome man ever to show an interest in her, the first really handsome man she'd ever met, for that matter. But what was he doing here?

She'd been so surprised to see him burst into her room when she'd thought she'd never see him again. But he obviously thought that she was the culprit in Judith's abduction, and he was treating her like a common criminal because of it! He was going to be quite embarrassed and deservedly so when she corrected him—if she ever got a chance to.

It infuriated her that he'd threatened her into silence. Would he really ravish her? But she'd get her explanation out first, surely, and then . . . what if he didn't believe her? He *did* seem positive that she was guilty, and he was quite angry about it. What if he'd rather ravish her than believe her?

She shivered. Oh, my, she wished he hadn't mentioned

that. She couldn't get the thought out of her mind now. And then she realized, incredulously, that he was touching her! She swatted his hand away, but it came back to caress her cheek again. Gooseflesh spread down her back and arms. His fingers moved toward her neck. She drew in her breath and held it, waiting . . . waiting . . .

He tilted her head back. He was standing so close behind her that the back of her head touched the buckle on the belt of his trousers. And he was looking down at her with such heat in his dark eyes.

"You can't imagine how much—"

He cut himself off. He took his eyes off her face and raised them to the ceiling instead. Katey seized the moment to bolt out of the chair. She didn't mean to knock it over, but she was glad to see the small barrier lying on the floor between them when she turned to glare at him.

"You drag me in here, threaten me, then make improper advances! If I didn't know you, Boyd Anderson, I would be screaming right now. That's still an option! How dare you treat me in this high-handed fashion?"

He picked up the chair and set it aside without taking his eyes off her. Those dark, expressive eyes were slowly roaming over her curves in such a way that her stomach actually fluttered. She was reminded of their time on his ship. So often she'd caught him staring at her like this when he didn't think she'd noticed. Grace had said he was having carnal thoughts about her. He'd had them then, and he was having them now. But now he wasn't trying to hide them!

"It's occurred to me that your activities here change everything," he said in a low, husky tone. "You're much more sophisticated than I thought, aren't you, Katey?"

When his eyes came back to hers, she couldn't help but

blush because she understood what he was insinuating. That the blush might make him think he'd guessed correctly didn't occur to her. But he was quick in closing the space between them. Too quick.

"Do you know how often I've dreamed of having you alone like this?" he said, cupping her face in his hands.

For the briefest moment, Katey was mesmerized by his touch. It was tender, it was romantic, and he wasn't the only one who'd had such dreams since they'd first met. He was about to kiss her. She knew, deep down, that she'd be lost if he did, because she wanted him to! He made her feel excitement of the unfamiliar sort, and while she was obviously no more prepared to deal with it now than she had been on his ship, it was still thrilling beyond measure.

"I'm almost glad you've shown your true colors," he continued.

That broke the spell. He was still accusing her of something she hadn't done, and he thought he could take liberties because of it?

"Stop it!" she said, and slapped his hands away.

But his hands didn't fall far. They went to her hips instead. And before she could even think to step away from him, he was pulling her closer to him. She gasped and placed both hands on his chest to shove him away, but it didn't work! As she was pushing, she couldn't help but notice how hard and muscular his chest was, how warm she felt pressed so closely against his big body.

Desperate to tamp down the hot swirl of sensations that were overwhelming her, she said, "I'm going to sock you! You've been warned."

"Don't do that, sweetheart. I don't want you to hurt your hand."

Reluctantly, he let go. But he looked amused! And

while he'd released her carefully enough that she didn't stumble back, his amusement sharpened her fury. "How kind of you, but this has gone on long enough. What are you even doing here? Judith's a Malory, you're not!"

Her last few words came out as a shout, she was so flustered, which made his calm reply seem like a whisper in comparison. "No, I'm not, but I have a sister and brother who have both married into that family."

That surprised her. But it must also have reminded him of what he'd accused her of because his eyes narrowed as they gazed at her.

"How could you do this?" he demanded. "Do you even know who you've crossed? Malorys never forget a wrong against them. I can't believe you would knowingly stir up this hornet's nest."

Her back stiffened. "Why don't you examine what you just said? You can't believe it because it's not true! I had no part in this."

"Then explain what you were doing in that room with Judith."

"Oh, finally you're asking what you should have asked to begin with?" she said scathingly. "I was helping her! I was on my way back from Scotland when—"

"My God," he cut in, his expression now as incredulous as his tone, "you're Geordie Cameron's wife, aren't you?"

"Who?"

But he didn't hear her and was saying to himself, "Now it makes sense. He even said this was your idea."

"Who?" she asked again, but again he didn't seem to hear her.

"You've got one minute to explain. Tell me you're innocent, that you were coerced, that you were convinced no one would be hurt by this."

He was giving her a list of excuses to pick from if she didn't have any ready for him? Was he just being sarcastic? Or was he really hoping she could give him a good reason to let her go?

"I rescued Judith," she said quickly. "She'll tell you."

That should have been enough to make him start apologizing. It should at least have caused him some doubt. But she could tell by his expression that she'd said it too late, that he didn't believe her.

"Conveniently for *you,* she isn't here to corroborate that, is she?" he said curtly. "But let me tell you what is obvious. You were keeping Judith in a locked room. We heard your accomplice remind you to lock the door when she left. If you had rescued her, you would be taking her home right now, not detaining her in the same town where you arranged to exchange her for the fortune you demanded."

Katey gulped. That sounded so, so—incriminating! "Well, before you do anything rash, let's go find Judith," she suggested reasonably. "I assume you'll believe the child when she tells you I snuck her away from those people who had her and—"

"Jeremy would be back here to tell me if that was the case. Now, I gave you a chance to tell me something plausible. You haven't."

At which point Katey lost all patience with him. "Are you just pretending to be dense or does it come naturally to you? Why would they come back here? Judith will have already told her relative that I helped her. He isn't going to assume as *you* have that I'm guilty. He surely knows the truth by now and he'll think you do as well. So why would he come back here? He doesn't know that you've been ridiculously stubborn in detaining me. If anything, he'll assume you thanked me properly for my help and will soon be catching up with him."

"It's my sister's niece you stole, Jeremy's cousin, and her parents have been out of their minds with worry for two days now. Jeremy isn't going to delay a single second in getting her straight home to her family. Come on."

twelve

KATEY'S FIRST PANICKED thought as Boyd dragged her downstairs was that he was taking her to jail. He mumbled something about letting the authorities figure it out, that he couldn't trust his own instincts where she was concerned. So all she could think to shout at him was "Wait! *Wait!*"

He didn't. And he reinforced her conclusion when he said to the wide-eyed innkeeper as they passed the man, "Caught her sneaking into my room. I'm surprised to find thieves in a nice town like this."

Katey gasped at that accusation, but Boyd wasn't stopping so she couldn't let the innkeeper know who the real culprit was. He pulled her straight out the door, and his horse *would* have to be right there.

He tossed her up in the saddle none too gently. With his hands off her for a moment, she started to slide off the horse to the other side, but Boyd mounted behind her too quickly. With Boyd's arms on either side of her now as he gathered the reins, she felt like she was being caged.

A deep sense of rage settled over her. *Pigheaded, arbitrary, thinks-he-knows-it-all blackguard!* she screamed to herself. And to think she'd liked him! Too much! How many times on that voyage with him had she been tempted to tell him the truth, that she wasn't really married. Ha! She'd been right to hold her tongue.

But she wasn't holding it now. "You should have done this to begin with," she yelled at him. "Instead of detaining me against my will. And don't be surprised if you're the one who ends up in jail, Mr. High-and-Mighty. When I get done telling the constable how you held me prisoner in that room, manhandled me, and falsely accused me, we'll see who's laughing."

"Then I guess it's a good thing that's not where we're going."

He sounded amused, as if he was sure her threats were desperate attempts to perpetuate her lies. But if she'd been paying attention instead of railing at him, she would have noticed that he'd galloped out of town and was only now slowing down to a less grueling pace. She frowned, staring at the now familiar highway up ahead.

"Where are you taking me then?"

"To London. It was your idea," he reminded her.

She gasped. "I never said we should go to London, I said we should find Judith!"

"And she'll be at home. I warned you Jeremy wouldn't waste any time taking her back to her parents. They'll be in London long before we can catch up to them."

"My God, I can't believe you're carrying this to this outrageous extreme!" she exclaimed. "All you had to do was *listen* to me."

"I did," he said, sounding angry again, "but all you did was claim to be innocent when I caught you red-handed! *That,* sweetheart, doesn't work. So what was the truth? You got separated from Cameron, didn't you? You moved Judy without telling him? Did you have a fight with him? Decide to keep the fortune all to yourself?"

Katey stared incredulously before her, hearing new charges that were so preposterous they didn't deserve to be answered. "If you'd just use your head for what it's supposed to be good for," she retorted, "you'd realize how ridiculous all those allegations are."

To which he leaned into her back to say, "I can't think straight when you're within touching distance, when the only thing on my mind is carrying you to the nearest bed, so I don't dare just take you at your word, Katey Tyler. I'm sorry."

She drew in her breath sharply. It wasn't just his words that affected her. It was also his chest pressed against her, his arms tight on either side of her, and his warm breath against her ear. The shiver that ran through her body had nothing to do with the brisk autumn air blowing against her face.

It took several minutes for her to get her own desires under control and to drum up enough nerve to point out, "You don't call this touching distance?"

"You noticed that, did you?" He chuckled. "But there's no longer a bed nearby, so I think I can manage to restrain myself long enough to turn you over to the Malorys. Judith's father can sort this out and figure out what to do . . . with . . . you."

It wasn't just how he tried to not end that statement. She also felt him stiffen, as if he'd just realized something he should have thought of sooner. Of course he'd already admitted he wasn't thinking straight . . .

"What?" she demanded as she glanced back at him. "Did you overlook something pertinent? Like you have no right to be taking me anywhere?!"

Instead of answering her, his eyes latched on to her mouth. "You might want to keep your lips out of my view, Katey. Really. Unless—?"

"I get the point!" she exclaimed, and whipped her head back around.

The chill wind hit her in the face again due to his fast pace. But had the clouds overhead darkened? It was going to rain, she was sure of it, and he was foolishly racing them down the highway on horseback!

"This is absurd," she grumbled. "I was going to London, but I'm not going by horseback! I demand you take me back for my coach and driver. And my maid is going to be frantic with worry when she can't find me. And my clothes! I'm not dressed to travel like this!"

"Do you ever keep quiet?"

"Do you ever listen to anything that's said to you?" she shot back. "I'm not dressed to ride a horse like this. My skirt—"

"Tuck it under your legs," he suggested. But he also pressed closer to her again, leaning over her shoulder to see what she was complaining about. "Nice calves. I had a feeling they would be."

"Keep your eyes to yourself!" she snapped, blushing, and shrugged him away from her.

"I'm trying!"

My God, she almost laughed. If she weren't so furious with him, she probably would have. What an outlandish rogue he was turning out to be. This lust of his had been present on the voyage, but while she'd known about it, they had both had to pretend it didn't exist. Her supposed marital status had served as a firm barrier that had helped them accomplish that. That barrier had crumbled today and he'd become entirely too bold.

She tucked her skirt tight under her inner thighs on both legs, but that didn't help with the wind. "I'm still cold," she complained. "I'm blocking most of this wind from you, so you're not feeling how brisk it's gotten. I need my coat. No, I need my coach! There is absolutely no reason to make this trip this way when I have a perfectly good coach ten minutes back."

"No," he said simply.

"Why?!" she wailed.

"Because I'm not letting you out of my sight. Do you *really* think I'd trust your driver to take us where I tell him to go? Someone will be sent back to deal with the rest of your cohorts in good time."

She gritted her teeth. "Mark my words, it's going to rain. Look up at the sky if you don't believe me."

He barked a short laugh. "When doesn't it look like that in this country?"

"You're saying it's not going to rain?"

"I doubt it. It's looked like that all morning and it hasn't rained yet."

"I'm still cold."

He leaned his chest against her again to say suggestively, "Well, you could turn around to face me. I guarantee that will warm you very fast. Or you could put my jacket on."

"I'll take the jacket."

She heard his sigh as he leaned away from her again. A moment later, his jacket was draped about her shoulders. Katey didn't thank him, but she quickly put it on. She wished it didn't smell like him, though. It made it seem as if she were surrounded by *his* warmth.

A few minutes of silence passed as she snuggled deep into that warmth. Her legs were resting on his with her sitting in front of him on the saddle. His arms on each side of her hugged her more tightly, too, until it felt as if he were actually holding her in his arms. Him, him, him. God! She needed to think about something else!

"You didn't say what gave you pause a while ago, when you mentioned the Malorys," she said.

"It merely occurred to me that you don't need to be scared of any constables, sweetheart. You *do* need to be scared of Anthony Malory, though."

She rolled her eyes. He really and truly did think she was guilty, while she was sure she'd have nothing to fear from Judith's father. Boyd was going to be the one who would have to account for his mistake, and she relished that. But that was assuming that Judith would think to mention Katey's part in this little adventure, and if she hadn't, *if* Katey would be allowed to speak to the child first before . . . before what?

"This isn't the first time you've implied the Malorys are to be feared. Just who are they?"

"One of the more powerful families in this realm, and very family-oriented. Hurt one and you've hurt them all. But Judy's father, well, he beat your husband, Geordie, so severely it's doubtful he'll ever look the same again. He's been so out of his mind with worry that he'll take heads off before he asks questions."

Katey stiffened. "I told you, I don't know this Geordie person. And Judy was much too sweet to have a father like the one you're describing, so stop trying to scare me."

She felt him shrug when he replied, "Don't say I didn't warn you. Anthony isn't likely to lay a hand on you. I didn't mean to imply that. You're a woman, after all. But he can make sure you spend the rest of your life behind bars. In fact, my first thought when I found you knee-deep in this was to rescue *you*."

She decided to humor him by asking, "I suppose you mean from prison?"

"Yes. I could get you out of the country instead. That's still an option. Think you could manage to convince me to do that?"

She snorted. She should have known he wasn't being serious, that his thoughts had taken a sensual turn. "That doesn't deserve an answer."

"By the end of the day you'll think otherwise."

"By the end of the day," she shot back angrily, "you'll be on your knees begging my forgiveness, which *won't* be forthcoming, I promise you. In fact, if I ever see you again after today, you'll be lucky if I don't shoot you. You, sir, are a . . . a . . . a stubborn jackass!"

She heard his chuckle. "But you like me anyway, don't you, sweetheart?"

"Oh!" She wasn't going to say another word to him. Odious man. But he *would* be sorry!

It started to rain. Big drops. She smirked for all of two minutes, until she was quite drenched.

"Now look what you've done!" she said accusingly.

"Sorry, but I didn't summon up this downpour."

"I'm freezing!"

"You're nothing of the sort," he said, but his arms did close around her a bit more tightly.

"I'm going to catch my death and it will be your fault. I *told* you I was going to London. We *could* have been riding in my nice, warm coach! But, no, you couldn't be sensible about this, could you?"

She sneezed to make her point. It wasn't a feigned sneeze, but it wasn't a true sign that she was catching a cold either. Raindrops had gathered on the tip of her nose, tickling the sneeze out of her.

But it was enough to make him ask, "I don't suppose you know of any shelter nearby?"

She blinked. He was going to be sensible? A bit late, but still . . .

"As it happens, there's a small town about ten minutes from here. You just passed the road to it. Go back. There's an inn there."

He turned around. It took him less than five minutes on horseback to reach the town she'd stopped at that morning, but then he'd spurred his mount to a gallop again to get them out of the rain sooner.

She pointed out the inn when they were in the center of the small town in case he hadn't noticed it yet. He whisked them straight inside, leaving her in front of the fireplace in the common room to start warming up, while he paid for a room where they could wait out the storm.

She wasn't really cold. The rain might have brought a little chill to the air, but the weather wasn't even close to wintry yet. She'd merely been trying to make Boyd feel guilty, not that she thought he was capable of remorse. Yet. But he would be when he finally found out what a colossal mistake he'd made.

She kept an eye on him while she held her hands out to the fire. Unfortunately, he was keeping an eye on her. She sighed. There'd be no slipping out a side door without his noticing—yet.

She also thought about making a scene now that they were around other people again. Having a constable summoned could go either way, though. Without her servants here to verify her story, Boyd might be believed instead, and she could well end up in jail after all. She decided not to risk that. Besides, she would rather make her way back to Northampton, collect her belongings and her servants, and put what had turned into a ridiculous adventure behind her.

"Come on," he said, taking her arm to escort her upstairs. "If this rain doesn't stop within the hour, I'll see if I can find a coach to hire for the remainder of the journey."

Concessions? So he could make them? But he should have thought of coaches before he galloped them out of the much larger town of Northampton. He wasn't likely to find one to hire here. But she didn't mention that. Anything that would separate them long enough for her to escape she would agree with.

To that end, she said as soon as he ushered her into the room, "I'm starving."

He ignored her and went straight to the fireplace to get it lit. She wished he'd forget that she'd said she was freezing. He was so single-minded!

Annoyed, she said, "Did you hear me? I'm starving?"

He glanced over his shoulder at her. "Really?"

"Yes, really. I haven't eaten since yesterday," she lied, but for good measure added, "My maid had just gone to fetch us food when you burst into my room."

He still got the fire going before he stood up, dusted his hands, and said, "All right, I'll see about getting some food sent up and maybe a hot bath, too. Dry off while I'm gone, but stay the hell away from that bed. Is that clear?"

"I didn't say I was tired," she quipped.

He just stared at her until a blush appeared on her face. She knew what he'd meant. He'd mentioned her and beds in the same breath enough times for her to never forget just how much he wanted to get her into one.

"We're clear," she was forced to say.

He ran a hand through his wet hair and glanced at the comfy bed. "This is probably a bad idea," he said in a half groan. "We should just wait out the storm downstairs. We can get food down there as well."

That wasn't going to help her to get away from him! "*You* wait downstairs," she quickly said. "I'll take that hot bath you mentioned. Really. It will probably keep me from catching a cold."

He stared at her for another long moment before he nodded and left the room, closing the door behind him. She immediately heard the scraping of a key in the lock and ground her teeth in exasperation. Well, no wonder he'd so readily agreed. He knew damn well he'd be locking her in!

But Katey wasted no time in examining other options. The room had two windows that overlooked the street, and the street was empty because of the rain. One of those windows was even directly over the slanted porch roof at the front of the inn. And it wouldn't be that far of a drop if she dangled from that roof.

Ten minutes later Boyd stood at that same window that Katey had left open in her escape. Although he'd tossed a coin to one of the inn workers downstairs to get his horse stabled, he could see out the window that the horse wasn't where he'd left it and had a feeling Katey had gotten to it first. It was just as well.

As soon as he'd left the room and Katey's presence, he'd started having doubts about her involvement in Judith's abduction. It just didn't feel right labeling her a criminal. She befriended animals, for God's sake! And with that thought he began to think he'd *wanted* her to be guilty. Then he could put her from his mind, finally, as unworthy of his regard, and for a married woman, she'd been on his mind far too long as it was.

But whether he was making excuses for her now and she was actually guilty as sin, he wasn't going to chase her down. Judith was safe now. And he couldn't really bear the thought of Katey Tyler in jail.

thirteen

KATEY RODE QUICKLY back to Northampton despite the rain. Halfway to her destination, she rode out of the storm. Although the road ahead of her was completely dry, the solid bank of clouds wasn't breaking up. And while the clouds weren't as dark as they were farther south, the rain could still drift north and drench her again. But that was the least of her worries.

The storm clouds were probably making it seem later than it was, but the day was still nearly gone. There was no way she could gather up her servants and her belongings and reach London before nightfall. She was afraid to travel that same highway again anyway because she didn't want to risk running into Boyd again.

She'd delayed him by taking his horse, so she didn't expect him to be *right* behind her. But she didn't expect him to give up and go home, either. He'd proven to be too stubborn for that. But he wouldn't find her in Northampton again. She'd leave his horse there for him to find, not that she felt the least bit guilty for taking it after what he'd done, but she'd have no further need for it once she was on the road in her coach again—heading in some other direction.

She made quite a sight riding into town wet and

bedraggled, wearing a man's jacket. Even her hair had come loose, and she hadn't wasted time to stop to rebraid it. She probably should have. She was attracting far too many curious looks, though that might be because her calves were showing. Embarrassed, she dismounted so her legs would be properly covered again.

Leading the horse behind her now, Katey walked by the town's marketplace, which reminded Katey just how hungry she was now.

The market was closing down for the night, not that she had any coins to buy anything. But a few customers were still making their purchases, and one woman was shouting at a fruit seller whose stand Katey was passing.

"Just point me toward the nearest docks, mon!"

"I've already told you, you dafty woman, we don't have docks."

"I ken ye dinna hae any, but which way tae the nearest town that does? Did I no' say my husband is trying tae kill me? I hae tae leave the country, ye ken?"

Katey stopped in her tracks. She wasn't just hearing an interesting shouting match. Was that the same Scotswoman she, Grace, and Judith had spent half the morning trying to lose? With the woman's back to her, she couldn't be sure. But having twice been accused by Boyd of being Geordie Cameron's wife, she had a name now to put to Judith's abductor. And here was a Scotswoman trying to escape her husband, which made her think of what Boyd had mentioned about Anthony Malory beating Cameron senseless over what the man's wife had done.

Katey didn't really have any doubts by then, which was why she stopped a young boy running past her and whispered for him to fetch the constable. She'd detain Mrs. Cameron until he got there, and she was angry enough not to care how she did it. The woman had stolen and mistreated a child, chased them all over Northampton and the surrounding area trying to get the child back, and if it wasn't for her, Katey's memories of Boyd Anderson wouldn't be utterly ruined now. The woman wasn't going to walk away from all the trouble she'd caused without retribution if Katey could help it.

She approached the woman from behind. "Mrs. Cameron?"

The Scotswoman swung around immediately. Katey almost laughed at how quickly the fruit seller took off in the opposite direction to escape any further harassment. And Katey had no trouble recognizing her now. Her hair was still in wild disarray, and her eyes had a wild look to them as well.

"How'd ye know my name, eh?" she demanded in the same belligerent tone she'd been using with the fruit seller. "From the inn? We paid for that room, though we should've got our money back. Bluidy lock was broken on the door!"

Katey realized the woman didn't recognize her, but that didn't surprise her. Her clothes soaked and disheveled, her hair wet and windblown, Katey looked nothing like she did that morning, and in fact, she probably looked as wildly unkempt as the Scotswoman.

"I'm not from the inn."

Katey didn't point out who she was, though. She needed to detain the woman until the constable arrived, and engaging her in a conversation seemed to be the best way to do that.

Mrs. Cameron squinted her eyes at Katey. "Then where do I know ye from? Ye seem familiar tae me—never mind. If ye can tell me which way tae the nearest docks,

I'll be thanking ye. Otherwise I'll be finding someone who can."

Common sense would suggest heading to the nearest coast, but Katey merely said, "I'm afraid I can't help you there. I'm not all that familiar with this part of the country."

The Scotswoman snorted with impatience. "Then I dinna hae time tae waste chatting at ye. Good day."

Interesting how she'd put that, as if her words were the only ones that mattered. And she was already glancing around for someone else to accost with her demand for directions. But Katey needed to keep her talking. She'd rather wait to accuse her until the constable was there to arrest her.

"What's your hurry?"

"None of—"

Katey cut her off, "Did I actually hear you tell the fruit merchant you were running away from a husband determined to kill you? That was quite an exaggeration."

"That was the bluidy truth, womon. He took a beating that's made him dafty in the head. I barely recognized him. And now he wants tae take it oout on me."

"Take what out?"

"That he got blamed for what I did. Chased me down the road, he did, swearing he was going tae kill me afore the Mal—er, afore they got their hands on me like they did him. But here now, this isna any of yer business and I'm ooot of time. Geordie will be riding intae town any minute."

She started to walk away. Katey glanced anxiously behind her, but there was no sign of the constable yet, or the boy that she'd sent for him.

"Wait, Mrs. Cameron. I look familiar to you because you stopped me on the road earlier today. You were looking for your daughter, which we both know was a lie. You don't have a daughter any more than I do."

Mrs. Cameron swung back around. Her expression was momentarily surprised, but quickly turned angry as she poked a finger at Katey's shoulder. "Sae ye did steal her from me? I'd hae my fortune now if no' for ye. Where is she?"

"She's back with her family, where you won't be getting your greedy hands on her again. The constable is on his way to apprehend you. Did you really think you'd get away with this?"

Katey braced herself to stop the woman from taking flight, but Mrs. Cameron actually looked thoughtful, then amazed Katey by saying, "Aye, that's no' a bad idea. Jail will be a safe place tae hide from Geordie, I'm thinking."

Katey was thinking that Geordie Cameron might be daft for marrying this woman, but if anyone was *really* crazy, it was her.

"Come on then," Mrs. Cameron continued, and she even grabbed Katey's arm to take her with her. "Let's find yer constable, eh? I'll be needing ye tae say I'm guilty. They're no' likely tae believe me if I'm the only one saying it."

That was doubtful, but Katey had expected to have to make the charges. She hadn't expected the woman to insist on it and be the one to lead them eagerly to the constable's office. And a good thing she did, since Katey spotted the boy she'd sent off for the constable playing at the end of the square with a dog. A coin might have got him to do as she'd asked, but without one, he'd simply ignored her request!

She was still suspicious of the Scotswoman's motives. Could she really prefer a jail cell to facing her husband's anger? Apparently so. But what she should have been suspicious of instead was why Mrs. Cameron insisted that she go along with her.

fourteen

KATEY SAT ON the cot with her legs scrunched up, her chin resting on her knees, her lips twisted sourly. She was creating one of her tales in her mind, of Boyd Anderson being walked up to a gallows. His hands weren't tied, but his mouth was gagged. He was being asked if he had any last words to say, but he couldn't answer because of the gag. But he could remove it easily enough, couldn't he? Very well, she was going to have to tie his hands, since she had no interest in hearing what he might have to say.

She delayed opening the trapdoor under him. She was savoring the moment. He didn't look frightened, though. Looked damned stubborn, actually, just as he did when she'd last seen him. Maybe because he was confident that he wouldn't be hung for stupidity, which was what he'd been convicted of. So if she put herself in the scene, let him see her, then he'd know he had something to worry about . . .

"Ah, so here you are," Grace said drily. "I should have known. I looked everywhere else. Why didn't I think to look in—jail?"

Katey glanced up as the cell door was closed behind her maid. Grace had a highly developed sarcastic sense of humor.

"I'm glad you're seeing some humor in this," Katey said with a sigh.

"Did I sound amused? Really? I assure you I'm not. I assure you I'm quite angry. Good deeds are not supposed to end this way."

And that was exactly how Katey had felt, until she'd started hanging Boyd Anderson in her mind. Dispensing a just punishment to him, even if it was only in her imagination, had got rid of, or at least calmed down, some of her anger. She knew very well that she and Grace would have been in London by now if not for his stubbornness. She certainly wouldn't still have been in Northampton and run into Maisie Cameron again and ended up in jail herself because of it.

But Grace was here now, and surely her identical version of events had convinced the constable that she was innocent. "Now that you've arrived, we can be on our way, so let's just put this—"

"Whatever made you think that?" Grace cut in curtly. "No, I'm joining you. Apparently, I'm a member of your gang of abductors."

That certainly wasn't what Katey had been hoping to hear. "This is so silly. You'd think with us both telling them exactly the same thing—"

"Did we?" Grace cut in suspiciously. "Or did you get creative?"

"I did not!" Katey said indignantly.

"Well, the constable didn't ask me much, but why haven't *you* talked your way out of here yet?"

"I did," Katey replied with a small degree of triumph. "Mr. Calderson, our jailor, even believed me."

"I should have guessed," Grace said, and rattled the door that prevented them from leaving.

Katey glowered. It was an impressive glower for a change. Grace even looked contrite over that last bit of sarcasm—but only briefly.

While the maid was momentarily silenced, Katey explained, "I haven't been released yet because of who Judith's family is. They're apparently very well known in this country. Mr. Calderson recognized their name immediately and said he doesn't dare let me go until he hears from a representative of the family."

"So you've been in here all afternoon?" Grace asked incredulously as she sat on the cot next to Katey. "I looked everywhere for you—twice! I was sure I had to just be missing you by moments, that—"

"Didn't you question the innkeeper?"

"Of course I did."

"Then you should have thought to look here sooner. He saw me being dragged outside. He didn't tell you?"

"*He* probably would have, but *he* wasn't there by the time I discovered you weren't in the room. His wife had taken over at the desk and she claimed she hadn't seen you."

"Well, I wasn't even in Northampton. That blasted American who came to rescue Judith was determined to take me back to London to answer to the Malorys, and he carted me off to do just that! If I hadn't climbed out a window to escape him—"

Grace shot off the bed and said stiffly, "Now I know you're spinning one of your tales. All things considered, the truth would be appreciated—*right now!*"

Katey didn't take offense. Grace was understandably upset. They'd done nothing wrong, yet they were both sitting in jail right now. And Katey *had* spun one too many tales in her life, giving Grace good reason to doubt her.

Katey sighed. "That was the truth. The man got it set in his mind that I was guilty, so it didn't matter what I told him to the contrary. But at least I got away from *him*. And Mr. Calderson assured me that I won't have to wait it out here. He's checking with his sister to see if she'll put me up. He sounded confident that she would."

"Behind lock and key, I suppose?"

"Well—probably. But at least we'll be in a more comfortable room than a jail cell."

It wasn't a horrible jail cell, actually. With fresh air coming in through a barred window, it didn't stink. It even had a boarded floor. Vermin moved in the cracks, which was why Katey was keeping her feet up on the cot, but still, it was better than a dirt floor.

"What American was involved?" Grace asked as she moved to sit next to Katey again. "I was told the child was on her way back to London with a member of her family and her family's English."

"No, I think you were sleeping in the coach when Judith mentioned she has American relatives, too, and this was one of them. You even know him. You're the one who warned me on *The Oceanus* to be cautious around him when you sensed that he was overly taken with me."

"Anderson?" Grace said incredulously. "The owner of that ship? But he *was* taken with you. I've never seen a man so interested in a woman that it was obvious he was having carnal thoughts about her. He's the very last man who would doubt you, so why did he?"

"I suppose it's how it looked, me keeping the girl in a locked room in the same town where her abductors had been holding her."

"But surely she would have pointed out that she'd already been rescued—by us."

"I'm sure she would have, but another relative quickly took her away without asking her what had happened. Boyd was left behind with me and jumped to the wrong conclusion."

"Didn't you explain?"

"Of course I did, but he had it set in his mind that I was a criminal, so he refused to listen to anything I said."

"But he liked you!"

"That might have been part of the problem."

"That his rationalities are reversed?" Grace shot back. "Of course! Hug your enemies, toss your friends in jail. Makes perfect sense!"

Grace's sarcasm was back. Katey tsked and said, "No, I think it was just that he felt he was *too* biased in my favor. He mumbled something about letting the authorities figure it out, implying that he couldn't trust his own instincts where I was concerned."

He'd said something else, but she wasn't going to repeat that to her maid, when it caused a pleasant fluttering inside her just remembering it. *I can't think straight when you're within touching distance, when the only thing on my mind is carrying you to the nearest bed, so I don't dare just take you at your word, Katey Tyler. I'm sorry.*

"How nice for him," Grace said, "but I don't see *him* sitting here in jail keeping you company while we wait on clearance from some English lords, who, by the way, don't look favorably upon Americans and will probably not rush to clear up this injustice."

Grace had had a run-in with a nobleman on one of their first few days in London. The man had pushed her aside when she'd been getting into a hack that she'd hailed, had stolen it out from under her, more or less, then said something condescending about her waiting on her betters. Grace had disdained the gentry ever since, despite that being the only bad incident she'd encountered with the upper classes—until now.

Katey felt compelled to point out, "We've met some very friendly people on this trip so far, both in England and in Scotland."

"None of which were lords."

"True, but you can't toss them all in one basket just because one was rude to you, especially when most everyone else has been kind and helpful. Even Mr. Calderson, our jailor, apologized to me three times for not being able to let me go."

"You made your point," Grace grumbled, then sighed. "I hope they're at least out looking for that crazy Scotswoman. I'd hate to think that the rescuers are in jail while she's still running around free."

"Oh, she's here with us. No one told you? Or maybe I should say, she made sure *we* were here with *her!*"

Katey explained what had happened when she got back to town and ran into Maisie Cameron, ending with "I'd no sooner told Mr. Calderson about the whole adventure when Mrs. Cameron pointed a finger at me, called me a liar, and said it was all my idea. She wanted to be in jail to escape her husband, but she was still angry enough at me for ruining her plans to want a little revenge, too."

Grace lifted a tawny brow. "Why am I *not* surprised? I knew that woman wasn't right in the head."

Katey nodded. "A candidate for Bedlam was how Mr. Calderson put it. But I don't blame her for the predicament we're in. It's Boyd Anderson's fault that we're not going to be sleeping in a lovely hotel in London tonight. He might as well have put me here himself. He ruined a perfectly nice adventure with his ridiculous assumptions."

"I hate to mention it, but this *isn't* an adventure anymore. This is a tragedy."

"It's nothing of the sort. It's just turned into an inconvenience and a small delay, is all."

"A gross miscarriage of justice," Grace insisted.

That was harder to disagree with, but Katey replied, "It's quite annoying, and I'm as angry as you are—"

"You could have fooled me."

"—*but* Mr. Calderson assured me it doesn't take that long to reach London on horseback, and he immediately sent a man off to the Malory household to get this cleared up. We might even be released later tonight."

They both knew that wasn't going to happen. It was already dark. Even if the man reached London tonight, it was highly unlikely that he'd turn right around to return to Northampton. It was nothing to him, after all, if a couple of Americans rotted in jail overnight.

Mr. Calderson did move them to his sister's house, but that didn't stop Grace from complaining, especially when their room turned out to be even smaller than the jail cell! One of them grumbling and fussing was more than enough, so Katey tried to control her own anger. She wasn't used to feeling angry. She was much more used to cheering up other people and entertaining them, so she shared a greatly embellished version of her "hanging Boyd Anderson" story with Grace that evening to pass the time. And listening to it definitely cheered Grace up. She was even laughing before Katey was finished.

But when they finally gave up waiting to be released that night and extinguished the lamp to get some sleep, all those strange emotions that had disturbed Katey earlier in the day caught up to her and kept her eyes open, staring at the dark ceiling.

Anger, hurt . . . *how* could Boyd Anderson treat her like a common criminal? He knew her! They weren't strangers. She'd crossed an ocean with him. He thought she was a married woman with two children—well, no, he'd decided now that she must have stolen those children, too. But that had been a guess on his part, based on his contention that she had abducted Judith!

She imagined how awful he was going to feel when he learned the truth, but that didn't help to soothe her hurt feelings. The trouble was, she hated him for the high-handed way he'd treated her today, but she didn't *want* to hate him, and the contrary emotions were causing a pain in her chest and tears to come to her eyes. And she hated him for making her feel so confused.

She got back to hanging him in her mind and opened the trapdoor this time . . . then cried herself to sleep.

fifteen

KATEY DISCOVERED THAT buying a comfortable English coach—at least a new one—as Judith Malory had suggested, wasn't something that could be accomplished in a day. The man at the first coach yard she'd visited had said three weeks. The second coach builder had said he could have one made for her in a month. He had a waiting list!

It was bad enough that all the passenger ships departing for the Continent in the next few days had filled their lists already. The best Katey could do was to buy passage for two on a ship that sailed next week. She was still smarting over that, so she wasn't about to delay leaving London even longer for a coach. This was all Boyd Anderson's fault. Mr. Calderson hadn't released them until yesterday afternoon, apologizing profusely when the man he'd sent to London returned and said the Malorys had indeed corroborated Katey's version of events.

On the way back to their London hotel, Katey told Grace, "I think we'll just revert to our original idea and buy a coach *after* we get to France."

"You don't think we'll run into the same problem there?" Grace asked.

"Yes, but at least we can begin touring the country while we wait."

Grace nodded. "Then what's next on the agenda here before we leave? A new wardrobe? Hiring a coachman for a coach you don't own yet?"

Katey raised a brow at her maid's sarcastic tone. Her own mood was taking a downward swing. She hated being dependent on other people's schedules. She wanted to leave England now, not next week. She'd wanted to buy a coach today, too, not next month. She'd even briefly thought of buying her own ship so she wouldn't have to deal with someone else's schedule anymore and could just stick to her own. But she could just imagine how long *it* would take to build a ship!

She'd only been half-serious yesterday when she'd told Grace they wouldn't be leaving for six more days and had ended with "I should just buy a ship so we don't run into delays like this again."

Grace had rolled her eyes at her and replied, "Buying a coach is a good idea, buying a ship isn't. We aren't sailing around the world. We only need a ship to get to the next continent."

"And then the one after that."

"Yes, but how many months later will that be?" Grace had asked. "You said it yourself, that crossing Europe by land is going to take a *long* time. Besides, there aren't that many continents for us to visit—are there?"

Whatever schooling Grace had received in Danbury hadn't included geography. She readily admitted she'd only stayed in school long enough to learn to read and write. Katey's education had been much more extensive, and while her tutor had been diligent in teaching her about the world, she hadn't had picture books that showed her what he was talking about, so it had been hard for her to imagine how different Europe and Africa were from America. Her tutor had only given her a taste of what was beyond the horizon, leaving her wanting to see it for herself. She knew from her tutor's lectures that it would be more convenient to sail from country to country rather than traveling over land.

"It's too bad we can't rent a ship," Katey had ended with a sigh.

Grace had chuckled. "That's funny. Waiting for the next ship to leave for the port you want to go to is only a small inconvenience, a small price to pay for seeing the world."

But Katey was definitely learning that patience wasn't one of her strong points. "Well, what about a new wardrobe?" Grace prodded.

"Why do I need a new wardrobe? I'm already carrying around trunks of clothes I'm making no use of, so why on earth would I buy even more?"

"Because you have nothing but serviceable, everyday clothes that you used to wear at home in Gardener. You don't have a single fancy dress or wrap. What if you're invited to a nice dinner or—"

"Invited by *who*?" Katey chuckled. "We're not exactly meeting people who give fancy dinners."

"You could. You should at least be prepared. Or will you be declining invitations just because you don't have anything appropriate to wear?"

Katey conceded that point. "I suppose it wouldn't hurt to have at least one special dress, would it? And I did want to get another comfortable traveling ensemble. There might be time for that if we find a seamstress today. Very well, tell the driver to turn around. I think I noticed some shops a few streets back."

Grace spoke to the hack driver, but after resuming her seat she said, "Now that we've got that off our list of immediate business, are you going to visit the child, to make sure she got home all right?"

"I don't know—actually, I think not. I wasn't pleased with the end of that little adventure, so I'd just as soon forget it. She was a delightful girl, though. I'll at least jot off a note to—"

"Coward."

Katey stiffened. "Excuse me?"

"You heard me right. You're afraid that if you go anywhere near a Malory house you'll end up running into him again."

"You're quite wrong there. I would love to run into Boyd Anderson again so I can put that pistol I bought the other day to good use."

Grace snorted. "You wouldn't shoot him."

"I hung him, didn't I?"

Grace burst out laughing, but when she wound down, she said with a fond smile, "What you do in those little tales you create is just daydreaming out loud, Katey. Pure fantasy like that has no bearing on what you'd *really* do if given the chance. But that was funny, the way you hung him. It's too bad that was only your imagination getting angry."

"I don't know why you keep thinking I'm incapable of anger, that you're the only one who gets to experience that emotion. I was furious over that whole incident."

"Maybe, but you're avoiding the point."

"Maybe because I don't want to discuss him?" Katey was quick to reply.

"I meant about the child. Jotting off a note without expecting a reply isn't going to tell you that she got safely home. What if it wasn't really a relative who ran off with her that day? What if Anderson was one of the kidnappers and he took off with you just to get you out of the way so you wouldn't suspect what was really going on? What if Judith never got home?"

Katey laughed now. "You've listened to too many of my tales!"

"I'm being serious."

"Then pick a subject that isn't so absurd. *The Oceanus* belonged to him. And during the crossing we heard it mentioned that it was just one of many ships that belong to the shipping company his family owns. That man is no pauper, Grace."

"Neither are you, but that didn't stop him from pointing a finger, did it?"

That statement had some validity. "Very well, I'll make sure I get a confirmation when my note is delivered. I *have* been assuming that everything is fine in regard to Judith. But I don't have to go by the Malory residence myself to do that."

"Fair enough," Grace said. "I just didn't want to see you leaving any loose ends here—speaking of which, we've got time before we sail for another jaunt to Gloucestershire."

"No," Katey said immediately. "Actually, I was thinking about a nice drive along the southern coast, perhaps as far as Dover, or maybe all the way to Cornwall if we don't dally. We didn't get a chance to visit the southern shires before we left for Scotland."

Grace crossed her arms, looking stubborn, before she said, "I wouldn't be doing my duty if I didn't mention that you may never get back to England once we leave here. You might get to Italy and decide that's the country where you want to put down roots. You already said Scotland would be a nice place to live, so I know you're going to be looking at all of these countries we visit with an eye toward where you plan to roost when you finish seeing the world.

"So think about it," Grace continued. "You know you'll end up regretting that you didn't make a greater effort to meet your mother's family, when we're on the other side of the world."

sixteen

KATEY SHOULD HAVE known that sending a note to Judith's house would elicit more than a simple reply. When the hotel maid came to her door to tell her she had a visitor waiting for her in the lobby, she almost sent the maid back with the response that she was indisposed.

She was afraid it was Boyd. He could have been at the Malory house when her messenger arrived and followed the man back to her hotel. She didn't want to see him again. Ever. Not even to witness his groveling on his knees now that he'd discovered just how wrong he'd been. But she followed the maid downstairs anyway, refusing to believe that the anticipation she was experiencing had anything to do with excitement at the thought of seeing him again.

She didn't have a chance to feel either relief or disappointment when she saw that her visitor wasn't Boyd Anderson. She was too surprised by the man standing there waiting for her. He was incredibly handsome, and it had nothing to do with the warm smile he was giving her. Extremely tall with a lean, strapping physique that went perfectly with his height, he was the kind of man a tailor would love. He was elegantly clad in a dark brown frock coat with buff breeches, his cravat neatly tied, not too extravagant. His clothes were the height of fashion, yet understated. No dandy here. His coal black hair fell in waves to just below his ears, his eyes had a slight exotic slant to them and were the most beautiful cobalt blue . . . Judith Malory's eyes, she realized!

He had to be a relative, and while she hadn't gotten a good look at Jeremy Malory before he'd hied off with Judith that day, she realized this could be him. The resemblance was too close from what she remembered, though she could have sworn he was younger. Not that this man was old. Late thirties or early forties would be her guess.

"Miss Tyler? I'm Anthony Malory, Judith's father." He took her extended hand and squeezed it warmly.

Well, she hadn't expected that! This was the man Boyd had tried to frighten her with? How absurd!

She returned his smile. "Call me Katey. I hope Judith has recovered from that nasty business?"

"Thanks to you, yes. You cannot begin to understand how grateful my wife and I are for your assistance. You're a remarkable young woman, Katey."

She couldn't help but blush. "I just did what anyone else would have done."

"You're wrong there. Most people would have minded their own business. You saw a little girl in need and rescued her. You quite charmed my daughter, you know. She's done nothing but talk about you since she got home."

Katey grinned. "I was rather taken with her myself. She's so smart for her age, I found myself treating her like an adult!"

He chuckled. "She has that effect on all of us! And she's looking forward to seeing you again. My wife, Roslynn, is having a small family dinner tonight and we'd like you to join us."

Katey almost laughed, remembering her conversation with Grace that morning. She would never have dreamed that she would be forced to say, "But I don't have anything to wear!" that very day. But she had to say it. The Malorys were English nobility. They probably went to bed looking elegant!

"I'm going to have to decline. I don't have anything appropriate to wear to a London dinner party."

Anthony laughed and said, "Your presence is desired, not your wardrobe. And Judy will be crushed if you don't come." Then he added drolly, "Wear a sack if you must, I promise you my family won't care. So no excuses. I'll send a coach for you in a few hours."

And how could Katey refuse now? Anthony Malory was a stubborn man, but very nice for all that, and she *would* like to see Judith again, so she shyly agreed. Grace, of course, had to tell her at least three times, "I told you so," as they dug out the nicest dress Katey owned. Far from being a sack, it was a simple pink frock with mother-of-pearl buttons. When Katey put it on and Grace arranged her hair in a loose braid that draped over her shoulder, she felt more at ease about attending the Malorys' dinner. And before long she was on her way to the fashionable town house on Piccadilly

That was another surprise. From the street, the Malory town house looked so narrow, but inside it was huge. It was probably three times the size of her home in Gardener. And so grand looking! Gilt frames, crystal chandeliers, shiny marble on the foyer floor. Everywhere she looked she saw elegant details. Katey felt quite out of her element. These people were rich aristocrats—what the devil was she doing there?

But that thought didn't last long. Anthony Malory's

idea of "small" seemed rather large to Katey as a butler ushered her into a room full of people who were all saying thank-you to her. Even the butler thanked her!

Katey noticed that Roslynn Malory wasn't dressed as elegantly as the other women in the room. Sir Anthony had probably told her about the silly issue of "clothes" he'd had to deal with when he'd invited Katey to dinner, so she had merely dressed in a skirt and blouse. That extra effort alone made Katey feel welcome, but the hug Roslynn gave her relaxed her completely.

Anthony greeted her warmly, but Roslynn pulled her back into the foyer for a private moment. "I'm so glad Tony convinced you to join us this evening. He said you put up a good fight." Katey blushed, but Roslynn laughed and assured her, "I'm joking, m'dear. I just want you to feel welcome here. I'm hoping you will agree to accept our hospitality for longer than this evening, but we can talk about that later. Before Judy comes down, I thought you might like to know more about this unfortunate incident, as we now understand it. My cousin Geordie Cameron has always coveted my fortune, you see."

"So it really was your cousin that your husband pummeled?"

"Don't let *that* surprise you. It certainly wasn't the first time. Before I married Tony, Geordie tried to abduct me several times. I knew what he was up to. He was going to force me to marry him so he could get his hands on the fortune my grandfather left me, and he didn't care how he accomplished it. Tony put a stop to that, and we were sure we'd have no more trouble from him! And Geordie was sincerely contrite back then, so while Tony might blame him for all this, I don't. I even received a note of apology from him today and the assurance that his wife won't trouble us again, though we already knew that. Calderson's man explained when he came here to get Judy's story about what happened that Maisie Cameron and her cohorts had been apprehended."

Katey realized immediately that the Malorys didn't know that she'd been the one accused of being a cohort and had spent time in jail because of it. She started to mention it, but abruptly changed her mind. Judith was safe at home, and the Malorys were relieved and grateful for her help. They didn't need to know she'd suffered further consequences from it.

A squeal of delight interrupted her thoughts. She saw Roslynn roll her eyes, then turned to see why. Judith was bounding down the stairs to them, and the child latched on to Katey with an exuberant hug.

"You came! I'm so glad. Father teased me that you might not. And you look so pretty in that dress."

Katey chuckled. Had everyone heard about her limited wardrobe? "Look at yourself, all fancied up. You didn't tell me you were the prettiest girl in England!"

Judith beamed at the compliment, yet Katey didn't doubt it was true. The girl had her mother's magnificent copper-gold hair and her father's exotic blue eyes, and both parents were stunning in their looks. Katey had a feeling Judith was going to be *too* beautiful when she grew up. Even now, full of happy delight, she glowed like an angel.

"Have you met everyone?" Judith asked, then before Katey could answer, said, "Come with me, I'll make sure you do."

The child wouldn't leave her side after that. And like a perfect hostess, which she was probably already being groomed to become one day, she introduced Katey to her relatives and supplied some commentary about each person afterward.

Her uncle Edward and aunt Charlotte were there. They also lived in London. Her cousin Jeremy and his new bride—the ex-thief, Judith whispered—lived in London, too, and had only just returned from their wedding trip.

Katey was rather stiff as she was introduced to that handsome young man, the impetuous fellow who'd raced off with Judith that day in Northampton. It would have been better if he'd stuck around long enough to meet her *then*, which would have kept her from becoming familiar with the inside of a jail cell.

She nearly said as much, but it wasn't in her nature to be rude, so she held her tongue. And it certainly wasn't his fault that Boyd Anderson couldn't recognize the truth if it hit him over the head.

"I'm sorry we didn't meet the other day," Jeremy apologized as he shook her hand. "But I'm sure Boyd explained why it was imperative that I get Judy home immediately."

"Oh, he did," Katey replied, and congratulated herself on not sounding sarcastic.

She'd half-expected to find Boyd at the Malory house, actually. She was disappointed that he wasn't there. Not that she'd already decided what she would have said to him if he were, she just knew it would have been blistering.

Which is why it was just as well that he wasn't in attendance, because it didn't take her long to realize that Judith's family didn't even know about his blunder. How could they unless he told them? He obviously didn't want to put his foot in that nasty puddle. He'd probably thought the Malorys would never meet her so there was no need for him to confess. But she didn't want to put a damper on the evening by mentioning his silly accusations, either.

As for Jeremy, Katey could honestly say she'd never met a more handsome man, but she was still somewhat annoyed with him. She could see now why she'd briefly thought that Anthony might be Jeremy when she'd seen him at the hotel. Judith's father so closely resembled the younger Malory that she would have thought Jeremy was Anthony's son or brother, if she didn't already know he was Judith's cousin.

But Jeremy's wife, Danny, was so beautiful Katey nearly gasped when she saw her! She wore an emerald silk gown, and her hair was snow-white and cut unfashionably short, but she had the most exquisite features. Katey was sure she'd never meet another woman as beautiful as Danny Malory, but then she was introduced to Judith's cousin Derek and his wife, Kelsey, and she had to amend that—and she began to wonder how one family could have so many amazing-looking people in it.

They were all dressed so grandly, too. Danny in her emerald silk, Kelsey and Charlotte in dark velvets, even the men were wearing jackets and lacy cravats, and it wasn't even a formal affair! If they weren't all so warm and genuinely pleased that she was there, she would have been terribly embarrassed in her simple cotton dress, which seemed out of place amid their rich apparel and sparkling jewels. But she didn't even think of that until later, because Judith barely gave her any time to think at all with her running stream of commentary.

"Their son, Brandon, is the Duke of Wrighton, you know," Judith told her after she pulled Katey away from Derek and his lovely wife.

That information meant absolutely nothing to Katey.

Her tutor had been American-born and had never taught her the different tiers of the English nobility. A lord was a lord to her, no more, no less.

"You'd never guess, but Derek met Kelsey in a brothel," Judith continued in another whisper, then added, "No, it's not what you're thinking. It's quite an interesting story, what she was doing there."

Katey could imagine—no, actually, she couldn't! But the secrets this child was revealing to her were most definitely scandalous and things Judith shouldn't even know about at her age. Thieves and brothels, and hadn't she mentioned pirates before, too? Surely these unusual aspects of some of the Malorys' lives weren't public knowledge, so why was she sharing them with Katey?

"I wouldn't tell just anyone that," Judith said, seeming to read Katey's thoughts. "You're special."

Katey blushed furiously. That was one of the nicest compliments she'd ever received. But she wondered about the child's uncanny perceptions.

"I'm nothing of the sort—but why did you say so?" she asked.

Judith shrugged. "It's odd, but I feel like I've known you forever."

That really *was* odd, because Katey felt an affinity for the girl, too. But then Judith reminded her of herself at that age with her friendliness, her curiosity, and her thousand and one questions!

"It was probably because we talked so much about ourselves when we met, and later in your coach," Judith suggested. "I've never talked so much to anyone else like that, ever, who wasn't family."

Katey smiled and glanced about the room. "And you certainly have a large family."

Judith giggled at that, a sound that reminded Katey of how young she was. "This isn't even half of them! I believe the count is up to eight separate Malory households in London now, though you might want to ask my mother to confirm that. But even that doesn't account for all of my family."

Katey found that hard to fathom. She was an only child with no aunts and uncles, no cousins, not even grandparents—at least none that she knew of. It must be nice, she thought, to have so many relatives. And maybe she should go to Gloucester again and this time actually knock on the Millards' door.

Dinner was announced shortly after that. The table was extremely long, giving Katey an idea of just how many family members occasionally showed up to eat at it. With just ten of them present tonight, Roslynn seated the group at one end of the long table, putting Katey between Anthony and Judith, while she sat across from them.

There wasn't a single pause in the conversations, which ranged from horse racing and the merits of Derek's newest stallion, to the ladies' opinions on the latest fashions that had lower waistlines. Charlotte liked the new style, while the other three women still favored the comfort of the French Empire style.

When Charlotte asked Katey her opinion, she had to admit, "I'm afraid the closest I've been to a seamstress in five years is a visit to one this morning. I did order one fancy dress and took the seamstress's advice. She said she would only make gowns in the new lower-waisted style."

"How rude of her," Kelsey said.

"And probably a whopper," Danny added. "I know how shopkeepers operate. She just wants you to tell all your friends where you bought the latest fashion."

"It doesn't matter," Katey tried to assure them. "It's going to take her four days to make that single gown. I didn't have time to look around for a different seamstress."

"That's ridiculous! It doesn't take that long to make a gown," Roslynn said. "She was probably just looking for an excuse to charge you more. I'll send my seamstress to you tomorrow. She'll make you as many gowns as you like in whatever styles you prefer and in quick order, too."

"Thank you, but that isn't necessary. I'm traveling, so I don't need a wide variety of clothes. And my ship sails next week."

"Going home to America?" Anthony asked.

"No, I have no family left there, so I doubt I'll ever return."

"She has family here in England, she just doesn't want to visit them," Judith piped in.

Katey's blush made Roslynn gently scold her daughter. "That's privileged information, puss. Katey will mention it if she wants to. You don't do it for her."

Judith's lower lip trembled slightly, which made Katey leap to her defense. "That's quite all right, really. I do have family here, but I've never met them, and I didn't think I'd have time to visit them before I sailed to France. But I couldn't obtain passage any sooner than next week." She paused to smile at the child and squeeze her hand under the table. "After our discussion, Judith, I've been reconsidering visiting them, and now that I have a little more time in England, I probably will. But your mother is right, I'd rather not discuss it."

She'd said a lot for not wanting to discuss it! But the Malorys took the hint, and Anthony changed the subject by asking, "What's luring you to France? Shopping?"

"No, it's the next country I'm visiting on my tour."

"How many countries are you planning to see?" Edward asked.

"All of them," Katey replied. "I'm actually going to tour the world."

"The world?" Jeremy nearly choked on the bite he was taking. "Hell's bells, most people just want to tour the Continent, but you want to see the whole world?"

"Why not?" Katey asked. "It's something I'm longing to do after spending my entire life in one small village. Now that there's nothing holding me down, I'd like to see the rest of the world."

"Don't look so surprised, puppy," Anthony said to his nephew. "Everyone has different goals. Katey's is just a grand one."

"But a world tour is going to take—forever," Jeremy pointed out.

Katey grinned. "Not quite that long, though I did get carried away here. It's been more than a month since I arrived from America and I've only seen England and Scotland so far. So I do know now that I can't spend so long in one place, which is why I'm so annoyed with the shipping schedules. I should have been leaving for France tomorrow, not next week."

"Well, since you are delayed, may we invite you to stay with us until your ship sails?" Roslynn asked. "That's the least we can do after you rescued Judy for us."

"Yes, please do, Katey," Judith added hopefully.

"Thank you, but if the visit with my family goes as I hope it will, I will probably want to spend the rest of my time in England with them. I will let you know. But you certainly don't have to thank me for helping Judith. That was an adventure for me, so I have her to thank for that!"

They adjourned to the parlor after dinner. Katey was

late arriving after taking a few minutes to freshen up. Seeing more of the house, she was once again awed by its opulence. Did the Millards, who were also aristocrats, live like this, too? Is this the kind of wealth her mother had given up for love?

For several moments she stood just inside the door to the parlor watching the Malorys, the laughter and teasing going on, the obvious love they shared. What a wonderful family they were, and so lucky to have each other. She wished she didn't feel so out of place among them, despite how nice they'd been to her, but she did. And they made her miss her mother.

Grace had been right, she did have to meet the Millards before she left England. She would never forgive herself if she didn't. One of them might even look like Adeline or have a similar personality. God, she so wanted to discover that she had a relative who was like her mother.

"Who are you?" asked a deep voice behind her.

Katey turned and couldn't help the frisson of fear that passed over her at the sight of the big blond man standing there eyeing her so intently. In a billowing white shirt open at the neck, tight breeches, knee-high boots, and hair to his shoulders, he looked even more out of place in the Malorys' house than she did. But something else about the man had her holding her breath. His look was downright menacing, almost as if he were a . . . a . . . what the devil was it? A flash of gold at his ear gave her the answer. He looked like a pirate!

seventeen

"WELL, GOOD GOD, James, you could have given us some warning," Anthony said to the new arrival. "When did you get back to town?"

"Just this afternoon."

A lot suddenly happened at once. Jeremy bolted across the room and enveloped the large blond man in a bear hug. That would surely have knocked a slighter man back out of the room, but not this one, which was a good thing, since he wasn't alone. Entering the parlor right behind him were a woman and a child.

Katey scurried out of the way. The big man might look downright menacing, but obviously he wasn't, and even more obvious, he was yet another member of Judith's family. Judith bolted across the room, too, but to hug the little girl who had come in with her parents and pull her aside to start whispering in her ear.

The woman who had come in with them—good grief, yet another beauty!—was making her way around the room hugging everyone, as if she hadn't seen them for months. And perhaps that was the case, she thought, when she heard Anthony questioning the blond man named James.

"How did that trip go?" he asked. "You were able to find Drew?"

"Yes, and Gabrielle Brooks was with him as we'd suspected. We just hadn't thought that she was the one who'd
commandeered his ship."

"She actually stole it? How?"

"She had some help from her father's loyal crew. And
she was desperate. They'd brought her word that her father was being held prisoner by a bunch of rogue pirates
who *used* to be his associates."

"But why'd she steal it? Wasn't Drew her escort while
she was here in London?" Anthony asked. "She could have
just asked him to take her to the Caribbean, couldn't she?"

"You don't recall that scandal about Gabby that made
the rounds right before she left?" James's wife asked Anthony. "Drew was responsible for that, so she wasn't about
to ask him for anything at that point."

"Ah, an angry woman with the means for revenge,"
Anthony guessed with a knowing grin. "I quite understand."

"Thought you might," James said drily. "But they
patched up their differences by the time we found them."

"So Drew didn't need to be rescued after all?"

"Not a'tall. But Gabby's father still did, and that was a
grand fight if I do say so m'self, pulling him out of that pirates' nest. Sorry you missed the fun, old chap. You would
have enjoyed it."

"Did Drew return with you?" Roslynn asked.

"No, he'll be staying in the Caribbean for a while. We
attended his wedding before we sailed home."

Anthony laughed. "Don't tell me, more pirates in *your*
family now?"

That got him a glower from the handsome blond man
and Katey abruptly changed her mind. James Malory *was*
absolutely menacing. Could expressions be lethal?

"Don't be an ass, they're your family, too," James replied.

Anthony was either very brave or he simply didn't notice the other man's glower, because he said with a grin, "Beg to differ, old man. You're the one with five barbarian brothers-in-law, not me."

"And *our* nephew by marriage is one of them," James pointed out.

"Bloody hell, forgot about him," Anthony grumbled, then put an arm around his brother's wide shoulders to steer James toward Katey. "Well, come and meet Judy's heroine. You heard what happened? I know Judy rushed over to see Jack the very day after she got home."

"Yes, Jack told us all about it in less than ten seconds. We'd barely got in the door! But you know how she will string all her sentences together when she's excited."

"Indeed." Anthony rolled his eyes. "Judy does the same thing. She didn't get that habit from me! I swear we were never that excitable when we were that age."

"We weren't girls" was James's droll reply. But then on a sober note, he added, "Sorry I wasn't here to help, Tony."

"Not to worry, old man. Your son and brother-in-law filled in for you nicely. And it's over, thank God, so no need to belabor it."

When they reached Katey, Anthony made the introductions. Even though James Malory wasn't that much taller than she was, when he wrapped those massive arms around her—he actually hugged her!—she felt very, very small.

"We are in your debt," James told her. "You helped my dearest niece, who is also my daughter's best friend. If you ever need anything, Katey Tyler, anything of any sort, you come to me."

She didn't doubt he was quite sincere. And she had a feeling "anything" really meant anything, even of the dangerous sort.

His wife, "George," joined them to add her thanks. And listening to them, Katey got the impression that while James Malory could easily be a danger to some people, his friends and family certainly had nothing to fear from him, and Katey had just been placed in the latter group, which banished that brief bit of nervousness she'd felt earlier at his arrival.

One more person had arrived with James and his family, but he'd been tardy in coming through the door. Unfortunately he'd snuck in behind Katey. If she'd had just a little warning, she might not have made a fool of herself.

"Mrs. Tyler?"

She swung around to face Boyd Anderson. With the most derision she'd ever mustered, she said, "Ah, if it isn't the man who would make criminals out of innocents. It's a shame the Malorys have to call a blackguard like you a relative."

Shamefaced, he said, "I've come to apologize for not believing you."

"Apology denied," she replied coldly. "Now go away."

"Please—"

"Deaf as well as stupid?" she cut in without pity. "Then let me see if I can make you understand. You could beg on your knees, and it would make no difference. You, sir, are an idiot!"

He got down on his knees. She snorted, took out her pistol, and shot him. She missed, of course, but it was nice to see him looking fearful.

Unfortunately, all of that only happened in her imagination afterward and *not* in a room filled with a dozen witnesses. Boyd did surprise her. She did swing around to face him with a gasp. He was dressed more elegantly than the last time she'd seen him, in a well-tailored black jacket that fit snugly to his wide shoulders, a white, lacy cravat tight to his neck, his gold-streaked brown curls in fashionable disarray. But the sight of this handsome man didn't steal her breath; instead her instinct for self-preservation overrode her good sense, and she snapped, "Don't talk to me! Don't you dare even come near me. Actually—"

She turned to Sir Anthony, who was now frowning as he glanced between them. She felt a hot blush coloring her cheeks because the Malorys couldn't have helped but hear her being so rude to their relative. She simply couldn't stay here now.

"I'm sorry, but I need to leave immediately," she told her host. "Thank you for your hospitality."

She didn't give him a chance to reply, didn't pause but a moment on her way out the door, just long enough to bend down and hug Judith and whisper to her, "I'll visit again before I sail, but right now I have to go."

She almost reached the front door, but Boyd was fast on her heels. His hand on her arm stopped her briefly and brought her around to face him.

"Katey, you have to let me explain."

"Get your hand off me!" She stared down at it until Boyd removed it, then told him, "I don't *have* to do anything except ignore you, which is going to be very easy to do."

"Will you please listen to me for a—"

"Like you listened to me? You dragged me across the countryside against my will—*in* a storm, I might add. You manhandled me, locked me in a room, all without listening to me even once!"

"Maybe I didn't manhandle you enough, since you managed to escape," he said in frustration. "I could have tied you down in that room, but I didn't."

She gasped indignantly. "Do you actually think that exonerates you? I can't believe I'm even talking to you, but no more. I will give you exactly the same courtesy you gave me, though. Whatever you say will fall on deaf ears. Isn't that how it went?"

She was glad to see at least a slight tinge of color mount his cheeks, but that's all she stood there to see. She turned and rushed out the door. She heard him call her name again, shouting it actually, but she didn't stop and even ran down the outer stairs. The coach Anthony had sent to fetch her was still in front of the house, and within moments she was inside it and on her way back to her hotel.

eighteen

BOYD'S FIRST INSTINCT as he stood at the door and watched Katey drive away was to follow her, but James had sent their coach home and it wouldn't be returning for several hours. It was Edward's habit to do the same thing. Since Piccadilly was a high-traffic street, the family preferred not to add to the congestion of it by leaving their vehicles at the curb.

Derek's driver was the only one left, and while he probably wouldn't hesitate to take a Malory anywhere he or she requested, he'd no doubt want permission first to drive off with an Anderson. And then there'd be no catching up to the coach, which was already disappearing in the distance. But Boyd knew that someone inside Anthony's house had to know where Katey was staying because she'd been invited here.

He'd found out she was innocent of the charges he'd laid on her as soon as he got back to London. Anyone who didn't have his mind *and* body clouded with desire as Boyd had been would probably have believed her immediately, since she *had* been telling the truth. But he'd gone straight to Anthony's house to assure himself that Judith was home.

As soon as he'd walked into the parlor, Jeremy, still there and sitting with Judith on a sofa, said to him,

"D'you know what it's like being scolded by a seven-year-old who's too smart to be condescended to?"

And Judith piped in, "I just wanted to thank Katey properly. You would have, too, if someone had risked her life to save you. You could have taken me back for just a few minutes to do that. But you had us miles down the road before you even listened to me!"

Jeremy gave Boyd a you-see-what-I-mean? look. However, to his young cousin, he said, "So it would have taken more'n a few minutes, wouldn't it, puss, as far down the road as we were? But I'll find out where she's staying when she gets to London and take you to visit her m'self so you can thank her properly. I'll be wanting to thank her as well. Hell's bells, the whole family's in her debt. So stop worrying about it, she'll get thanked."

But Judith had asked Boyd directly, "Did *you* at least thank her before you left?"

Boyd didn't know how he'd managed to get a single word out, he'd been so poleaxed, but he said by way of excuse, "I was overcome by her beauty, so that might have slipped my mind." Jeremy rolled his eyes at that, but Boyd quickly continued, "But you can be sure I'll help to find her to rectify that oversight."

"Would you?" The child beamed at him, driving the ax in a lot deeper.

He'd gotten out of there fast before they could notice how guilty he felt. He'd even thought about riding back to Northampton that night, but he doubted that Katey would still be there. Besides, he felt she'd be looking for him as soon as she got to town, with a gun, or a club, or a parasol to break over his head. And it would be easier for her to find him than for him to find her, since she could locate him through the Malorys.

But that didn't stop him from beginning his search for her yesterday. He had to make amends for his error, somehow. There was no getting around that. And he deserved whatever she felt like dishing out, of course. *How* did you make up for something like this? But a Skylark crisis had erupted yesterday morning that took up a good deal of his time. One of their ships had limped into port after getting damaged in a bad storm. Extensive repairs had to be arranged. The cargo had spoiled and had to be disposed of. Couldn't just dump it in the Thames.

And then Georgina and James had returned this afternoon and he'd spent the rest of the day with them, hearing about Drew's little adventure.

Several times he'd started to tell his sister about his blunder. But he couldn't bring himself to ruin Georgina's homecoming, and besides, he was still hoping to find Katey and set things right with her before his family found out.

Now, he had to return to a room full of Malorys who had heard what Katey said to him—she hadn't said it quietly—and watched her leave because of him. Had she already told them? No, they would have pounced on him immediately for an explanation if she had. But they'd be wanting one now. He was surprised they hadn't followed him to the front door to get it already.

Actually, when he walked back into the house and shut the door, he saw James and Anthony standing in the doorway to the parlor. Watching him. Those two wouldn't have let him just leave, if the thought had occurred to him, without making a clean breast of it. If he weren't anticipating finding out where Katey was staying, he might just have tried it anyway, because walking back into that parlor felt like walking to a guillotine that had his name on it.

Boyd passed between the two Malorys he admired

most for their superlative skill in the ring. He'd only experienced that skill once himself, when he and his four brothers had tried to trounce James for scandalously announcing to a roomful of people that he'd ruined their sister—not in those exact words, but New Englanders could read between the lines as well as anyone else.

They'd tried to be fair in taking James on one at a time. That simply hadn't worked. But James had given them enough excuses that day to forgo fairness, and truly, it had taken all five of them to finally bring him down. He was that good with his fists.

Every eye in the room turned to Boyd when he reentered the parlor. Most waited patiently for an explanation, expecting him to volunteer it. Judith's disappointment overrode her patience.

Looking crestfallen, she asked him, "You didn't fix it and bring her back?"

She actually thought he would? So simple, the way a child looked at things. Fix it. All's better. He wished this were that simple.

He was shaking his head at Judith when his sister said, "Boyd, tell me you didn't insult that young woman?"

He winced. "Depends on how you define *insult*."

"Barbaric to the bloody end, eh?" James guessed.

"Don't start," Georgina told her husband, then said to her brother more carefully, "I take it more happened that day than we're aware of?"

But Anthony wasn't in any mood to drag it out and pointedly asked, "What'd you do, Yank, to get her so angry she won't even stay in the same room with you?"

How had Katey put it? "I manhandled her, locked her—"

"What?"

The question came at him from every direction because no one had actually heard him, he'd been mumbling so low. And perhaps it wasn't wise to be that blunt.

He cleared his throat and said, "I didn't believe her when she explained why she was there."

"In Northampton?" Georgina asked.

"No, at the inn where I found her with Judith," he corrected.

To which James started laughing. "Accused her of being the culprit, didn't you? I can see why that would have annoyed her."

And when Boyd didn't deny it, Jeremy piped in, "Hell's bells, Yank, I told you what Cameron claimed, that it was his wife—"

"I know," Boyd cut in. "But we found Judy in that inn being kept behind a locked door rather than on her way home. Which made me begin to doubt Cameron's tale. You even agreed that he must have lied to get Anthony to stop pummeling him."

"That didn't end it," Anthony put in, which got him a frown from his wife for sounding so smug about it.

"You beat my poor cousin for nothing," Roslynn scolded. "Judy confirmed that it was none of his doing."

"Beg to differ, m'dear. His whining over the years that he didn't get your fortune was what gave his wife the idea, so he was still ultimately at fault. That it wasn't *his* idea is the only reason he's not dead."

Roslynn snorted, obviously in disagreement with that contention. Boyd actually started to relax his guard somewhat, with people's attention drifting elsewhere. But then he caught James's unnerving gaze on him, and unfortunately, that Malory was too perceptive by half.

All humor gone now, James said, "Just a bloody moment. If you didn't believe her, and she's still angry at you—

tell me you were as incompetent as I would expect you to be and you *didn't* follow through on your suspicions?"

Boyd sighed. "I was very competent."

"Oh, good God," James replied, guessing. "He put the chit in jail."

"No, that wasn't an option, even when it occurred to me that she might be Cameron's wife. But I did try to drag her back to London with me, without her permission. I was going to bring her straight here so Anthony could decide what to do with her. But we ran into a storm, and when I found us some shelter, she escaped."

After only a moment of shocked silence, everyone started in with varying degrees of disbelief and censure, all directed where it belonged, and so much that Boyd barely caught a word of it. It was actually an amazing relief not to have to keep that guilt to himself any longer. And when he did finally hear something he could reply to, it wasn't even directed at him.

"How the devil are we going to make up for this?" Anthony asked his wife.

"It's not your error," Boyd pointed out.

Roslynn snapped at him, "The devil it isn't. You're a member of this family."

Even though she'd said them in anger, Roslynn's words were still music to his ears. The Malory men might still deal with him almost exclusively in a derogatory manner, but that's how they treated each other as well. It was simply their way. Now it was time for him to accept that he really was a member of this family. Georgina had seen to that, and so had Warren, because they were both happily married to Malorys.

So Boyd took a leaf from Judith's book and said, "I'll fix it. I've no idea how yet, but I *will* fix it."

nineteen

"YOU'RE BACK EARLY," Grace said when Katey walked into her room.

"He was there—so I left."

It wasn't necessary to say who "he" was. "You gave him his setdown first, though, right? Before you left?" Katey's grimace was enough for Grace to conclude, "You didn't? I swear, Katey Tyler, I didn't raise you right."

Katey snorted as she dropped into the nearest chair. "You didn't raise me at all. And he caught me by surprise or I would have said much more to him than I did—or possibly not. There were too many people there for me to behave like a harridan as he deserves."

"And now you've lost your chance."

It took Katey a moment, but then she started chuckling. "Lost my chance to behave like a harridan—is that really what we're bemoaning?"

Grace grinned as well, albeit a bit sheepishly. "That did sound terrible, didn't it? But a setdown can be delivered genteelly. You've got the finesse for it, my girl, I know you do. And it's really going to stick in my craw if that man doesn't at least get—hung."

They both laughed now. But then Katey sighed and leaned her head back on the chair, closing her eyes. And

Grace went back to repacking the clothes Katey rarely wore anymore. The maid had been giving them all a good cleaning and pressing before they set sail again.

The trouble was, Katey *would* probably still get a chance to "hang" Boyd, so to speak, and she wasn't sure she wanted it now. Because the Malorys knew where she was staying. He could get that information from Sir Anthony easily enough. He might even come around in the morning to say whatever he'd been going to say tonight.

Katey had already concluded that she didn't want to hear it. She didn't really want to see him again either. Castigating him would serve no purpose. He knew by now he should have believed her. He'd want to apologize, no doubt. She had no intention of forgiving him for his appalling stubbornness. Actually, she'd much prefer he just wallow in guilt.

She said as much to Grace. "Blistering his ears gives him a chance to apologize, and once he does that, he's going to feel exonerated. Whether I forgive him or not, *he'll* feel that he corrected the matter with an apology and not give it another thought. But if he never gets that chance, then his guilt will never go away, will it?"

"That is positively wicked of you, Katey Tyler," Grace said, grinning again.

"You think so?" Katey nodded and made the decision. "Then we're going to leave first thing in the morning so he has no opportunity to find me."

Grace rolled her eyes. "For that tour of the southern shires?"

"No, for Gloucester."

Katey's impromptu decision certainly made Grace happy. Katey, on the other hand, experienced a nervous stomach before they even left the hotel the next morning. She wasn't sure why she'd felt so hesitant recently about meeting her relatives. It was something she'd looked forward to for a long time. And they *could* open their arms to her. But she'd somehow got it into her mind that they wouldn't.

Spur-of-the-moment decisions didn't always work, but sometimes they did. She and Grace didn't have to search for a coach to take them out of London. The same coach and driver that had been sent to fetch Katey last night was there again this morning, and seeing them, the driver quickly jumped down from his perch to open the door for them.

Grace was impressed enough to ask the man, "Don't tell me you've been here all night?"

"No, ma'am, but my job now is to take you ladies wherever you'd like to go until you set sail. Sir Anthony's orders."

That was a pleasant surprise, not to have to worry about transportation for the trip to Gloucestershire. Katey sent the driver to the door of Sir Anthony's house so she could pick up her coat, too, on the way out of London. She'd left it behind last night when she'd run off so quickly and didn't have another one that was as warm and comfortable for traveling. She would have gone to the door herself, but she doubted anyone other than the servants were up and about at that hour. She was wrong.

Judith bounded down the stairs to the coach, having heard the driver mention Katey's name at the door, and didn't even hesitate to enter the vehicle and plop down on the seat next to Katey. Katey didn't have the heart to scold her. The coach could have been empty. She could merely have sent the driver to pick up her coat. A little girl shouldn't just get into a vehicle if she didn't know who was in it.

Instead Katey said, "Do you always get up this early?"

"D'you always retrieve things this early?" Judith countered with a grin.

"I'm leaving London," Katey said by way of explanation. "So now was the only time I could fetch my coat. I'm going to visit my relatives in Gloucestershire after all, before I leave England altogether."

"*That's* where your relatives live?"

"Yes, why?"

"Haverston is there, the marquis's estate."

"Who's that?"

"My uncle Jason. He's the head of the family. Remember I mentioned his gardens to you?"

"Oh, yes, the gardener."

Judith giggled. "I think he'd love hearing himself called that. He does love his flowers."

"Isn't that where that French coach got buried?" Grace said with a grin.

"Indeed. You simply must see that! He's made it a beautiful setting in one of his greenhouses."

"I doubt we'll be anywhere near your uncle's house, Judith. Gloucestershire is a big county. And we don't have any spare time for detours. Our ship sails in four days. So we're going straight to the inn at Havers Town where we stayed before . . . Now what?" Katey asked as the child's blue eyes grew wide.

"Haverston is near that town!" Judith exclaimed. "Oh, this would be perfect."

"What would?"

"If you'd stay at Haverston."

Katey shook her head immediately. "I couldn't possibly. And there's no need, really. We're only going to be there a night or two."

"But *we* need you to stay," Judith said earnestly.

Katey frowned. "What do you mean?"

"There was quite an uproar last night after you left. I'm sure you can imagine. None of us knew what Boyd had done until then. My parents were beside themselves, trying to think of a way to make it up to you. This isn't nearly enough, but I'm certain it would make them feel much better if you would accept our hospitability while in Gloucestershire. You simply must."

This was so silly, Katey was thinking, when Judith continued, "The house there is big and comfortable, you'll like it there. And it's good to have friends in your corner when you're going to face the lions."

It took Katey a moment to figure out what Judy was talking about, but then she burst out laughing. Judith must have remembered Grace saying that Katey hadn't had the nerve to introduce herself to her relatives before. The "lions" were the family she'd never met, and the "friends" on her side were the powerful Malorys. Amazing that a child would even think of such things, but Katey was getting used to being surprised by this one. It was all in the upbringing, she supposed. Judith was nobility, but obviously she hadn't been restricted to the nursery and nannies who treated her like a child. She spent most of her time with adults who loved and respected her.

Still, it wasn't the Malorys who owed her anything. "I can't just show up at your uncle's door—"

"You can if I'm with you."

"Your parents aren't going to let—"

"They'll be with us, too, at least my mother will," Judith interrupted yet again. "My father's already gone out for the day. But don't worry, we won't delay you. You don't have to wait for us. We have more'n one coach and will catch up with you on the road."

And with that settled, at least in Judith's mind, the little girl rushed back into her house before Katey could think of any more reasons to refuse.

Once they were on their way Grace said, "Do you think they'll actually come?"

"Of course not. That's just a child's wishful thinking. Her mother isn't going to rush off to the country just to afford us some hospitality. The idea is ludicrous. Besides, she's probably still abed."

"That's too bad. I would have liked to see that coach covered in flowers."

twenty

No one, at least none of the adults who knew of his desire to make amends to Katey, had bothered to tell Boyd that she had been invited to Haverston. He had to hear it from Jacqueline, because Judith wouldn't think of leaving town without telling her best friend where she was going and why. But he didn't hear about it soon enough, which left him racing for Haverston, and still, it was impossible for him to ride fast enough to arrive before dark.

He could have arrived much sooner if he hadn't gone to Katey's hotel that morning. Even though the clerk had told him she'd checked out earlier, Boyd hadn't believed him. No one had indicated last night that Katey was leaving England right away. He thought she might have asked the hotel staff to tell him she was gone if he came by. He knew she was angry at him and didn't want to see him. But after he'd stubbornly waited in the hotel lobby, hoping to catch a glimpse of her walking by, he'd left.

Angry at himself for missing her, he concluded that she'd changed hotels just so he couldn't find her. After he'd inquired at other hotels in the vicinity, he still couldn't find her.

When he finally returned to Georgina's house, he'd

been relieved to learn she'd merely gone to Haverston. He knew the way there because he'd been to the Malory ancestral estate several times over the years when he happened to be in England during the holidays. That was when the entire Malory clan, his sister included, gathered at Haverston for Christmas.

Boyd would have found the ride pleasant what with the vibrant colors of autumn still dotting the landscape and the temperature somewhat mild, but the weather had turned foul, casting a gray pall over anything that could be seen through the downpour. At several points that afternoon, it was raining so hard that it was difficult for him even to make out the road in front of him.

He was soaked through long before he arrived. The butler told him the family was still at dinner as he led Boyd straight upstairs to dry off and change clothes. The butler hadn't given him a choice to do otherwise, so Boyd had to tamp down his impatience to see Katey. He did request that his arrival not be announced, though. After his last meeting with Katey Tyler, he had no doubt that she would conveniently disappear with some excuse if she was warned that he was there. And it didn't take him long to change clothes and run back downstairs.

His hair was still quite damp, as were his boots. He'd only tossed a few extra clothes in his valise before he rushed out of London, so he was without a coat, since the one he'd brought was still wet from the ride. He knew he was dressed too casually in his white, long-sleeved shirt and black britches for a dinner at Haverston, but that wasn't going to keep him away.

When he reached the dining room, he didn't budge from the doorway, even when the family noticed him and started their greetings. Katey *was* there, and he wasn't going to let her run off on him again. She probably realized that he was barricading the doorway, preventing her escape, because she merely glanced at him briefly before ignoring him while she continued eating.

Well, at least she wasn't running off, or even trying to. That should have been a relief. It wasn't. And he was incapable of ignoring her in the same way. In fact, he couldn't take his eyes off her.

She was wearing a white blouse with a dainty lace collar that was buttoned high to the neck. Her ample breasts filled out the blouse. Hell, her breasts filled out anything she wore much too amply.

Get your eyes off her breasts! he snarled to himself.

Her hair was arranged in the long braid she favored, though the tail of it wasn't looped through her belt today. Instead her braid was laid over her shoulder with the tail end resting in her lap. The thick raven braid provided a stark contrast to her soft white blouse. And her pink cheeks . . .

He realized abruptly that she was blushing. Because she knew he was looking at her? He couldn't seem to pull his eyes away even to end her discomfort or greet his in-laws. If given the choice, he could look at her for the rest of his life.

But he couldn't continue to just stand there blocking the doorway. Jason Malory, Third Marquis of Haverston, was at the head of the long dining table and, treating him like any other member of his family, told Boyd to take a seat while motioning for one of the footmen to bring him a plate. The days of the Malorys squaring off on one side of a room against the Andersons on the other side were long gone.

It was just a small gathering. In addition to Judith

and her mother, who had brought Katey to Haverston for some reason, Jason and his housekeeper, Molly, were there, seated together at one end of the long table. Molly was actually Jason's wife and Derek Malory's mother, though no one but the family knew that, and as far as Boyd knew, Molly insisted on keeping it that way.

Boyd wondered whether she had been introduced to Katey as the housekeeper. Not that it really mattered to him. His main concern was making sure Katey stayed in the room long enough this time to hear his apology.

To that end, he took the seat across from her, which still placed him close enough to the door to prevent her from bolting out of the room. Someone mentioned something about the rain when a crack of thunder sounded in the distance. He barely heard the comment, or the thunder. He was still staring at Katey, willing her to look at him. But she wouldn't. As far as she was concerned, he wasn't even in the room.

Which was as it should be, he supposed. She was a married woman, after all. She shouldn't be paying attention to unmarried men apart from extending common courtesy, but she wouldn't even afford him that. Well, of course not, she was still furious with him. And where the hell *was* her husband?

He'd assumed she was meeting that lucky bastard in England, but she'd never actually said she was, merely that she was on her way to meet him. Was that the reason for the world tour that Judith had mentioned was on Katey's agenda? Her husband was in a different country?

Boyd hoped not, because in the back of his mind he'd been expecting to have to deal with her husband at some point, for his high-handed treatment of her. Actually, he would have welcomed that. He needed something to relieve him of his guilt. Katey's forgiveness wouldn't quite do it, but a thrashing by her husband—no, that wasn't likely to happen. He didn't just admire pugilists, he excelled at the sport himself. He could just imagine how much more guilty he would feel if he beat her husband senseless instead.

He repressed a bitter laugh. Whom was he kidding? If he was going to beat any man bloody, he'd relish its being the one man who could claim Katey as his wife.

His frustration was adding to his impatience. He wanted to apologize immediately, but he couldn't. He needed to get Katey alone first. He couldn't very well explain at the dining table the reasons for what he'd done in Northampton, not when those reasons involved his lustful feelings for her. She was a married woman. Surely she would understand.

"Where's your husband, Mrs. Tyler?" he blurted out in frustration.

She glanced up at him, but only to raise a brow and ask with feigned curiosity, "Which one?"

He flinched. He couldn't deny he deserved that. Just one more mistake he needed to apologize for, thinking she could be Cameron's wife.

But Katey wasn't interested in his reply. With her eyes back on her food, she said, "I don't have a husband."

Incredulous, he said, "You lost him?"

He was about to add his condolences when she said, "Never had one to lose. I've never been married."

Two things happened to him at once. A sense of relief overwhelmed him. He could stop feeling guilty for desiring a married woman. She was available!

But then he thought of the hell he'd gone through on that voyage with her because he'd been forced to keep his distance, because he'd *thought* she was a happily married woman and the mother of two small children. And how different their encounter in Northampton might have been if her marriage hadn't stood between them.

The possibilities stunned him. He might even have made love to her that day! And he wouldn't have dragged her off to face the Malorys' wrath, would he? With his mind unclouded by his desire for her he would have seen her for the sweet, delightful wench that she was. He would have had no trouble believing her then. But that hadn't been possible because she had lied about being married. His mood darkened as he wondered if she'd told that lie to keep him away from her. His tone had a sharp edge of anger when he asked, "Then why were you using the name *Mrs.* Tyler?"

"For convenience. I used that guise as a cloak of protection, to keep unwanted attention at bay. It worked very well," she added smugly, and peeked up at him to see his reaction.

Red-faced, Boyd said, "And your two children?"

She stopped pretending a fascination with her plate and lifted her head to stare at him directly. "They weren't mine. You guessed correctly about that. They were my neighbor's nieces. She needed someone to escort them to a relative in England. That was the impetus I needed to begin my world tour."

The other people at the table had been following this conversation, glancing back and forth from Katey to Boyd. Jason reminded them that they weren't alone in the room when he asked, "It sounds as if you two know each other from some prior meeting."

Boyd tore his eyes off Katey long enough to glance at the eldest Malory. "She was a passenger on my ship during my last Atlantic crossing."

Which made Roslynn gasp. "You knew her and still thought she was guilty?"

"I didn't *know* her," he said in exasperation. "We barely spoke on the voyage."

"We spoke plenty," Katey disagreed.

"Not about anything personal," Boyd shot back, his eyes returning to her.

"We spoke enough for me to be glad I'd tacked a *Mrs.* onto my name."

"Oh, my—," Molly began, then made an effort to change the subject. "Perhaps we should adjourn to the parlor for dessert?"

With that suggestion the Malorys filed out of the room. But Boyd didn't follow them. Katey didn't move either. They were too busy glaring at each other to even notice they were alone now.

twenty-one

"WAS I so transparent?" Boyd asked.

It was as if two minutes of silence hadn't slowly passed while they stared at each other across the table, oblivious of everything else in the room. Katey hadn't expected him to show up at Haverston. When Judith and her mother had caught up to her coach and led the way to the ancestral estate, Roslynn had mentioned that Anthony might join them if he didn't get delayed in Kent, where his brother Edward had sent him on business, but she hadn't said anything about Boyd.

And then there he was, suddenly standing in the doorway, his hair wet, his dark brown eyes gazing intently at her, stealing her breath. She hadn't expected to ever again feel that thrilling burst of excitement at the sight of him, but there it was, too, and she had to stomp on it immediately or she was going to be the one making a fool of herself.

The torrential rain had delayed her visit to the Millards. Instead she spent an enjoyable afternoon with the Malorys, who managed to relax her tense, nervous stomach with their amusing wit and easy banter. A fresh start in the morning would be better, and she hoped to sleep off the sense of dread that had revisited her. She was just so afraid that if the meeting with her mother's family went badly, all her hopes would die right there, and she had such big hopes again that these people could fill in the gaping hole her mother's death had left in her heart. If the meeting went well, on the other hand, she would be so pleased she might even delay her departure for France. But she had no idea how that meeting would go until it happened.

She certainly hadn't planned on this private meeting with Boyd, not after she had more or less decided to let him wallow in the guilt of never getting to apologize to her. But there were two sides to that coin. Ignoring his apology would work just as well, she supposed. She wasn't going to let the man off the hook. If he thought she would ever forgive him for what he'd done, he was wrong.

Now, in response to his question about whether he'd been transparent, she said, "Yes, you were—well, no actually. My maid brought to my attention that you were more interested in me than you should be. 'Having carnal thoughts' was how she put it. I might never have figured out for myself what all those intense looks were about, if—"

"You made your point." His groan sounded nearly agonized.

The groan made Katey remember those days aboard his ship and how exciting it had been, knowing that he wanted her. He'd given her one of her fondest memories, her first experience of being desired by an exceptionally handsome man. And then he'd ruined it. He was now part of one of her worst memories instead. And that was worth crying over.

"Why don't you just shoot me and get it over with?" he continued.

"I prefer hanging."

She hadn't meant to say that, it just slipped out. If she'd said it to Grace, she might have laughed, since it was now somewhat of a joke between them. But there was nothing amusing about it this time.

"Of course," he agreed. "Not as messy. A woman would—"

"Do *not* make light of this!" She stood up as she said it, her expression as angry as she sounded. "I don't even know why I'm talking to you. You behaved like a fool. I wasn't articulate enough to sway you to reason. Nothing else needs to be said about it."

"That doesn't even scratch the surface!" he protested. "Please sit down."

"I think not. If it hasn't occurred to you yet, nothing you can say will make a difference. So why don't you save us both this embarrassment?"

"The explanation I have isn't appropriate for innocent ears."

He tossed that out there like a broadside, and that's how it was felt. He was going to talk about his desire again? Perhaps she ought to sit down after all. Her wobbly knees were insisting on it!

"I thought you would understand," he went on. "But you've blown me out of the water with your confession that you aren't married. Not that that doesn't delight me more than you can imagine, but I was sure a married woman would understand what it's like to want someone so much it clouds your mind and negates good judgment."

"That's your excuse, what you told me that day? That you couldn't think straight with me near? 'Within touching distance,' wasn't that how you put it? That you didn't dare to take me at my word because of it? But wait, this gets better. Because *you* couldn't control your carnal thoughts, it was preferable, in your mind, to drag me *all* the way to London and throw me to the wolves there, which is what you thought was going to happen. I lost my driver because of you. My maid is still upset. And to top it all—"

He cut in with a wince, "If it's any consolation, as soon as I left you in that room, putting some distance between us that day, my gut instinct kicked in. I couldn't believe that you would hurt a child."

"Maybe because I wouldn't! But, no, that doesn't help one little bit, Boyd Anderson. What good are instincts if you ignore them?"

"Then you tell me, how could I trust my instincts at that point, when my very *first* instinct at finding you there, *and* thinking you were guilty, was to run off with you? I told you that. Did you think I was joking? My first thought was to save you from being arrested, to sneak you out of the country if need be."

That might have been preferable, all things considered, but she didn't say that aloud and asked instead, "Then why didn't you?"

He ran a frustrated hand through his damp hair before he said, "Because I'm an honest man and the crime appalled me. I saw firsthand what Judith's parents were going through, and you can't put people through that kind of emotional hell and not pay an equal price for it. And I was afraid that whisking you away would solve nothing, that you'd just do the same thing again in some other country. But for it to have even occurred to me, to help you escape—I knew I wasn't thinking rationally."

She stiffened. "So we've come full circle to that? Your excuse that you can't think clearly when you're around me? You, sir, simply don't think!"

"Damnit, Katey, you have no idea what it's like to want someone as much as I want you!"

She drew in her breath sharply. "Nor do I want to know, thank you."

She couldn't believe she managed to say that, when it was taking every ounce of will she had to ignore what those words did to her. He still wanted her! Even her anger didn't put him off.

"Well, you're going to hear this," he continued with a stubborn look. "You have been on my mind since the moment I met you. Even after our voyage together ended, I still couldn't get you out of my thoughts. I should have, but I couldn't. You were even in my dreams. I didn't expect to ever see you again. And then there you were in the flesh, and all I could think about was kissing you, putting my hands on —"

"Stop it!" Her cheeks bloomed with color as a wave of heat rushed over her. But she was staring at his mouth. He'd said he'd wanted to kiss her. She couldn't seem to tear her eyes away. What the devil was happening to her?

"I'm sorry," he continued. "I was really hoping you might understand at least a little, but I realize you can't, since you've never experienced anything even remotely similar, have you?"

"You don't really expect me to answer that, do you?" she replied indignantly.

He was beginning to look dejected. She looked away from him. She was appalled that inklings of remorse were sneaking up on her. Just because he looked miserable? He was *supposed* to look miserable!

"At the risk of making you blush again, I have to say one last—"

She jumped to her feet and quickly interrupted him, "If you mention wanting me again, I promise you, this conversation will end right now."

He sighed. "I was merely going to say that because of my—well, what I was feeling, I was afraid I would have believed anything you said, true or false, because I *wanted* you to be innocent. And I was furious because I was sure you weren't. So I knew damn well there was no way I could trust my own judgment. I had to let someone else sort it out."

She recalled that he did suggest excuses she could use that day that would allow him to let her go, but they'd all been based on the premise that she was guilty and just provided some acceptable reason for her involvement in Judith's abduction. That did support his assertion that he had really thought she was guilty while he was with her that day. Apparently, he didn't start to have any doubts until he'd walked away from her.

Katey halted those thoughts abruptly. Was she now looking for an excuse to forgive him?

She moved around the table, but when he stood up, she turned around so she could back out the dining room door, afraid he was going to try to stop her. She even held up a hand to put him off, not that it would have done any good if he was intent on keeping her there. She might be tall, but Boyd Anderson was lean, hard brawn. There was no question who would win that little battle.

"I've listened to you," she said, stopping in the doorway. "Now give me the same courtesy. You have in so many words blamed 'feelings' for your despicable treatment of me. I find that reason unacceptable. I understand you're sorry—well, you haven't actually said so, but—"

"Of course I am!"

"So am I," she continued, giving him only a minor frown for interrupting. "However, being sorry after the fact is rarely helpful. This is one of those times. You had other options. But you chose the easiest path."

"*What* other options?" His tone was sounding frustrated again.

"You could have sent someone after Jeremy. You could have kept me at the inn, in that comfortable room until they returned with the truth, instead of taking me out in a storm!"

"When I was this close to bedding you?"

There was no space at all between the thumb and finger he held up to her, causing heat to rush up her cheeks again. "You could have at least waited until my maid returned. She would have confirmed everything—"

"That's just it, Katey. I couldn't wait another moment. But I did let you go. That should count for something."

She gasped. "The devil you did, I escaped from you! And I could have broken my neck doing so, you know. Climbing out of windows, scampering across rain-slick roofs—do I look like a child who would delight in such things?"

"I wasn't gone that long, Katey. I could have caught up with you easily, but I decided not to." He sounded rather proud of himself. "Judy was safe, so—I let you go."

"Oh, I see. So instead of dragging me the rest of the way to London where you thought I'd be tossed in jail, you *allowed* me to escape so that I could run into Maisie Cameron and end up in jail anyway, after she raved like a lunatic and—"

"You better be lying," he cut in.

"You'd like to think so, wouldn't you?"

"Katey," he said warningly.

She snorted at him. "You're no longer in any position to threaten me, and you better keep that in mind. You'll be getting no information out of me that I'm not willing to volunteer. But I wasn't keeping it a secret. If you hadn't dragged me out of Northampton, I would have been comfortably ensconced in my coach on my way to London, right behind Judith, and I never would have run into Maisie Cameron again. The authorities would have caught up to her soon enough, since she was more afraid of her husband at that point than she was of jail. I didn't need to be the one to take her to the constable."

"Then why did you?"

"Because there she was in front of me when I got back to Northampton, and because it was the right thing to do. But Maisie knew I'd thwarted her plans, and while she was happy to get behind bars to escape her husband's wrath, she was also delighted to get even with me by accusing me of the whole plot—just as you did!"

"Good God," Boyd said, looking quite sick to his stomach. "I had no idea, Katey."

She scowled at him. "Isn't this where you should be gloating? That *is* what you had planned for me, after all, right? To end up in jail. Well, I did end up there, and my maid, too, and even my driver, which, by the way, is why he quit on me."

"The constable didn't believe you either?"

"Oh, he did. But he wasn't about to let me go without getting clearance from the Malorys first. Their name is well known even up north. It wasn't until nearly noon the next day, when his man got back from London with the information he obtained from Judith, that we were finally released."

"You can't imagine how sorry I am, Katey."

He said that with great feeling. She didn't doubt he meant it. But it was still too late for apologies.

"No, I can't," she said. "Nor do I care to try. Do you really think a few words, no matter how sincere, are going to make me forget the anger and humiliation I felt at being branded a common criminal, all because I tried to help a little girl in need?"

"For God's sake, you have to let me make this up to you somehow." His expression brightened as an idea occurred to him. "You said you lost your driver? I'll drive you anywhere you want to go for as long as you like!"

She rolled her eyes toward the ceiling. "I've already replaced the driver. You call that making amends, giving me something I already have?"

"Katey, give me a bone here!" he said in exasperation. "There must be something you want or need that I can help you with."

"There's only one thing you have that—"

She stopped abruptly. Bringing up his ship, which had popped into her mind at his mention of transportation, was out of the question. He might be contrite, but not enough to give up his ship, even if she offered to pay for it. Besides, the inconvenience of planning her tour according to shipping schedules was a mere annoyance. She didn't really want her own ship.

But he was suddenly looking much too sensual. The intense heat in his eyes nearly paralyzed her. What the devil had she said?

She drew in her breath sharply. "Oh, good grief, you are so off the mark it boggles the mind. There was nothing—inappropriate—in what I was about to say. It was certainly *not* what you are thinking."

"Then what do I have that—?"

"Nothing!" she snapped, flustered at the turn their conversation had taken. "I lost my train of thought. I can't recall what I was going to say. So don't mention it again."

His sigh was heartfelt. *She* felt it, right to her toes. And the heat was still in his dark eyes. . . .

He leapt across the space between them and drew her hard against him. His kiss was as hot as his expression had been, just as she'd guessed it would be. And she didn't push him away from her. Oh, no, she wrapped her arms around him. Those feelings of excitement and desire that she'd had in that room in Northampton when he'd touched her were back again, churning her insides, making her . . .

"You're not very good at lying," Boyd observed.

She blinked the brief fantasy away, and blushing for even having those thoughts intrude *now,* with him standing right there before her, she started to ramble. "Actually, I'm wonderfully good at it. I excel at it. You would be quite surprised, not that it matters in the least. And I've given you much more time than you deserve. I have to rise early in the morning to finish my business here, so I'm going off to bed. Please extend my good-nights to the Malorys, if you will."

"Katey—"

She squealed as he reached for her, because that kiss she had just imagined was still too fresh in her mind. She bolted out into the hall and straight up the stairs. He probably hadn't been about to put his hands on her to try to stop her, but she'd let him get to her, frazzling her senses more than she could withstand in one evening. Good grief, she'd been babbling like a loon!

It was that look of his there at the end, when she knew exactly what he was thinking . . . and wanting to do to her. And in her mind she'd let him! And how the devil was she going to sleep now, when she had already imagined how that meeting could have turned out, if that man did deserve to be forgiven?

twenty-two

WHILE THE PEOPLE in Gardener hadn't socialized much other than on Sundays and holidays, Katey's mother had still taught her the finer points of proper etiquette as they had been taught to her years ago, and visiting people in the rain was on the "must never do" list. Dripping rainwater in people's foyers and tracking wet, muddy footprints across fine carpeting was a sure way never to get invited again. Not that the homes in Gardener had had any fine carpets, but Adeline had made her point.

When Katey looked out her window the next morning, she didn't see a drizzle, she saw a steady downpour. The rain that had blown in yesterday continued and showed no signs of letting up. She waited an hour, then extended that to two, but finally she put off the visit to the Millards' for another day. As long as she and Grace were back in London by tomorrow night to sail the following day, they could afford to spend another day at Haverston, and it was still in the back of Katey's mind that she might cancel her departure from England if all went as she hoped with the Millards.

When she'd arrived at Haverston yesterday, she'd been awed and amazed. Sir Anthony's house had been sparkling elegance, but the marquis's country estate was a mansion!

It literally extended over acres of land and was too big to sparkle: light got lost in such huge rooms. But the marquis's residence had warmth—sofas so richly upholstered Katey was afraid to sit on them, fireplaces twice their normal size, paintings hanging from the wallpapered walls that were bigger than she was! Judith had given her a brief tour that lasted an hour and didn't even cover half the mansion.

She hadn't been to the greenhouses yet, though, to see the coach that had been turned into a garden ornament. Judith had been saving that tour for after dinner last night, when the lamps would be lit to give it a special prominence, but Katey had defected to her room after dinner because of Boyd.

She decided to see it now before breakfast. She wasn't going to wait for the rain to stop first since it didn't look as if it was going to. A lot of greenhouses were out back. Judith hadn't exaggerated about Jason Malory's love of growing things. They were all big and mostly made of glass, and Katey only had to mention "the coach" for a servant to point her to the right one.

He offered to fetch her an umbrella. She didn't want to wait and so declined, since the run wasn't that far from the house. But before she reached the entrance of the greenhouse she was laughing at how quickly she'd been drenched. She wasn't cold, though. Inside, the greenhouse was warm and humid. A pathway led through the rich foliage, some plants potted, some on trellises, some even hanging from the ceiling beams, but many were just planted in the rich soil underfoot.

She slowed her step when she saw the coach up ahead and was wide-eyed and feeling amazed once again. Jason had even hung two chandeliers above it, in a greenhouse! She arrived to find one of the workers lighting them.

Now that was extravagance and she said to the man, "In the daytime?"

The old fellow chuckled at her. "Only on dark days like this, miss."

Katey sat down on one of the benches that had been set near the coach. The servant soon finished his task and left her alone there. The coach was an amazing sight. The wheels had been removed, making it seem as if it were planted in the ground! Flowers and vines surrounded it. But it certainly didn't need any extra light. Entirely white and gold, it was probably blinding when sun came through the windows. But the chandeliers did give it a unique glow, making it look almost ethereal, and bringing fairy tales to mind.

She felt her nervous stomach settling down. Even her agitation from last night went away. The setting was so peaceful, and she felt some of that peace flowing through her.

She didn't even stiffen or jump up to leave when Boyd appeared and sat down next to her. Their talk last night had aroused some powerful emotions in her, but she wasn't the least bit aggravated by his presence now. As she looked at him, she thought, why did he *have* to be so handsome? He was dressed as he'd usually been on his ship in an open-collared shirt and an unbuttoned jacket. He wasn't fashionably attired with a cravat, yet his clothes fit him splendidly, too splendidly, hugging his lean, muscular body.

"So you don't really mind the rain after all?" he asked.

She'd wiped her face off on her long sleeves, but beads of water still clung to her braid, and wet patches dotted her lime green dress everywhere. She saw that he was just as wet as she was, and he hadn't wiped his face yet. She had an urge to remove the raindrops from his cheeks with her . . . tongue . . .

She blushed immediately at the direction her thoughts had taken, but he probably assumed it was because of his question. She tried hard to keep her tone conversational, just as his had been. "Not when it's my choice to go out in it," she answered.

He grinned. "I get the point."

"Not so dumb after all?" She grinned back at him.

Good grief, was she teasing him? Well, it certainly felt better than yelling at him, but where had her anger gone? She hadn't forgiven him, not even a little. Maybe it was the setting? It was making her feel as if she were in a fairy tale . . . or one of her fantasies . . . where Boyd Anderson often appeared.

"I thought you were visiting your relatives this morning. I didn't expect to find you still here."

"How did you know I was visiting relatives?"

"I asked Roslynn. I'd rather not leave things to chance where you're concerned."

She blushed again, and her whole body suddenly felt warm. She was reminded why she'd told him she was married to begin with. He disturbed her on a level she just wasn't familiar with. He had revealed his feelings, or rather, desires, when he'd thought she was a criminal. And he wasn't hiding them now when he knew better, because he also knew she wasn't really married. Could she withstand his flirtations this time? Or was she still *too* attracted to him to enjoy just a little romance and then move on?

"Cat got your tongue, Katey?"

She blinked away her thoughts. "I'm not going visiting in the rain. It can wait until tomorrow."

He grinned and reminded her, "You just admitted you

don't mind rain. Dare I hope you were reluctant to leave Haverston without seeing me again?"

She rolled her eyes at him. "Not a chance. I've just never met my mother's family, so I want this first meeting to be perfect."

"Ah, understood. Did you let them know you'd be delayed?"

"They don't even know I'm in England."

He raised a brow. "You're not going to let them know you're in the area before you appear at their door?"

"So they can pack up and leave?"

It was obvious she wasn't joking now, which made Boyd frown. "Why would you say that?"

She'd never mentioned the Millards to him. They certainly hadn't come up in any of their conversations aboard his ship.

She didn't want to explain the situation now, either, so she said, "They're my mother's family, but they disowned her when she married my father and moved to America. They may not want to meet me. In fact, I almost didn't come here."

He started to reach for her hand. It would have been a natural thing for him to do—if they'd been friends and didn't have his blunder standing between them. He put his hand back on his knee, but she knew what he'd almost done, and those warm, sparkly sensations were filling her again. . . . What the devil?

"Did you consider they might not even be in residence now?" he inquired.

"We stopped in Havers Town on the way here and made inquiries at several shops. The Millards are here."

"Would you like an escort? I would be very pleased to accompany you. Moral support if you need it."

Was he just trying to make amends, or did he really want to offer his support? It was hard to tell what was on his mind—other than lust, which was easy to recognize with him. But his eyes weren't filled with it just now, and he was being cordial and—nice.

Katey groaned to herself. What was she thinking? It didn't matter how he was behaving now, she'd seen him at his worst—arrogant, stubborn, deaf to reason, and she'd had to suffer all that plus a lot more that she *did* blame him for. He might not have put her in jail, but she wouldn't have ended up there if he hadn't forcibly removed her from Northampton that day.

She stood up abruptly. "Thank you, but this is something I have to do alone. And I believe I'm ready for breakfast now."

He called her name, but she hurried off without stopping. And she wouldn't have stopped at the breakfast room either if it had been empty, because she heard Boyd right behind her. But it wasn't empty.

The smaller, more casual room for eating had a wall of windows that caught the morning sun when it wasn't overcast or raining like today. It was set up for a buffet today. Judith and her mother were already seated at the table, and Katey took a seat between them. That kept her from having any more private words with Boyd for the moment, and she was determined to try to keep it that way for the remainder of her visit.

twenty-three

KATEY SKIPPED LUNCHEON, but realized how silly she was being trying to avoid Boyd. He was stalking her, anyway, at least that's how it seemed when she couldn't turn around without finding him nearby. Somehow he got her to agree to a game of chess. Did Boyd bring out a competitive streak in her? She'd been unable to lay him low with words so she was going to demolish him with a board game?

It turned out to be an enjoyable experience that lasted most of the afternoon. Judith stood by her side and whispered moves she could make. Boyd accused Katey of cheating because of it! "Who's playing against me?" he asked at one point. "You or Judy?"

"Getting nervous?" Katey smirked as she captured his second knight, leaving him with no move for retaliation unless he wanted to lose his queen, too. "Judith's just confirming for me that my strategy is working. She and I seem to think alike."

Glancing from Katey to Judith, he exclaimed, "My God, you two even smirk alike. How about helping me instead, Judy? I'm the one who's losing here."

The child giggled, but stayed right where she was. And Boyd proved he wasn't losing at all when he captured

Katey's queen four moves later. And that about ended that round. When the queen goes, all hope goes with her.

Boyd played so aggressively! Katey wasn't used to that. All of her prior games of chess had been with her mother, and played leisurely as an enjoyable means of passing the time. But she shouldn't have been surprised by Boyd's style of play.

She'd sensed his aggressive nature the first day she'd met him when it had been so obvious that he was going to pursue her. The man had overwhelmed her then, so much so that she'd had to put a stop to it by inventing a husband. She had thought she'd be better able to handle flirtations of that sort with time, but apparently not, at least not with Boyd.

But for the moment his aggression was centered on a game, and Katey was enjoying herself too much to end it. He won that first game and they immediately started another. And he continued to go out of his way to distract her and keep her from concentrating, all deliberately. There was a lot of laughter, and she realized later that there shouldn't have been. Chess was a serious game, but he'd turned it into more fun than Katey had ever had playing it.

She didn't exactly demolish him at only one win out of three, but his victories had been difficult, so the games had been close enough to suit her.

"Who taught you to play?" he finally asked her when they put the chess pieces away.

Dinner had been announced, and he offered his arm to escort her to the dining room. She took his arm without thinking, too relaxed in his company to remember that she shouldn't be touching him.

"My mother," she said. "We used to play once or twice a week in the evenings."

"Did you lose to her so easily?"

She sputtered a laugh. "You call that easy? I nearly had you all three games!"

"Nearly never counts—except like this."

He demonstrated what "this" was when he pulled her aside next to the doorway, out of view from anyone in the hall, and trapped her there with an arm on either side of her, her back to the wall. Judith had run ahead. They were alone in the room now. And while he wasn't actually touching her, she sensed he would be at any moment.

"Don't," she said—or did she? She was staring at his mouth, breathlessly waiting for his kiss as he slowly leaned in closer to her.

"Katey?"

It was Judith calling from the hall to see what was keeping her. Boyd sighed and stepped away from her. Then he put her hand back on his arm and continued to escort her to the dining room as if he hadn't almost kissed her.

Katey was incredulous. Did he think she'd forgiven him? He certainly seemed to be acting as if it were a foregone conclusion. Not once today had he mentioned his regret, but then she hadn't once mentioned the incident either, so he could be basing assumptions on that. He *did* make assumptions too easily, she reminded herself, including ridiculous ones. . . .

"Boyd," she began.

But they'd reached the dining room, and what she would have said couldn't be said now with the Malorys already gathered there. But *he* got another word in.

"Sit next to me?" he whispered.

Katey took her hand from his arm and said simply, "No," as she moved to the seat next to Judith again, rather than the two empty seats on the other side of the table. She saw that Boyd was slightly frowning now as he took one of those seats across from her. That was too bad. He needed to remember what she'd told him last night in this very room, and now that they were back in it, maybe he would. Just because she had been somewhat sociable with him today for the Malorys' sake didn't mean anything had changed.

She vowed to ignore him for the rest of the evening. That would make her point. And it would have worked well if her eyes weren't drawn to him so often. So she started a conversation with Jason Malory, to keep her attention directed away from Boyd.

She hadn't had the nerve last night to ask Jason about his neighbors. The large man had intimidated her too much with his serious looks and reticence yesterday. He was blond and green-eyed like his brothers James and Edward—only Anthony had the dark Gypsy looks. Judith had tried to assure her that Jason was only a tyrant where his brothers were concerned, that he was like a big, cuddly bear with the rest of the family. Whether that was true or not, he was much more friendly today, had spoken to her several times, and had even stood with his arm around Judith and watched the chess game for a while.

So she asked him what he could tell her about the Millard family. Unfortunately, it wasn't much.

"They were never very sociable here in the country," he told her, then added with a grin, "Not that we've ever been a whirl of parties out here. But they weren't part of the London circle either. Neither was I, but my younger brothers all were, and I don't recall them ever mentioning the Millards being part of that crowd. I think the Millards favored Gloucester, at least that's where I heard your grandmother Sophie was from, before she married the earl, so they did most of their socializing in that city."

"Did you know my mother, Adeline?"

"I'm afraid I can't recall ever meeting Lady Adeline. There was a rumor that she'd married some baron on the Continent. Not so?"

"No."

"Her older sister, Letitia, I vaguely recall seeing in Havers Town from time to time when I was much younger. Actually, now that I think of it, I used to see her there quite often. Seemed like every time I went to town back then, there she was, doing some sort of shopping or other. She used to be a friendly girl. Always stopped to have a few words with me."

"Used to be?"

"If I happen to come across her these days, she completely snubs me. For whatever reason, she never married. It turned her quite disagreeable, or that seems to be the general consensus. Oddly, I have few memories of the friendly girl, but the bitter one I recall clearly. I suppose an unpleasant person tends to stand out in one's mind."

That little bit of information was more than Katey's mother had ever given her, including the names of her relatives. "My father" or "the earl" or "my mother" was how Adeline had always referred to them, and she'd never even mentioned a sister! And Katey would meet them tomorrow. Hopefully.

twenty-four

KATEY HADN'T PLANNED on taking Grace with her to the
Millard estate. Her maid had a way of either attempt-
ing to bolster Katey's courage with her sarcastic remarks,
which could goad Katey into showing her maid that she
was wrong, or adding to any nervousness that was beset-
ting her. But Boyd's appearance at Haverston changed
Katey's mind about leaving Grace behind. Returning to
the marquis's estate after her visit to the Millards' just to
collect her maid was the worse of two evils—with Boyd
still there.

But Grace surprised her. She barely said a word on
the short drive to the Millard home, and it really was a
short drive. Haverston was in the country on one side of
the small town of Havers, and the Millards lived out in
the country on the other side. The drive between the two
estates was less than twenty minutes. It seemed odd to
Katey that with such proximity the two families didn't
know each other better, but as Jason had said, this part of
Gloucestershire wasn't known for much socializing.

"I'll wait here in the coach," Grace said when they
pulled up in front of the stately country manor. "Just
don't forget I'm out here if you plan on a long visit."

Grace's reticence was almost palpable now. She had

pretty much pushed this visit down Katey's throat, but now she was obviously just as worried about the outcome as Katey. If it didn't go well, Grace would be blaming herself.

But that was only in the back of Katey's mind as she stood at the front door of the large country manor. The estate wasn't nearly as big as Haverston, but it was still imposing, and in the forefront of her mind was a fear she'd never known. No, that wasn't so. She'd felt the same fear the first time she'd come to Havers Town. She'd succumbed to it then and hadn't got this far, right to her relatives' door. She was about to do the same thing again, to turn around and race off in any direction other than here . . .

"Can I help you, miss?"

The door had opened. An old fellow stood there in the kind of meticulous black suit that servants usually wore. The Millard butler? No, her *family's* butler. Damnit, it was *her* family who lived here. They might have disowned her mother, but that didn't negate her being a part of them. And that disowning had happened long ago. Adeline might never have forgiven them for it, but perhaps her family now regreted their actions. And Katey would never know either way if she didn't tell them who she was.

"I'm Katey Tyler."

The old fellow's look was completely blank. He didn't recognize the name Tyler at all. Well, perhaps he was new to the household, or more likely, perhaps the family didn't discuss personal matters with their servants. Or perhaps a name like Tyler simply wouldn't be remembered twenty-three years later.

"I would like to speak to the lady of the house, if she's available?"

"Come inside, miss." He extended an arm. "That wind is a bit chilly."

She hadn't noticed the wind until he mentioned it. The rain had stopped at some point in the night, but a solid bank of clouds kept the sun from shining this morning.

The butler showed her to a large room furnished as a parlor. That she'd even been let inside meant that her grandmother must be at home. And her queasy stomach worsened. But mixed in with that uncomfortable feeling was a good deal of awe that tightened her throat with emotion. This was the house her mother had grown up in! Had she sat on that brown and rose brocaded sofa? Had she warmed her hands at the fireplace? Who was the man in the portrait above the cherrywood mantel? Brown-haired and distinguished-looking, he was not tall, but was quite handsome. Adeline's father? Her grandfather? An even older ancestor?

God, how much family history must be in this house! And the stories. Would they tell them to her? Would they share their memories?

"My mother is sleeping. She hasn't been feeling well. Can I help you?"

Katey swung around. The woman was middle-aged with faded brown hair and emerald eyes. Katey's eyes. Her mother's eyes. She could feel some moisture gathering in her own. This had to be her aunt. She had only a vague facial resemblance to Adeline, but those eyes . . .

"Letitia?"

The woman frowned. It changed her appearance dramatically, adding a sternness that was actually intimidating. At least Katey found it so. Someone else might not be impressed at all, but this was Katey's aunt, one of her few remaining relatives, and the woman didn't know that yet.

"It's Lady Letitia," the woman said with a heavy dose of condescension, as if she were speaking to someone she was sure was far below her own class. "Do I know you?"

"Not yet, but—I'm Katey Tyler."

"And?"

No open arms. No delighted cries. No joyful tears of welcome. Like the butler, her aunt didn't recognize the Tyler name.

Katey had been sure the Millards would at least remember the name of the man they had refused to allow into the family. Surely the two sisters must have discussed her father at some point. They weren't that far apart in age, perhaps five or six years. But Katey was making assumptions based on little information.

And the best way to get beyond that, before her nerve completely deserted her, was to say, "I'm your niece. Adeline was my mother."

Letitia's expression didn't change. Not even a little. But it had already been twisted sour, apparently at the realization that she was dealing with someone from the lower classes.

"Get out."

Katey questioned her hearing. Surely she was mistaken. But if she wasn't, perhaps young Judith's idea might be useful after all. Anything was worth trying at that point, if there was nothing wrong with her ears.

"I've come a very long way to meet you," Katey said, trying to ignore the desperation in her own tone. "The Malorys of Haverston were nice enough to—"

"How *dare* you mention those scandalmongers!" Letitia cut in, her voice rising angrily. "How *dare* you presume you'd find welcome here, you little bastard! *Get out!*"

Katey bit her lip to stop it from trembling. She couldn't stop the tears though, or the pain that rose up to choke her. She ran out of that room, and out of that house.

twenty-five

"WHAT DO YOU mean it sailed!" Katey shouted at the dockhand who'd just told her she'd missed her ship.

"Cast off with the morning tide," the fellow said with barely a glance her way as he went about loading crates into a wagon. "Most ships do."

He was the only one standing near the berth she'd been directed to whom she could question. And finding an empty berth, she wasn't exactly in a calm state of mind.

"Why wasn't I told that! Why wasn't it printed on these tickets?!"

"Did you look at the tickets?"

She snapped her mouth shut and marched off. No, she didn't examine the tickets closely. She wasn't accustomed to sailing. She'd only sailed once before! And she couldn't believe she'd missed her ship!

"It's really gone?" Grace asked hesitantly when Katey climbed back in the coach. The hesitancy came from hearing the door slammed shut as well as the shouting that had just taken place outside.

"Yes."

"The sun's only been out an hour. How early did we need to get here?"

"Too early. I see now why that ticket fellow had

mentioned that we could board the night prior to sailing if we cared to. He shouldn't have made it sound like a mere option. He should have stated that it was the only option."

Grace sat back with a sigh. "So we're back to the ticket office?"

"And another long delay? I think not. I'm going to find Boyd Anderson instead."

"What for?"

"To rent his ship."

Grace started to laugh. Katey didn't. When the maid noticed that, she said, "You weren't joking?"

"No, I wasn't. He pretty much begged me at Haverston to give him a way to make amends. And I'm not talking about demanding the use of his ship without recompense. I did say rent it, didn't I?"

"Yes, but you can't just rent a ship and its entire crew at a moment's notice."

"I can if it belongs to *him*."

"I'll wager he won't agree to something like that," Grace predicted.

Katey remembered Boyd's expression when he'd beseeched her to let him do something, *anything*, to make things right with her. "I'll take that wager."

They had returned to London early enough yesterday to collect the clothes that had been finished and delivered to her hotel—and to find a new hotel. Hers hadn't had any rooms available. She'd left so early in the morning for Gloucestershire that she hadn't thought about reserving her room for another night upon her return. But at least the hotel clerk had held her packages for her and directed her to another hotel.

She supposed that she was going to have to start paying

better attention to these details if she was going to continue traveling around the world. Ship schedules, coaches, guaranteed hotel rooms, things she'd been taking for granted, well, things she just wasn't used to arranging yet. She'd done well until they'd left Scotland, but then they hadn't run into any obstacles on that pleasant tour, all of which had deluded her into believing that everything else would go just as smoothly—instead of steadily downhill.

Katey sighed. She knew she was letting what had happened in Gloucestershire affect her outlook on everything else. She was upset—well, she was more than that—but she was going to have to put it behind her. This horrible impatience, the anger that came with it—the hurt—these things were so alien to her, and she didn't like how they made her feel.

She hadn't given Grace a word-for-word account of that brief interview with her aunt. God, her mother had been so right. They really were snobs of the worst sort, the Millards, and that's all she'd told her maid. She'd been too hurt to want to discuss it.

She'd never been called such a horrible name before in her life. She knew it could be used in a derogatory, nasty way, that it didn't only imply illegitimacy, which in her case wasn't the situation at all. So her aunt had called her a bastard just to show how little she thought of her. It still hurt. It hurt even more that the hopes she'd had about still having a *family* had soundly been dashed.

She wanted to get far, far away from England and these terrible emotions that she'd never experienced before she'd come to this country. Wait on another ship's schedule? When she had another option?

Of course, there she was again taking things for granted. Grace could be right. Boyd might laugh at the suggestion that he rent his ship to her. The idea really was ludicrous if she cared to think about it. But if he did agree, she could be sailing in the morning, or even later today. If he did agree, she wouldn't be seeing the last of him either, as she'd thought on her way to the docks this morning. That was a daunting thought, but, though she'd only admit it to herself, an exciting one, too. But she would insist that he not sail with his ship. That would be the smart thing to do. It wasn't as if he captained it. That would be a much better arrangement, *The Oceanus* at her disposal and its owner left far behind in England.

And just to make sure that Grace couldn't accuse her later of *wanting* to see Boyd again, she'd stop by the ticket office first. If she could get passage on another ship within the next day or so, then she would forget about involving Boyd Anderson.

twenty-six

"OUT OF THE question!" Boyd told Katey.

They were sitting in his sister's parlor. James was there with one arm leaning on the mantel and thankfully keeping his mouth shut. Boyd's nerves were strung taut as it was. He didn't think he could handle one of James's cutting remarks today.

Georgina was present also and sitting next to Katey on the sofa, pouring tea for the four of them. She merely raised a brow at him for his sharp tone. She, too, was mostly trying to stay out of the conversation after it had taken such an amazing turn.

Boyd still couldn't believe Katey was even there, much less what she'd asked of him. He'd come bounding into the room after being woken with the information that he had a visitor and who it was.

His clothes were askew because he'd dragged them on so quickly. Georgina had stepped forward and, without remarking on it, lined up the buttons on his shirt in the right order. He barely noticed, unable to take his eyes off Katey.

Not for the first time, he'd thought he'd never see her again. This time, however, she'd snuck off from Haverston before he'd even woken yesterday morning, and Roslynn had told him Katey's ship was sailing today. Nor had he been able to locate her after he got back to London. He'd spent the rest of the day and most of the night frantically trying to find her new hotel, but with no luck. Which was why he'd still been abed at this late hour in the morning.

But she'd found him. And she'd gotten right to the point of her visit. No cordial greetings from her, even after they'd spent an agreeable day at Haverston that had given him quite a bit of hope that they could put that unfortunate Northampton mistake behind them. Of course she had turned stiff again that second evening. She might not have railed at him again, but that stiffness was a clear reminder that he hadn't been forgiven.

"You asked if there was something I needed that you could help with," she'd bluntly stated, her emerald eyes locked to his. "As it happens, I find myself needing a ship. Would you be willing to rent yours to me?"

"Rent it?" He started to laugh, but cut it off so abruptly, it sounded as if he were choking. He ended asking, "Why?"

"Well, I have a lot of traveling on my agenda. I'm seeing the world, you know. And I'd much prefer to just go where I'd like to go without having to wait for a ship scheduled to go there, and—I missed my ship this morning."

A little pink showed up on her cheeks for having to admit that her ship had sailed without her. He was used to that, too, and how that bit of color enhanced her . . .

"There are no other ships leaving today?"

He stared at his brother-in-law incredulously and thought about cutting out James's tongue for asking that. Here was a golden opportunity, and James had just risked losing it for him! But that was unfair. James had merely followed his own lead. Instead of saying, of course, rent *The Oceanus* as long as you like, he'd asked her why she wanted to.

Wake up! She's thrown you for an incredible loop. Don't mess it up with logical questions.

"Apparently there was a storm in the region recently that damaged a large number of ships," Katey said to James.

"She's right," Boyd added. "One of our Skylark ships also limped into port from that storm. Most of the cargo was lost. It's still being refitted. With so many damaged ships sitting in the harbor, it's taking much longer than usual to get them all back to sea."

Katey continued, "I already experienced one delay last week because of that storm, or I would have sailed sooner than today. But now—" She gritted her teeth before she said, "Eight days! Eight more days I was told, unless there is a cancellation in the meantime. But I was also told how unlikely that would be. Foreigners who visited here for the summer are anxious to get back to their homes before the colder weather sets in."

There was no doubt that she was frustrated by the delay. It was obvious in her expression and tone. So she'd thought of him and his offer to help her in any way he could? Understandable. Boyd decided to jump on it. This was a boon for him the likes of which he could never have imagined.

"You can rent *The Oceanus*," he said.

"Just like that?"

"Yes."

She was surprised. Georgina was surprised. You could never tell by looking at him what James was feeling, but at least he was still just listening without comment. Had

Katey really anticipated an argument? But then she blew the wind out of Boyd's sails.

"I don't expect this to inconvenience you," she'd added. "You don't captain your ship. There's no reason for you to come along."

Boyd wasn't going to budge on this one. When he'd told her that was out of the question, he'd meant it. And now they were staring at each other in a brief battle of wills that was lasting longer than the two other occupants in the room were comfortable with. Boyd could see it in Katey's eyes, that she wanted to insist, but he knew his own expression reflected his adamancy, so she held her tongue.

James actually helped him out, probably without intending to, when he said, "It's an unusual situation. Doubt if I could send my ship off for an extended trip whether I captained her or not. But the Yank here always sails with his ship. Besides, I envision being stuck with him under roof if his ship leaves without him, which won't do a'tall."

He made it sound as if he were joking, but Georgina and Boyd knew he wasn't. James merely tolerated his brothers-in-law when they came to visit. Anything longer than a brief stay they would hear about most unpleasantly.

"It's not subject to debate, anyway," Boyd stated, settling the matter. "I go where my ship does."

Katey sighed. "Very well. If you must, I suppose you must. As for the particulars, I only have a small entourage. My maid and a driver I've already hired. Can your ship accommodate a coach? I'll be ordering one as soon as I get to France and will expect it to travel with me."

"You'll be paying their salary in the form of 'rent.' My crew will be most accommodating about whatever you want to transport with you."

Georgina gave Katey a thoughtful look. "It will take

time to have a coach made. Are you sure you want to spend that long in France, as cold as it's getting?"

"I didn't really plan my trip around the weather," Katey admitted. "But I do want my own coach. Depending on hired ones has already become tiresome. But I am not going to remain in England to have one made. I was told that would take three weeks."

"Or longer." Georgina chuckled. "The last one I ordered took over two months to build."

"Only because you tried to turn it into a bedroom, George," James remarked.

"I did not!" Georgina said indignantly.

"Those special seats you designed certainly felt like mattresses," he rejoined.

"Oh, stop." She snorted even as she gave her husband a wicked grin. "What better place to add extra comfort than where you'll be sitting for long durations. That coach was designed for our trips to Haverston, if you'll recall." Then she returned her glance to Katey. "But I've thought of a way of eliminating that delay for you."

"Oh?"

"Yes, my sister-in-law Roslynn just had a new coach delivered. I wouldn't be a bit surprised if she would offer it to you."

"I couldn't," Katey said.

"She would insist, I know she would," Georgina replied. "Believe me, she complains constantly that she has nothing to spend her money on. She didn't even need this coach, yet she ordered it anyway. And I saw the other night how upset she was over the way you were mistreated after helping Judy." Georgina spared a glare at Boyd for having been responsible for that upset. "I'll wager it would delight her to do this small favor for you."

"Really, I couldn't. Judith's family owes me nothing for my help." Katey turned a look on Boyd, just as his sister had. "You, on the other hand—"

"I know," he cut in. "Believe me, Katey, I wouldn't be putting my ship at your disposal if I didn't have a very big hole to crawl out of."

"Well, let me just find out how Roslynn feels about it," Georgina said. "If I'm right, the coach can be delivered to *The Oceanus* later today. Then you could skip France for the time being and travel somewhere warmer—unless you like the cold, of course."

Katey grinned. "I don't mind the cold, but I hadn't really thought about some of the difficulties of traveling in it. I would insist on reimbursing Roslynn for the coach, however—if she's agreeable to the idea."

"Wherever you'd like to go is fine with me, Katey," Boyd added. "But Georgina's suggestion has some merit. You'd probably enjoy seeing the European countries much better in the springtime and summer. And there are many warmer destinations to choose from for the winter months. Then we could return this way next year."

"You're quite right. There's no reason not to see the countries with milder climates first, then return north later."

"How long did you actually plan on traveling, Katey?" James asked curiously.

"As long as it takes to see the world."

Such a remarkable statement, but, damn, that was sounding nice to Boyd. This trip of hers could take years. And he'd either be in sublime heaven, or she'd drive him positively insane.

twenty-seven

"Dug yourself a big hole, did you?"

Boyd had just returned from the wharfs where he'd spent most of the afternoon with his captain, Tyrus Reynolds, getting *The Oceanus* ready to cast off tomorrow.

The remark, coming from James, had probably been uttered because Boyd looked a bit downtrodden. He hadn't been having second thoughts. He'd been having miserable thoughts with *positively insane* remaining in his mind, while the *sublime heaven* had slipped away because it was so unlikely that it should never have occurred to him.

The trouble was, Katey Tyler wasn't the least bit like other women her age, so he didn't quite know how to approach her. Instead of thinking about settling down and starting a family of her own, she was flitting about the world. Instead of getting married, she claimed she already was, so men would keep their distance from her. Hell, she should already *be* married at her age, but she wasn't and didn't appear to have marriage anywhere in her future plans.

If Boyd weren't so distracted, he would never have entered a room with just James and Anthony Malory in it. He wasn't sure if he could stomach any of James's derogatory remarks today, much less any that Anthony might add. The two brothers could easily go at each other's throats verbally and delight in doing so—unless a common enemy was around. Then they joined forces. Nicholas Eden, who had married their favorite niece, was frequently one of their targets. So was every Anderson other than Georgina.

But Boyd needed someone to talk to about his predicament. And none of his brothers were currently in England, so he couldn't bend their ears about it. Nor was it a subject he could comfortably discuss with his sister. But these two—two of London's most notorious rakes in their day—well, if anyone would understand, they would. They'd probably bedded more women, and in all varieties, than most men could even dream about.

So Boyd dropped down on the nearest sofa and said, "You can't imagine how big a hole. She nearly drove me mad with lust on that last voyage with her aboard."

Anthony had already heard about Boyd's "rental agreement" with Katey and said drily, "And now you're putting yourself back on a ship with her? Smart move."

"Rather impulsive even for a Yank," James added.

"What choice do I have? I don't just owe her for that mistake I made in Northampton. I want her."

"That, dear boy, has been painfully obvious," said James. "You behave like a bloody fool around her."

Boyd flinched, his defenses rising. "You think I'm not aware of that? You think I wouldn't rein it in if I could? That's why I made such a blunder in the first place. I couldn't trust my own instincts about her innocence that day, when all I could think about was bedding her."

"Sounds like a man in love, don't it?" Anthony said to his brother.

"No, in *lust* is more like it," James disagreed.

"*Do* you love her?" Anthony persisted.

Boyd felt like pulling his hair out. "How the hell would I know? The intense desire I feel for her when I get near her leaves no room to explore any other feelings."

"Then what exactly *are* your intentions?" Anthony continued with a slight frown. "I don't think I'd care to hear about her getting hurt by you, or anyone else for that matter. She's a remarkable chit."

"Agreed," James said. "There's much about her to admire. There aren't many who would have done what she did to rescue Judy. Most people, women especially, would have ignored the situation or just gone for help, and then it would have been two adults' words against a child's, and you know bloody well the child wouldn't be believed."

"And they were mistreating my baby," Anthony said, getting worked up again about it. "The bastards hadn't even fed her! But Katey Tyler saw a child tied to the floor and didn't fob off the rescue to someone else. *She* got Judy out of there without giving it another thought."

"I think what my brother is getting at is, don't let this lust of yours burn the wench. She might be traveling around the world, but she doesn't strike me as being very worldly, if you catch my drift."

Boyd sighed. "You're both off the mark. I've been thinking of settling down for a while now, including getting married."

"Back in Connecticut I hope?" James quickly remarked.

Boyd snorted. "When my entire family spends more time here now? No, I was thinking of running the Skylark office in London on a permanent basis."

James groaned. Anthony chuckled. Boyd ignored the dramatics and continued, "So I could use some advice on how to win the wench to my favor."

Anthony glanced behind him, then at James, then exclaimed to Boyd, "You're asking *us*?"

James did the chuckling this time and said to his brother, "Come now, dear boy, who better should he ask for advice of this sort? And she's not one of ours where we'd have grounds to object because we don't want any more Andersons in the family. He'd probably even make a good husband. Warren did, and who in their right mind would have predicted that?"

Anthony shrugged. "Well, if you're game for this, old man, I suppose I can chip in." And to Boyd, he said, "Let's start with the basics, shall we? Has she ever given you any indication that she even likes you? All I've seen is her running in the opposite direction from you."

"She blushes a lot in my presence," Boyd answered. "I used to think that was a good indication with a wench, but I'm not so sure anymore."

Anthony laughed. "That's no indication a'tall. Could be you just embarrass her with that rampant lust you've owned up to."

"Put a lid on it, puppy, and help the boy out," James admonished.

"But it's obvious, ain't it?" Anthony rejoined. "He's going to have to resort to seduction."

"My thoughts exactly," James agreed.

"That sounds—underhanded," Boyd remarked.

"Well, you might be accustomed to a straightforward approach with women, but do you really think that would work with this one when you have so many marks against you already?" Anthony said.

"You need to sneak up on her emotions, dear boy. Catch her off guard," James added.

Anthony hooted at his brother. "That's how *you* had to

operate, old man. I preferred charm. Worked every time, you know."

"I don't believe barbarians possess any of that," James put in.

"Now who's *not* being helpful?" Anthony quipped.

James sighed. "Quite right. Habit, you know." Then he said to Boyd, "Sorry, Yank."

Boyd grinned slightly. "I'm used to it."

"Down to particulars then," James said. "Once you ascertain that she has some sort of feelings for you other than murderous ones, then you progress to slowly whittling down her barriers, and she'll likely have a lot of them in your case. So don't rush it. Remember, subtlety."

"And eye contact," Anthony added. "It's amazing what you can achieve with your eyes. They are your first line of expression, you know. Dozens of things can be said with a sensual look that words might otherwise muck up."

"But keep your eyes above water, if you know what I mean," James said next. "A woman doesn't like catching you staring at her breasts. Insults them for some reason."

"Never understood that m'self, but he's quite right," Anthony put in.

Boyd was beginning to wonder if he should be taking notes about all of this, but then James said, "Let's see a demonstration, lad."

"Of?"

"What you're capable of expressing to a woman with a look. And remember, keep it subtle."

Boyd felt distinctly uncomfortable with the suggestion, but he gave it a try—and bowled both Malorys over with laughter. Serious laughter that had him feeling as if he were the brunt of a joke. He started to get up to leave before his hot temper kicked in. He'd asked for their help, but he should have known better.

But James wound down first and said, "Show him how it's done, Tony."

"He's not my type," Anthony replied. But that got him one of his brother's unbending looks, so he amended, "Oh, very well."

Anthony took a moment to compose himself, then Boyd was given the full brunt of what the ladies of London used to experience when he'd targeted them. Easy to see how this particular Malory's tally was legendary in the matter of seductions. Charm didn't even come close to describing a look like that.

Assured now that they weren't just pulling his leg, Boyd was quick to grumble, "He's got remarkable eyes to begin with. It's no wonder that would work for him."

"So he does," James concurred. "But that doesn't mean the rest of us are a lost cause. Now give it another try yourself, lad, and this time, imagine Miss Tyler is standing in front of you."

That was easy enough to do when Katey was never far from Boyd's thoughts. So he brought her image to the forefront of his mind, her beautiful emerald eyes, the dimples that suggested a smile that wasn't really there, her skin that looked as if it would feel like silk, her plump, luscious lips, the long, black braid he wanted to tuck into his belt instead of hers, her magnificent curves . . .

"Good God," James said, breaking the image of Katey in Boyd's mind. "Forget charming her until after you've taken care of that lust. You'll bloody well sink your ship in flames with looks like that one."

Anthony chuckled. "What can I say? Some of us have it and some of us don't." He was giving James a pointed smirk when he said that, which got a snort out of the golden-haired Malory. But then to Boyd, Anthony suggested, "Just practice, Yank. Use a mirror if you have to. It's worth getting right. The battle is won if you can get the lady all aflutter before you've even touched her."

"Back to the overall strategy then," James said thoughtfully. "If you really are thinking about settling down and it's marriage you want in the end, let her know you aren't adverse to the idea. But by all means, be subtle about it. Don't barrage her with your New England frankness. Give her some time to see that there's more to you than impulsive decisions."

"She's a New Englander, too," Boyd reminded them. "You haven't noticed how *she* gets right to the point?"

James chuckled. "Threw you quite a curve, didn't it, her asking for your ship?"

"Have you ever heard anything so preposterous? I can't even imagine what would make her think of such a thing as renting a ship. A small boat, yes, of course. But a fully crewed three-masted ship!"

"Actually I find that a logical thought progression m'self," James said. "You wouldn't, having lived your whole life in a shipping family. To you, ships are your business, a livelihood, but not everyone sees them that way. Even I owned a ship just for pleasure—"

"And pirating," Boyd cut in.

James lifted a golden brow. "We aren't really going to rehash that, are we?"

Boyd flushed a bit. "No. Sorry."

James let it slide. "The point I was making was, I paid for my crew, for all repairs, for everything that had to do with my ship, out of my own pocket. I didn't sign on cargoes or passengers to cover the costs. And here you have a young woman who has the means and desire to travel the world. She's already accustomed to renting vehicles and has progressed to the next step of wanting her own coach instead. I wouldn't be surprised if she thought about buying a ship as well; she just doesn't have the patience to wait for one to be built. And they aren't a common commodity. It's rare to find a seasoned vessel up for sale when you want it. There are plenty available when you *aren't* shopping, but when you actually want one, well, you know what I mean."

"Her lack of patience is rather notable," Anthony added. "Or she wouldn't have come asking to rent your ship because of a mere eight days' wait. It's not as if she has anywhere to be anytime soon."

"That was eight more days on top of the wait she'd already experienced, for the ship she missed this morning," Boyd reminded them.

"Quite right. Forgot about that," Anthony said. "But still, what's her hurry? Did she say?"

"I wasn't going to ask," Boyd said.

"You know," James began, "come to think of it, I could sell her the ship I recently purchased. I only bought it on a whim for the next time George gets it in her mind to visit your old hometown, and that isn't likely to happen again until next summer. It came in handy to chase after your brother and aid in getting his new father-in-law out of that pirate prison in the Caribbean, but I've got all winter now to have another ship commissioned for when I might need one again."

"Don't do that," Boyd protested. "Don't even mention it to Katey. This is the only means I have of getting rid of this guilt. For a woman I do *not* want to see the last of, I couldn't have asked for a better boon than to sail around the world with her."

"Unless she continues to hold it against you."

Boyd slumped down in the sofa. "*The Oceanus* is my peace offering. She implied—"

"*Never* go by what a woman merely implies, Yank," Anthony said, then snickered, "Especially one you've recently enraged."

"That isn't even remotely funny," Boyd grumbled with a glare.

"Well, it was to the point," Anthony replied with a shrug. "But if I were you, I'd get it spelled out in no uncertain terms before you cast off that putting your ship at her disposal squares it between you two. No point in even trying seduction on the chit if she hates your guts."

twenty-eight

FOUR DAYS AT sea and Katey hadn't seen Boyd even once since the morning they sailed down the Thames into the English Channel. And their conversation that morning before they cast off had been brief. They had merely discussed their immediate destination, after he'd told her he had to send that information to his Skylark office before they sailed.

"I would suggest the Caribbean," he told her. "It's an area I'm very familiar with, since it's always been one of Skylark's trading routes. The waters are warm, the weather always balmy, the beaches pristine. At most any time of the year it will feel like summer."

She hadn't intended to be disagreeable just to be disagreeable, though that would certainly be the case *now* after the man had ignored her for four days. She hadn't really expected that, nor how quickly it had aggravated her. Possibly because she had intended to ignore him and he wasn't around to notice!

But that morning she'd said, "I don't want to spend long weeks again at sea, at least not this soon. I would also prefer to stay on this side of the world since we're already here. So let's just sail south, shall we?"

"To?"

"You're the sailor, at least you likely know much more about the world than I do. You implied there were many choices to choose from. Let's hear them."

He didn't have to think about it for more than a few seconds. "The Mediterranean then? It's a large body of water that comprises a number of seas within it. It offers access to the south of Europe on the north side of it, Spain, Italy, Greece, even the southern coast of France, and a large number of islands around them, all of which will still be quite warm. In fact the entire area offers spring-like weather all year long. Then on the south side of the Mediterranean is Africa, and to the east—"

"Africa sounds interesting."

"Yes, but it's not a country you're actually going to want to travel inland in."

"Why not?"

"Because it's mostly desert. Besides, we can stop at a few of its open ports once we get beyond the Barbary Coast, to give you a feel for the country. You can decide then if you'd like to see more of it."

"The Barbary Coast?" She'd never heard the name before. "Why can't we stop there?"

"It's mostly just pirate bases and—"

"*Wait* just a minute. Pirates?"

He gave her a slight wince, but quickly tempered it with a shrug and an unconcerned tone. "Pirates are an unfortunate fact of life in many parts of the world, but they are particularly active in warmer waters. Surely you knew that before you began this trip?"

She simply stared at him incredulously. She'd known nothing of the sort, but she was too speechless to say so at the moment. Her tutor either hadn't been aware of these "facts" or he hadn't thought it an appropriate subject for a child.

Boyd had continued teaching her about this missed history lesson whether she wanted to hear it or not. "The Caribbean, Asia, in the Mediterranean, just to name a few—pirates have been around for centuries. But *The Oceanus* is outfitted to deal with them. She's fast and she's well-armed. Skylark shipping has had enough run-ins with pirates to make it mandatory for all our ships to carry cannon now. So it's just as safe to travel by ship as it is by land, at least on a Skylark ship. But as for land travel, highway robbers are just as prevalent, you know."

"No, I didn't know. In fact, I had no idea about any of this."

"I didn't mention it to make you nervous," he assured her. "Really, you can travel the world without ever seeing a pirate ship. And Skylark has a few routes in the Mediterranean, which include certain trade agreements. So the privateers from those countries, who also have agreements with their own governments, will for the most part ignore us. It's only the Barbary Coast pirates who would see us as fair game, but as I said, we will avoid their territory. Tyrus is very familiar with those waters."

"It's really safe?"

"I won't lie to you, Katey. Nothing is ever one hundred percent safe. But I don't anticipate any trouble or I would never have suggested the area to you. Skylark ships do regularly travel there just as sea traders have been doing for thousands of years. But as for traveling inland—I assumed when you said you were traveling the world it was to see as much of the world and its many differences, cultures, and beauties as possible in a reasonable time frame. To see the *entire* world would take a lifetime. That wasn't what you had in mind, was it?"

He'd looked so appalled when that thought had

occurred to him, she'd been hard-pressed not to laugh. "No, you're quite right," she said to put his mind at ease. "A little flavor from each region will do."

With their immediate destination settled, she'd turned to head to her cabin. He stopped her.

"Katey, am I forgiven?"

A little stiffness entered her tone. She couldn't help it. "Your generosity has breached the silence. I'm talking to you, am I not?"

"But am I forgiven?"

"You've allowed me to pay for the use of your ship. Whether this will make my traveling experience more enjoyable, though, remains to be seen. Ask me that again in a month."

"Katey—"

"I think it would be best if this not be mentioned again. So I'll say this one last time. You wanted a way to make amends. I've supplied you with an opportunity to do so. It's a grand gesture you've made. I'm well aware of that. But so far you've merely saved me from eight— seven now—days in London. Annoying days to be sure, but days where I would have been free to find some sort of amusement to pass the time. That doesn't equal the one day of detention—"

"*That* wasn't my doing!"

"—that you were indirectly responsible for, the manhandling, the frustration, the anger . . . yet," she went on as if he hadn't interrupted. "So I repeat, ask me again in a month, after I've seen a bit more of the world with your help."

Perhaps that was why she didn't see him again after they sailed. She had been a bit harsh in her response. A bit? No, quite overdone. He might well be regretting his magnanimous offer now, and she couldn't blame him if he was. Of course his gesture was enough. It was much more than she could have expected. Hadn't she contemplated buying her own ship? Now she had one at her disposal without the wait and without the much larger cost. She would have had to pay for a captain and crew either way.

She also had her own coach now, thanks to Roslynn Malory, and a luxurious one at that. She had her own driver now, too. John Tobby was a strapping fellow in his midthirties. He claimed to be a good shot, and good with his fists as well. And as big as he was, he could be quite intimidating if need be. Which might just be needed, since he'd agreed to act as her guard as well as her driver. She'd made sure of that before hiring him. And hiring him had been too easy. That she was taking him around the world with her had been an incentive, rather than a deterrent. She wasn't the only one who wanted to see more of the world.

Unfortunately, John might not last for the duration. He'd never sailed before, and he wasn't the only one they hadn't seen since the start of the voyage. The poor man had been beset with a terrible bout of seasickness before they even reached the English Channel. Which had Grace moping about. The maid had been enjoying some friendly flirtation with John, which was cut off abruptly when he barricaded himself in his cabin. She, too, had realized that he might abandon them now as soon as they reached a port. Especially since she already knew they would be doing a *lot* of sailing.

Katey sighed to herself. She stood at the rail alone, spyglass in hand. They had sailed through the Strait of Gibraltar early that morning. Captain Reynolds had given her the spyglass that very first day at sea, telling her he'd keep the ship as close to the coastlines of the countries they passed as the shoals would allow so she could view them. They had made good time, the wind quite cooperative. The weather was already noticeably warmer, too, enough that she no longer needed to bundle up to stand there at the rail for hours at a time, as she'd been doing each day.

The spyglass had been a nice gesture, but after the first day of using it, it wasn't nearly as entertaining. The landscape began to all look the same, rocky coasts, beaches, and lots and lots of trees. Those had at least been interesting along the north half of France, which like England, had been filled with autumn colors, but everything was still green farther south. Then there were only fishing villages to break the monotony, or the occasional coastal town that she couldn't really see much of through a spyglass.

It didn't take long for Katey's particular brand of creativity to kick in and she was seeing things through the spyglass that weren't really there. She saw the Millards' parlor again. An old, kindly-faced woman was there this time, sitting on the sofa with her, the grandmother she hadn't got to meet. She was holding Katey's hand and telling her childhood tales about her mother. And her aunt Letitia was on her other side, smiling, laughing, a completely different woman from the one Katey had actually met. She'd apologized profusely for her previous nasty reception, explaining that she'd thought someone had been playing a cruel joke on her, that she hadn't believed Katey was really who she'd said she was.

This meeting went so differently it brought tears to Katey's eyes. It was merely her imagination, yet it filled her with such profound feelings, because it was what she had wanted so badly to happen, to have the only family she had left really be a family for her, a loving family. And because it was never going to happen now, she'd cried herself to sleep that night and didn't let the Millards into her daydreams again.

Which had Boyd showing up quite often after that on the other side of her looking glass. She even came up with a perfectly good reason for his absence during those first four days. It certainly wasn't seasickness the way her driver was suffering, though that was the first thing to occur to her. But Boyd was a shipowner. He wouldn't sail with his vessel if he was prone to that malady, now would he? No, she had him laid low by something as simple as a cold that turned so severe overnight that he was now running such a high fever that it made him delirious. And the ship's doctor, Philips she'd thought was his name, couldn't sit with him day and night, so she'd been asked to share some of that duty.

Cold compresses, warm sponge baths. She took liberties she would never think to take if it were anything other than one of her risqué fantasies. Of course she was there when he finally woke up, miraculously without clammy skin or sweaty hair, perfectly healthy and staring at her with those velvety brown eyes.

He put a hand to her cheek. She didn't move out of his reach. She tilted her head toward his touch.

"Do I owe you my life?"

"No—well, maybe a little."

She grinned. She would have had him do the same, but she'd so rarely seen him grin. He was usually so intensely serious around her, so filled with passions that weren't exactly amusing. So she couldn't quite imagine him grinning. But she didn't need to. In her fantasy, it was enough that she knew he wanted to.

"Then let me express my gratitude."

She held her breath as he drew her down for a gentle kiss, but their lips didn't touch yet. With her leaning forward, it was an easy matter for him to pull her over him, all the way to the other side of his bed. She was now lying beside him with him leaning over her, and damn, she did manage to give him a grin, though it was a wicked one. And that was fine. He was going to kiss her. She waited for it with bated breath. She was already feeling that thrill again that only he had ever made her feel.

It was powerful when it happened. Too powerful, as if it were really happening. Anticipation. That's all it was for her, because she'd never been kissed for real, so she had nothing in her mind to repeat or let her know how she should be feeling, just wishful assumptions of how it would be if Boyd did ever kiss her. But, oh, my, for that alone to stir her senses so much . . .

"Will you join us for lunch, Miss Tyler? We should discuss our first port, now that we've reached the Mediterranean."

Usually she could snap right out of a daydream when reality called, but not this time. It took several long moments and a deep breath before she was calm enough to glance aside at Tyrus Reynolds, who had come to stand next to her at the rail. She was used to the captain's booming voice now, enough that it no longer startled her. A middle-aged man with black hair and gray eyes, bushy brows, and a beard, he was actually slightly shorter than she was.

"Us?"

"Yes. Boyd asked me to extend the invitation to you."

"He's still with us? I was beginning to wonder."

Her tart reply brought a slight grin to his lips. "At noon then in my cabin?"

NO CHOICE BUT SEDUCTION   205

"Certainly."

He returned to the quarterdeck. She returned to using her spyglass. She had expected invitations of that sort sooner. She and the other passengers on the Atlantic crossing had taken most of their meals in the captain's cabin with him. It was a common courtesy, since his was the largest cabin on the ship. But she hadn't been invited until now, which was quite odd, now that she thought about it.

twenty-nine

THE CABIN WAS exactly as Katey remembered it, comfortable, carpeted, the seats plush, without the stiffness of being new. It was a room designed for work, but also designed for entertainment. The dining table was long enough to seat ten. Occasionally *The Oceanus* had transported only passengers, with little cargo. There was a small section for musical performances in the corner with three chairs, a harp, and a glass-faced cabinet that held an assortment of musical instruments. The captain himself played the harp. One of his officers was handy with a cittern. On the Atlantic crossing, one of the passengers had had a splendid voice and joined them most evenings, providing excellent entertainment.

Katey had wondered before, why Boyd didn't claim this larger cabin for himself. Being the owner of the ship, he no doubt could have. Of course she had no idea what his cabin looked like. It could be just as large as this one for all she knew.

Her own cabin was a decent size this time around. Very little bumping into things if she was careful, which hadn't been the case before. There was enough room for the full-size bed, the wardrobe, a bureau, a small table with four chairs, and her clothes trunks. There was even a bookcase filled with an assortment of reading material she'd been pleased to find. She guessed the room was reserved for special passengers, which she supposed was an apt description of her on this voyage.

She entered Tyrus's cabin relaxed. That ended abruptly as soon as she clapped eyes on Boyd sitting next to the captain. Both men wore jackets, but that was the extent of their formal attire.

American men could dress impeccably, but they tended not to fancy themselves up with frilly cravats and lacy cuffs as the English gentry did. With Boyd, however, she had a feeling he'd look magnificent to her no matter what he wore, simply because she found him so handsome. That gold-streaked hair, the darker slash of brows, the even darker brown eyes that could be so expressive they provoked her senses to unrecognized heights, and, oh my, his mouth, the thin upper lip, the full, supple lower one, lips she'd caught herself staring at much too frequently on that first voyage. Her attraction to him should have been severely tempered after what he'd done, but it was still there and still just as strong.

If she didn't have so much on her agenda, plans she was *not* giving up, things might be different. If marriage was a part of those plans, she might not fight so much what this man could make her feel. She could enjoy a mild flirtation here and there, to add a little spice to her travels, as long as she didn't take any of it seriously. But not with Boyd Anderson. She'd sensed from the start that a flirtation with him would get her burned. She had no doubt of it.

The tension she was feeling now that she was in Boyd's presence again annoyed her though. She was also still miffed that he'd more or less hidden himself away from her until now. She should have been grateful that he was going to keep his distance, but it was quite demoralizing to be ignored when she wasn't expecting to be ignored.

Both men had stood up at her entrance. Tyrus pulled out a chair to seat her. A crewman from the galley was there to serve them and was even semiformally dressed in a waistcoat. He offered her a napkin with one arm, a salad with the other, then left the room to return to the galley for the next course.

Katey picked up her fork before she glanced at Boyd again. His eyes hadn't left her since her arrival, but at least he was keeping his look impersonal enough to not embarrass her.

"You look a bit peaked," she told him. "Have you been sick?"

She could have bit her tongue out. That damned fantasy was still in her mind, obviously. But did she have to sound concerned?

"No!"

He said it too quickly and too forcefully. She lifted a brow over that reaction, but realized he might be just as tense as she was, so she made an effort to at least put one of them at ease.

"Actually it's gone," she said, and it was. "There's ample color in your cheeks now. Must have been an odd reflection of the light."

Tyrus cleared his throat and introduced a neutral subject. "Will you have wine with lunch, Miss Tyler, or wait until dinner before partaking?"

"I'm invited to dinner tonight?"

"Certainly. Consider it an open invitation for the voyage."

She smiled in concurrence. He'd probably just been giving her a chance to get her "sea legs," as she'd heard it called, before doing any socializing. And that's what dinners with the captain were, the only real chance to socialize at sea.

Another crewman showed up, though this one wasn't from the galley. He bent down to whisper something to Tyrus, who immediately stood up.

"I'm needed topside," he told Katey. "I'll only be gone a moment."

The captain appeared embarrassed to be leaving. Boyd noticed it, too, and said, "She's a grown woman, Tyrus. She doesn't need a chaperone."

"She's an *un*married woman," Tyrus rejoined. "I'd say she does need one."

Boyd simply shrugged, replying, "Then by all means, do hurry back."

Having been discussed like that, as if she weren't sitting there, was embarrassing enough to put the blush on her cheeks, but that wasn't what made her blush. She was now alone with Boyd, and the expression in his eyes was no longer impersonal. The moment the door closed on the captain's back, Boyd was looking at her as if she were the first course.

"Stop it," she blurted out.

"Stop what?"

"Looking at me like that. It's highly im—"

He cut in with some blurting of his own. "Marry me, Katey. Tyrus is legally empowered to officiate at sea. We can be sharing a bed tonight."

She sucked in her breath over such rudeness. And he had to be joking. There was no other excuse when a marriage proposal, crude as that one had been, was too impulsive, even for him.

"Now you add insult to injury?"

He looked as if he wanted to bang his head on the table. "I'm serious. Put me out of my misery."

She was angry enough to say, "Misery becomes you."

A long moment passed while she glared and he slowly began looking contrite as he realized just how far out of bounds he'd just stepped. The proposal was inappropriate enough considering all that had happened, but for him to mention sharing a bed in the same breath!

He finally sighed, "I'm sorry. That wasn't planned. Believe me, I did not—"

"There we are," the captain said, returning. "That didn't take long at all."

Katey managed a smile for the man. She would have liked to have heard the rest of Boyd's explanation, but it was probably better that she not.

"No, indeed," she told the captain.

The main course arrived on Tyrus's heels. While they were served, he mentioned a few interesting Spanish ports that could be reached by morning or even later that afternoon.

"We'll be passing the port of Málaga first, possibly before evening if the wind remains steady. Cartagena and Valencia can be reached within the week."

"If you want to stop at only one Spanish town for now," Boyd added, "I would recommend Barcelona in the Catalunya region. Our country has been trading with them for over forty years now."

The two men began to mention the merits of each town and some of the things that could be seen, including evidence of the Roman occupation so many centuries ago. They were halfway through the main course when another crewman came in to whisper in Tyrus's ear again.

The captain stared pointedly at Boyd with disapproval as he stood up this time. Tyrus looked as if he might even say something scathing, but tight-lipped, he excused himself instead and marched out of the cabin.

Katey couldn't help noticing that Boyd appeared entirely too smug over that abrupt departure, causing her to suspect that both of those "emergencies" the captain had to deal with were contrived—by Boyd. With that thought she stood up to leave. She wasn't going to deal with yet another outrageous proposal, if that's what this was all about.

She paused at the door though with the realization that he could just have come by her cabin if he wanted to talk to her alone. He didn't have to resort to any elaborate scheme. Grace wasn't always there with her—well, mostly she was. They preferred to pass the time aboard ship in each other's company rather than alone. But she was usually alone when she stood at the rail with her spyglass—and crewmen passed her by frequently, so she wasn't really alone there either.

She stopped trying to talk herself out of leaving and put her hand on the doorknob—and felt his hand cover hers. She was startled enough to swing around. She couldn't have made a worse mistake. He was too close. Their bodies were actually touching. And then their mouths were, too.

Oh, God, she'd known what this would be like. She'd had too many daydreams about him kissing her like this and had cut them off abruptly because it had been too exciting, thinking about it. Yet she'd done so again, and again. She hadn't been able to resist. But this . . . it was so much more than she could possibly have imagined.

He drew her up against him with his arm around her back. His other hand moved around her neck, his thumb resting under her chin to keep her mouth at the angle he wanted. Any angle would have been sublime for her. She was afraid she was going to swoon, so many sensations were coming at her all at once. Her heart had never pounded so hard, or so loud she could hear it in her ears. Her blood had never raced so swiftly.

Her own arms slipped around his shoulders. In the back of her mind she told herself it was to keep from falling, certainly not because she wanted to hold him. Yet there really was no chance of her falling when he was now crushing her so closely to him. Her breasts tingled with that hard contact. Her stomach swirled. And when his tongue thrust between her lips, heat seemed to wash over her from head to foot. It was her racing blood she was sure. It was the taste of him that she'd craved for so long. Anything he did right then would have been—

The opening door banged into them. They leapt apart, but not soon enough for Tyrus not to guess what they'd just been doing.

"Damnit, Boyd—," he started to explode.

"Not now!" Boyd cut in even more sharply.

He was in no condition for a reprimand. He was himself leaning on the wall for support. And the tone he'd used was apparently one the captain recognized as adamant, because Tyrus didn't say another word, not with Katey still standing there.

Katey was amazed she *was* still standing and that she hadn't yet moved. Her feet urged her to bolt out of there immediately, embarrassment urged her even more, but she resisted with every ounce of will she had left. She couldn't let this happen again. Boyd's kiss had been too powerful, had sapped her will, had thrilled her beyond measure. And it would happen again if she didn't make sure it didn't. And there was only one way to do that.

"I lied," she said to Boyd, her eyes locked to his. "I'm very good at it. Didn't I already mention that to you, that it's something I excel at? I do it all the time. Ask my maid, she'll tell you. It's a habit from childhood, you know."

"Lied about what?"

"About not being married. I really am."

thirty

ANTHONY WAS LAUGHING as he and James left Knighton's Hall together. He had been frequenting the sporting establishment for many years. The owner tried to keep him supplied with sparring partners, but most of them found employment elsewhere after a round or two with him. He was renowned for being unmatched in the ring, unless James was around. He'd even given up hope of any good matches, until his brother moved back to London and started joining him at Knighton's again a few times each week.

The only other man willing and capable of giving Anthony a decent workout was Warren Anderson, but Warren was rarely in London. And Anthony's niece Amy objected to her husband's getting bloodied in the ring just for a little exercise. Anthony had been meaning to give the youngest Anderson a try. Boyd was reputed to be pretty good with his fists. But Boyd was rarely in town, either.

At least James was still willing to accommodate him occasionally, though their matches could be brutal and James was usually the winner. His fists *were* like bloody bricks, after all. But not today.

"Don't try and tell me you let me win that round," Anthony said, laughing. "I have witnesses!"

"One lucky punch and you're going to crow about it all week, aren't you?"

"A week? Half a year at the very least."

James would probably have lifted his right brow over that remark, if Anthony hadn't cracked the skin above it. Instead James merely snorted as he headed toward Anthony's carriage. They'd ridden over together to Knighton's, so James couldn't escape Anthony's amusement just yet.

"Coming home with me for luncheon?" Anthony asked before he gave his driver directions.

"No, you can drop me off at my club."

"Ah, of course!" Anthony chuckled. "It prob'ly *will* take drinking the rest of the afternoon to help you forget that I knocked you out."

"For all of two bloody seconds!" James growled.

"Time is irrelevant. What's important is it landed you on your arse!"

"Put a lid on it, puppy, before I do."

Anthony just grinned. There was nothing he enjoyed more than being one up on his brother, this brother, anyway. Nothing could dent his humor today, certainly not James's sour looks. Or so he thought.

But one of his footmen rode up suddenly just as the carriage started off. His driver reined in, hearing the man shouting to get their attention.

"You might want to come home now, m'lord," the footman said as he stopped his horse next to the carriage. "Lady Roslynn is a bit upset—with you."

"What'd I do now?" Anthony asked.

"She didn't say. But her Scottish brogue was in evidence."

"Doesn't that usually mean Roslynn is angry about something?" James remarked, his own humor suddenly looking much improved.

NO CHOICE BUT SEDUCTION 217

"Not always," Anthony mumbled. "But it can."

James was the one laughing now. "I think I'll join you for luncheon after all, dear boy. Indeed, I find I'm suddenly quite famished."

Anthony ignored his brother and told his driver to make haste getting home. He had absolutely no idea what could have upset his wife. She'd seen him off at the door this morning with a kiss and the teasing admonishment for him not to come home with a bloody nose, since she knew where he was going and with whom.

It didn't take long to reach the town house on Piccadilly. Anthony bounded inside. He hoped he'd find Roslynn upstairs in their room, where James wouldn't follow, but no such luck. She was in the parlor, in front of the fireplace, tapping her foot. Her arms were crossed over her chest. A sharp gleam was in her hazel eyes. Not upset. Definitely angry. He groaned mentally.

"I'll be hearing an explanation for this, mon, and I'll be hearing it now! I canna believe you kept this a secret from me."

"What?" he asked carefully.

She marched over to him and slammed a piece of paper in the center of his chest. He almost didn't catch it before it floated to the floor. He didn't glance at it yet. Roslynn wasn't done blistering his ears.

"Why did you no' tell me, eh?" she demanded shrilly. "Did you think I wouldna understand? It runs in your family after all!"

She spared a glare for James after that last comment. He'd stopped in the doorway to lean against the frame. He raised that golden right brow at her, despite how it must have smarted him.

To Anthony he said, "Read that bloody note. I'm dying to know what she's just accused *me* of."

"You? I'm the one she's yelling at and I'd rather hear it from her." He put an arm around Roslynn's shoulders and said tenderly, "Sweetheart, I don't keep secrets from you. What's this all about?"

She shrugged off his arm, crossed her own over her chest again, and just glared at him. At which point James muttered, "Bloody hell," and walked over to snatch the note out of Anthony's hand.

"'Keep your bastard at home,'" James read aloud. "'I don't want her here again, upsetting my mother and bringing back memories of a daughter that are better left dead—just as she is.' It's signed 'Letitia.'"

Anthony couldn't think of anyone by that name of his acquaintance. "Who?"

James shrugged, not recognizing the name either. But Roslynn obviously knew exactly who had sent that note.

She snapped, "You even brought her into my house and said nothing about it!" Then her fury got the better of her and she ran out of the room.

thirty-one

"WHAT AM I missing here?" Anthony said incredulously to his brother as he stared at the empty doorway his wife had just passed through. "*Who* am I supposed to have brought into this house?"

Something must have clicked for James because he started laughing. "I do believe she thinks Katey Tyler is your daughter. That's priceless."

"The hell she is," Anthony growled. "Where'd you get that idea out of that note?"

"Because it's just occurred to me who Letitia is." At Anthony's blank look, James went on, "Good God, you don't know that Katey went to Gloucestershire to visit the family she'd never met? Her mother's family?"

"I knew that, yes."

"And?"

"And what?" Anthony said in frustration. "This is no time for you *not* to get to the point."

James rolled his eyes toward the ceiling. "But that says it all, dear boy. Even I heard Judy and Jack talking about it. It's why Katey went to Havers Town specifically, because her family lives there. Did no one mention to you who her family is?"

Anthony frowned. "Come to think of it, no, I can't

recall that they did. However, yes, I did know that's why they invited Katey to stay over at Haverston for her visit, since her family lived nearby. But not much more was said about it, and I wasn't curious enough to ask when I assumed her family must be some Americans who'd settled into the neighborhood. Roslynn may even have thought she mentioned it to me . . . *who* are we talking about, James?"

"The Millards."

Anthony dropped into a chair, his face gone white. James, seeing his new reaction, was no longer amused.

"Don't you dare tell me I've got a niece I never knew about!"

"Look who's talking!" Anthony shot back. "You didn't discover Jeremy's existence until he was sixteen!"

"Beside the point," James mumbled, then said on a drier note, "So it's true? It's ringing a bell for you now?"

Memories were coming at Anthony with a vengeance. Old ones, over twenty years old, pleasant ones, not so pleasant ones. It was possible. It was more than possible. It could all be coincidence, and yet his gut instinct was telling him otherwise.

He closed his eyes and dredged up an image he'd nearly forgotten. The image was vague, it was so long ago, but the eyes were like emeralds, the hair raven, so pretty with her adorable dimples and laughing eyes. Adeline Millard. The only woman in his youth who'd tempted him to marry. And Katey Tyler had those eyes, and that hair, even those dimples . . . oh, God.

"The bell getting a bit deafening, is it?" James said, still watching him.

"As if you'd just fired your pistol next to my ear," Anthony replied with a bit of awe.

"Hold on. I think I need to sit down." Doing so, James

NO CHOICE BUT SEDUCTION   221

added sardonically, "All right, let's hear how the amazing circumstance of having a full-grown daughter just happened to slip your mind all these years."

Anthony didn't give him a typical rejoinder. He was too incredulous and more than a little shocked by the memories and what could be the resulting circumstances, which were still flooding into his mind.

"God, I couldn't have been more'n twenty-one I don't think," he said to his brother. "I went home to Haverston for Christmas that year. Come to think of it, you were there as well and getting on Jason's nerves as usual. We rode over from London together."

James shrugged. "We always did, until I took to the seas. And never mind putting me to sleep with the long version. The short one will do."

Anthony did spare him an annoyed look this time before he continued, "I don't recall what I went to Havers Town for that day, probably some last-minute trinkets to buy for the young 'uns. Adeline was there doing some shopping as well. Now I'd seen the Millard girls here and there over the years when we were all children, but this was the first time I'd seen Adeline all grown up."

James thoughtlessly lifted that sore right brow, winced slightly, but still said drily, "Knocked you on your arse, did she?"

"You could say that. I definitely took a fancy to her and turned on the charm, if you know what I mean. I ended up sticking around after the holidays, and before long I was quite smitten. So was she. I was even thinking— bloody hell, don't you dare laugh, James—but I was even thinking of settling down with her, that's how taken I was. If I hadn't had marriage on my mind, I never would have bedded her. She was our neighbor, after all."

"I get the picture."

"But then she went off on a European tour without a by-your-leave! I had no warning, not a clue that she'd been planning that trip. And no good-bye. I don't mind admitting I was crushed. I heard years later that she married some baron in Europe and had settled down in his country, so she wasn't coming back."

"A lie the family spread to keep the scandalmongers at bay?"

"Obviously."

"Then explain to me this: why didn't they just rope you in if they knew you were the father of her child? That *is* a very good reason to get married. Jason would have demanded it if he'd found out. You know how he is. And you and her apparently *wanted* to get married. I don't get it."

Neither did Anthony, except . . . "They never did open their door wide to me."

To which James snorted doubtfully. "You're a Malory. You were a *prime* catch."

Anthony raised a brow this time. "Your memory failing you, old chap? You and I had begun causing scandals before that Christmas, and Jason had already shocked the ton as well when he made his bastard his legitimate heir. You may not have noticed it, or just didn't give a damn, which was more likely the case, but we were already starting to get the snub from the more prudish in London."

"The Millards snubbed you?"

"It wasn't quite that bad. Let's say Adeline's parents tolerated me, but it was obvious they would have preferred I wasn't courting their youngest daughter. I even got the impression they were humoring me, that they were sure I'd lose interest and hie m'self back to London. They may even have thought I was just toying with Adeline, but because I was a Malory and also a neighbor, they didn't just show me the door. Letitia, on the other hand, was very blatant in her dislike of me and never tried to hide it."

"So you remember her now?"

"Too clearly," Anthony said with a sigh. "To put it mildly, she was a cold bitch."

James grinned. "You call that mild?"

"Exactly my point, cold as in glacial. Every time I called on Adeline, I had to deal with scathing remarks from her sister. It was a very real rancor she had, as if I'd personally insulted her."

"Did you?"

"Of course not. I was in the bloom of first love, James. I was bloody well nice to everyone! I would have thought it was because she hadn't married yet herself, and she was at least six years older than Adeline."

"Ah, missed her boat, did she? So it was merely the bitterness of an old maid spilling out on her younger sister's beau?"

"As I said, that's what I *would* have thought, but she wasn't caustic with others, only with me. And I had occasion to watch her around other people. She could be just as sweet as Adeline was—all right, that's a bit of an exaggeration. She wasn't *that* sweet, but you get the point."

"Well, not that it matters, other than to explain why she was so nasty in that note she sent you. So what is your conclusion? Is Katey yours?"

Anthony closed his eyes again with the thought. He was still having trouble believing that he might have a full-grown daughter.

"She's the right age to be mine. There's even a slight

resemblance to Adeline, though not enough that I would have noticed right off. But she also has her eyes, her hair, even her dimples."

"Why do I detect a *but* in your tone?"

"None of that is conclusive. You have to agree it could simply be coincidence."

James nodded, but added, "It's not coincidence that Adeline is Katey's mother."

"No, there is that. But we don't know Katey's exact age, do we? She'd have to be twenty-two for me to be her father. And Katey told Judy that her mother had eloped with the American Tyler and got disowned by her mother's family because of it. When did she even meet that American? She'd been trysting with me at the time!"

"*If* Katey is twenty-two, I'd say there is a lie in that story somewhere. But if she isn't, hell, Adeline could have returned from Europe early, met the American, hied off with him, got pregnant on the ship taking them to America, all without you knowing any of it, since you were back in London by then. And Katey herself says Tyler is her father. It's only Letitia Millard who has implied that you are."

"But Letitia would be in a position to know, wouldn't she?" Anthony said. "And what Katey believes to be true is merely whatever Adeline told her. It's not uncommon for a mother having a child out of wedlock to hide that shameful fact from the child. Molly is a prime example. She refused all those years to allow Jason to tell their son that she was his mother."

"Do I detect a hopeful note there?"

Anthony flushed slightly. Some of the shock was wearing off, and he couldn't deny that awe and, yes, even delight were taking its place. If an unexpected daughter had to show up on his doorstep, he couldn't have asked for a nicer one. The girl had pluck, she had courage, and she'd already endeared herself to his family. Incredibly, he realized he'd be proud to claim Katey Tyler as his daughter.

To his brother, he said, "Judy would be thrilled. She took to Katey as if they were—"

"Sisters?" James cut in with a laugh. "Sorry, old boy, but you don't claim a daughter who isn't yours just to thrill the one who is."

Anthony slumped a bit in his seat with a sigh. "I know. This has thrown me for quite a loop, you know. I'm not thinking clearly yet."

"When do you ever?"

Anthony ignored the goad to add, "Adeline would have told me, wouldn't she? I mean, *why* wouldn't she? She could have come to me at any time. I was staying at Haverston. I was very accessible."

"You're not going to have your answers unless you pay a visit to the Millards yourself. You do realize that, don't you?"

"Yes."

"And you'll probably have to pry the facts out of them. They aren't going to welcome you."

"I'm aware of that, too."

"Well, also keep *this* in mind. This could be a hoax cooked up by Letitia, for whatever reason. You admit she disliked you, unreasonably so. Katey shows up, giving her the means for a little revenge."

"Revenge?"

"Exactly. How would you feel if you take Katey in, believing her to be yours, grow to love her, then several years down the road Letitia drops the bomb that she lied, that the chit isn't yours at all."

Anthony rolled his eyes. "That's a bit far-fetched, but I get the point. I still have no idea why Letitia despised me, but I won't just take her word on this. Oliver Millard is deceased, but Adeline's mother is still alive. I'll go straight to her."

"If they let you in the door. You know, Katey never said, but considering Letitia's note, I'd hazard a guess that she didn't have a cordial visit with these relatives of hers. And she *was* in a tearing hurry to leave England, so much so that she was willing to let the Yank off the hook of his guilt by renting his ship. To put that unpleasant meeting behind her most likely."

Anthony shot out of his seat with a gasp. Mention of Boyd recalled their last conversation with him. Oh, good God, he didn't really advise Anderson on how to seduce his own daughter, did he?

James, guessing exactly what Anthony was thinking by the murderous look that came over him, began reasonably, "Now wait a minute, Tony—"

There was no place for reason in Anthony's mind just then. He cut in, "If he's already seduced her, I'm going to have to kill him."

"We're talking about George's brother here," James reminded him.

"No, we're talking about *my* daughter."

"A daughter you only just found out is yours. If she even is. So the lad has lusted after her. Why wouldn't he? She's a pretty chit. If he manages to get lucky, he'll just have to marry her is all. You even said he'd make a good husband, if you'll recall."

"No, *you* said that, I didn't. And you know bloody well

I'm going to have to kill him if he's laid even one inappropriate hand on her."

James sighed. He did know that. He'd given what arguments he could merely for his wife's sake, but the fact was, if Katey did turn out to be his niece, he'd be right there helping Anthony kill the Yank.

thirty-two

"FEELING ANY BETTER?" Tyrus stuck his head around the door to ask.

"God, no."

Boyd didn't lift his head from the pillow to say it. He didn't even open his eyes. Any sort of movement *at* all usually prompted another mad dash for the chamber pot. His seasickness didn't take into account that his stomach was already empty.

"When's the last time you ate?"

"Before we left Cartagena."

Tyrus sighed sympathetically since that was nearly two days ago. "You're going to starve yourself on this trip. I can't believe you even suggested the Mediterranean to her, where she's going to want to make port every few days. What was the point of you even coming along, when you knew you'd end up spending most of the voyage sick in bed?"

Boyd knew that very well. To make amends to Katey, he was going to go through this again and again, when he had thought he'd come to the end of this sort of suffering with his decision to landlock himself. But it wasn't as if he weren't used to this malady. He'd been dealing with it for over fifteen years. Grin and bear it had been his usual outlook. That just didn't take into account having on board a woman who he wanted to spend every minute with.

"I need help, Tyrus, not criticism."

"Would you like for me to get one of Philips's drafts to knock you out till we make port again?"

He should. *The Oceanus's* doctor made a potent concoction that could put him to sleep for a good ten hours whether he was tired or not. The ship could go down with a blast of cannons and he wouldn't know it. And the drink didn't even taste foul as most beneficial drafts tended to. But he wasn't going to sleep through this voyage or, as Tyrus had said, he might as well have remained in England. This was his chance to win Katey, and he was going to do everything possible to accomplish that. *If* he could get his arse out of bed.

"I didn't mean that kind of help," Boyd said. "I'm serious about her. I want to marry her. But I made a really big mistake treating her like a criminal. I can't court her properly because of that. It stands squarely between us."

He'd told Tyrus about the Northampton incident. They'd been sailing together for over seven years. Sail into any port after a long voyage and they'd be off to find the nearest tavern together. Tyrus was probably the closest friend Boyd had aside from his brothers.

"Are you forgetting her confession?" Tyrus reminded him. "That she's really married?"

Boyd snorted. "You missed her saying just the opposite the very next day. And looking damned guilty when she admitted she lied to us."

"Which lie? I'm losing track."

"She's not married, Tyrus. While she was in England, she told my family she wasn't, that she'd only pretended to be so men would keep their distance from her. It was a ruse that worked amazingly well on the Atlantic crossing, if you'll remember."

"I remember she had you so tied in knots that I couldn't talk to you, no one could, without getting our heads snapped off. I don't mind admitting I was afraid that's how this voyage was going to go as well."

"There's a big difference between believing she isn't available and knowing she actually is. I know damn well her confession the other day is true."

"You mean it's the one you *want* to believe," Tyrus replied skeptically.

There was that, but he was onto her tactics now, simply because they were so obvious. Deliberate on her part? Was it a subtle, or rather, not so subtle point she was making? Or did she really think she could still fool him, after that kiss they'd shared?

God, that had been sweet, to finally taste her, touch her, hold her in his arms. His desire had gone through the roof, but he'd managed to keep it under control so he didn't frighten her with it. He had no idea *how* he'd managed that, as much as he wanted her.

But she had shocked him with her remark about being married, right after that kiss. A definite cold dousing that had been. He hadn't known what to believe. And he'd spent the rest of the day brooding over it in his cabin. And then she approached him the next morning on deck.

"I have a confession to make," she'd told him, staring down at her feet instead of looking at him. "I lied."

He'd tried not to growl at her. "Forgetful? You made that confession last night."

She still wouldn't look up at him. "That's the lie I'm talking about. Really, I've never been married."

"Then why—?"

"You shouldn't have kissed me," she'd said primly. "That isn't part of our rental agreement."

And so he understood, vaguely, what had prompted the lie. And once again, he was too delighted to get angry with her. He *had* been a little annoyed though. She couldn't keep jerking his cords like that. But she didn't stay there to discuss it. Pink-cheeked with embarrassment, she'd run off.

To his friend he said, "She's changed that story three times already since we set sail, so it's not just hopefulness on my part."

"Three?" Tyrus choked out.

"That's not even counting the first two times prior to this trip. So if I catch her in an appropriate mood, one where she doesn't currently have a 'husband,' and drag her before you to marry us, do *not* ask questions. Just do it."

"Just what do you mean by appropriate?" Tyrus asked suspiciously. "I'll tell you right now, bucko, I'm not wedding anyone not properly dressed for it."

Boyd actually laughed. "I didn't mean straight from bedding her, though that would be about as appropriate as it gets, wouldn't it?"

"Then what did you mean?"

Boyd took a moment to see if he could explain how he would know when the right time was. He'd had no difficulty recognizing it in Cartagena.

They had spent two days in that ancient seaport, there was so much to see, and Boyd had offered to escort Katey and her maid on tours through the old Roman forums, what little was left of the castle on the hill, and the Roman amphitheater where gladiators had once tested their skills and died, or went on to fight in other arenas across the extended Roman empire. There wasn't much left of those ancient ruins since their building blocks were constantly being confiscated for the erection of new buildings, but enough was left for Katey to get the flavor of the area she wanted. Cartagena had passed through many hands over the centuries, and most of them had left their marks. All of which had put Katey in a delightful mood. In awe, bubbly with excitement, she'd actually been treating him like a friend instead of her worst enemy.

Forgetful? That's probably all that was, the easy camaraderie, yet it had allowed him to get close to her again. And when he got too close he made her blush. And when she blushed, he knew he was affecting her so much that she had to hold up a "husband" like a sword to back him off. She'd done exactly that again, before they left Cartagena.

He said to Tyrus, "You already know she has this grand agenda of seeing the world, and it's a fine goal, but because of it, she has it set in her mind that marriage can't be part of this agenda. And yet I know that she isn't immune to me. If anything, I get the feeling that she's afraid her trip will end if she lets me into her heart."

"But who better to marry than a man with a ship who can take her anywhere she wants to go?"

"Exactly."

Tyrus chuckled. "What rotten irony, that you want to settle down on land—with a woman who wants to sail around the world."

"I know."

"But you still want her?"

"Absolutely. And if it means not retiring from the sea, so be it."

"Does she know what the sea does to you?" Tyrus asked carefully.

"No, nor will she. My family doesn't even know. You're the only one who does."

"She's going to find out if you do manage to get yourself married to her before the end of this voyage. It will be hard to miss if you're puking all over her in bed."

"*Not* funny, Tyrus. But I'll assure her that it's not going to end her world tour."

"Don't be dense, man. If she loves you, she'll end it— for your sake. And then she'll always have it in the back of her mind, the regret that she gave up her goals for you. Bitterness will show up, then resentment, then—"

Boyd sat up. "When did you get to be such a damned doomsayer?"

Tyrus shrugged. "Just pointing out some very real possibilities that could show up later."

"Well, don't. She doesn't know that I was ready to give up the sea, nor does she ever need to know that. She *does* know that I've always sailed with my ship. Enough said. I've managed to bear with this for nearly half my life. I think I can manage a few more years so she can have her tour of the world."

Since Boyd hadn't dashed for the chamber pot with his abrupt movement, Tyrus raised a brow. "The seasickness leaving you a bit early this time?"

It did seem to be gone. "For the moment."

"Well, she did ask after you yesterday, at both luncheon and dinner. Being evasive in my replies doesn't sit well with me. You need to come up with a reason for her, for why you aren't joining us for meals—if you don't want to confess the real reason."

"You're joking, right? What reason could there possibly be to avoid her when she *knows* I want her? Hell, I *want* to spend every minute with her. In fact, what I really need is some time alone with her, without interruptions, where we can get to know each other better and she can't run off every time I get a little too close to her emotions."

Tyrus chuckled. "It's too bad you can't be shipwrecked together on some deserted island. You can't get much more alone than that."

Boyd snorted. "I'm not wrecking my ship just to . . ."

He didn't finish. In fact, what just occurred to him was outlandish and more than a little silly, yet it fascinated him, which must have shown in his expression.

Tyrus, guessing his thoughts, exclaimed, "Now just a damn minute! I'm not going down with this ship just so you can court your lady!"

"There aren't any deserted islands in this area, are there?" Boyd replied thoughtfully.

"Did you hear me? We're *not* wrecking *The Oceanus*!"

thirty-three

KATEY WOKE TO a warm, balmy breeze against her cheeks. It caused her to stretch luxuriously before she even opened her eyes, but she cut that short abruptly when she felt her damp nightgown clinging to her skin. Dampness? As if she'd soaked it in a feverish sweat, or put it on before it was completely dry from washing, neither of which . . .

Confused, she opened her eyes to find Boyd leaning over her, a palm tree behind him, the fronds moving gently in the warm breeze. A dream then? Well, she might as well enjoy it if that's all it was!

She smiled up at him. He seemed surprised by that, but only for a second. She hoped he was going to kiss her. This wasn't one of her daydreams where she could control his actions and make him kiss her. She had to take what she could get in a real dream. But he must have seen her wish in her eyes. He started to lean closer to her. Excited anticipation had her stomach already fluttering sensually. His mouth was almost touching hers—

The shrill call of a bird gave her a start. Boyd glanced toward the sound behind her. She twisted her head back to look in the same direction. She didn't see a bird, but was amazed by so much greenery at the edge of a pristine beach, towering pines mixed with palm trees of varying sizes, and sprinkled here and there, flowering bushes.

It was ironic that she was putting this tropical flavor into her dream. Just a few days ago Boyd had asked her how much she knew about the Mediterranean, and she'd had to admit it was next to nothing.

"My tutor, while quite brilliant, didn't have a wealth of material to work with," she'd told him. "At the most he had an old map of the world that wasn't even up-to-date. He was able to spark my curiosity about the world, but without pictures I wasn't able to envision any of it, which is why I always wanted to see it for myself."

And just yesterday Boyd had suggested they take a day off to enjoy a beach on one of the islands in the area—just the two of them. He'd made it sound innocent. And it would have been a fun thing to do! He even told her to think about it, not to answer immediately. But there was nothing to think about and she'd told him no. It wasn't that she didn't trust his passions, she was beginning not to trust her own. But she didn't tell him that!

She fantasized about this man constantly. She had no doubt any longer about how much she wanted him. But there was also no doubt that he'd end her trip if she gave in. And lust, which was what motivated him, wasn't enough to base a marriage on. It would be a nice benefit to marriage, but love had to be there first.

But the tropical atmosphere of Cartagena, which they had just visited, as well as his suggestion for an outing on a beach, were both still fresh in her mind, and thus it didn't surprise her at all that her dream was filled with the same tropics.

She looked back at Boyd. He was smiling down at her this time, a warm, intimate smile, as if they had just shared something. The intense, sensual moment when he'd been about to kiss her wasn't there again—yet. This was a more relaxed moment, just as nice, but not nearly as intense. It allowed other things to intrude, the sound of a crackling fire nearby, the smell of fish . . .

How rude for that to be in her dream! Wait, smelling things in dreams?

Katey scrambled to her feet so fast she stumbled and backed away even more as she stared wildly around her. She was barefoot, her toes sinking in warm sand. She was in her nightgown and it *was* damp. Her hair was loosely flowing about her, and that was damp, too, as if she'd swum ashore. She was on an empty beach with no ship anchored nearby, no ships at all on the horizon, nothing but endless blue waters as far as she could see.

And Boyd was there lying on his side in the sand beneath several palm trees, wearing just his breeches and a long-sleeved, white shirt opened halfway down his chest. He was leaning on his elbow as he watched her, concern in his expression now. A little campfire was burning near him, a fish roasting on a spit he'd fashioned above it. It was such a peaceful, idyllic setting, and yet the horror that filled her mind turned her cold with dread.

"My God, your ship sank?" she gasped out. "Did anyone else survive? Grace? Oh no, no—!"

He leapt immediately to his feet to grasp her shoulders. "Katey, stop it! The ship is fine. Everyone aboard her is fine!"

She stared at him wide-eyed, wanting to believe him, yet how could she? "Don't try to tell me I'm dreaming. Dreams aren't real like this."

"No, of course not."

"Then how are we here? And why can't I recall getting here?"

"Because you slept through it." Her eyes narrowed at him, but before she could snort her disbelief, he added, "Have you ever sleepwalked before?"

"Done what?"

"Gotten out of bed, walked around in your sleep."

"Don't be absurd."

"Then maybe you were on your way to find me? You were in your nightgown out on the deck, and that *was* my first thought—hope."

"Don't start," she warned him.

He shrugged, but she could tell he was trying not to chuckle, and he wasn't done coming up with other explanations. "Too much to drink at dinner then? I know I had too much myself, but I noticed you were doing a good job of emptying that bottle of wine next to you on the table as well. I think Tyrus ordered up two extra bottles last night we were emptying them so fast."

He had been at dinner, for a change. He usually wasn't. But last night he had been present, and a lively conversation between the captain and him had distracted her enough that she had tipped that bottle to her glass more than she should have. She didn't recall emptying it though, nor being drunk, though how would she know when she'd never been drunk before!

"I'm not used to wine with dinner," she admitted. "But wouldn't there be some sort of aftereffect if I had too much of it? I recall my father groaning horribly one morning after drinking too much the night before."

"Head not aching?"

"Not at all."

At least now it wasn't. But she didn't add that aloud,

since the brief pain she had felt when she shot to her feet a few minutes ago she attributed to just rising too quickly. And it was already gone.

He shrugged. "Perhaps you simply have a high tolerance for alcohol? Some people do. They can drink barrels of the stuff and wake up feeling no different than any other day."

"Whether I do or don't, I'm sure I didn't go to bed drunk." She tsked at herself for sounding so prim about it.

"You recall getting into bed then?"

"Yes—of course," she answered, but actually, she didn't.

Getting ready for bed was a standard nightly practice, done by rote. With nothing out of the ordinary occurring to make it stand out in her mind, how was she supposed to remember? And right now she was having trouble thinking clearly about anything.

"The deck was dark, Katey. I couldn't actually see you clearly. You could have been hurt, could have been looking for help. I suppose you might even have been in shock. Did you have an accident?"

She shook her limbs briefly. "No, nothing hurts. I feel fine."

"Then it probably was my second guess, that you were sleepwalking."

She sighed at him. "I'm telling you, that isn't something I do."

"How would you know if you do your walking then get back into bed, all without waking?"

"Someone would have told me, seen me, if it's something I'm prone to do."

"Not if you never go far."

"There has to be a better explanation than this, Boyd,"

she said, somewhat exasperated. "To even suggest that I walked ashore is so—"

"Wait." He chuckled. "I can see now why you're having trouble believing this. No, that's not what you did. But you did appear on deck last night. I certainly didn't imagine that. I was manning the wheel. I do that often, take the night round at the helm. And I did doubt my eyes, I was so amazed to see you walking slowly across the deck in your nightgown. I tied off the wheel, but before I got down to you, you fell over the side! There was no time to call for help. I was terrified you'd drown if I didn't immediately dive in after you."

"You saved me?" she gasped, her eyes widening with that realization.

He didn't answer that directly, but merely replied, "I would have thought hitting the water would have woken you, but incredibly, it didn't. Actually, if you hit the water hard enough, it could have knocked you out. I've seen that happen before. But whichever case it was, my worst fear wasn't realized."

"What?"

"That you would sink immediately and I wouldn't be able to find you in the dark depths. But you didn't. However, by the time I reached you, the ship was already beyond shouting distance. It was quite disconcerting, watching it sail on without us."

She could imagine. No, she couldn't. She was still having a hard time believing any of this.

He led her back toward the little bit of shade under the palms. "Sit down. Relax. It's early morning. Tyrus will have noticed we're missing by now. They'll probably find us before noon today."

She was still too shaken to take his advice. Relax? Was

he joking? Another glance around them pointed out just how alone they were on that strip of beach, without a single thing anywhere indicating habitation. And he was entirely too unconcerned over their situation. For all intents and purposes, they appeared to be shipwrecked!

The thought immediately brought back her original fear. "The ship wouldn't have crashed, would it?" she asked anxiously. "With no one at the wheel and no one else on deck to even notice if it was going to run aground?"

He smiled at her. "No, I was due to be relieved within the hour last night. And she was set on a straight course away from land."

"Then they've been looking for us since the middle of the night?"

"Possibly. Langtry, who was to relieve me, might have thought I left the deck mere minutes before he arrived, though, in which case, as I said, they won't have found us missing until this morning. Or they could have turned around last night. Either way, it won't be long. Tyrus knows these waters well. He won't rest until he's retraced the ship's course to find us."

"Unless he thinks we've drowned," she predicted, her thoughts still frazzled.

"He'll have his spyglass trained on the water as well."

"He gave his spyglass to me."

Boyd was trying *not* to grin again, she was sure, when he replied lightly, "You don't really think that was his only spyglass, do you, or that there aren't a good dozen on the ship?"

She could tell he was just humoring her now. It didn't annoy her. It actually had the opposite effect since it pointed out that she was probably being silly in her fears. They hadn't drowned. He'd gotten them on land.

They'd be back on the ship before dark. Nothing to worry about.

She sat down in the sand again. She tried to be demure about it, but that was rather hard to do in a nightgown. He joined her, sitting cross-legged next to her. His feet were as bare as hers, though she noticed his shoes drying out in the sun nearby. At least he still had them, though that must have been hard, swimming with shoes on . . .

"By the way," he said offhandedly and with a slight grin. "Are you married today—or not?"

thirty-four

ARE YOU MARRIED today, or not?

Katey didn't answer Boyd immediately and kept her eyes trained on the gentle waves rolling in toward the shore. She wasn't sure if she wanted to answer at all. He made the question sound like a joke, and that's probably how he was seeing it now. Which was her fault. She should have just stuck to her guns.

He'd believed her lie about being married that afternoon in the captain's cabin, after they kissed. It even looked as if he were going to avoid her again, because of it, when he missed dinner with her that evening.

Perversely, the very next time she saw him, she confessed, yet again, that she wasn't really married. A big mistake, that, especially when she ended up changing her tune once more before they left Cartagena. The man could disturb her too much at times. He'd claimed *he* couldn't think clearly in her presence? She seemed to be having the same problem these days!

"Let me rephrase that," he said during the long silence. "Why haven't you married? You're certainly old enough. In fact, before long you'll be an old maid."

She glanced at him, just in time to see him pour sand from his fist on top of her hand, which was already half-buried in the sand, since she was leaning on it. His silly remark, and the sand, set an irresistibly friendly mood.

"An old maid, eh?"

"Absolutely. In this bright light, I can already see a few wrinkles." She laughed. He grinned. But then he added, "So why haven't you?"

She shrugged. "I nearly did. Before I left home, I was desperate to have something new happen in my life. And I was asked by every bachelor in Gardener, all three of them. Two were old enough to be my father. The third could have been my grandfather he was so elderly. You can see why I declined."

"I can't believe you only had offers from old men."

"Believe it. Gardener was a dying village. All the young people had moved on."

"Your parents gave you no other options? Surely they didn't expect you to find a husband amid such limited prospects?"

"My father died long ago. My mother often talked about an extended trip to one of the big cities along the coast, maybe even New York, but we never got around to it, and then she died, too."

"I'm sorry."

"So am I," Katey replied tonelessly, glancing back at the incoming waves.

He dribbled two more fistfuls of sand on her hand before his next question, as if he'd had to work up the nerve to ask it. "So you do plan to marry someday?"

"Yes, maybe even before my trip is over. It would be exciting to marry a Persian prince, don't you think? If I'm lucky enough to meet one, that is. Or maybe I'll end up in a harem. I've heard of such exotic things, and my marriage will have to be extraordinary, at least very exciting. I won't settle for less than that since my life before this trip has been nothing but boring."

"A harem?" he choked out. "You're joking, right?"

She peeked at him with a grin. He did really look horrified. She felt like patting herself on the back. She hadn't lost her touch.

"Of course I am."

He poured more sand on top of her hand before he said, "You wouldn't find having an affair with a shipowner exciting?"

The image came too swiftly to her mind, of the two of them lying in a bed, limbs entwined, passionately kissing. She blinked it away. At least he hadn't said marriage, which is what she'd thought he might be leading up to. She didn't want to sit here all day feeling angry at him for hounding her about something that wasn't going to happen. The present mood was too cordial. She didn't want it to end abruptly.

So she continued in the same teasing tone, "I suppose it could be under the right circumstances, like during a terrible storm at sea where the ship might sink, or—well, you get the idea."

"I'll try and drum up a storm for you," he said.

She laughed, delighted with him for playing along. Life was too short for the seriousness that he usually brought to the table.

Of course, his high passion, which he'd mentioned more than once in regard to her, no doubt accounted for some of that seriousness. But she could hardly blame the man for being overly attracted to her when she'd been having the same problem since she'd first met him. She might wish he could control it a little better, but it was nothing to hang him over.

Suggesting marriage, though, just to solve his problem, was preposterous. *That* was worth hanging him for. The very idea! No romance involved, not the least bit of courting on his part. Good grief, they'd only shared one kiss together, and that was *after* he'd proposed!—those kisses she'd fantasized about didn't count.

But she tried to continue in the same light vein, and staring down the beach with nothing in her view but lush foliage, she said, "When you order up that storm, how about ordering a carriage, too. Or do you think we're close enough to a town to walk to one?"

"You don't seem to have much confidence in Tyrus," he admonished.

"It was just a thought. But we are somewhere along the Spanish coast, aren't we?"

He shook his head. "Not unless I got seriously turned around in the water. This should be one of the Balearic Islands. I had just sailed past them last night right before you appeared on deck, so I knew which direction to swim in. They aren't all populated. It looks like this is one that isn't, though I could be wrong. Most islands, even well-populated ones, can still have long stretches of empty shoreline."

He leaned to the side to feed a few more twigs to his little fire, and to turn the fish over on its spit. Not seeing anything else lying around other than a pile of dry twigs next to the fire, his shoes drying in the sun, and his jacket tossed over a nearby bush to dry as well, she wondered how he'd obtained a fish for their lunch.

"How did you catch that?"

He chuckled. "I'm not going to pretend I'm an excellent fisherman. It got trapped in that little pool over there when the tide went back out. I found it flopping about in the puddle that was left."

She saw the indent in the shore he was talking about. There wasn't much sand there. Dirt and trees had encroached too close to the water, and dirt wasn't as malleable as sand, so the hole was being further eroded by the tides, rather than filling back in. It was a nice-size fish, probably enough for lunch and dinner. At least they weren't going to starve while waiting to be found.

"And the fire?" she asked curiously.

He grinned and pulled a small glass lens out of his pocket to show her. "I've been carrying this around with me for years now, ever since I watched someone break a spyglass open to hold the lens toward the sun to get a fire started. I found this much smaller version, small enough to barely notice it in my pocket, I figured it might come in handy someday, though, ironically, I almost tossed it away this year, since I never did end up needing to use it and I frequently misplaced it, as small as it is. It's a good thing I didn't. I don't think you would have liked raw fish. Hungry?"

"Not yet." She smiled. "I rarely am when I first wake up, and I did just wake up."

Instead of smiling, she thought he actually winced slightly. Odd. Or was she mistaken? But the sun was getting up pretty high. It could even be close to noon already, and she never slept this late.

Come to think of it, how could he possibly have gotten her to shore without her waking? Water would have been splashing in her face, his arm would have been uncomfortably tight around her, pulling her along. Normal sleep couldn't have survived that much activity. Either she'd drunk more than she remembered last night or hitting the water had indeed knocked her unconscious. She supposed she was lucky to have finally woken up at all.

She realized suddenly that he'd risked his life to save

her. He wouldn't have been able to keep them both afloat for long if he hadn't found land. And she would have sunk to the bottom, without even knowing she was about to die if he hadn't jumped in after her. She owed him . . .

"What?"

She blushed. She'd probably looked quite amazed there for a moment, enough for him to notice.

"Nothing," she said, glancing down in her lap, then, "Do you see rain on the horizon?"

Oh, God, she didn't really just give him such a blatant invitation, did she? But maybe he wouldn't relate her question to his remark about drumming up a storm for her so they could have an affair. And a peek back at him showed he didn't even look at the sky for storm clouds. There was no need. There hadn't been a single cloud of any sort in that blue sky and they both knew it.

His eyes did widen, though. He understood perfectly. And now would be the time to tell him she'd been teasing, whether she had been or not. Quickly, before it was too late. But no words came out as she stared at him. Sun sparkled in his golden curls. That intensely sensual look entered his eyes.

He dove at her. She shrieked with laughter as she fell back in the sand, because she'd caught his playful smile. But now his smile was gone as he settled carefully on top of her. So was her laughter. And she was staring up at a man who wanted her so much, he'd made a fool of himself a number of times because of it. God, she could say the same thing about herself. And she was so tired of fighting it . . .

thirty-five

DAYDREAMING ABOUT KISSING just wasn't the same as this. While some of those daydreams had actually stirred Katey's pulse and caused her some private blushes, none of them was comparable to the thrill of really having Boyd's mouth on hers. Her pulse had started racing even before their lips touched, just in anticipation! And it was such a deep, scintillating kiss. If he didn't have that lens in his pocket, they could probably have started a fire just from the sparks flaring between them.

It wasn't all raw passion as she'd worried it would be from him. Close. Indeed, very close. But he was also bringing some nice skill into play that was unexpected. Considering what a powder keg of passion he'd always been around her, and their last stirring kiss, this was a nice surprise. It was as if he were trying to mesmerize her with it and to allay her fears at the same time, to draw her in with a slow seduction of her senses, to make her *want* to kiss him back, and, oh my, it worked extremely well.

"Don't wake me. Don't you dare. I think I would die if I woke right now."

His voice, and yet she *could* have said exactly the same thing, she realized. But his mouth had moved across her cheek so it was by her ear that he said that, just before his tongue plunged inside it. She nearly shrieked. Goose-flesh spread down her body so quickly and so powerfully, she tingled everywhere. She did wrap her arms around his neck. Tightly. It felt as if she *had* to hold on or she would be lost in that maelstrom of sensations he was provoking.

Lips to lips again, he gently sucked on hers and tickled them with his tongue, not intentionally, but her skin everywhere was already getting too sensitive. She pressed her lips more firmly to his, to end the tickles. He must have thought she was trying to increase the tempo when she did that, because the passion he'd miraculously been keeping harnessed was suddenly released. His kiss became voracious, and it sucked her right in to the same steamy vortex.

Having her own passion fired to that degree was mildly alarming, but merely because she hadn't known she was capable of such passion. She didn't mind that she was, it was just unexpected. Though with as much as she'd daydreamed about this very thing happening, she shouldn't have been surprised at all. Nor could she have ordered a nicer setting for her fantasies to come true in. A warm, tropical island with a balmy, ocean-scented breeze just the right temperature for taking off one's clothes. What more could she have asked for—well, other than a bed, but soft beds were for perfect daydreams. This was real and much more preferable.

And private. There wouldn't be any doors opening to interrupt them here. That thought was in the back of her mind. Here, only she could interrupt this and she wasn't about to. That she owed him was merely an excuse. She'd thought about this too often to go on any longer without experiencing it. And there wasn't anyone else in the entire world that she'd rather experience it with.

He was working on the buttons of her nightgown without breaking their kiss. She wouldn't even have noticed if the back of his hand hadn't brushed against her breast. There were too many buttons, of course, because it wasn't really a nightgown she was wearing but a thin robe that buttoned from neck to feet, one that she preferred because it was so much softer for sleeping in than her cotton gowns.

He'd find that out soon. Would his passion override patience and have him ripping the robe to finish the job? She hoped not, because this robe was all she had to wear for their rescue later. But the thought disappeared as his hand slipped inside what he'd opened so far and caressed her thighs and then moved between them.

Oh, God, she was too sensitized for that! Just the accidental touch against her breast had hardened her nipples a moment ago. But this, his finger sliding over that kernel of raw sensual pleasure! She jerked. She couldn't help it, had no control of it! He did it again. She moved again, pressing herself closer to him then pulling back, gasping against his mouth. She thought she could feel his lips forming a smile against hers just before he thrust his finger inside her.

She gasped and went right over the edge. So quickly it happened, it just burst upon her, the most incredible ecstasy that spread out wildly from her loins, throbbing around his finger, draining her slowly, deliciously. She was nearly in shock she was so amazed.

"What was that?" she gasped.

"Just the beginning," he said as he showered her face with tender kisses.

He stood up to remove his clothes. They weren't done? Excitement swirled in her belly again. She quickly finished unbuttoning her robe, but kept it on. It would make a nice blanket for them in the sand, she thought before she glanced up and had no more thoughts.

Boyd was standing there naked, had just dropped his breeches to the ground. Her eyes flared wide. She'd always thought he was a fine figure of a man, too perfect in her eyes, but this was pure magnificence. Long, lean lines delineated by thick muscle. His chest was broad, spread lightly with a mat of golden hair that didn't travel much below his nipples. His midsection looked so hard there was simply no give or take to it. She thought she could stand on his belly without making a dent. Even his thighs were corded with muscle, thick, strong, there'd be no racing on foot with him! And those arms that had held her, *how* had he kept from crushing her? His shoulders and arms were so muscular. It was no wonder he wore loose-sleeved shirts. Any tightness there would probably have him splitting seams.

All of that was seen as a whole, but what her eyes locked onto was the shaft that protruded from his loins, the pinnacle of his maleness, and awe was definitely in her voice when she said, "Oh my, that is an amazing appendage."

He went absolutely still with that statement. Should she not have mentioned it? Was she shocking him too much? She didn't care. She was too curious not to say anything, and, yes, *she* was shocked. She hadn't expected anything like this, especially after she'd recently seen those statues in England, several of them. They had each portrayed that unique part of the male body as so small it was barely noticeable. How misleading! And in comparison, Boyd was monstrous, yet oddly, it didn't frighten her.

Utterly fascinated by what she was staring at, she even said, "Can I touch it?"

He fell to his knees in front of her with a groan. She took that as a yes. With a single hand at first, she covered the length to feel the texture, silky smooth, warm, supple, and yet hard. Amazing.

She heard him groan again and glanced up to see his eyes hot on her. "That hurt?"

"No," he choked out.

"Good, because I'm not done."

She ignored a gurgle in his throat. With both hands now she cupped that long length, forming a steeple with her fingers on either side of it and gently tugging as her palms slid across the velvety surface toward her. She did it again, and again. Each time her fingertips left him, the shaft would sway and bounce about. It bounced against her breast once. She felt scalded by it. But it wasn't as unyielding as it had seemed at first. Incredibly hard, yes, but it was still malleable.

"You're killing me."

She glanced up sharply at him with an accusing frown. "You said it didn't hurt."

"It's not that kind of hurt. My God, Katey, I want you so much I'm going to explode."

Her expression softened as she said, "Then what are you waiting for?"

He'd been serious. His passion had reached the explosive point. In a mere second she was on her back in the sand again and he unerringly buried himself inside her. She was still wet from her own orgasm, so he slid in as deeply as he needed to go without pausing for anything, including her virginity. But the pain of that breaking was over before she even registered the sharp tear. She was overwhelmed. She held on for dear life. It was the most primitive thing she'd ever done, exploding with such intense pleasure again, before him, so she was still arching up to enjoy that second orgasm to the fullest when he released himself into her.

He fell to the sand beside her, seeming utterly spent, but he had enough strength left to draw her to his side and, with one arm around her, keep her there. Her cheek pressed against his chest, she smiled dreamily, just as exhausted, just as replete, and there was something else she was feeling. Was it happiness? She had no regrets, not a one. She had enjoyed her foray into lovemaking immensely. And she was overly pleased with the man she was curled up against. So maybe it was something as simple as happiness.

Eyes at half-mast, lazily twirling a finger around his chest hair under her hand, she finally took note of where her gaze was directed and her eyes grew wide. That magnificent appendage of his was gone!

She sat up. "Where did it go?"

She was serious. She really didn't know. Opening his eyes to see what she was accusing him of, Boyd burst out laughing.

"It will be back, I promise you," he told her with a wide grin.

Later she was going to laugh with him about how little she knew about the male body. But just then, before her eyes, he actually fulfilled his promise.

thirty-six

KATEY LAUGHED AS she ran out of the water. She and Boyd had been playing in it like children, though there'd been nothing childlike about the many kisses they'd exchanged with waves lapping over them. But this was her first time in the ocean, or in any big body of water for that matter, aside from last night when Boyd had led her to the island, which she still didn't remember.

Boyd had been amazed when she'd told him, "It's a good thing I wasn't completely awake when I fell off the ship, or I probably would have panicked, since I can't swim."

"What do you mean you can't?"

"I never had occasion to learn, since we lived inland."

Of course he would find her inability to swim unusual, with his growing up in a harbor town. She'd already known that his family and their shipping company were based in Bridgeport on the coast, but she heard much more about his home port while they had shared that beached fish for lunch.

She even told him, "I almost visited your town one summer with my father. A shipment he had ordered for his store from Bridgeport was late, and he was going there to find out why. He offered to take me along and we were going to leave the next morning, but then in rolled the wagon with his shipment, so we didn't have to go. I was quite disappointed."

It was incredible that they'd grown up so close to each other, yet really, worlds apart. Her father had only ever ordered supplies that once from Bridgeport. Danbury, much closer, was where he got most of the stock for his store. But what if they had met much sooner? Would they have become friends? Would they have even noticed each other? Probably not. He was at least ten years older than she was, in his early thirties. While their ages made no difference now, it would have when she was still a child and he was already a man.

But she really did surprise him about not being able to swim and he'd asked her, "You're not afraid to be in the water?"

They were already standing in it waist high when that subject came up, and she hadn't even thought about any danger when she'd run in with him, hand in hand. "With you near, of course not. We already know that you swim just fine for both of us."

She'd been teasing. It simply hadn't occurred to her to be afraid of the ocean. But he'd glanced toward the shore at the mention of his heroics. That struck her as odd, but only for a second. And then he'd tried to teach her to swim. What a failure that had been! She was too busy having fun to pay attention to a swimming lesson, and he soon gave up the attempt.

She lay down in the sand now to let the sun dry her. He dropped to his knees next to her and shook the water off himself like a dog. She shrieked as the water from his hair rained down on her.

"You did that on purpose!"

"You noticed?" He grinned unrepentantly.

She grinned, too. He was such a different man! Relaxed, playful, teasing, full of smiles, boyish ones, sexy ones. She liked this Boyd. Maybe a little too much.

"Where's your nightgown?" he asked, looking beyond her to their little camp. "As much as I love the fact that you are unselfconsciously flaunting your beautiful body before me, I don't want to see you get sunburned."

She chuckled. "Flaunted? Is that what I've done? I didn't exactly have anything appropriate to wear for that swim, now did I?"

"I know, not even drawers, which was a pleasant surprise, finding you don't wear any under your nightgown."

"To sleep? Please," she said drily. "I'd sleep naked if I didn't have a maid who barged in most mornings to wake me."

"A nice thing about marriage is that maids stop doing that."

Katey stiffened. He wasn't going to ruin this idyllic tryst by getting serious on her again, was he?

"Tyrus can legally wed anyone at sea."

He was. "How nice for him, but unless Grace wants to take her flirtation with our new driver beyond that, which I'm almost certain she doesn't, Tyrus's extra services won't be needed."

He just stared at her. She squirmed a little. *Why* couldn't he just enjoy this time with her and let it go at that?

She tried to tease him back to his previous playfulness. "Oh, you meant me?" She said it lightly, but he wasn't going to be teased away from this subject.

"Katey—"

"Don't start. Please. This has been fun. We might even do it again sometime without the dramatics of falling off a ship first. But nothing has changed. I've already told you why I'm not ready for marriage yet."

"You can't stick to this map you've laid out for your life. Not after today, which was a very big detour."

"It was nothing of the sort. And if you're talking about my virginity—" She snorted. "Do I really look like a society miss who would swoon over its loss?"

"You look like the most aggravating woman in the world, is what you look like!"

"Why thank you. I do try!"

She shot to her feet and went in search of her robe. Arguing with him when she didn't have any clothes on just felt wrong. They shouldn't even *be* arguing. *Why* did he have to be so stubborn?

She expected him to follow her to drive his point home. He didn't, and when she glanced back to see him sitting exactly where she'd left him, she had a feeling she knew why. Even that infuriated her right now, since she suspected it had a lot to do with his persistence.

She was too agitated to fasten any more than half her buttons before she marched back to accuse him, "Hiding the evidence that even when you're furious with me, you still want me? Ha! You're worse than a tomcat. Admit it, you're just perpetually on the prowl!"

He stood up to show her just how accurate her guess was. She blushed to her roots. But that wasn't the only effect his desire had on her.

"Do you really think this has anything to do with anyone other than you?"

Hearing that just clinched it. She threw herself at him, wrapping her arms around his neck, wrapping her legs around his hips. Her aim was precise and she groaned with pleasure. She was exactly where she wanted to be.

"Now I dare you to argue with me further," she said before she kissed him.

She merely had to hold on after that. He did all the rest. But she'd never done anything so aggressive in her life. It was his fault, inflaming her like that. Is that what he experienced so often, urges so powerful he could barely control them? He obviously had more strength of will than she did.

thirty-seven

IT WAS LATE afternoon if the position of the sun was any indication. Neither of them felt like arguing anymore. Lovemaking took the bite out of heated emotions, leaving tender languor in its place.

She didn't like leaving their argument open-ended though, but she wasn't sure how to make him understand that while she would love to marry him if she was ready to take that step, now wasn't the time.

They sat side by side on the beach, shoulders touching, just watching the waves roll in. He held her hand in his lap, toying with her fingers, which also satisfied her need to touch him. There was still no ship on the horizon. If they weren't found before the sun set, was it going to be as chilly on the beach as it had been on the ship in the evenings? They could keep each other warm, but it was going to be uncomfortable without some sort of shelter.

"Do you think we'll get lucky with another beached fish for dinner?"

"I think we'll be rescued before then, or are you getting hungry again? You have been quite—active today."

She grinned at the delicate way he described her passion. "I was just thinking of what-ifs. Like we should spend some time making some sort of windbreak for shelter, before it gets dark. And maybe look for some fruit, in case the tide leaves only water behind tonight. Surely there must be some, with all this vegetation."

"You aren't showing much faith in Tyrus."

"You thought he'd find us by noon, but it's long past that now."

He licked a finger and held it up to judge the direction of the wind, not that they had more than a gentle breeze at the moment. "The wind might be running against him," he admitted. "He may have had to take a round-about course in order to swing back this way. I'll have to build a bigger fire if we're still here by dark."

"And a shelter?"

He rolled his eyes. "All right, let's gather some palm fronds, but only near the shore. We need to stay on the beach to be seen by any ships that pass by."

He helped her to her feet, but instead of letting go so they could start their chore, he gave her a gentle hug. "You might be the most aggravating, stubborn woman of my acquaintance, but you're still the only one I want to spend the rest of my life with, and that's all I have to say about that."

He walked away, leaving her standing there with her mouth hanging open as she stared after him. The man was getting under her skin in a permanent way, and she didn't doubt that was his plan.

She headed down the beach in the opposite direc-tion. The sand was a little too warm under her bare feet after being heated all day by a steady sun, but the palm trees were up in the grassy area, which she moved toward quickly. Boyd's shout turned her back in his direction. He was waving at her to join him, so she marched that way instead.

"We'll get this done faster if we split up," she said as she reached him.

"Then we won't get it done faster. I'd rather have your company."

That was hard to argue with in her mellow mood. "All right, but I get all the easy-to-reach fronds."

"I think we'll find all we need on the ground."

Ten minutes later, with their arms nearly full, they headed back to the campfire, which was down to mere embers after being neglected. He immediately set about feeding it again. She sat down to watch him.

"I would like to ask you one question without getting knee-deep in argument again," she said carefully. "Would you be willing to wait for me?"

She thought she'd have to explain, but his mind apparently hadn't drifted too far from the same thoughts. "That implies you want to marry me—eventually," he replied just as carefully.

"I never said I wouldn't want to."

"I know, just not now. But you won't look at the broader picture. Marriage doesn't have to bring your trip to a halt, it will instead give you someone to share it with, at least in my case. Did you really think I'd ask you to end this goal of yours? I own a ship, Katey. I'll take you anywhere you want to go in it."

He was making all the concessions. It nearly brought tears to her eyes, she was suddenly so filled with emotion. But he was overlooking one hindrance that couldn't be ignored.

"Marriage means children, and children need stability. They don't need to be dragged around the world on a ship. And I am not ready to give up my travels when I've barely begun them, to start a family sooner than I'd planned to."

"My sister-in-law Amy manages to raise her family just fine on board my brother's ship. They sail with the children's nurse and their tutor."

"That's wonderful for her, that she doesn't mind, but I'm only traveling by ship because it's necessary to do so to get where I want to go. I certainly don't like the sea well enough to make it my way of life as you have. Too much wind, the air is too salty, and there have been a number of times when I thought I was going to be seasick like my driver, Mr. Tobby, has been, though at least that passed quickly."

He had an immediate answer for that, too. "I'll be ready to give up the sea when you are. In fact, I'd just about made the decision to settle in England myself this year, at least that was my thought before you entered my life. And you have family there, too."

"No, I don't."

"But I thought—"

"So did I. But they want nothing to do with me, and just as they disowned my mother, I've now disowned them."

"I'm sorry."

She shrugged. "I'm over it."

She wasn't, but she didn't want to talk about that, any more than she wanted to talk about marriage. And yet they *were* discussing it again. And she was losing the battle. He was making her rethink her goals, and that frightened her. But while he had some nice answers for the future—she wouldn't half mind settling in England someday—he had no answer for right now. Because there wasn't one. If they married now, she *would* get with child—if she wasn't already. How could she not, as lusty as Boyd was? And that would end her trip. Permanently.

But, oh, God, to marry *him*, to know his touch every day instead of giving it up after today, which she'd have to do? She had allowed herself this one day of bliss, but she didn't dare let it happen again. Unless she was willing to marry him now.

Give up the world for him? When he didn't even love her? Yet her emotions were screaming at her to do just that, which was a good indication that she was having his problem. She simply couldn't think straight with him so near.

She was about to tell him she'd give it more thought when she saw the ship on the horizon. . . .

thirty-eight

"GET OFF THE beach, Katey, quickly. Don't argue, just do it!"

Being told not to argue didn't stop her from doing so. "But you said we had to be seen for Tyrus to find us!"

"That's not *The Oceanus.*"

"How can you tell from this distance?" From delight over their imminent rescue, to confusion, to the beginning of panic, her tone was on the rise.

"It's a two-masted brigantine, the type favored by pirates in this area."

He didn't need to say another word. She scrambled for the bushes behind them. He took a moment to shove several armfuls of sand over their little fire so not much smoke escaped. He also tossed the palm fronds they'd gathered under the nearest palm so it would look as if they'd dropped from it. He then grabbed his shoes and jacket to leave no obvious evidence behind and dove into the shrubbery after her.

She was lying prone, just peeking over the edge of the highest part of the beach. The ship appeared to be just slowly sailing by the island.

"They didn't see us." She was trying to sound positive, but her whisper ruined the effect.

"That's hard to tell yet."

"But why would they even look in this direction when they're sailing that way?"

She pointed her thumb in the direction the brigantine was traveling, which was away from the island. Boyd glanced down at her, started to say something, but changed his mind. And that hesitation worried her more than whatever he might have said.

"What?" she demanded.

"Nothing. You were right."

"No, I wasn't," she said, her voice sounding quite panicky now. "And tell me, why wasn't I?"

He sighed. "The Barbary corsairs don't just chase down merchant ships for free cargoes. They're also in the business of supplying the Turkish sultans on the eastern side of this sea with slaves. Even their larger ships are oared by slaves. Finding a few people on a deserted beach, without any dwellings nearby, would be easy pickings for them that would merely require a brief stop while they send in a small crew in a skiff."

"Slaves? You know, I was only joking about a harem. I would rather not find myself in one. Really."

"I know." He took her hand and pulled her to her feet. "Let's go. I need to find somewhere to hide you while I take care of this."

"While you what?" she shrieked.

She glanced behind her to see what he was talking about. The two-masted ship was turning around—in the direction of the island.

"Maybe they just forgot something from wherever they came from and are going back—"

"Stop fretting, Katey. I'm not going to let anything happen to you, I promise."

That sounded as reassuring as he'd meant it to, but he wasn't taking into account her vivid imagination. Stop fretting? She'd be gibbering in a moment.

"What is there to take care of? They land, they look around, they find nothing, they go away."

"That would be ideal," he agreed. "And as long as they don't leave the beach, then all is well. But if they come inland looking for us—let's just say I prefer to meet trouble head-on before it finds me."

"You'd fight them? With what?" she demanded. "You don't have a weapon."

He picked up a sturdy branch as he dragged her along behind him. It actually looked like a bent club. "I do now."

Oh, sure, he was going to take on bloodthirsty and no doubt *armed* pirates with a stick? But she realized she didn't want him facing any pirates at all, even if he did have a better weapon to do it with. She simply couldn't stand the thought of him getting hurt.

"Let's just keep heading for the other side of the island," she suggested.

He stopped to grip her shoulders. "One of us has to stay near that beach, and it isn't going to be you. If Tyrus comes in range and sees pirates anchored here with no sign of us, he'll sail on by to continue looking for us elsewhere. So if they dally too long looking for us, I'm going to take out that first group of pirates, and the next if they send in another skiff. Hopefully they won't waste any more than that and will move on."

"Would the pirates chase *The Oceanus* if she does show up before they leave?"

"Only if they are very, very stupid. Skylark ships are all well armed for just such a contingency. Haven't we already discussed this subject?"

She vaguely recalled him saying something to that effect. He continued to drag her along until they ran out of easy paths. She kept to herself all the little ouches she wanted to cry out because she was stepping barefoot on little pinecones. Tall pines, other trees, bushes grown bigger than she was, and tropical vines spread among it all— it was now a solid mat of green they were standing in. And no wonder no one wanted to settle on that coastline when no clear land was anywhere to be seen.

"Get behind those bushes there, hunker down, and stay put until I come back for you. If you're capable of silence, now would be the time to prove it," he added with a wink.

He left her immediately after saying that. It took her about five minutes to finally get irked over it. Implying she was a chatterbox was rather rude, and she groused mentally for another ten minutes about that, all of which took her mind off of the pirates for a bit. Did he do that intentionally? She doubted it.

But then a local bird screeched nearby, making her start and look for other signs of wildlife. What she actually saw was that Boyd had pretty much left her at a dead end. Without a long knife or other tool to cut through the thick vegetation behind her, she had nowhere to run if she needed to, except back toward the shore, where the pirates were probably even now landing. Had that much time passed? Boyd was going to do something foolish, she was sure, and get himself caught or killed. And then they'd come looking for her.

With that alarming thought, Katey scrambled to her feet and headed back toward the shore, but she wasn't going right back to where their camp had been. As soon as she found an opening in the path to the left, she took it and moved off in that direction for quite some ways.

Thankfully, she didn't run into another dead end. The foliage wasn't as thick nearer to the shore. She also picked up all the stones she could find along the way, lifting the lower hem of her robe to form a pocket to pile them in. She wasn't going to be completely defenseless.

When she got far enough down the shoreline, she inched her way back toward the beach so she could at least see what the pirate ship was doing. Maybe it had already left! She could hope.

But the ship was still there, anchored rather close. Any closer and it would have run aground. And a small boat was only now rowing swiftly toward the beach. It had taken them this long to come ashore!?

The beach wasn't a straight line, it was curved slightly, not enough to call it a cove or a bay, with their camp at the center of that arch. She was far enough away that she didn't have to lift her head far to see where the campfire had been buried. There was a little boat beached there, empty, so the one rowing in wasn't the first? Then where were the men who had been in it? No one was on the beach right now, it was completely empty aside from that little boat. And where was Boyd?

What she should do was keep moving in the opposite direction, but the fear that came over her was entirely for Boyd. She had to know that he was all right. And until she saw that with her own eyes, she wasn't going anywhere except to find him.

Crouched over and keeping a fist around her improvised sack of stones still bundled in her robe hem, she ran from tree to bush to tree, keeping hidden, but making quick progress back toward their camp. When she was halfway there, she stumbled across yet another boat!

This one had been pulled all the way up to the grass

line out of the sand and shoved under the bush she'd stopped to crouch behind, or she would never have seen it. A large, broken, leafy branch was even lying over it, as if an attempt had been made to hide it. Why? And how many boats were those pirates going to send in? This made three. Could they really have a crew that big? Or maybe only a couple men had manned each boat. That made better sense. And Boyd might be able to easily handle two men at a time.

Some of her fear left her, though not enough to turn her around. But a word caught her eye just as she was about to dash to the next bush. Neatly painted in white lettering on the edge of one of the two wooden planks in the boat used for seating was a single word. Bent over right next to the boat, she had no trouble making it out. *Oceanus.*

She stared. And stared. She was going to kill him. The implication was mind-boggling! No, she wasn't going to touch that thought. Not now. She felt heat wash over her. Angry heat. She tamped it down, took a deep breath. But she *was* going to kill him. Later. If the pirates hadn't already done so yet.

thirty-nine

KATEY FOUND BOYD. He was still alive. She wasn't sure if the pirates lying at his feet were still breathing, but Boyd looked fine. The sounds of men fighting would have led her in the right direction if the landscape at the top of the beach hadn't been clear enough to allow her to see for some distance.

She counted three bodies down, yet three more pirates were still standing. Six of them had been on the first boat with more on the way.

The pirates had weapons. She could see pistols and long knives tucked in their belts. One of them who was still on his feet even had a pistol in his hand, but he was holding it as if he was going to use it as a club rather than fire it.

They were trying to subdue Boyd without hurting him, she realized! He must represent cargo to them that they could sell later, which was probably the reason they had came ashore. Apparently, they didn't care if they got hurt in the process.

Breathless, utterly fascinated, Katey couldn't take her eyes off Boyd. He was fiercely laying into one of the men still standing, not with his improvised club, but with his fists. He held the man with one hand and was punching his face with the other. A second man came too close and Boyd merely backhanded him away. It didn't even look as if he'd broken a sweat yet, though she wasn't really close enough to tell. But he didn't even look winded from his exertions!

The third man was dragging one of the downed pirates out of the way. All three pirates couldn't get close enough to Boyd with the bodies of their mates cluttering the ground at his feet. And he wasn't moving from that position, which gave him his advantage.

A fourth pirate went down now. The last two men must have realized they weren't getting anywhere with their careful tactics. They still didn't point their pistols at Boyd, but with one man shouting an order, the two charged him in unison. That managed to knock him down, and all three were sprawled on the ground now.

Katey started to move closer. But new activity on the beach caught her attention instead. The other boat had landed! Six more men were jumping out of it. As soon as they came a little farther up the beach, they would see what was happening on the other side of the rise—and join the fray. Boyd wouldn't be able to handle six more. He had to be tiring. But even if he wasn't, this new bunch would take him by surprise while he was still grappling on the ground with those other two.

She didn't get past that thought. Stepping out on the beach to draw the new arrivals' attention in her direction, she pretended to be surprised by them. One of them saw her and nudged the man next to him. He also said something that had them all turning to look at her. In seconds, all six were running toward her. They didn't even send one of their men to find the first arrivals. Apparently, she was a more interesting find.

She gave a shriek, a loud one, that wasn't the least bit faked. She hoped Boyd had heard her, or the chance she'd just taken in revealing herself would have been really stupid. She had no idea how long she could keep from being captured, but she did *not* want to be used as a bargaining chip for them to capture him, too. So she couldn't go too far or Boyd wouldn't be able to catch up to help her. Yet she couldn't let the pirates get within reach of her, either, or it would be all over.

She remembered her rocks only because her little improvised sack banged against her knee as she leapt back off the sand. She paused a moment to loosen the tight grip she had on it that had closed it and make it an open pouch she could reach into. Making sure she wasn't going to run into anything behind her first, she turned to face the pirates just in time to see them come over the rise near her. Much too close. If they decided to charge her as a group as the other two had done to Boyd . . .

She threw a rock at them. They stopped and laughed at her as it landed several feet in front of them. Backing away slowly, she threw another rock, harder this time. They laughed again as it sailed past them, hitting no one. What made her think throwing stones would be a good weapon when she didn't know how to aim them? All she was doing was entertaining them! But a moment later she realized her rocks were a better weapon than she'd thought, because they'd done exactly what she'd intended, kept the pirates' attention on her long enough for Boyd to take over.

Seeing him running up behind them now, his thick, clublike stick in hand, she kept the pirates distracted with a few more rocks. And Boyd went immediately to work on them with barely a pause. He swung his club to one side, then the other. Two down. One of those moved, wasn't unconscious. A quick punch to his face and he didn't move again.

The other four had turned about with the noise. Three charged Boyd immediately. He sidestepped one and swung his club in an arc to catch the other two at once. It didn't knock either of them down, but the one it hit first screamed and put a hand to his smashed ear. He was temporarily immobilized by pain.

The last pirate didn't move. Instead he pulled a long-barreled pistol from his belt. But he'd turned his back to Katey. What he was going to do with that pistol she didn't know and didn't want to find out, especially when he might have decided that one slave, her, was good enough and Boyd was too much trouble to bother with.

Without even thinking about it, she took the largest of the rocks she had left, let the others slide to the ground so she could grip the big one with both hands, and, coming up behind the pirate, slammed it against the back of his head. He dropped to the ground. She stared down incredulously that she'd managed to knock him out.

Glancing back up, she saw that Boyd wasn't nearly finished yet. He was having a fistfight with two of the pirates. He must have disarmed them in the fight. They no longer had their weapons, and he was winning. Their faces were getting bloody, his wasn't. The other man was still holding his ear and shouting in some foreign language, probably swearing. But he was also reaching for the gun in his belt, and he definitely looked angry enough to use it.

Katey went cold with fear. It was hard to even think, she was suddenly so afraid—for Boyd. She started to shout to him with a warning, but realized he might not hear her in his efforts, and distracting him just then might be the worst thing she could do, when the two men he was fighting were as brawny as he was. So she lifted the heavy rock she still had in her hand, but remembered in time her lousy aim. Fast running out of options, a flash of light, sun against metal, made her look down, and she dove at the pistol by her feet that the unconscious pirate had dropped before he hit the ground.

She didn't take a chance either that her pointing it at that angry pirate would make him drop or lower his weapon, which he already had in hand. He hadn't fired it yet, but probably because he didn't have a clear shot at Boyd, with his mates in the way. And he wasn't looking at her and didn't notice she was also armed. His hearing might currently be impaired, too, so she wasn't going to trust shouting at him, either. But he'd hear a shot fired she was sure, so she simply did that, fired off a harmless shot.

She definitely had his attention now, and everyone else's. She nearly knocked herself over from the blast. Damned old-fashioned pistols, too long-nosed and too heavy for her. And she knew as well as everyone else that it only had one shot in it. But once again, her action allowed Boyd to minimize the danger. He'd only paused a second from her shot. And since she was facing the angry pirate, Boyd gave him some attention, too, going straight for the remaining pistol in the man's hand. With it in his own hand now, he slammed it against the man's other ear. That time he went down for good. Boyd then cracked the barrel against another head and smashed it into the face of the last man.

All of them out of action! She shared Boyd's thrill of success. Actually, he just looked tired. But she was so excited by his victory, she was nearly jumping up and down with it—until she remembered the ship anchored nearby.

"Will they send in more?" she asked him as he bent over, a hand on each knee, to rest a moment.

He glanced up at her to say, "Probably. So gather up the pistols here while I tie up the first bunch. I think I'll just shoot any others that show up."

She noticed he hadn't said a word about her presence, that she hadn't stayed where he'd told her to stay. To keep him from realizing that she hadn't followed his instructions, she asked, "What are you going to tie them with?"

"I already made some ropes while waiting for that first boat to land. Palm leaves, fresh or dry, are quite sturdy if manipulated just right, and tie together easily. I'll need to make more though. I wasn't counting on this many pirates coming ashore."

"Wouldn't vines work?" she ventured. "They're all over the place."

"Too slippery, and they can snap at their joints, so they're not as dependable. Besides, I merely need to make sure that if any of them wake, they don't become further problems. I'd as soon not have to kill them. They might be guilty of piracy, but they make no difference in the greater scheme of things. Their captain will just replace them and go on about business as usual."

He sounded disgusted as he said that, but then he quickly walked off to take care of the business of tying. She stared at the spot he was heading to, where he'd left the first bunch of bodies.

He'd have to work quickly. He had twelve men to tie up before any more arrived. No, actually, she'd just have to help him to get it done speedily. So she gathered up the pistols as he'd said, and she ran as best she could over those tiny pinecones and needles to join Boyd. He already had three men tied and was stripping the leaves off another palm frond. She dumped the pistols on top of the pile that he'd taken the time to collect from this first crew and started helping him strip leaves. He was pretty good at tying them together. Well, he was a sailor. He would be. And he was soon heading back to the second crew with six more improvised ropes in hand.

She followed him. He didn't object. But when she started to help him tie the men, he told her to keep a watch on the ship instead. It figured he wouldn't trust her to make a decent knot out of a leaf end.

But he was only tying wrists behind backs for the moment, so he was almost done when she was forced to say, "They're lowering another small boat in the water."

She heard Boyd's sigh behind her. He had to be seriously exhausted by now. My God, he'd taken on twelve pirates and won! Granted, they had been trying to capture him without doing any real harm to him, but still, it had been his exertions that had brought them down, and he'd made it look so easy! She might have helped a little by distracting them, but it had been his brawn and skill that had ended the danger quickly. Now he had to face even more coming ashore.

A glance back at him showed he hadn't paused in what he was doing. Nor did he rush to finish it. He took time to make sure the bonds would hold.

Looking back toward the ship, her eyes widened and she was delighted to say, "They may have changed their mind."

"What do you mean?" He stood up to see for himself.

The little boat that had been put in the water and filled with men hadn't launched to shore; in fact, the men in it were climbing rapidly back on the ship. A moment later Katey and Boyd saw why. Another ship had sailed into view.

forty

THE OCEANUS HAD come into view. Katey couldn't recognize it from such a distance, could barely even tell that it was three-masted from the angle at which it was coming toward them, but Boyd had no trouble doing so. With rescue imminent and the danger over—the pirate ship had sailed off with cowardly haste—she sat down on the beach to wait.

Boyd spent the time making more ropes and tying up the feet of many of the pirates. He didn't want them getting loose too soon, he explained, but he didn't want them to never get loose, either.

"If their captain doesn't come back later to look for them, they should have no trouble chewing through each other's bonds with their teeth. But he'll probably be back before dark, especially since he will have already noticed that *The Oceanus* isn't going to give chase."

"You're being too kind to men who wanted to turn you into a slave."

"You think so? There's an arsenal of weapons here, I suppose I could kill them."

He was only teasing. If he'd had any intention of doing that, he would have done it before he started tying them up.

But the pirates he was being so lenient with had given

her quite a few real scares today, so she mumbled at him, "I don't see why we aren't going to take them with us and turn them over to the authorities."

"Which authorities would that be?" he countered, obviously trying not to grin over her apparent ignorance. "We don't know which port these fellows are based out of, and many different countries border this sea. They could be privateers with agreements from their country to operate in this area, in which case those authorities would just laugh and let them go with a pat on the hand. And I'm not joking. The Barbary Coast pirates, which *would* end up behind bars, don't usually come this far north. They prefer easy merchant vessels that aren't armed, since their tactics are to board quickly, subdue fast, and reap the easy rewards."

When he was done with his task, he sat down next to her on the sand, their shoulders touching. Recalling what she'd found hidden in the bushes farther down the beach, she moved away from him. He didn't remark on that, might not have noticed since he was staring at his ship, which was close enough now to have started lowering sails so as to stop.

"Are you ready to leave? We can use one of these boats to row out to the ship." He'd waved toward the two pirate boats on the beach in front of them.

"Why one of these? Why not the one you used to get us here?"

She was staring at him now. Was that a flinch? No, he'd have to have a guilty conscience to flinch. But the silence grew thick enough to cut.

Her words became the knife. "You were just going to abandon it here, weren't you? A cost of doing business, or in this case, the expendable cost of a seduction?"

"I can explain," he finally got out.

"Of course you can. But is it going to help?"

"From the sound of your voice, probably not," he said with a sigh.

She stood up and glared down at him. "Did you really think I wouldn't get angry? No, wait. What you *thought* was I'd never find out that this little outing was all arranged *by you*. Does that sum it up accurately?"

He stood up as well, his posture suddenly defensive from her sarcasm. "You aren't the only one who can lie, so don't even think about getting angry because I took a clue from you, to arrange a little time alone with you with a lie."

"If that was *all* you did then you might be right. *Might be!*" she added sharply. "But you did much, much more than that, didn't you? My God, you even got me wet! What'd you do, dunk me in the water after we got here just so it would *seem* like you swam us ashore?"

"No, a wave washed over the boat on the way in, so that wasn't necessary. Though I probably would have done exactly that!"

They were shouting at each other by this point. She was so furious she was shaking. The details he had cooked up! She was getting more and more incredulous as each one occurred to her. The list would unfold and hit the sand, it was so damn long.

"The fish?" she demanded.

"A gift of the tide as I said."

"The convenient lens you carry around in your pocket?"

"A pretty good lie if I do say so myself," he shot back smugly.

She bristled more. How dare *he* get angry and sarcastic?

Or was this his reaction to guilt? And he had a *lot* to be guilty about.

"The pirates? Did you arrange them, too, so you could 'save me' and play the hero?"

"They would have been a good idea, wouldn't they?" he shot back with a feigned thoughtful look that just scratched her bristles even more. "But pirates are rather hard to hire these days and probably aren't the least bit trustworthy. Sorry, they weren't part of the plan."

He was leaving it at that. He didn't point out that he *did* save her. Though it wouldn't have made a bit of difference to her at the moment.

"Is this island even deserted?" She was pacing now in the sand in front of him, too angry to stand still.

"No, it's one of the larger islands in the Balearic chain, though this corner of it isn't settled, so it wouldn't have been an easy trek to reach one of the villages. You'd be surprised how big an island is—if you're on foot."

"Of course you would have shot down the suggestion to find out if a settlement or town was nearby, if I'd made it," she guessed.

"Of course."

"Your ship was hiding on the other side of this island all the time, wasn't it? So it didn't just arrive in the nick of time. You probably told Tyrus exactly when to pick us up." She was mortified with the thought: "My God, they all know about this, don't they?"

"No," he said quickly, and with no heat now. "Most of them think we just went on an outing for the day."

"Oh, sure, so I went on an outing in my bedclothes?!" she replied scathingly.

Looking down at her robe, he blanched. She realized

he'd missed that detail, or he just hadn't thought that far ahead in his elaborate scheme.

But before she remarked on that, he told her, "Put these on."

It was a good thing he said it first, because he then started to strip off his belt. For one brief second, what they had done on the island, together, before the pirates showed up, filled her mind and made her nearly gasp. But she was far too angry right now to let those memories intrude, and he was merely handing her his belt to wear. He gave her his coat, too.

"Your belt buckle is too big," she mumbled after fastening the belt around her waist. "It's obvious that it belongs to a man."

"Slide the buckle around to your back, the coat will cover it. There, now it looks like you're wearing a dress instead of nightclothes, albeit a thin one. But considering the warm weather, thin is pretty normal around here."

It didn't really look like a dress, but as long as she wasn't looked at closely, it would do. Except for anyone who had helped him.

"Tyrus knows, doesn't he?" she gasped, red-cheeked with embarrassment.

Boyd nodded. "If it helps, I had to twist his arm and call in every favor he owes me. He was *not* going to assist me in this. He doesn't handle secrecy very well. And I had to convince him he'd be marrying us when we returned to the ship, or he never would have agreed."

"That *isn't* happening!"

"Obviously," Boyd replied with a sigh.

His explanation hadn't helped at all. If anything, it had stoked the fire more. And now she had mortified embarrassment to add to it.

"I can't believe I bought that ridiculous sleepwalking story even for a minute. No, actually, I can't believe you even came up with it. If you're going to lie, at least make it sound reasonable."

"I suppose I should have asked for lessons first."

She gasped.

He looked immediately contrite and said quickly, "I'm sorry."

"I don't believe you are. In fact, I'll never believe you again. You, sir, can't be trusted! You have let this lust of yours cloud your judgment far too many times. But this! This is beyond redemption! And how did you get me here without my waking?" She drew in a sharp breath with the realization. "You drugged me, didn't you? With what? How?"

"Don't be absurd. Dr. Philips might make me a potent sleeping powder occasionally when I need it, but it didn't even occur to me to use that. I wouldn't do that to you, Katey. You have my word."

"Then how did you accomplish this?"

"It wasn't planned. I thought about it, certainly, after I suggested that we go ashore together and you flatly refused. But there was no way to get you ashore without your waking, so I gave up the notion—until you imbibed so much wine last night you don't even remember stumbling out of Tyrus's cabin. Admit it. You don't remember, do you?"

She didn't, but she still didn't believe him. His cheeks had turned too red at the mention of that sleeping powder. "I wouldn't remember, would I, if you'd slipped that powder in my glass?" she said sharply.

"Damnit, it would have been much easier and much less nerve-racking for me if I had, but I didn't!"

"Liar!"

"Are you even listening to me?"

"Do you deserve that courtesy?"

"You asked for an explanation. Caught red-handed as it were, why would I bother with anything but the truth right now? So listen to me carefully this time. I did not drug you! I didn't fill your glass with wine, either, you did. I wasn't even sitting next to you. I *did* nudge Tyrus to order more wine when I saw that you'd already emptied the bottle by your plate. I wasn't nearly as drunk yet myself, so I recognized a golden opportunity when it presented itself. And you even drank a quarter of another bottle before you marched off to find your bed. Without even a good-night, mind you. That's how tipsy you were."

Since she couldn't deny that, and she *did* remember pouring herself several glasses of wine, she didn't immediately call him a liar again and scoffed instead, "What was nerve-racking? You wouldn't have done it if you thought I was going to wake."

"It was a chance I was willing to take. If you had woken, I knew it would have taken days for you to get over your anger—"

"Make that years—no, centuries!"

"Which is why I was so glad you didn't wake. I was sure you would when that wave doused us, but you didn't. All you did was snuggle closer to me in my lap."

She blushed furiously, hearing that. She wasn't responsible for what she did in her sleep.

To put him back on the defensive she said, "If you aren't lying, why did you get so red-faced at the mention of that sleeping powder?"

"Not for the reason you think."

Bright color spread up his cheeks again. Her brow

knitted suspiciously, yet her curiosity had kicked in, too. "Why do you take it?"

"It doesn't matter," he said, looking even more embarrassed.

"Why?"

"It really isn't important—"

"It is to me. I want to know why you're looking *and* sounding guilty."

"It's because I suffer seasickness. There, are you happy? That's something my family doesn't even know, Katey. It's why I don't captain my own ship. It affects me for a good four days every time my ship casts off. It's why you won't see me for the next four days when we sail out of here."

"Four days? Forever is more like it. Do you really think I believe that? The truth now."

"That is the truth. And it's why I got desperate enough to do this."

The word *desperate* made her think of his lust. She had *thought* he'd risked his life jumping overboard to save her, that she owed him for that. If that had never occurred to her, would she have instigated their lovemaking today? She didn't know, and she was too angry to figure it out.

"All of this so you could make love to me?" she choked out, glaring at him.

"If I just wanted to bed you, I wouldn't have brought you to shore. I was in your room, Katey, and you *were* inebriated. It would have been a simple matter to make love to you there. Hell, you probably wouldn't even have remembered it come morning! But that's not why I gave us this day together. It's because I was spending more time getting sick in my cabin than I was courting you."

"Courting me?" she sputtered. "You call blurting out 'marry me' courting?"

"Since you're the only woman I've ever wanted to marry and the only one I've ever *blurted* that at, I guess I need lessons in courting, too."

"I'm beginning to think you need lessons in life. I see now why Anthony Malory referred to you and your brothers as barbarians."

"He and James do that deliberately, to get a rile out of us."

She snorted. "Don't kid yourself. In your case, it's absolutely true!"

She definitely struck a nerve that time. Tight-lipped, he started to reply, then saw that his crew was about to lower a boat in the water. He waved them off that notion, marched down the beach, and dragged the *Oceanus* skiff out of the bushes.

Having followed him, Katey heard him say, "There, are you happy? We've saved the damned boat."

She wasn't happy. She was about as unhappy as she could be. And during the short ride to the ship, having expended her anger, she was choking back her hurt feelings. Boyd was silent, too.

But before they climbed aboard, he did say to her, "Do you really wish today hadn't happened?"

She didn't answer him.

forty-one

BOYD HAD DRUNK too much wine himself last night during the dinner he'd shared with Katey. Sober, he would have come to his senses and never pulled such a stunt. But he'd acted on the idea as soon as it had come to him. There hadn't been enough time to think it through.

Looking at Katey's stiff back in front of him in the boat as he rowed them out to the ship, he reprimanded himself. Whom was he kidding? Desperation had brought him to this, and desperation would have to see it through.

But he *hadn't* planned to make love to her. He'd never dreamed that would have been a result of his day on the beach with her. He'd just wanted some time where they could get to know each other better, without her maid nearby as had been the case on their outing in Cartagena. And he'd needed it to be on solid ground. Spending most of his time in his cabin on this trip was getting him nowhere. And when he did steal a few minutes with her on the ship, his desire for her kept him making a fool of himself.

The Malory brothers had given him good advice, but he wasn't like them. He was a sailor. He'd never been in one port for long. He'd never had time to be subtle with a woman, so it wasn't something he'd attempted before.

And his feelings kept getting in the way with Katey. Wanting her so damn much, he couldn't even be himself with her. Until today. Briefly. Too briefly. He should have killed those damn pirates for interrupting what had been the sweetest day of his life.

Katey's silence was killing him. She hadn't answered his question, but that was an answer in itself. Of course, now she wished today hadn't happened. But before she'd found out how he'd arranged for them to be alone on the beach, she'd seemed to have no regrets. But she still wouldn't marry him. Stubborn woman. But, my God, she did ask him if he'd wait for her! Now, he'd be lucky if she didn't spend the rest of the voyage in *her* cabin. Actually, he'd be lucky if she didn't leave *The Oceanus* altogether at the next port.

Reaching the ship, she climbed the ladder rather hastily, so he was surprised she was still standing there when he came over the side behind her. Tyrus was there, too, looking utterly ashamed, which was probably why she hadn't walked away. She wasn't going to let him escape her anger.

"There she is, Cap'n," a crewman shouted from the quarterdeck. "We didn't lose her."

The crewman wasn't talking about Katey, of course. He'd just lowered his spyglass, but he wasn't facing in the direction of the pirate ship.

"What ship is he talking about?" Boyd asked Tyrus.

"Theirs," Tyrus said, nodding behind him. "By taking the same northern Mediterranean course and checking they found us a few hours ago and came aboard. Their ship was following us, but we lost sight of her when we came around the isle."

Boyd turned abruptly to see whom Tyrus was talking about and then went perfectly still. Leaning against the railing, both of them looking as inscrutable as ever, stood Anthony and James Malory. James looked no different from the way he had the last time he'd boarded *The Oceanus*—and stolen her cargo!—all those years ago when he'd amused himself by living the life of a gentleman pirate in the Caribbean. His white shirt was loosely tucked into tight breeches, his blond hair was windblown, and a gold earring flashed in his ear. Anthony wasn't looking quite as immaculate as usual, either, with the sleeves of his white shirt rolled up because of the heat. Boyd was incredulous. He hadn't even noticed them there when he'd climbed aboard. He couldn't think of a single reason why they would be there. And then he did, and he blanched.

"Georgina?"

"She's got a pretty big bone to pick with you, but otherwise she's fine," James said.

"My brothers?"

"No idea," James replied. "But they're probably as well as the last time you saw them."

The color came back to his cheeks with his immediate relief, but a frown quickly followed. "Then what are *you* doing here?"

This question hadn't been directed at one of them in particular, but Anthony answered, "I came to collect Katey and kill you."

Since he spoke without any change in expression whatsoever, Boyd assumed Anthony was just being annoying as usual. But Katey latched on to his remark.

"That sounds like a splendid plan to me on both counts," she said to the Malorys. "But you might want to wait to kill him until he's back on dry land. Here on the ship, he'll no doubt gain your sympathy with his seasickness. It will probably start up any moment now," she added as the ship dipped low in the water. "Hard to kill a man if he's puking all over you."

Boyd groaned inwardly. "Thanks, Katey. Just the two I would have preferred didn't know about that."

"You are quite welcome," she snapped at him. "And as long as I'm talking to you for the moment, I'll say good-bye now. If I ever see you again, Boyd Anderson, please pretend you don't know me. You're as good at pretenses as I am, so I'm sure you can manage it just fine."

She stomped off in the direction of her cabin, all four men watching her go. James actually waited until she was out of sight before he doubled over with laughter. Boyd steeled himself for a good deal of humor—at his expense. He didn't have to wait long for it.

"His entire family in shipping and he can't 'stomach' the sea," James said with another round of laughter. "Priceless. And I guarantee his family doesn't know. I suppose we should keep it to ourselves," he said to his brother.

"The hell I will," Anthony replied. "I'll be shouting it from the rooftops until every member of Skylark and his family hears it."

"That implies he'll be breathing to suffer the shame," James said, still obviously amused. "So you aren't going to kill him now?"

"Only a little." Anthony slammed his fist into Boyd's face.

Boyd was caught completely off guard. He really wasn't expecting that. But Anthony was fast. He would probably have got in that punch even if Boyd was anticipating it.

Picking himself up off the deck, Boyd snarled, "*Why* are you two here?"

"That was already answered," James put in, leaning against the rail again with his arms crossed.

James's making himself comfortable to watch the entertainment should have given Boyd warning, but damned if Anthony didn't get in another punch. This one didn't knock Boyd down, but his cheek exploded with pain. He ignored it and raised his fists. He wasn't going to be caught off guard a third time.

He even smiled slightly as he told Anthony, "You know, I've waited years for this, an opportunity to test my skills against a master, which I've always considered you to be."

"Should have said so, Yank. I would have been glad to accommodate you."

"*But* I'd like to know why you're granting my fondest wish." Then Boyd added politely, "If you don't mind?"

"If Katey wasn't furious with you, which implies you didn't manage to seduce her after all, I wouldn't be holding m'self back," Anthony informed him.

Boyd rubbed his cheek gently. "You call this holding yourself back?"

Anthony ignored that question. "Since you didn't succeed, I don't have to kill you. However, I do need to make it very clear that seducing my daughter is to be removed from your list of choices. In fact, where—"

"Your *what*?"

Anthony didn't pause at that interruption. "—she's concerned, you don't get any choices. She'd have to be so in love with you that it makes her literally sick before I'd ever consider letting yet another Anderson into the immediate family. And since that obviously isn't the case, you, dear boy, will bloody well stay away from her."

Incredulous, Boyd looked to James for answers. "He's delusional, right?"

" 'Fraid not, Yank."

"But she's as American as I am! How can she be his daughter?"

"In the usual way it's done, I would imagine," James said drily.

"You know what I meant," Boyd replied, his frustration mounting.

James shrugged. "It's a long story. Suffice it to say, she *is* a Malory. Which is too bad for you, ain't it?"

That "too bad" held a lot of meaning, and some of it came to him immediately. For the third time, Boyd was caught off guard and knocked to the deck. But this time he came up swinging.

forty-two

"WHEN ARE YOU going to tell her?" James quietly asked his brother.

They stood at the rail of James's ship, watching *The Oceanus* in the distance trying to catch up to them. It wasn't going to happen unless he allowed it.

The Maiden George, as he'd rechristened his ship when he bought her a few months ago to take Georgina to Connecticut, had been named for his wife, but also in fond memory of *The Maiden Anne,* the ship he'd lived on for so many years. This ship was faster, but only because he'd removed all of her cannon before they set out to find *The Oceanus.* He could do nothing but run if attacked, but if attacked, he could run damn fast.

Sailing unarmed had made the voyage a bit dangerous, considering the rampant pirate activity in the Mediterranean, but speed had been preferable with Anthony climbing the walls with his impatience. And with good reason. They *had* instructed Boyd on how to go about seducing the chit. So it *was* imperative they find him and Katey before that happened.

James had let *The Oceanus* catch up to them once, deliberately. But that had just turned into a shouting match that had infuriated Anthony, because he couldn't reach the Yank to pound on him some more. Katey, who was now on board *The Maiden George,* hadn't come up on deck to hear it, which was a good thing. Women tended to get all sympathetic when they witnessed the battered face of someone they knew, and Boyd's face definitely fit into that category. Which was possibly what Boyd had been hoping would happen, since he'd shouted for them to stop so he could talk to her.

Katey hadn't seen his condition when she'd returned to the deck of *The Oceanus* with her servants and baggage, ready to change ships, because Boyd had already been carried off to his cabin by then, quite unconscious.

"Well?" James prodded his brother.

"I'd prefer to wait until I no longer look like a panda," Anthony mumbled.

James chuckled. "It's only one black eye he gave you, not two. But I'll allow he did give a good accounting of himself. Surprising, that. Don't think you were expecting it either, were you?"

"I've never had him in the ring. From the sound of it, he'd been hoping for an invitation. I wish he'd mentioned that before today. I would have much preferred to know ahead of time that that fight was going to last so bloody long."

"I suppose I shouldn't be surprised, come to think of it," James said. "The puppy spent more time admiring my pugilist skill in Connecticut than he did trying to trounce me with his brothers. But they were all pretty handy with their fists, those Yanks. The third worst beating of my life, as a matter of fact."

"There were five of them on you at once. Perfectly understandable, old man. The Andersons aren't exactly small men. And the other two beatings?"

"You and the elders, of course," James reminded Anthony. "When I brought our niece home after stealing away with her that summer so long ago."

"You *allowed* that beating because you were feeling guilty, or so you finally admitted. When was the third time?"

James chuckled. "Had an entire tavern full of miscreants jump me in the Caribbean once."

"Mouthed off at the wrong time, did you?"

"So I mentioned it to you?"

"You might have, but I've had one too many shocks lately. It's not coming to mind."

"They actually thought I was dead. I was beaten so badly that night they dumped me off the dock to hide the evidence. That's how I met Gabrielle's father and ended up owing him my life, a debt he called in this summer when he asked me to sponsor his daughter for the Season. He and his first mate pulled me out of the water."

Anthony laughed. "Now I remember. You mentioned it when you explained why you had a pirate's daughter under your roof. But you do realize that the very least of those fights was three to one, and that one you allowed. You've never gone down one-on-one, have you? Not even with me."

"Neither have you. We *are* wise enough to end our matches before we bruise each other very badly."

"Of course. Can't have the wives getting annoyed about it."

"So when are you going to tell her?"

James threw that back out to catch Anthony off guard after getting his mind off it, but Anthony just gave him an aggravated look and the warning "Don't push. It's not exactly a subject one raises everyday. She isn't going to like being told that the man she thought was her father all these years really wasn't."

"He's still the man who raised her. This news isn't going to make her love him any less."

"Of course not, but she's going to be shocked no matter what is said. Adeline and her husband lied to Katey. And they're both dead, so she would never have learned the truth. The Millards didn't bother to tell her," Anthony ended in disgust.

James harbored that same disgust. "Letitia Millard admitted that she barely let Katey in the door. Hell, she wasn't going to let *us* in at all. Damned annoying, that closemouthed woman."

They were both remembering the day they visited the Millards. They hadn't spent more'n ten minutes in that house, and they'd had to barge their way in when Letitia herself answered the door that day. She'd tried to close it in their faces. And she'd absolutely refused to allow them to see her mother.

She did verify what she'd said in that note, that Katey was Anthony's bastard, but they weren't about to take her at her word. The woman was too angry. She'd gone red in the face at the mere sight of Anthony. And she'd been shrieking at them to leave. She didn't even recognize James.

But James's curiosity didn't keep him quiet. He'd asked her directly, "What do you have against my family?"

Her reply had been "Who are you?"

"A Malory, whom you seem to despise."

She'd merely snorted and called for her servants to toss them out, an attempt that had ended rather abruptly with the footman sprawled on the floor and the butler running in the opposite direction.

They'd had to push their way past Letitia again to get upstairs to find her mother. She kept shouting that her mother wasn't well enough to deal with them. Unfortunately, she'd been telling the truth about that.

The room smelled of medicine, candle smoke, and sickness. It was closed off; even the draperies were drawn tightly shut. And the old lady in the bed seemed unconscious rather than asleep. A young maid sat beside the bed knitting. She didn't seem all that concerned over Sophie's condition, but then some servants didn't care about their employers, with one job being as good as the next.

Letitia had followed them upstairs, of course. Still furious at them and her impotence at being unable to prevent their intrusion, she had at least stopped shouting.

"Don't wake her. She's had this cold for a week now. She's not strong enough to fight it off."

Letitia whispered that information in a hiss. It was apparent that she loved her mother, but also that she was overprotecting her. Which was understandable. In her mind, Sophie was all she had left. But love could be smothering, too, and being entombed in stuffy darkness went much too far in that direction.

"Fresh air would be more beneficial, don't you think?" James remarked.

Letitia wasn't open to suggestions from them. "Fresh air is too chilly this time of year."

"Light isn't," Sophie Millard grumbled from the bed.

Letitia was quick to say in a defensive whine, "The dark helps you to sleep, Mother, and sleep will help you to get better."

"I've had too much sleep, and too much smoke from these candles. If it's day, give me some light." She motioned for the maid to open the drapes. "I'd like to see who my visitors are."

The old lady didn't sound as if she were at death's door. But she was obviously sick, her voice gravelly from too much coughing. And she was pale, which the light revealed as the young maid did as she was told. But they weren't there to tire her out. If Letitia could have been believed, they wouldn't even have come upstairs. But Letitia's anger and lack of welcome put anything she said in a doubting light. And it wasn't going to take much to get the verification they'd come there for.

Anthony had come to the same conclusions and got right to the point. "It's been many years, Lady Sophie, but perhaps you remember that I was courting Adeline before she left England twentysome years ago."

The old woman squinted her eyes at him before she said, "You have a very memorable face, Sir Anthony. *Very* memorable. Is that what you were doing?"

"Excuse me?"

"Courting my daughter? The rest of my family were under the impression that your intentions weren't the least bit honorable, that you were merely amusing yourself with her."

Anthony had turned a little red in the cheeks. But since he had gone on to be quite a notorious rake, he was in no position to address the insult even if the accusation in this case was far off the mark.

He merely said, "I had hoped to marry her."

James's own impatience had kicked in by then, his curiosity for once running rampant. Anthony might have been reluctant by then to burden a sick woman with unpleasant memories, but James wasn't. He'd been about to ask the question himself, but it wasn't necessary.

"I see," Sophie had said, her tone as well as her expression turning sad. "Then perhaps you will like to know that she bore you a child."

"I'd already told him that, Mother," Letitia was quick to complain. "He wouldn't believe *me*."

Sophie had sighed but replied with disapproval, probably not for the first time, "Your attitude, Letty, leaves room for doubt."

James almost grinned but restrained himself. Anthony, having just heard it repeated and able to believe it this time, that Katey was his, was in shock again.

But he reined in his emotions enough to say, "Thank you, Lady Sophie. I hope you'll be feeling better soon. Perhaps we can then discuss this in greater detail."

"I will look forward to it, Sir Anthony."

They had allowed Letitia to push and pull them out of the room after that. And she told them on the way back downstairs, "Don't come back. Those memories just make her unhappy. She doesn't need that at her age."

They didn't reply. They had the answer they'd come for, but Katey wasn't aware of that information yet. She hadn't questioned Anthony's remark that they were there to collect her. She'd simply come aboard *The Maiden George* and had thus far remained in the cabin she'd been shown to. She hadn't yet asked why they had come to fetch her. She seemed angry and preoccupied with Anderson and was stewing over it privately. But she'd probably get around to asking before the day was out.

James supposed he could wait till then, to find out how his brother handled that question, and how his new niece responded to the answer. Not for a moment would he admit that he was just a little bit nervous over her reaction. So he could imagine how Anthony was feeling.

Both her parents might be English, but Katey had been born and raised in America, after all. And even though James had been married to one for eight years, the thought processes of Americans still boggled his mind sometimes. Bloody hell, quite frequently, actually. So it could well turn out that Katey wouldn't like being part of the Malory family.

Hard to imagine, yet still possible. Particularly since Boyd Anderson had siblings firmly rooted in the family now, and Katey rather obviously still hadn't forgiven Boyd for treating her like a criminal. Or had he incurred her rage for some other reason now? That wouldn't surprise James. The Yank *was* a hothead, after all.

forty-three

"FEELING BETTER?" GRACE asked, poking her head around the door.

"I wasn't sick," Katey said.

"No, but you were in that 'don't say one word to me' mood you've developed lately," Grace humphed. "I recognize the signs by now."

Grace herself was in a complaining mood, quite understandably.

Earlier when Katey had found Grace on *The Oceanus*, Grace had yelled at her, "You were on a picnic! You couldn't tell me before you left? I had to hound the captain for an hour before he could be bothered to explain your disappearance."

"Pack our trunks, we're changing ships" was all Katey had said.

"When?"

"Now, or as soon as the other ship gets close enough to board."

"But—why?"

"Because the Malorys have come to fetch us."

"But—why?"

"I don't know and I don't care. They might even have been joking. Those two brothers seem to be in the habit of doing that and making it sound like they're serious. Actually, they probably were joking, since they also said they were here to kill Boyd, and they couldn't have meant that."

"So we're not leaving then?"

"We are. Whatever reason really brought them here, I'm going to hold them to their remark about 'fetching' us. They have a ship and I don't even care where it's going, though my guess would be back to England. I'm just happy to be leaving *this* ship."

"What about your rental agreement?"

"It was only a verbal agreement, and besides, I really doubt Boyd will mention that at this point. Renting *The Oceanus* was a good idea and it would have continued to be a good idea—if its owner hadn't insisted on coming along."

"But—"

"No more buts," Katey had cut in, still too angry for long explanations.

That picnic excuse Grace had been given had just fueled Katey's anger, since she would wager Boyd hadn't once thought about her servants and how her absence would be explained to them. Or did he actually think they wouldn't notice that she wasn't on the ship all day? Or maybe he thought she was a thoughtless, imperious employer who merely gave her servants orders without taking the time to explain anything to them.

Tyrus had come up with the excuse of a picnic, which had been better than no excuse at all, and certainly better than the truth, which he had been privy to. But that excuse still made it look as if Katey had been inconsiderate for not giving Grace prior warning.

"I'm sorry I didn't think to leave you a note," she said

to Grace now as she sat up in her bed looking as guilty as she felt. "It was a—a spur-of-the-moment decision to go ashore. Boyd wanted me to catch the sunrise from the beach."

Lying to her maid! Not for the first time, of course, but that was a *real* lie, not the sort she cooked up to entertain Grace.

"Did you?" Grace asked curiously as she set about unpacking Katey's trunks again.

"No, but we saw it from the rowboat on the way in. It was lovely, reflecting on the few thin clouds near it, and on the water."

Katey blushed immediately. She wasn't used to lying for real, certainly not to Grace. She needed to stop elaborating and just change the subject!

"It sounds like a nice outing," Grace said with a sniff. "What turned it sour?"

Katey groaned inwardly. "When does that man *not* do something to annoy me? He brought up the subject of marriage again and wouldn't drop it."

Grace turned to her wide-eyed. "Again? When was the first time?"

"That was on the spur of the moment, too. Out of the blue, without even leading up to it, he just asked me to marry him. I was insulted."

Grace gasped. "How can you be insulted over a compliment like that?"

Katey was *not* going to tell her maid that Boyd had mentioned bedding her in the same breath. "It was his abruptness," she hedged. "For some reason he doesn't think that I might like to be courted first."

Grace chuckled at that and said in her superior I-know-more-than-you voice, "I had a feeling you were smitten. I don't know why you've kept it to yourself. Why don't you put both of you out of your respective miseries and marry the man?"

"I'm not smitten."

Grace snorted. "I know you, remember? You've been giving all the signs since you met up with Boyd Anderson again. You're well and truly smitten, so don't try to deny it."

Katey shook her head. "Attracted, certainly. How could I not find him handsome? Infatuated, maybe a little. But his emotions run in extremes and I'm not so sure I'd want to deal with that for the rest of my life."

That was the biggest lie yet. She'd found out today what Boyd was like when he wasn't lusting after her. He'd shown a completely different side of himself, as if he were two different men. And the relaxed, playful one would be easy to fall in love with. Too easy.

"I wasn't planning on marrying until I've finished this trip."

"Love doesn't care about plans, Katey. It never does. It just happens."

"I disagree. It can be avoided, nipped in the bud. Steps can be taken to keep it from happening."

"So *that's* why we've jumped ship, as they say? It's not just because you're furious with him again, you're running from love?"

Katey gritted her teeth. "No, I already told you. The Malorys came here to fetch me, at least that's what they said. And it seemed a good time to take a vacation from Boyd Anderson. A permanent one."

"Because you're furious with him."

"Fine! Because I'm furious with him!"

Back came Grace's I-know-more-than-you tone. "Putting distance between yourself and him isn't going to weaken what you're feeling."

Since what Katey was feeling was rage, she certainly hoped that wasn't the case. She wouldn't like to sail all the way back to England stewing with this anger. But she knew that wasn't what Grace was talking about.

"I don't love him," she insisted again. "It might have been sneaking up on me a little, but it's already fading. And never seeing him again will take care of any remaining feelings I have for him."

Please let that be true, she said to herself. As for her anger, she *could* curb that, she was sure. It might take a few days to settle down, but with the cause of it no longer in her immediate vicinity, it would be much easier to set aside than if she had to see Boyd every day.

"I'm still incredulous that you wanted to abandon ship just because of a spat with him," Grace remarked.

"I can't enjoy this trip if I'm constantly in an aggravated state."

"Well, that's true enough, I suppose." Grace added, "He followed us, you know."

"What?"

"They even had a shouting match from ship to ship when *The Oceanus* sailed up alongside this ship."

"What?!"

Grace nodded. "I went up on deck to listen, but that blond lord ordered me to return to my cabin, and, well, I didn't feel like arguing with him."

Katey stared at her maid wide-eyed for a moment, but then she almost grinned over her last remark. Perfectly understandable for Grace not to want to argue with James Malory. Neither would Katey.

She tried to sound nonchalant as she asked, "So you didn't hear what they were shouting?"

"No, but what do you think? He's asked you to marry him, but they're hying off with you. He no doubt wants you back on *his* ship so he can finish courting you."

Katey rolled her eyes. "He was *not* courting me. I doubt he knows the first thing about it."

Grace snorted. "Neither do you. Sure, you don't have a house where he can come calling on you, but what do you think all that was about in Cartagena, when he spent the entire day with you? And that picnic? And wanting to watch the sunrise with you?"

Katey would have banged her head on a table if there had been one in front of her. Two out of three of the things Grace had just mentioned were lies, and the one that wasn't just didn't wash when she knew very well that every single thing that man had done was because of his physical desire for her, not because he wanted to court her.

But Grace wasn't finished. She had only paused long enough to dig a small box out of one of Katey's trunks. "And this?" Grace said, handing the box to her. "I found it in your cabin when you went on that picnic. It could have been delivered earlier. Since it's still unopened—you didn't see it?"

"No." Katey frowned as she took the little package and removed the thin silk wrapping.

When she opened the small wooden trinket box, her eyes widened. Dangling from a gold chain was a lovely scrimshaw pendant, delicately carved and an immediate reminder of home—and Boyd. She draped the chain over her neck before she examined it more closely.

Grace was smirking now. "Pretty, but of course he couldn't have given it to you because he was *courting* you. Not that it matters now. His ship is no longer following us, or if it is, it's fallen far behind. I went up to check before I came to tell you the Malorys are holding dinner for you."

Katey blinked and flew off the bed, yelling, "Why didn't you say so?!"

"I just did. And there's no need to fly into a panic. So you keep them waiting. It's—"

"No, I do *not* keep *them* waiting." Katey grabbed one of the dresses that Grace had just put in the standing wardrobe. "One brother scares the heck out of me. *And* you. Don't deny it, you just said as much. He seems to be cloaked in menace all the time, that one! I've yet to feel relaxed in his presence. The other, Judith's father, well, he's been nothing but nice, I can't deny that. But I get this strange feeling around him that nearly makes me just as nervous."

"Strange how?"

Katey didn't pause in changing her clothes. "It's hard to describe. It's as if for Judith's sake, I want to impress him. He saw me as his daughter's heroine."

Grace laughed. "You can't get much more impressive than that."

"I know. And I guess I just don't want to tarnish that image he has of me. I shouldn't care, but for some reason I do."

Grace fastened the back of Katey's dress. "Impressing and not disappointing are pretty much the same thing so it's understandable that you'd feel that way about Judith's father. You did form a fast close bond with that child. I don't doubt you and Judith will remain friends and keep in touch."

"You think that's all it is?"

"Why else would you worry about what Sir Anthony Malory thinks of you?"

forty-four

IT WAS AN unpleasant dinner. Katey couldn't think of a more appropriate word to describe it. She was uncomfortable. The two Malory men were just as uncomfortable. And it didn't help that James had nearly insulted her when he'd remarked on the pendant she was wearing close to her heart, asking if it was made of ivory.

She'd smiled and told him, "No, it's called scrimshaw, carvings that have become popular in New England recently. It's made of whalebone."

He'd looked appalled. "You're wearing—whale?"

She'd stiffened and said, "I think it's beautiful. A lot of thought and talent went into making it."

"Quite right," he'd amended. "Very pretty."

For whatever reason, they seemed to be as nervous as she was tonight. Or perhaps they were just responding to her mood.

The food was delicious though. The Malorys even attempted to make normal conversation, but it was pretty terse. And she caught quite a few pointed looks between the brothers, as if they were communicating without words. Their odd behavior began to worry her. She had intended to ask what they were doing in the Mediterranean. Now she was quite sure she didn't want to know.

"Pure foolishness on his part, taking you through that particular sea," James was saying to her. "There is ample warm weather in the Caribbean. That's where Boyd should have sailed you."

"I didn't want to travel that far yet," Katey replied. "He did suggest it. I declined."

"Then the fault was yours, m'dear," James didn't hesitate to scold. "You have to take into account what is happening in the part of the world you intend to visit. Most of the pirates in the Caribbean were done away with toward the end of the last century. The few that are still operating there are mostly just the annoying sort that will ransom you back to your family if you're captured."

"What my brother is getting at," Anthony added, "is that pirates are much more prevalent in the Mediterranean. The governments who have suffered losses because of them haven't become sufficiently annoyed to declare war on them. They will eventually, but in the meantime, if those pirates capture you, they won't ransom you to your family, they'll sell you into slavery. A very big difference."

Katey didn't take offense. When someone scolded her out of concern for her, she tended to feel guilt, not anger. But Katey felt neither emotion now. At least they were no longer tiptoeing around with their words, which enabled her to relax just a little.

"I was assured that we would be relatively safe if we avoided the Barbary Coast, which we did," Katey told them. "Was I misinformed? Is that why you came looking for us? Do you know something about this area that Boyd and his captain don't know?"

"My brother is being overly dramatic," Anthony said. "You were probably fine."

"Not so fine," Katey was forced to say. "Had we stayed

on ship, we would have been, no doubt. But going on that outing so far from any settlements left us exposed. Some pirates did show up today. They spotted us on the beach and came ashore to capture us. Boyd took care of both boats they sent. You didn't notice their ship scurrying away at the first sight of *The Oceanus*?"

"We saw the smaller vessel, but since you were on the empty side of a populated island, we assumed they were merely local friendlies who stopped to see if you wanted a ride out of there."

"Two boatloads, eh?" James said thoughtfully. "What was the head count?"

"Six per boat. Boyd wasn't quite done with the first group when the second boat arrived."

"He had weapons?"

"If you want to call his fists weapons. With the apparent intent to sell him into slavery, they were doing their best not to seriously hurt him. They thought they could bring him down with their bare hands. They thought wrong."

To that James raised a golden brow at his brother. "Feeling better, old man?"

"That he's good with his fists?" Anthony grumbled. "Or that after bruising them on twelve faces he was *still* good with his fists?"

James ended up chuckling. "Good point."

But Anthony said to her with a frown, "You must have been terrified."

Katey blinked with the realization that she'd been nothing of the sort, at least she hadn't really been afraid for herself. In fact . . .

"I was worried, yes, but at first about Boyd. He'd hid me inland, then went back to 'take care of them,' he'd said. I was too nervous to stay put. When I got back to the beach, I saw another boat landing, but Boyd wasn't quite finished with the first group, and he couldn't see the new arrivals. That's when I panicked. I was afraid the new group would surprise Boyd and overwhelm him. So I stepped out to draw their attention to me, to give him a little more time to finish with the two he was still fighting."

"They didn't try to overwhelm you?"

Her lips twisted with disgust. "They probably would have, but they were too busy laughing at my attempt to hit them with the rocks I'd gathered. Not *one* of the stones I threw landed anywhere near them. It was a pathetic attempt to do them harm, but it worked rather perfectly as a distraction, if I do say so myself."

Anthony sat back in amazement. "So once again you come to the rescue."

She chuckled at him. "Certainly not. I merely gave Boyd time to sneak up behind them and drop two of them with his club before they even knew he was there! You know, as I look back on it, and I can say this now that the danger is over, it was quite an exciting adventure, the second I've had since I began this journey. I even managed to knock one of the pirates out when they turned their backs on me to deal with Boyd's timely arrival. And he made quick work of the last three. You should have seen him. He was quite magnificent, particularly since he barely took a scratch himself."

The brothers exchanged glances before Anthony asked carefully, "Katey, you haven't developed fond feelings for Boyd Anderson, have you?"

"No."

She said it so quickly, Anthony didn't delve further. He

merely added, "Glad to hear it, because he's not exactly in our good graces just now."

James grinned. "When has that barbarian ever been?"

Anthony disagreed. "You weren't here, old man, but I had reason to be grateful to the Yank recently."

James feigned a surprised look. "Never say so."

"It was certainly brief, mind you, but I felt it none-theless."

"And long gone," James said.

"Most definitely," Anthony agreed with a sour look. "But I'll have to allow it sounds as if he acquitted himself rather well today—before we arrived."

"You can allow that if you must, but I bloody well won't," James said to his brother, then glancing at Katey, he added, "Katey, m'dear, don't make the mistake of see-ing my annoying brother-in-law as your hero just because he managed to take down twelve miscreants today. With those pirates not wanting to hurt him, as you said, the advantage was completely his. Any man who is the least bit handy with his fists could have done the same thing."

"Oh, I wouldn't make the mistake of thinking that," she said tight-lipped. "Certainly not."

Especially since they would never have been on that isle to begin with, or run into those pirates, if Boyd hadn't jumped on his *golden* opportunity, as he'd put it, to get them there. But she wasn't about to mention that to the Malory brothers.

James, however, picked up on her tone and remarked thoughtfully, "That's right, you're currently annoyed with him, aren't you?"

"Whatever gave you that idea?" she said sarcastically.

James replied with a grin, "The 'pretend you don't know me' remark you made to him would have sufficed, but we could also see that you'd been chewing his head off on the beach."

She groaned inwardly, realizing they'd probably had spyglasses trained on the island. But this was one subject she wasn't going to discuss. The Malorys, however, apparently felt they knew her well enough by now to delve.

One of James's golden brows went up. "Would you like to discuss it?"

"No."

"It's nothing that would require punishment?" James pressed in a more menacing tone. He even rubbed his knuckles against his cheek so she'd understand what sort of punishment he was talking about.

"No, don't hurt him!"

"Wouldn't dream of it, dear girl," Anthony assured her, albeit with some color in his cheeks.

James chuckled to himself. Katey had no idea why. She saw nothing amusing about the subject. But then these English lords did seem to have a quirky sense of humor.

With dinner pretty much finished and the conversation no longer to her liking, Katey waved away the dessert that was offered to her. "I should be getting back to my cabin," she told her companions. "It's been a long, eventful day."

Anthony said quickly, "Katey, don't go yet. I need to have a few words with you." He looked at his brother. "Would you mind?"

James understood, but he started laughing in reply. "Leave?" In other words, he wasn't budging.

forty-five

KATEY HAD NODDED that she would stay, but she quickly wished she hadn't. Anthony didn't get right to the point of whatever he wanted to talk to her about. He didn't even stay at the table. He marched over to the captain's desk, James's desk, since he captained *The Maiden George* himself, and poured himself a drink from a decanter of spirits there. He even drank it straight down—then paced the floor between the desk and the dining table.

His nervousness was palpable, causing hers to escalate dramatically. She was just about to shoot to her feet and rudely run out of the room with merely a yelled "Good night" when Anthony pinned her with his eyes. Such beautiful eyes he had, purest cobalt blue, exotically slanted just enough to be noticeable, and riveting. She didn't move.

"Tell me about the man who raised you, Katey," Anthony began.

She blinked. What an odd way to refer to her father. "My father?"

"Yes."

Oh, good grief, he just wanted to hear her family history? "What would you like to know?"

"What sort of man was he?"

"Kind, generous, cheerful, oh, and very gossipy." She chuckled. "Of course he had to be. It kept his customers amused."

"Were you close to him?"

She thought about that for a moment, but had to admit, "Not really. He died when I was only ten, so I don't have many memories of him that stand out in my mind. And he was rarely home. He spent every day in his shop. He ran it himself. It was a small shop in a very small village. And it was the only place in Gardener for the villagers to gather, so he kept it open late each day. If I wanted to spend time with him other than on Sundays, then I had to go to the shop. Half the year I was usually in bed by the time he got home."

"So you barely knew him?"

"I wouldn't say that. I knew him as well as any child that age knows their parents. I loved him, he loved me. He always had a smile, or a hug, for me. But I was much closer to my mother. I spent hours with her every day, either helping her in her garden, or helping her in the kitchen, or with the house chores we did together."

"She worked—in the *kitchen*?"

It sounded as if he'd had to spit out those words, that they wouldn't come out on their own. How odd. What did it matter where she worked? Oh, wait, he was a lord. To him, only servants worked in kitchens.

She chuckled with understanding. "No one had servants in Gardener, Sir Anthony. While my family could have easily afforded them, my mother wanted us to be like everyone else, and besides, she enjoyed her chores and I enjoyed doing them with her. It wasn't as if we had anything else to do to greatly occupy our time. She didn't give in and hire Grace until I was much older. But mother took over running the store after my father died, so her time was much more limited after that, and more of the chores came to me, now that I think of it."

Anthony made a sound that could easily have been likened to pain. He also marched straight out of the cabin without a by-your-leave. And had his complexion gone white? He'd turned too fast for her to be sure. Katey was frowning when James rose, too, and quickly followed his brother.

But he glanced back at her and ordered, "Stay put," then slammed the door shut behind him.

Katey humphed to herself. What the devil was that about? She didn't budge, though, much as she wanted to. If anyone else had given her that order, she'd be marching off to her own cabin in high dudgeon at that very moment. But from that particular man, well, she stayed put. Even when something banged against the wall outside and her immediate impulse was to investigate, she stayed put.

~~~~~~

Outside, James had Anthony pinned against the wall he'd just slammed him into. "Don't even think about abandoning ship," James snarled.

"I wasn't jumping."

"I'm talking about Katey in there and leaving her clueless. Have you flipped your bloody gourd, Tony? What the deuce got into you?"

"You heard her. Good God, she grew up in absolute drudgery and it's my fault!"

"So you *have* flipped your gourd. It was Adeline's choice to leave England. You didn't put her on the ship that took her to America. And you certainly didn't keep her there. She could have come home at any time."

"But she never would have got on that ship in the first place if I hadn't been dragging my feet about proposing, so bloody nervous that she wouldn't give me the answer I wanted. If she had been more sure about me, she would have come to me and we would have married. Then she would have continued living in the style she was accustomed to, and Katey, God, Katey wouldn't have been raised like a servant!"

"What are you suggesting? That no one except the upper crust can live happy lives? Don't be such a bloody arse, Tony, and a snobbish one at that."

"No," Anthony growled back, "but we're talking about *my* daughter. She shouldn't have had to live like that. She should have been pampered just like Judy and—"

"Stop and think about that before my fist helps you," James interrupted. "You do realize that had any of that played out differently, you never would have met and married Roslynn. Then you wouldn't have two other daughters to be comparing this one to, would you? Judith and Jaime would never have been born, would they?"

Anthony dropped his head back against the wall with a sigh. "I might have overreacted."

"Might?" James snorted.

"It's just—why would she even want me for a father at this late date? She's a young woman of means. There is nothing that I can give her that she can't give herself."

"Yes, there is. A family. It would take her an entire lifetime to produce a family the size of the one you're going to hand her due to a quirk of fate."

forty-six

THE TWO MALORYS had been gone too long. It wasn't unreasonable to think they might have forgotten about her. So it wasn't unreasonable for Katey to risk defying James Malory's order. Besides, it had been an incredibly eventful day. She was due for a good, long sleep, if she could get out of her mind those hours she'd spent with Boyd *before* the pirates showed up.

But the two men hadn't actually gone that far off, she found as she tried sneaking out of the cabin unnoticed. They noticed, both turning their heads her way when the door opened, so she innocently inquired, "Is everything all right?"

"Certainly. I was merely contemplating tossing my brother overboard," James said drily as he let go of Anthony's jacket and pretended to be merely dusting off his lapels.

"And I was explaining to this arse why he shouldn't," Anthony replied cheerfully, and shouldered his way past James to usher Katey back into the cabin.

She sighed as she took her seat again at the dining table. What about her could Anthony be so interested in, that it couldn't wait until morning? She should just be rude and say she was exhausted. She wasn't. The day had been too invigorating. But they didn't know that. Maybe if she faked a yawn . . .

"Now where were we?" Anthony said.

He didn't take *his* seat. He was back to pacing, and he didn't look all that cheerful now, either. That had no doubt been feigned.

"You were about to get to the point," James prompted him.

James didn't return to the table, either. He sat sideways on the edge of his desk, just enough to have one leg comfortably dangling. His crossed arms looked rather menacing, though, so Katey took her eyes off him. Anthony ignored him altogether.

"Ah, yes, I was about to ask if you had a happy childhood, despite all that drudgery?"

James groaned.

Katey frowned. "What drudgery? If you mean my chores, I never minded them. It was time I got to spend with my mother, and later, with Grace. Besides, cleaning our house, growing and cooking our food, that was just a part of my life. There was no one else to do it. Everyone in Gardener saw to themselves. I know you might find that appalling. You come from a different way of life. But for us, it was simply normal."

Anthony winced. "I haven't thoughtlessly insulted you, have I? That certainly wasn't—"

"Not at all," Katey assured him. Then a memory came to her that caused her to chuckle. "It's funny. Your daughter had exactly the opposite reaction to my chores when I mentioned them in our conversations. She complained she never got to help with any!"

"Judy did?"

"Indeed. You might want to give her her own garden

before she gets much older. Children happen to like growing things, at least I did."

"But—she'd get dirty."

Katey felt he was teasing with that appalled look on his face at the mention of dirt. She grinned at him. "I know, but playing in the dirt can be fun. It smells good and it makes wonderful mud pies!"

James rolled his eyes. Anthony returned her grin and said, "Can't recall ever wanting to muck around in the dirt m'self, but I can say without a doubt that our eldest brother would probably agree with you."

"Ah, yes, the gardener. I enjoyed meeting him and walking through his gardens."

James practically spit out a laugh over the way she'd referred to Jason. She glanced at James and added, "I know, someone already told me I probably shouldn't call him that. But he is a gardener, you know. It might just be his hobby as he called it, but I've never seen so many beautiful flowers and in so many varieties. Judy warned me I'd be impressed, but seeing Jason's handiwork firsthand truly amazed me."

Anthony cleared his throat to draw her attention back to him. "I believe we've gotten a bit off topic."

Katey frowned. "Why so much curiosity about my past?"

"I knew your mother—well."

"Ah, of course." Katey smiled, beginning to understand. "She lived close to Haverston before she met my father, and you grew up there, didn't you?"

"Indeed, though truth to tell, I was full grown and merely home for the holidays before I really got acquainted with her. But I suppose I just wanted to know if you and she had led a normal life in America."

"Normal for Gardener, yes."

"That bears some significance?"

She smiled. "It was a very small village of old people with no industry other than a few farms on the outer edges. I was the last child born there, and the few other children left were nowhere close to my age and soon gone. No one ever moved there anymore, other than people looking for a quaint, quiet village to retire in." She chuckled. "We were definitely quiet. Nothing ever happened of interest. No one ever entertained. The highlight of every day was someone reading aloud from the Danbury newspaper in our shop. Old Hodgkins rode over to the larger town twice a week to buy up a few copies just for that. Gardener was, without a doubt, the most boring place you can imagine."

"Good God, so you had a horrible childhood?"

"I didn't say that! It was just boring—for a child. My parents didn't seem to mind. They had things to keep them busy. Myself, I groaned each day my tutor sent me home. Really, I did. I would have much preferred to stay with him and talk about the world!"

"Why didn't your parents move somewhere more lively or at least to that bigger town nearby?"

She shrugged. "I heard them talking about it once. Shopkeeping was all my father knew how to do. In Gardener, he never lacked for customers with his store being the only one in the village. In Danbury, or some other larger town, he would have had to compete with already established shops, and with a family to feed, I think he was afraid to try that. After he died, I was hoping my mother would move us, but she jumped feetfirst into running the shop herself. She actually enjoyed it."

"But your mother had money, didn't she? Isn't that what you inherited?"

"Yes, and quite a bit of it, but she refused to touch it herself. It came from her father when he died, and she despised her family for disowning her. She wouldn't even talk about them. I didn't even know how many Millards were left until I came to England."

"They disowned her?"

"You didn't hear about it back then? It was because she eloped with an American who was in trade, or that's what she implied."

James interjected, "And an excellent time to get to the point, Tony—before I die of old age."

Anthony shot his brother a cold look. "*You* weren't invited, so why don't you go to bed."

"I can't, dear boy. It's my bedroom you're dragging your feet in." Anthony flushed slightly with that reminder, but James wasn't finished. "Katey, what my brother—"

James was finished this time. Anthony leapt across the space between them and knocked James backward with enough force that they both tumbled over the other side of the desk to the floor.

Katey shot to her feet. Incredulous, she demanded, "Are you both insane?"

James's head came up first as he stood back up. "Certainly not." He gave his brother a hand up.

"Apologies, Katey," Anthony said as he came back around the desk, running a hand through his hair to straighten it. "Unfortunately, that was nothing out of the ordinary in our family."

"You mean between us, don't you, dear boy?" James added with a pointed stare. "You won't find the elders knocking each other around, so don't frighten her by implying all Malorys are like you and I."

"Quite right," Anthony agreed with an abashed look.

"James and I are just more—energetic. Call it brotherly competition if you like."

Still a bit shaken from their burst of—energy, Katey said, "Having had no siblings of my own, I'm afraid that's a bit hard to comprehend."

"Perfectly understandable. Perhaps it would make more sense to know that we're both avid pugilists. Exercise for us has always consisted of a good round in a sporting ring several times a week."

"You still do that?"

"She's not calling us too old to exercise, is she?" James said drily.

Katey blushed despite the grin he offered her to imply he was only teasing.

Anthony sighed in exasperation. "We've gone far from the mark again. So let me be blunt for a moment, Katey. You never actually answered my question about a happy childhood, if you had one. Is that significant? There are no painful memories you'd prefer not to discuss?"

She rolled her eyes at him. "If there were, I wouldn't be discussing them, would I? The fact of the matter is, my childhood wasn't very memorable, but it wasn't miserable, either. I was happy enough living with my parents and then, just with my mother after my father died. When I got old enough, I could have left Gardener like all the other young people did as soon as they could, but it never even occurred to me to do so until my mother died. The main thing I didn't like about my childhood was simply the sheer boredom of it from a child's perspective. But that *is* why I decided to travel for a few years to see the world, before I consider marriage and children of my own. I was hoping for the excitement I missed as a child, and some adventure. I've been finding a little of both." She grinned.

"Have you ever wished you had a larger family?"

She almost pointed out that wishing about the past was irrelevant, but held her tongue, mainly because she sensed his nervousness over the question. She found that quite odd, but even James seemed tense now, waiting for her reply. What the devil was wrong with these two tonight?

Hesitantly she said, "I am beginning to suspect that you're leading up to something I may not find palatable. So perhaps as your brother suggested, it's time to get to the point, Sir Anthony?"

He sighed and took his seat across from her again. "I said I knew your mother, but not just as an acquaintance. I was courting her before she left England, and my intentions were honorable. I wanted to marry her."

Katey stared at him hard, trying to assimilate that, but it just didn't make sense. "I don't understand. You're an exceptionally handsome man. And—"

"Thank you."

"—to be frank, my father wasn't. He wasn't ugly or anything like that, but between you two, I can't imagine my mother picking him over you, and yet you're saying she did? Did you do something that turned her against you? Are we talking about a tragic romance?"

"No, it was nothing like that. Her family didn't like me. I'm not even sure why. I wasn't quite the rakehell yet that I became in later years. But Adeline didn't share their feelings. I was quite sure she felt the same as I. My mistake was in not letting her know sooner that I wanted her for my wife. I erroneously *assumed* she took it for granted, that we were of a like mind and would be married. And then she was gone. Overnight. I can't tell you what a shock that was, to ride over to take her on a picnic to our favorite spot and be told she'd left England. They gave me some tripe about a grand tour that had been planned that *she* had never mentioned to me, and that she'd be back in a year or so."

"So you didn't resume your courtship when she returned to England?"

"She never returned, Katey."

She was frowning now with extreme confusion. "But she eloped with my father, so . . . you're saying she knew and fell in love with him prior to your courting her? That he suddenly showed up again and she ran off with him without even an explanation for you?"

"No, my guess would be she didn't meet him until after she left England, perhaps on the ship to America, or soon after she landed."

Katey realized that was the opinion of a man who had come in second place in the running for a woman's affections. She couldn't blame him for wanting to think it. She still found it amazing herself, that her mother hadn't picked Anthony over her father.

She said gently, "I'm sorry to say you're wrong. She told me—"

"Katey, some parents will make up a good lie to hide a sad truth. For whatever reason, she didn't want you to know the real reason she left England. I had no idea myself. She could have told me, but she didn't. All these years, I didn't know she ran off carrying my child. I still wouldn't have known if your aunt Letitia hadn't sent me a nasty note about it after you sailed on *The Oceanus*."

Katey's eyes widened. She put her hand to her mouth, but it was to stifle a surprised laugh. If she laughed when he seemed so sincere, she'd never forgive herself. But at least the fallacy wasn't his, but instigated by that harsh relative of hers.

"I met Letitia," she said quickly. "Frankly, I wouldn't believe a single word she told me. Why, she even called me a . . ."

The color drained from Katey's cheeks as she slowly stood up. Her eyes were riveted to Anthony's face, and she was seeing so much more in his expression now, dread, sympathy, understanding—and caring.

And even though she didn't need to hear it now, he said, "You're correct. I didn't believe her. I went to hear it from your grandmother. She wasn't well, so I didn't over-tax her to hear more details, but she confirmed it, Katey. You're my daughter."

The only sound that would come out of her mouth was a small, painful sound, a mewling. And before she made a fool of herself, she raced out of the cabin.

"Bloody hell," Anthony groaned.

"Did you expect squeals of delight and an exuberant father-daughter hug?" James asked drily as he moved to close the door Katey had left open in her escape.

"This isn't a good time for your pearls of wisdom, James."

"Perhaps not, but much can be said for bluntness. You should have just spit it out and saved yourself all that agonizing hearing about the bush."

"I was trying to break it to her gently."

"Oh, you did, dear boy," James said. "With the finesse of a sledgehammer."

forty-seven

TO HAVE EVERYTHING that she knew about herself and her life crack like a nutshell in her hand, the shards too small to piece back together, the only option to discard it, wasn't just a little traumatic for Katey. She was devastated. It wasn't that she was a Malory. Having one for a parent didn't automatically make her one of them, at least in her mind. She had no more history with that family than she did with the Millards. But at least she had *known* about the Millards.

And therein was the source of the trauma she couldn't shake. It was the lie, her mother's lie, her mother's deceit, that she'd kept the truth from Katey her whole life. Maybe Adeline had intended to tell her someday who her real father was, perhaps after she was married and starting her own family. Adeline wouldn't really have denied her grandchildren knowing where they came from, would she? She hadn't meant to die before she could make that confession. Life wasn't that predictable. Stupid piece of ice . . .

Katey cried her heart out for what Adeline had given up with one single life-altering decision. Why did she do it? Katey cried her heart out for what her mother had missed, and subsequently, what Katey had missed as well, life with the Malorys. *Why?*

Katey had put so much hope into the Millards, but now she was glad she hadn't grown up anywhere near them. She couldn't imagine what it would have been like, having someone like Letitia always around. Would she have grown up to be like her? The thought horrified her. But to have grown up in the midst of the Malorys, she realized, that would have been wonderful.

I can't imagine what it must have been like, not having something exciting going on all the time, Judith had told her that day in the coach. *With my family, there is always something interesting happening.*

When it hit her, it was like a ton of bricks. Judith Malory was her sister. My God, she had a sister! No, she had two of them! Some of her tears were happy ones.

Anthony came to her door numerous times the next day to make sure she was all right. She wouldn't open it, but from the other side she assured him, "I'm fine, I just need some time to myself to digest it all."

And put the shattered pieces of her life back together—if she could.

But even James had come by toward evening with some heavy pounding on the door and the gruff warning, "This ain't healthy, puss. Present yourself for dinner tonight or I break this door down."

She stayed locked in her cabin, ignoring that order. But she was still too immersed in her thoughts to really notice that he didn't come back to break the door. And the only time she opened that door at all was for Grace, briefly, and not to let her in.

She didn't want her maid to worry so she told her bluntly, "Anthony Malory claims to be my real father." To which she abruptly added, "I don't want to talk about it yet."

Wide-eyed, Grace started to reply, but Katey put a finger to her lips. "Not yet. It's a shock, yes, but please, Grace, I need a few days of solitude to—adjust."

Stubborn as usual, Grace at least pointed out, "You have to eat."

"No, I don't. I'm so upset, I'd just spit it back up."

"You *have* to eat. Do you want me to perish from worrying about you?"

"If I don't come out in a week, *then* you can worry." Katey had tried to sound teasing, knew she'd failed, and closed the door on any more arguing.

Grace set trays of food outside her door anyway. Katey left them there. She hadn't been exaggerating. The turmoil she was going through was physical, enough that she had no doubt her stomach wouldn't tolerate something as ordinary as nourishment. But she wasn't hungry. If she was, she was too upset to feel it.

She didn't stay barricaded more than the one day. After the second night's sleep that didn't include restless tossing, she woke with some peace of mind, and the gut-wrenching emotion inside her had gone away for the moment. She didn't know if she would ever forgive her mother for the lie, but this new family that she'd pretty much inherited overnight could fulfill the hopes that the Millards had failed to fill. If she hadn't just been told about her relationship with the Malorys for the sake of being told. *If* they actually wanted her to be a part of their family.

She joined her new relatives for luncheon that day. Both men rose abruptly as she entered the cabin. Both looked extremely anxious, still worried about how she'd received the news.

She smiled slightly as she took a seat at the table across

from Anthony. "Be at ease, please. It was just a shock. I'm sure it was for you, as well."

"Indeed, though I must admit it didn't take me long to be delighted."

"Me either," she replied bashfully. "Though I don't even know if your family is going to accept me, or if you'd prefer to keep this between ourselves."

"Good God, is that what you thought?"

"Dropped the hammer, but forgot the nails, eh, old chap?" James drolly put in.

Anthony ignored his brother to tell her, "You're going to be welcomed with open arms, never doubt it, Katey. Why, Judith is going to go through the roof with excitement when she hears. She took to you exceptionally well, you know."

Katey grinned, not just from the remark, but from relief. They did want her!

"The feeling was quite mutual," she said. "And I think being part of your family is going to be a wonderful experience. You could have kept the knowledge of being my father to yourself, without ever telling me. I'm glad you didn't. Thank you for that. But—"

"No buts allowed, puss," James interrupted.

That was the third time he'd given her an order since she'd come aboard *The Maiden George*. Having just begun to recover from a major emotional shock, Katey took offense this time. It was going to be a bit more difficult accepting that *he* was a relative.

"Don't be telling me what I can and can't do, *Uncle* James. I'm too new to your family for you to take that liberty yet. I'll let you know when you can."

Since she had just rendered the big man momentarily speechless, Anthony burst out laughing. "Bravo, m'dear. Spoken like a true Malory."

She blushed furiously. "I'm sorry." The apology was for James. "It's just going to take a little time for me to get used to it all."

"Don't apologize for speaking your mind," James replied. "And I won't apologize for trying to protect my brother—in my fashion. He's been on tenterhooks since he learned about this, afraid that it was too late to bring you into the fold, that you'd reject us out of hand."

Her eyes flared. "Are you joking? I know I didn't answer this question the other night, but I *have* always wanted to be part of a larger family. I had so been looking forward to meeting my mother's family and hoped I would be welcomed by them, but my aunt Letitia pretty much closed the door on that notion for me."

"Nasty old wench," Anthony said with disgust. "I'd say that's her forte, slamming doors in people's faces."

"Or trying to," James added a bit smugly.

Katey continued, "But even if those hopes had been realized, it's still been established that you're my father. I could never deny my . . . own—"

She paused to stare at Anthony, and her eyes got even bigger as the full impact of that statement hit her. He wasn't just *a* relative, he was the closest relative she could have. "My God, you really are my father."

His face began to waver as her eyes filled with happy tears. She stood up. So did he. They both rounded the table at James's end to get at each other. She threw herself into Anthony's open arms. He crushed her with his own emotion.

"If we weren't on a bloody ship, m'dear, I'd say, 'Welcome home.'"

Still seated beside them, without even turning to witness this long overdue reunion, James rolled his eyes.

forty-eight

IT WAS AMAZING how beneficial something as simple as a hug could be. The meaningful one Katey had received from her father caused her fears, even her nervousness, to instantly drain away. She was left with such a sense of well-being. And excitement. She couldn't wait now to get back to England to meet the rest of her new family!

Her father and her uncle, however, still seemed worried about the shock she'd undergone. They might also have sensed that she was all bubbly inside now and mistaken it for additional apprehension. So they continued to try, in their fashion, to make the transition easier for her.

"It might help if you hear how my brother met his son Jeremy."

Katey was ravenously eating from the plate that had been set before her. Relieved of all those anxious emotions she'd been experiencing, she had swiftly realized that she was famished! So it took her a moment to grasp the odd way her father had referred to his brother's first look at his newborn son.

"Met?"

"Indeed, and you'll be surprised how similar the circumstances were to ours. Would you like to tell it, James?"

James nodded. "Well, with the hope that this won't

bore you to tears, m'dear, I had no idea Jeremy existed. He knew all about me, though. His mother had been 'impressed' with me, I suppose, and had built me up to heroic proportions for the lad. It was about thirteen years ago that we came across each other. Pure luck it was, that I chose the tavern he was working in, to quench my thirst."

"So you recognized him?"

"Well, let's say he definitely had my attention. Even at twelve, his age at the time, he was nearly as tall as I was! And he looked so much like Tony here it was uncanny. Hard to miss that."

"I couldn't help noticing it myself when I saw the two of them together," Katey agreed.

"At least you didn't laugh," James said with a quelling eye on Anthony. "*He* thinks it's hilarious. So does my son, for that matter."

Anthony still chuckled at his brother. "If you weren't so touchy about it, you would, too." Then Anthony explained to Katey, "It's an old Gypsy trait that runs in our family. Pops up here and there rather strongly. I have it m'self, and two of our nieces do, Reggie and Amy. And Jeremy got a big dose of it himself."

For once James didn't change Regina's family nickname to the one *he* preferred, but Katey didn't hear about his peculiarity with names until later. At the moment, she couldn't help asking, "Gypsies?"

"That's another story, m'dear," James said. "Let's stick to one at a time to keep the confusion to a minimum, shall we?"

"By all means." She grinned at him.

"So there I was, arrested by this boy's amazing resemblance to my brother. But this meeting occurred in the Caribbean, and I knew Tony had never been anywhere near it, so I shrugged it off as merely a strong case of co-incidence. But the lad couldn't take his eyes off me, either. His mother had described me very well to him, you see. And then he comes up to me and asks me if I'm James Malory."

"That's when you knew?" Katey asked.

"No, but *that* bowled me over. And to understand why it did, I should mention that I didn't use my real name in that part of the world. I didn't want my activities there to ever be linked to my family, so I took on the name of Captain Hawke for the duration of the time I sailed in those waters."

"Why?"

Anthony chuckled. "That's yet another tale that is best left for later."

Katey raised a brow, intrigued, but James must have been in agreement with his brother, because he continued his first tale for her. "When I didn't deny the name, the brat tells me *I'm* his father."

"Why am I guessing you didn't believe him?" Katey speculated.

"Because by that point I did think he was Tony's."

"You didn't?" Anthony hooted. "All these years and you never mentioned that?"

"Put a lid on it, puppy, and let me get to the end of this. With Jeremy knowing my name, I had to allow that perhaps he hadn't been born in the Caribbean, but in England. And as soon as that thought showed up, it put him in range of Tony's stomping grounds. So while I didn't think Jeremy was mine yet, I did accept that he was probably a Malory. But the boy wasn't standing there silently waiting for me to open my arms to him. He was telling me all about his mother and the glorious week I'd spent with her—her take on it, mind you. She was a tavern wench. And I did actually recall her after he described her to me."

"One wench out of thousands?" Anthony snorted skeptically.

"Well, she carried three dirks, you see, one in each boot, and one quite visible in her belt. *That* I definitely remembered. The customers in her tavern knew from experience that she wasn't available to just anyone. She'd sliced up quite a few of them to make that point. And she was a pretty little thing, as I recall, which is why I did spend an entire week with her. I'd been intrigued by her reputation with those dirks when I heard about her. And besides, the brat stood there belligerently insisting I was his sire, daring me to call him a liar with his cocky attitude. I think that more'n anything else convinced me." James chuckled.

"A chip off the old block, eh?" Anthony smiled.

"Indeed."

Thoroughly fascinated with the tale by now, Katey asked, "But how did he end up in the Caribbean?"

"When he got old enough and started asking his mother so many questions about me, she got the notion that I should meet him. Quite brave of her, if I do say so m'self."

"Why?"

James lifted a golden brow. "Trust an American to ask that. You tell her, Tony."

Anthony chuckled. "The social sphere, m'dear, a bit particular to the aristocracy. He was a lord of the realm. A tavern wench showing up at his door with a child in hand, well, it just ain't done."

Katey was about to snort, but James got back to his tale. "I'd moved to the Caribbean by then, anyway, and finding that out, she moved her and her son there as well. But it's a big area. And she didn't know the name I went by there, so she had no hope, really, of finding me. She died not long before I discovered Jeremy, having jumped a little too eagerly into one of the many barroom brawls that inevitably occur in rowdy taverns like the one she worked in. The owner was used to Jeremy helping out, even at his young age, and kept him on. Frankly, the boy could have been likened to a guttersnipe when I found him—and certainly talked like one. Expected though, after being raised in taverns."

"I didn't notice that about him," Katey said.

James grinned. "He's come a long way. Course, he had both me and my first mate always on his arse about his grammar, so he learned quick. I took him to sea with me for a few years, but that got too dangerous, so I bought us a plantation in the islands with the intention of giving him a stable home. But I had a score to settle in England, which took us back there, and subsequently had a reunion with my brothers that brought me back to England for good. I merely had one last trip to take back to the Caribbean to settle my affairs there, and a damn good thing, since I met my wife on that trip."

Hesitantly, Katey asked, "Your family accepted Jeremy without any qualms?"

"My dear girl, that's been the point of my sharing this tale with you. Of course they did, wholeheartedly. You will find that Malorys are very, *very* strong on family ties. We nourish and protect our own."

"Yes, we even love our black sheep," Anthony added with a smirk toward his brother.

But James was quick to retort ominously, "Stuff it, old chap, before—"

Anthony cut in with a roll of his eyes, "Yes, yes, I know, before you help me."

Katey, glancing back and forth between them, had to ask, "Do you two—hate each other?"

"Good God, whatever gave you that idea?" they both nearly said in unison.

Katey choked back a laugh.

forty-nine

It seemed to take no time at all to get back to England. Long before Katey was expecting it, James announced they would be docking later that very day. The difference in the time getting them there so quickly had nothing to do with strong winds pushing them northward either, she realized. It was the simple fact that on *The Oceanus* she had anticipated seeing Boyd every single day, and when that didn't happen, time had dragged by at a snail's pace. And that had been more than half that voyage!

She knew why now. And it had been bothering her that many of her reactions to him had been tinged with anger because she'd thought he had been ignoring her. But his long absences hadn't been intentional at all.

Time was flying by on the return voyage because of the company she was sharing. Her father. Her uncle. Her *family*.

She and Anthony spent nearly every waking hour together. They took long, leisurely walks around the deck and talked. They stood at the rail together for hours and talked some more, barely noticing that the weather was getting colder by the day as they left the warm waters of the Mediterranean.

Lunches and dinners lasted three times as long as they

normally would in James's cabin! Anthony had years of Malory history to impart to her, and she soaked it all in, by turns surprised, shocked, amused. Good God, they were a fascinating family.

She did her share of talking, and not just about herself. Anthony got her to discuss her mother more and more, and each time she did, some of her anger at her mother would go away, until there was barely any left.

"So Adeline was happy in this village?" he asked her one evening during dinner.

She didn't have to think about that long before saying, "Not once did I ever catch her in a moment of melancholy, probably because she was always too busy for idle moments!"

Katey was trying to make light of it, but he was much too concerned about it to be amused. He seemed to have it stuck in his mind that a woman from his class couldn't step so far down the social ladder and live a happy life. Which was absurd. A certain way of life did not guarantee happiness.

James appeared to be of the same opinion. "My brother's a snob," he explained.

"The devil I am," Anthony shot back.

"You bloody well are, and a vain one at that!" But to Katey James added, "He's afraid your mother suffered a broken heart for having to give him up, for whatever reason. And considering that I know for a fact that he left broken hearts all over England during his rakehell years, I was having the same thought."

Katey understood and assured them, "If she did have a broken heart, she got over it by the time I was old enough to notice. But now that you've made me think about it— it's not something I ever really took note of back then—I doubt my parents shared a great love of the sort you mean." She paused, wincing over the word *parents*. "I'm sorry, but he raised me. I can't not think of him as my parent."

"Don't be silly, puss," Anthony said. "While I would have liked to have been the one to raise you, that doesn't make him any less your father, too."

She nodded. "Well, I can say with certainty that they did like each other. It might have only been that they had become great friends, or it might have been more, but they got along wonderfully, never arguing. They laughed a lot together, too. And they shared the same goals, raising me and running the store. They were even planning on enlarging it with a taproom before he died. Gardener didn't have a tavern."

They both stared at her with such horror over that news, she laughed. "Well, I told you it was a small village. And my mother gave up those plans when my father died. But she seemed to thrive, running the store by herself after that. She mourned, though, for quite a long time, so whether she loved him or not to begin with, I'm sure she grew to love him."

That appeared to be what Anthony needed to hear. "You have set my mind at ease, m'dear. Thank you."

Another time, when they were alone on the deck, she confessed her fabrication of tales and why she'd picked up the habit in the first place. Though since beginning her trip, she'd been getting more than enough entertainment, so that the imaginary sort was no longer necessary—one hope for the trip that had come true.

Katey felt she could talk to Anthony about anything—except Boyd. She definitely didn't want to talk about him. And anytime the Andersons were mentioned—they were part of the family now—she steered the conversation to other topics.

"Does your wife know about me?" Katey asked when they got closer to England, where Anthony had already told her he intended to take her home with him.

"Certainly. We haven't told Judy yet, though. We decided to wait until you were present to spring that delightful news on her. She would have been impossible to live with otherwise. The chit does *not* seem to understand the word *patience* when she's excited."

"Roslynn didn't mind?"

"She was a bit annoyed at me at first, but only because she mistakenly thought that I knew all along that you were mine and had kept it a secret from her. But she eavesdropped outside the door that day I found out, when James and I were discussing it, and she was in complete agreement that I go straight to your grandmother for the truth of the matter. So don't worry, m'dear. My wife is a very loving woman and will be all over you like a mother hen."

Katey gave him a relieved grin, but she latched on to that remark about Sophie. "So you met my grandmother? My aunt wouldn't let me see her when I was there."

"Must be a habit of hers, barricading the door," Anthony said, trying to make light of it, but the memory drew a frown from him. "I'm afraid we had to push our way in. The information I was after was too important to be denied. But what did Letitia expect after informing me about you and demanding I keep you away from there? The tone of her note was practically an assumption that I already knew about you, when how could I? What a miserable, hateful—"

"No need to elaborate!" Katey laughed. "I agree! But as

for her assumption, well, that might have been my fault for mentioning to her that I was staying at Haverston. Which had been Judith's suggestion, you know. She was sure it would pave the way a little, since I was 'going to face the lions,' which was how she put it. Are you *sure* she's only seven? Her perception and intelligence are absolutely amazing for a child that age."

Anthony chuckled. "I know what you mean. She bowls me over constantly with some of the things she says, which is why it's always a relief to see her and Jack together and giggling like normal seven-year-olds. But I can see why her strategy might have backfired on you that day. Your aunt has always had something against me, or perhaps it was against my family, I was never sure which, and she kept it to herself. I have no clue what her problem is."

"I hope my grandmother isn't like her."

"Not in the least. She wasn't well, or I would have pressed her for more information. But she promised we would speak again in greater detail when she's better. I'll take you to visit her m'self. I'm sure you're as curious as I am, to find out why your mother ran off with you to America, instead of coming to me."

Those were halcyon days Katey spent with her father and uncle, and she was grateful for every little tidbit about the Malorys they cared to share with her, which was a lot! But when she lay in bed each night, alone, the only thing filling her mind was Boyd.

She had overreacted to his high-handedness. What had he done except get past her defenses, and she was glad he'd done that. She even remembered at that last dinner with him, before she got so intoxicated, that he'd suggested they spend a day at one of the island beaches they would soon be passing, and despite how wonderful that had sounded, she'd quickly declined, afraid, considering how she felt about Boyd, to spend any time alone with him. She'd been right to fear that! Look what had happened! But she wouldn't undo those hours with him, not for the world.

From the moment he'd mentioned marriage and her in the same breath, she had been too thrilled—which brought on the panic. Because she *knew* he would be the end of her trip, that she'd gladly give it up for him. Every one of the reasons she had given him for why they shouldn't marry were true, but she'd held them up to convince herself more than him. Because if she did give in, she knew she would regret it later. She had too many doubts not to expect regrets.

And while he'd been working his way deeply into her mind and heart from as far back as that first voyage with him to England, she was afraid that he didn't feel the same, that it was all just lust on his part. What had he ever said to her to make her think otherwise? Not that she hadn't experienced a lot of that herself. Her passion for that man amazed her. But she felt much more than that. And the very next day after he'd been left in the wake of *The Maiden George,* she'd already been missing him.

fifty

"HERE WE ARE, only a day behind them, and we didn't have to toss the cannon overboard," Tyrus said as he came to stand beside Boyd at the rail.

Boyd didn't take his eyes off the busy London wharf to glance down at the shorter man. *The Oceanus,* like many other ships anchored in the Thames, would have to wait its turn to dock, which would take days. That was why a skiff was already being lowered to take him and some of the crew ashore now. Not for the first time, he thought Skylark should buy a private dock away from the congestion of the city.

He knew Tyrus made the cannon remark to get a grin out of him. It didn't work.

"If I thought it would have got us here more quickly, I probably would have ordered the cannon tossed over the side. They probably arrived here more than a day ago— that was a damn fast ship Malory had. But it doesn't matter. Katey will be ensconced at her father's house, so there's no point in even trying to see her."

"Is that going to stop you?"

Now that *did* get a grin out of Boyd. "Not a chance. But you know how the Malorys are. I've grouched about them enough times to you. So I think I need a little ammunition on my side in the form of my sister. At least Georgie can keep James out of it. Anthony I can handle, but not him and his brother together."

"I hate to mention it, bucko, but your real opposition is going to be the little lady herself. I warned you not to sneak her off the ship like that, but having done so, you should have been straight up about it."

"I was going to tell her before you arrived at the island, but the pirates showed up first. Hell, the night I took her off the ship I didn't even think I'd get her all the way to shore before she woke up, but when I did, I was so relieved not to be in the middle of a very long argument with her that I relaxed and got some sleep myself. I only woke a little while before she did, so on the spur of the moment I spun a crazy tale to account for us being there. I figured she'd find it amusing later, since she's so good at spinning tales herself. She might even have thought it was romantic on my part." Tyrus snorted at that, to which Boyd added, "*Some* women might have seen it that way. Of course, I thought I'd have her agreement to marry me by then, too."

"Did you tell her that?"

"Hell no. Her finding out before I could mention it took all amusement out of it. Besides, she wasn't believing anything I said by then."

As soon as Katey left *The Oceanus* for *The Maiden George,* he'd regretted not having made a full confession to Katey. That's why he'd gotten so furious with the Malorys once he caught up to them, because they wouldn't even let him see her so he could tell her that. He still didn't think she'd believe him. She'd been too angry. But he'd wanted to at least try before the seasickness brought him to his knees.

But for the first time ever, he didn't get seasick as soon as his ship sailed. Was the extreme emotion he'd been in the throes of responsible for that? Or was it the beating Anthony had given him? No, he doubted the latter. He'd sailed before after having a good fight with one of his brothers, and a few aches and pains hadn't stopped the nausea from overtaking him then.

Besides, the punches that Anthony had delivered were nothing he couldn't shrug off. He'd had worse from his brothers. He might have been knocked out briefly, but he'd managed to easily block the punches that could have broken bones.

He'd expected much worse from Anthony, so he had a feeling the older man had held back, and the reason was pretty obvious. Anthony assumed he'd gotten there in time to stop "the seduction," so he'd just administered a mere warning with his fists.

But did they know now? It was possible. Katey had just spent a lot of time with them and could have mentioned it. Boyd could be walking right into a situation where his head would be blown off by an angry father. God, why did Katey have to turn out to be a Malory? It was bad enough when the family had merely been grateful to her for rescuing Judith. But now she was one of their own, and the Malorys went above and beyond when it came to family.

~~~~~~

"No," Georgina said flatly to Boyd a few hours later when he'd reached her house in Berkeley Square. "You're lucky I don't take a whip to you m'self. I'm not protecting you from James, not this time."

Which didn't bode well for Boyd if that was her first reaction to his remark. All he'd done was kiss her hello and tell her he might need her help. He should have taken better note of her surprise at his sudden presence in her parlor, as if she'd thought he wouldn't dare show his face there.

With a sigh, he sat down next to her on the sofa. "What did your husband tell you?"

"That you intended to seduce that sweet girl on that trip and they got her out of your clutches before you could. But then I already knew that was your intention when they sailed off after you. You should have seen Tony. He was a volcano about to erupt."

Boyd rolled his eyes. "Yes, I know. He erupted on me."

A moment of sisterly concern filled her expression. "Did he hurt you?"

"Not really."

"He's losing his touch?"

He had to laugh at that. "That's doubtful. But I'm guessing James failed to mention the seduction was his and Anthony's idea?"

She pointed a finger at him. "Don't you dare try that tactic with me, Boyd Anderson. You're not passing the buck."

He chuckled at her. "It's true, you know. I asked for their help, and seduction was the first thing that came to their minds, but then that *is* their forte, so that's understandable. But the fact is, I wanted to marry Katey before we even sailed off together. Hell, I wanted to marry her from the day I first met her!"

"Why didn't you tell me this before you sailed?" she demanded.

"Because I wanted Katey so much, I wasn't thinking straight back then."

Georgina gave him a disapproving look, but asked, "And that's not going to get in the way now?"

"No."

She gasped in understanding, "Oh my God, you better hope James doesn't find out."

"Find out what?" James asked from the doorway.

fifty-one

AT JAMES'S SUDDEN arrival Georgina immediately jumped to her feet and stood like a barricade between her husband and her brother. Not that that would have stopped James from getting at Boyd if he'd wanted to, which was why Boyd stood up and braced himself.

But James told his wife, "Relax, m'dear. I'm not going to bloody him in your presence."

"So I'm going to have to stay stuck to his side for the next year?" Georgina said in annoyance.

James raised a single golden brow. "It's that bad, what I don't know?"

She hedged. "Depends on how you look at it."

"And how would that be?" James asked.

She started to answer, then clamped her mouth shut and took on a mulish expression. James shrugged and casually entered the room, removing his gloves and tossing them on a nearby table. But James Malory's demeanor could be deceptive. The man could be in a towering rage and still look utterly emotionless.

He stopped in front of Boyd. Georgina didn't try to squeeze between them. She had his word that he wouldn't bloody Boyd. Nothing had been said about not breaking bones, though. Boyd didn't take a defensive stance, but he didn't relax his guard, either.

"Let's hear it," James said without expression.

"We were merely discussing Katey, which you've probably already guessed. And perhaps you can better answer this. She was willing to abandon my ship for yours to come back here, but is she now in a tearing hurry to be off on her world trip again?"

"Not a'tall. She's delighted with her new family and is content to remain in England to get to know us. At least for the duration of winter."

"Really?"

James apparently didn't like how pleased Boyd sounded over that information. "What bloody difference does it make?" he snapped.

"Because that gives me reason to believe she'll marry me now."

"Oh? And what makes you think the rest of us will have you?"

"James Malory," Georgina began warningly.

But Boyd burst out laughing. "It's bad enough I have to fight Katey tooth and nail, as it were, to get her to admit she loves me, but I have to fight the Malorys, too?"

"I've got news for you, Yank. We ain't admitting we love you—ever."

Boyd rolled his eyes. "You know what I meant. I want Katey for my wife. I believe you understood that before I left England with her."

"That was before she became my niece. Now that she is, you can't have her."

"It's not up to you, it's up to her."

"Care to place a wager on that?"

Boyd didn't lose his temper, the subject was too important. "Her only objection to marrying me is her damn world tour. She assumed, for whatever reason, that once she marries and has children that she can never travel again. But if she's willing to forgo her trip for an entire winter, then perhaps this reunion with a family she never knew she had has changed her priorities, or at least made her put a higher value on family."

"You think that makes a difference, do you?"

Boyd sighed. "James, she asked me if I'd wait for her. What does that tell you?"

"It tells me you and she had a pretty serious conversation. What else did you have?"

Boyd didn't answer. Georgina quickly squeezed between them to cup her husband's cheeks. James wasn't stupid. Boyd's silence was the answer he didn't want to hear.

"You know this changes everything," she told him. "It did for us, with my brothers. They let us marry—"

"Insisted," he cut in to correct.

Georgina pursed her lips. "Well, if we're going to get particular, *you* did—"

"Don't go there," James warned.

She smiled sweetly at her husband, despite his scowl. Boyd managed not to laugh at them. Did these two really think he and his brothers had never figured it out? James had forced their hand when he'd let them all know their sweet, innocent sister had shared his cabin—and a lot more—with him. And he did it deliberately.

"And what about Amy and Warren?" Georgina continued. "As soon as you and your brother found them in bed together, that changed your opposition to him, didn't it? You would have dragged them straight to the altar if

Amy hadn't stubbornly dug in her heels and insisted she wouldn't have him until he proposed to her."

"You made your point, George," James said with a sour look that he then turned on Boyd. "I'm going to assume you didn't have your way with her without her permission?"

"That isn't even close to amusing, Malory."

"It wasn't meant to be. And since your indignation answers that, then, yes, unfortunately, this does change everything. But don't think you'll convince Tony this easily. He's very touchy right now about this particular daughter. Years lost, regrets, self-blame—despite how smoothly she's fitting into his family, it's all still sitting on his shoulders."

"Yes, but you're going to be on Boyd's side in the argument, aren't you?" Georgina said smugly.

Up went one of James's golden brows. "Isn't it enough that *I'm* not going to kill him?"

fifty-two

KATEY LOOKED OUT the coach's window. The Millard mansion loomed ahead. The trees on the drive and all around the mansion were barren now, empty of leaves—like the lives inside that big house. Her father was taking her there. Roslynn had offered to come along. Judith had wanted to come, too, but Anthony wouldn't let them. He'd merely said it was something Katey and he had to do alone, but Katey suspected he was afraid that their visit would turn ugly and he didn't want to subject them to that. After all, they would have to get past Letitia again to see her grandmother.

Katey held Anthony's hand in the coach and repeated to herself over and over that this other family of hers, the Millards, weren't important to her anymore. She had his family now, and they had welcomed her into their lives wholeheartedly. From the moment she'd entered that house on Piccadilly and Judith had come running to latch on to her waist with the biggest hug she was capable of, Katey had been filled with such peace.

"I knew it, I knew it," Judith had exclaimed in bubbling delight. "There had to be a reason I liked you so much, and there was!"

"And how did you know," Katey asked with a warm smile. "I thought they weren't going to tell you."

Roslynn Malory had appeared to say, "Tony sent a runner to inform us that you were back. I felt I ought to prepare her, but it's a good thing you didn't take too long getting here! Welcome home, Katey."

Roslynn came over to hug her, too. Katey had cried. In that moment, she really felt that she had a home again. And Anthony came in mumbling something about females and their contrary tears of happiness.

It had been quite a homecoming. The Malorys drifted in and out that day and the next, all of them coming by to assure the newest member of their family just how glad they were to have her. She had no doubts after that, not one. And last night at the family dinner Roslynn had arranged, Katey got to meet one of Boyd's brothers as well, Warren, the other sibling of his that she was now related to by marriage!

What a surprise Warren Anderson turned out to be. Married to her cousin Amy, Edward's youngest daughter, Warren looked nothing like Boyd. Much older, much taller, she would never have guessed he was Boyd and Georgina's brother if she wasn't told. She wouldn't have guessed either that he was a part of this family, from some of the derogatory remarks she heard the Malory men sending his way.

"Back again, Yank? What a pity."

That had been James's remark, but Anthony was quick to join in: "You really should take longer trips—and leave Amy and the children at home. They might miss you a little, but we certainly won't."

"Might as well give it up," James told his brother. "He's too dense to catch the hint."

They sounded so serious, Katey was surprised enough to ask Roslynn about it when she caught her alone. "Why do the Malorys ridicule the Andersons?"

"We don't," Roslynn was quick to assure her. "It's mainly just Tony and James. Those two form a solid front against opposition, and, well, the Andersons did try to hang James when they first met him. They also beat him senseless. And despite hearing how their sister loved him, they tried to keep him and Georgina apart."

"I heard about that," Katey admitted.

Roslynn chuckled. "Well, you've seen how James is, so you might understand why they'd have reservations about entrusting their only sister to him. But while it may sound as if they hold him in contempt, they aren't serious about it these days, and Warren knows that."

Katey understood—somewhat. And since Warren was amused and simply laughed off the remarks, he obviously knew the Malory men weren't *really* trying to insult him.

This was the older brother that Boyd had held up as an example to her, of a man who took his wife and family to sea with him. And Amy, vivacious, perky, bubbly with happiness, apparently didn't mind that arrangement at all. She was the second female in the family who had those dark Gypsy looks from their ancestor the way Anthony did. But she had one other thing that was most odd.

Laughing about it, Amy said, "I don't really tell fortunes, it's just that I get very strong feelings."

"She had me rush us back to England because she sensed there was going to be a new Malory in the family," Warren added. "As usual, she was right."

"I thought it would be a new baby!" Amy chuckled. "But I'm glad it's you instead, Katey. You and I are going to be best friends, you know," she said with absolute confidence, then she leaned forward to whisper, "Put that heartache away, m'dear. You're going to be more happy here than you realize. I've already bet on it."

Katey didn't find out until after Amy and Warren went home last night that Amy had never lost a bet in her life, that if she wanted something to happen, she merely had to bet on it and it would happen! Jeremy told Katey all about Amy's unusual ability and complained how often Amy had used those bets against him. Katey found the whole thing preposterous. A family joke, maybe, that she just hadn't heard the punch line to yet?

But Amy's remark about heartache had been too close to the mark, yet how could she know that Katey had stood for hours on the small balcony outside her room after she retired her first night there, watching, waiting, hoping for Boyd's arrival, and she did it again last night! With two days come and gone since her return to London, she was beginning to fear that he wasn't going to come back to England at all, that the angry things she'd said to him about never wanting to see him again had convinced him to give up on her.

But no one in the family knew that she had those fears, so Amy couldn't know! Katey let them see only her happiness to be there and be a part of the family, because that happiness was very real.

And then Anthony informed her over breakfast that morning that as soon as they'd docked, he'd immediately sent a man to Havers Town to find out Sophie's condition from her doctor. "I wouldn't put it past Letitia to try to claim your grandmother still isn't well enough for a visit. And the doctor informed me she is well. As hale and hearty as a woman her age can be. So if you'd like to head to Haverston today, I already told Ros to pack us for an extended visit."

They left London before noon, Anthony, Roslynn, Judy, and herself. They didn't arrive at Haverston until almost evening, though. Anthony suggested they wait until morning to ride over to the Millards, but Katey didn't want to wait. It wasn't quite dark yet and she wanted to see her grandmother right away so she could enjoy a few days at Haverston without this meeting looming over her.

She had thought she didn't need anything anymore to fill in the gaping hole in her life that her mother's death had left, because she had the Malorys now. But the same anxiety that had been present the last time she'd approached this mansion was back again. She'd been kidding herself. Deep down, she still wanted her mother's family to be part of her life.

fifty-three

"I'M SURE YOU'LL be delighted to know that as soon as Mother was feeling better, she gave me a severe setdown."

Those were the first words Letitia Millard said as she opened the door and extended her arm with an exaggerated flourish to usher Anthony and Katey inside. The exaggeration made it apparent that it wasn't her choice to let them into the house.

Anthony had promised he'd be on his best behavior for Katey's sake. She wasn't really sure what that meant, but it included a cordial nod to Letitia and the remark "Would it help to know I have relatives I'd prefer to shut the door on as well?"

"Sympathy, Malory? Keep it," Letitia said bitterly. "You know exactly where we stand."

"No, *you* do, I don't. But, that's why I'm here, ain't it? To find out."

Letitia made a sound of disgust and marched into the parlor. They followed her. And there sat Sophie Millard, Katey's only living grandmother. Katey's eyes and expression filled with wonder. Sophie wasn't nearly as old as she'd expected. She was merely in her midsixties. Her black hair was only just starting to turn gray. Her emerald eyes still held a lively sparkle. And Katey saw her mother so clearly. Had Adeline lived to this age, this is how she would have looked, Katey was sure.

A tightness filled her chest and throat, then the tears started. She wanted to run forward and hug Sophie, but her feet were rooted to the spot. Sophie might have dealt politely with Anthony and James when they'd visited a few weeks ago, but they were of the same social class as her. Katie feared that Sophie might treat her the same as Letitia had.

Oblivious of the emotion that was choking Katey, Anthony seemed just as surprised by Sophie's appearance and said, "Madam, you look splendid, years younger than you did in your sickbed."

Sophie chuckled at him. "What an odd compliment, but thank you nonetheless, Sir Anthony."

She hadn't even glanced at Katey yet, but that was Anthony's fault. Quite unintentionally, he frequently captured women's attention because he was incredibly handsome, so it was understandable that Sophie's eyes had gone to him when they walked in.

Sophie looked at Katey now and her eyes widened. There was no need for introductions. They had both recognized each other instantly.

"Good God."

That was all Sophie said. The seconds passed, an eternity in Katey's mind. She couldn't breathe. She was going to make a complete ninny of herself and faint.

And then she heard what she'd prayed to hear. "Come here, child."

Sophie was holding out her arms. Katey needed no other encouragement. She flew across the room, dropping to her knees on the floor in front of Sophie and putting her arms around her grandmother's waist, her cheek to her breasts. She was tall enough to manage it, and her tears came in earnest now as her grandmother hugged her back.

"None of that," Sophie scolded gently. "Stop those tears. You can't imagine how much I've longed for this moment, to finally meet you. Sit up here and let me see you."

Katey moved up onto the sofa with an embarrassed smile. She wiped one side of her cheek with her fingers; Sophie wiped the other side.

"Oh my, look at you," Sophie said in amazement. "You have her eyes. You have our dimples."

They both grinned, making those dimples more prominent. They were quite a bit deeper on Sophie's cheeks due to the looser skin of her advanced years, but this was where Katey had inherited hers from.

Anthony complained as he took a seat across from them, "I wish *I'd* seen the resemblance sooner. When I met Katey after her arrival in London, neither of us had any idea."

"A mother sees things differently, and a grandmother does as well," Sophie told him. "And shame on you, sir. When you implied you would be back for answers, you should have told me you would be bringing my granddaughter with you."

"That wasn't a guarantee. I had to find her first. She'd left England."

"Ah, very well, then you're forgiven."

Anthony raised a brow at Letitia before he said to Sophie, "It's beginning to sound as if you weren't told that Katey came here on her own, and instead of being made welcome, she was shown the door and told never to come back?"

"No, Letty only admitted her rudeness to you and your brother."

All eyes were on Letitia now. The woman didn't look the least bit embarrassed. In fact, her expression turned mulish when she said in her defense, "You have been in a decline ever since that solicitor you retained in America sent word of Adeline's death. Three times you've been sick enough to summon the doctor since then. This mourning has to stop. It's killing you! And *she*"—Letitia pointed an accusing finger at Katey—"would have just made it worse. She's going to bring back all the regrets and recriminations—"

"Stop it," Sophie cut in. "I'm not the one with regrets. I'm not the one who chased Adeline away. And my mourning began the day she left England."

Before their arguing got any worse, Katey said, "Why did she leave? She told me you had disowned her, but I'm beginning to think it was the other way around."

"I'm sure you're right," Sophie said with a heartfelt sigh. "Adeline's mistake was in going to her sister for advice about the baby instead of coming to me. With six years' difference in their ages, they had never been close. And Adeline didn't know that Letty had already convinced us that Sir Anthony was just amusing himself with her while he was at Haverston for the holidays."

"I sensed that your husband didn't think I was serious," Anthony said. "That he was just humoring me."

"Indeed, we all thought you'd get bored soon enough and hie yourself back to London. That a baby was the result instead seemed to support Letty's contention that you were just a rake, and she went straight to my husband, Oliver, with the news. What followed happened so quickly, all in the same day, I never even had a chance to assure Adeline that I would support whatever decision she made. I never dreamed that decision would be to leave home."

"But why didn't she come to me?" Anthony demanded.

"Oh, she was going to. Never doubt it. That was her first answer when Oliver gave her *his* heartless solution, that she'd be sent off to have the baby in secrecy, then be forced to give it away. They overwhelmed her with their anger when she protested. My husband, and Letitia especially, placed so much guilt and shame on her shoulders, it was a wonder she was able to make any decision at all that day. When she said she would go to you, my husband locked her in her room. But Letitia, with all the animosity she had for your family, went to her and warned her that you'd never marry her, that you'd only been toying with her. Adeline must have believed her."

"That isn't true," Anthony insisted.

"It doesn't matter if it was or not if she believed it long enough to decide on the action she took instead."

"But I wanted to marry her!"

"Did you tell her that?"

"No, I hadn't yet told her. I was working up to it. I wanted to court her properly first."

"And seduce her!" Letitia interjected, garnering a flush from Anthony.

Sophie shook her head sadly. "I doubt it would have mattered to my husband that your intentions were honorable. Letitia was Oliver's favorite, and she managed to fire his anger against your family from the day you first came to call, enough that he wouldn't consider a match there even if you had asked. She trotted out every scandal associated with your family that she'd been able to dredge up, that the marquis was raising a bastard as his heir, the duels James had been involved in over women, that you had already had numerous scandalous affairs since you moved to London, proving you hadn't gone there to look for a wife, that you were instead following in the rakish footsteps of your brother James."

"There was no need for James or I to marry when both of our elder brothers had male heirs by then," Anthony said in his defense. "I certainly had no plan to do so *before* I met Adeline. Falling in love with her changed that." Anthony's eyes suddenly narrowed. "Why was that allowed to even happen? If you all thought the worst of me, why didn't you just show me the door to begin with?"

Sophie admonished him, "You're a Malory. Do you really need to ask that? Oliver didn't want to insult your family. And besides, we thought you'd get bored soon enough and return to London."

"Adeline gave no clue a'tall that any of you had bad feelings toward my family. Why is that?"

"Because she didn't know, not until that day we learned of the baby. Prior to that, my husband feared that *she* would end up insulting you, she was so young and impulsive back then. So she was merely warned not to put much stock in your attention, that you were merely being neighborly. It was stressed that you weren't in the market for a wife. And we waited, and hoped, that you would just go away."

Anthony raked an agitated hand through his hair. "Good God, she should have known I would protect her and our baby from her father's heartless plans. I still don't understand why she didn't take the chance to come to me."

"Because she believed me that you wouldn't marry her, and why wouldn't she?" Letitia said haughtily. "It was the truth as it appeared, that your only interest was in racking up conquests back then. She was devastated, of course, but that was no more than she deserved for shamelessly succumbing to your seduction. And while our reactions may seem heartless to you, you know as well as I that intentions are meaningless if no one knows of them other than you. You had done nothing in your life up to that point to suggest that you weren't fast on your way to becoming a rakehell, which, as we're all aware, you more than succeeded at for many a year."

Even Katey knew that her father couldn't deny that, but Sophie took pity on him. "That was merely assumed, Sir Anthony, but these are the only facts that tell the story. My husband and Letty were checking on Adeline constantly, several times an hour, to make sure she was still locked in her room. A servant was even dispatched to keep watch on Haverston and put you off from visiting that day, if need be. Adeline knew that. So even if she had faith in you despite what Letty had told her, she obviously thought they could find her quickly if she went to Haverston. And she'd been told that Oliver was going to take her by ship to the Continent the very next morning to get her far away from you, that she wouldn't be coming home until after her bastard was no longer an embarrassment to our family. He never guessed how desperate she was to keep the child. Despite their close watch on her, she escaped out her window. We never saw her again. I had one letter from her telling me that she'd married and was going to raise her child in America. I never forgave my husband for driving her away from us."

"You never forgave me either," Letitia said bitterly, with a glimpse of hurt in her expression.

"Of course I did. You were both my daughters. I didn't pick favorites like your father did. And you were miserable enough already. You didn't need me adding to that with recriminations. How many times did I tell you to let it go, to release the past and get on with your life? But you never stopped hating the world for the bad hand you'd been dealt. But what *is* going to stop is your making decisions for me. Did it not occur to you even once that Katey's presence in our lives might help to heal those old wounds? How could you turn her away without even telling me?"

"You were sick!"

"That doesn't wash, my girl, and you know it."

"She's a Malory," Letitia snarled. "They'll never be welcome here!"

"Ah, to the heart of it," Anthony said, and his expression turned distinctly menacing, as did his tone when he added, "Care to let the Malorys know why we're so detested? Scandals don't generate this kind of personal malice."

fifty-four

THE SILENCE IN the room was thick with anger as Anthony and Letitia stared at each other balefully. Sophie glanced between them with annoyance. She was still rightly holding Katey's hand in her lap, almost as if restraining Katey from joining the fray.

"Are you going to tell them, Letty, or must I?" Sophie finally said when no response from her daughter was forthcoming.

Letitia clamped her mouth shut tighter, looking furious. She didn't want anything said, wanted her secret kept. Sophie obviously disagreed and had the last word on it.

But as if emotions weren't high, Sophie casually inquired, "How old were you, Letty, when you fell in love with him?"

"Fourteen," Letty mumbled.

"Too young. It should have faded away. She rarely saw him to foster it. But it hung on and got stronger."

It wasn't apparent whom Sophie was speaking to. Herself, the room at large? Her eyes remained sadly on her daughter.

Anthony, glancing between them, burst out, "You can't be suggesting she was in love with *me*!"

Sophie glanced at him and chuckled. "Goodness, no, you were still a child yourself back then. It was your brother Jason who caught her eye and her heart from the moment she first saw him."

Incredulous, Anthony said, "Serious, no-nonsense Jason? He's been the head of our family since he was eighteen. He never had time to socialize, much less think about romance."

"Well, he was quite the dashing figure back then. And Letty haunted Havers Town with the mere hope that he might make one of his rare appearances in town and give her a chance to speak with him."

Anthony's eyes widened. "I think I was with him one of those times. She stopped us to chat. I remember thinking she was wearing her heart on her sleeve, but Jason didn't notice it."

At the reminder of how insignificant she'd been in the eyes of her love, Letitia snarled, "He never noticed! Half the times I spoke to him, he had to be reminded who I was!"

"You expected more?" Anthony scoffed. "You weren't even out of the schoolroom yet. Besides, between raising the rest of us and running the estate, Jason always had too much on his mind."

"I think you misunderstand, Sir Anthony," Sophie said in a soothing tone that brought back a degree of calmness to the room. "This went on for years, even beyond her introduction to society. Letty had her come-out in Gloucester when she was eighteen. She tried to get out of it, but Oliver insisted. For two Seasons she ignored all offers. All she wanted was to come home so she could be near Jason again, even if she only managed to see him a few times a year. After two unsuccessful Seasons, Oliver stopped insisting."

"Why didn't she just tell Jason how she felt?" Anthony asked.

"It may not seem like it now, but she used to be quite shy. Besides, a lady is never that bold. You know that as well as I."

"When it's ruining their life, maybe they should be," Anthony replied.

"I was going to," Letitia admitted in a low voice. "I begged mother to invite him to dinner. It was a mistake. All he did was talk about his flowers and crops, which my father wasn't the least bit interested in, and he swore afterwards that we wouldn't be doing that again."

"I take it your parents didn't know about this great love you harbored?" Anthony asked Letitia.

"Of course not. And I never did manage to speak with him alone that evening."

"Why didn't you give up by then?" Anthony asked carefully. "My brother apparently gave you no encouragement a'tall, barely even knew you were alive. Why did you cling to hope that that would change?"

"Because I loved him! Even when we heard about his bastard and that he was going to raise him and make him his legal heir, I continued to love him. It was an indiscretion that obviously meant nothing to him, since he didn't marry the boy's mother, whoever she was. Then your sister died and he ended up raising her daughter as well. That was a fine thing he did, but the two youngsters were getting out of hand. And that's when he cut out my heart!" Letitia snarled. "Instead of looking closer to home for a wife who would be a mother to them, he called in a favor and brought home Frances instead, an earl's daughter. I'm an earl's daughter! I would have loved those children and been the perfect mother to them!"

"So he made a mistake in Frances," Anthony had to allow.

"A mistake? Is that what you call it? She despised him. Her father forced her into the marriage, but she didn't honor it. The whole neighborhood knew what a horrible match that was! They lived estranged all those years until he chalked up yet another scandal for your family when he divorced her."

Letitia's scathing tone made Anthony reply defensively, "So because you didn't have the gumption to state your case and at least make yourself a little more memorable to my brother before he was faced with needing an immediate wife—"

"How dare you!"

He raised a brow. "I'm a Malory, remember? You've already tarred me as scandalous, so I'll bloody well state it as I see it. Jason *was* desperate for a wife back then when our niece started turning into a hoyden. If you'd had the guts to go after what you wanted, instead of waiting for it to happen with no real effort on your part, then he might have remembered you when he was looking for a wife who would be a mother for the two young 'uns."

"You, sir, lived too long in the jaded bowels of London," Letitia shot back. "You no longer have any notion what a true lady must adhere to."

Anthony was obviously holding back a laugh. "Fine," he said in agreement. "You are quite right and I beg your pardon. You hold your tongue and hope for the best, which keeps you from even entering Jason's mind when he must pick a wife. So he ends up making the worst choice possible, when he could have had you instead. You're absolutely right, Letitia. Your ladylike way of keeping your feelings a secret was the better way."

Bright red shot up her cheeks, Letitia was so angry. "You're despicable!"

"Wait, let me finish first, and possibly you can come up with an epithet I haven't been reviled with yet."

"I'm sure that isn't possible."

"Touché! But what would you call your own actions, Letitia? Sterling? Without reproach? You know, Jason didn't want to marry back then. He didn't have time for a wife. But he made the sacrifice for the children's sake, to give them a mother. Because he didn't pick you for the role, your love for him turned to hate. And you painted his whole family with the same brush, hating us all by association, and made sure your father did, too. Under normal circumstances, your father would have come banging at my door and demanded I do right by his daughter, which I would have been delighted to do. But you made sure that wasn't going to happen. Was it jealousy, Letitia? You couldn't stand it that Adeline might win a Malory when you couldn't?"

She just glared daggers at him. Anthony shook his head in disgust. Katey, who'd kept silent as she listened to all that bile being tossed around, finally felt some herself. This was her mother who had been put through that hell back then, of being told she could bear her child, but couldn't keep it. Katey couldn't begin to imagine what that must have been like. And for what? An unrequited love that had turned Letitia so sour and bitter that she wanted everyone else to be as miserable as she was?

Katey stared at the woman responsible, who had spread her heartache around for everyone to share. "You made sure my mother couldn't marry the man she wanted to marry. You forced her to run away to another country, to abandon her home permanently just so she could keep her child. Did she have to be as unhappy as you, Letitia? Was that really necessary? She was your only sister!"

Letitia stiffened at this new accusation. "Look at me! I'm forty-six years old. I've never known the touch of a man. I've never even held a baby in my arms. Jason Malory took every ounce of love that I ever had, leaving none for me to give to another man. But I didn't want her to be unhappy. I never wanted that!"

Letitia suddenly ran out of the room. Katey didn't miss the tears in her aunt's eyes and felt a pang of remorse for causing them. Sophie was squeezing her own eyes tightly closed, holding in the pain she felt for her daughter.

Softly she said, "If it's any consolation, she doesn't like the way she is. She cries herself to sleep often. She thinks I don't know."

"I would as soon my brother never be told that he was unknowingly the cause of all this grief," Anthony said.

"But he wasn't," Sophie assured him. "A man can't be blamed for something that isn't even remotely his fault. He never knew. To him, Letty was just a neighbor he saw occasionally in passing. He had no idea that she harbored such tremendous feelings for him. I didn't know until years later myself, when she finally confessed all that to me. But maybe you should know this. It wasn't malice on her part. It wasn't even because of Jason. Yes, she had all those scandals from your family to use as ammunition to make her case, but it was simply you. She honestly thought that you would be an unfaithful husband, which would make Adeline unhappy in the end."

"She couldn't know that!" Anthony protested.

"No, but the path you took had already begun. You had already had a taste of the sophisticated side of London. By all accounts, you were following in your wild brother's footsteps. And you went on to become London's most notorious rake for more than a decade, which seemed to prove that she was right. While you might have been in the throes of first love and had the best of intentions, how long would that have lasted, Sir Anthony? Can you honestly say you would have been a faithful husband at that young age?"

Anthony opened his mouth, then slowly closed it. He sat back thoughtfully for a few moments, then finally raised his brow at Sophie.

"You've made your point, madam. A good one. While I love my wife, Roslynn, with all my heart and would never dream of being unfaithful to her, as you say, I spent more'n a decade sowing my oats, so I was quite ready to settle into matrimony with her. All those years ago with Adeline, who can say? Exemplary husband or worst husband imaginable? No, I can't honestly say which I would have been."

Sophie nodded and squeezed Katey's hand a little more. "It was an unfortunate event in our lives. But this lovely child came of it, and we can be grateful for that."

Anthony smiled at Katey. "Indeed, we can. Her mother didn't come home, but Katey has and is finally a member of my family. Thank you for giving us the answers we were missing. I would like to read that letter you had from Adeline, if you wouldn't mind?"

"I'm afraid I can't oblige you in that. I threw it away. It was too heartbreaking and I was rereading it too often. She blamed me as well, you see. And although I sent her countless letters m'self, begging her to come home and bring her new family with her, she never answered any of them. So I can only assume she never forgave me."

"Don't assume that," Katey said quickly. "In fact, that

she let you know she was all right and where she ended up speaks for itself. She didn't want you to worry. As for not writing again, I don't think she ever read your communications. She used to toss unopened letters into the fireplace. I can only guess that she didn't want to be reminded of her old life, when she was content with her new one."

Sophie hugged Katey for that. "We have so much to talk about, m'dear. Perhaps you'd like to stay here for a while so we can have a good visit?"

Katey would have liked that, but Anthony declined for her. "We're staying at Haverston, so she can ride over again tomorrow. She's only just entered my life, so my protective instincts are currently running rampant." He smiled to make light of it, but he was unmistakably serious. Unsaid was that he didn't want her having any more confrontations with Letitia. "For the time being, I would prefer to keep her close at hand, you understand."

fifty-five

IT WAS QUITE late when Anthony and Katey returned to Haverston. Sophie had insisted they stay for dinner, and Anthony couldn't refuse yet another suggestion of hers. Nor did they leave directly afterward. Katey and Sophie had too much to talk about that wasn't painful, and Letitia had thankfully not joined them again to put a damper on the remainder of the evening.

Settled into the coach, his arm around her shoulders in a paternal, protective fashion, Anthony was a bit hesitant in asking his daughter, "You're not upset with what you learned today?"

"No, actually, I'm relieved. I have a vivid imagination. I had expected much worse."

"I'll send Sophie an invitation to come to Haverston tomorrow—alone. I'd rather not expose Ros and Judy to Letitia, but I think they'd both enjoy meeting your grandmother. From some of the things she said tonight, I have the feeling Letitia has scared off most of their visitors over the years, so the old gal might appreciate the stimulation of a small gathering as well as being around children again."

"You're probably right. But I don't expect to avoid Letitia indefinitely. In fact, I expect her to get used to me eventually and lose some of her abrasiveness."

"You're more optimistic than I." He chuckled.

As late as it was, someone had waited up for them—the lights at the front of the house were still lit. It was probably Roslynn. She'd been dying of curiosity about what had happened all those years ago and had even pouted a little when Anthony refused to let her come along for the visit. He was surprised to find James in the wide entryway instead, leaning against the parlor doorway, brandy in hand.

"I was beginning to think you were staying the night at the Millards," James remarked.

Anthony grinned. "Didn't expect to see you here, old man. A little too curious to wait until we returned to London?"

James scoffed. "I was due for a visit with the elder. Haven't seen him since I got back from the Caribbean, you know, and then I sailed again with you."

"Sure," Anthony replied doubtfully, since he knew Jason had sent word to the family that he was coming to London next week for a visit.

But James wasn't quite done with his explanation. "And I brought the Yank with me."

Anthony stiffened. "Boyd? What the deuce did you do that for?"

But before James could answer, Katey gasped, "Boyd's here? Where?"

"When it looked like you weren't coming back tonight, he took himself off to bed, mumbling something about wanting to be fresh and clear—"

"That sounds like a good idea for me as well." Katey actually ran the stairs, shouting back at them, "Good night, you two!"

Anthony frowned as he watched her go. James started chuckling before he said, "Why am I not surprised?"

Anthony glared at his brother. "Surprised about what,

that she doesn't even greet you before she runs off? And how dare you bring that bounder—?"

"Put a lid on it, puppy." James came forward and shoved his brandy into Anthony's hand. "Drink that. You're going to need it when you hear what I have to tell you, or didn't you notice how her face lit up at the mere mention of his name?"

~~~~~~~

Katey's heart was racing. He'd come. For her. She didn't doubt it, and she didn't doubt either that he was filled with anxiety, still thinking he'd have to do battle to win her love. She wasn't going to let him spend another anxious moment.

She knew which rooms her family were in, so she knew which ones had been empty and were available to Boyd. The first one she checked was the right one—at least it was occupied. She had to wait for her eyes to adjust to the darkness before she could be positive. It wasn't cold enough yet for the fireplace to be lit.

She closed the door softly behind her and took several deep breaths. Just being in the same room with him again filled her with soothing peace. And it didn't take long for her to see well enough to approach the bed.

He was lying on his back, one arm thrown behind his head, his gold-streaked hair across one brow. His chest was naked, the blanket only covering him to his waist. Katey felt less peaceful when she noticed that. His mouth was slightly open, but he wasn't snoring. She heard only the deep, even breathing of sleep. He'd wanted to be fresh and clearheaded before he spoke to her in the morning. She couldn't wait that long.

She slipped out of her shoes and her clothes, leaving them in a pile next to the bed. She wasn't feeling at all peaceful now. She was getting quite excited and was surprised she'd been able to pause long enough to undress. But then she lay down on the bed next to Boyd and curled against his side. It didn't wake him, not even when she touched his chest. She was content to do just that for a few moments, but only for a few. She leaned closer, blew softly toward his ear to tickle him awake—and knew to the second when it worked and he realized he wasn't alone.

He turned toward her. She kissed him before he could say anything. If for some reason she'd been wrong and he didn't still want her, she didn't want to know it. But his body still wanted her. She had to resist the urge to laugh in sheer delight at how quickly his kiss turned hot and possessive, then was amazed at how fast her own body responded.

"Lavender—you have such a unique smell, Katey," he said dreamily as he cupped her cheek, then her shoulder. But then he groaned as his hand moved lower and he realized she was naked. "God, don't wake me. Or have I gone to heaven?"

He'd said something similar to her once before. "You're not sleeping," she replied. "But this is definitely heavenly, isn't it?"

He groaned and kissed her again. He struggled to get out from under the blanket without breaking that kiss, but soon he was lying on top of her, and her legs instinctively wrapped around him to keep him there. His lust had always been a problem. She had a feeling hers might be one now. She wanted him so much, too much to wait.

Apparently, he needed more. "You can't give me this and not marry me."

"I know." She kissed him again.

"You mean it?"

"We'll talk later!"

He grinned down at her impatience. "At least you finally understand what it's like—"

She gripped his hair and almost growled at him, "If you don't make love to me *right* now—"

With that look that had always been able to singe her, he said, "God, I love you so much, Katey," as he slid deep into her, satisfying her core need to have him there, satisfying her desire quickly after that, and satisfying her yearning heart with those impassioned words that had come from the bottom of his.

He held her gently in his arms afterward, as if she might break. "Did you mean it?" he asked her carefully.

Her passion spent, she only felt tenderness now and was overflowing with it. She turned to cup his cheek in her hand and look into his eyes before she said, "I learned tonight how horrible a life can turn out just because a few simple words were never said. They might have changed nothing, or they might have changed everything. But I'm not going to make the same mistake. Come what may, Boyd, I love you. So the next time I say I'm married, it's going to be true."

"You won't regret it, I promise you." He kissed each finger of her hand. "We have the rest of our lives to see the world. It isn't necessary to see it all in one year or two. When our children are older, they'll even enjoy it. They'll have experiences that you missed as a child, be able to see the world with their own eyes, and not just hear about it or read about it."

Tears nearly entered her eyes, she was so moved by how much he wanted to make her happy. "You'd do that for me, even as sick as sailing makes you? But it's no longer necessary. I was searching for excitement, new things, adventure, but it was all only to fill the void in my life, and to make up for the boredom of my youth. I don't need that anymore, Boyd, now that I have you."

Amy had warned her, *You're going to be more happy here than you realize.* Katey didn't doubt it now. She had the large family she'd always yearned for, and now she was ready to enlarge it even more with the man she loved. *That* was an exciting thought. *That* was going to be the adventure of her life.

~~~~~~~~~

In the morning Katey and Boyd went downstairs together to share their wonderful news with her family. Most of the Malorys were gathered in the parlor. Anthony and James were there with their wives enjoying some morning pastries. Jacqueline and Judith had their heads together whispering, both able to fit in the same armchair. They stopped to stare wide-eyed when they saw the couple come in, holding hands, smiling.

Anthony noticed them immediately as well and slowly stood up. He didn't need to ask what was going on after his talk with James. And he waited silently for the couple to reach him. Only Georgina and Roslynn looked concerned over what he might say or do. Apparently, it wasn't a foregone conclusion yet.

But Anthony put his hands on Katey cheeks and said, "Are you sure this is what you want? I can still kill him myself instead if it isn't."

Boyd snorted, but Katey gave her father a beautiful smile, her dimples in full view, and replied, "Love me, love my husband."

Anthony groaned. "So it's to be like that, is it?"

James chuckled behind him. "She's a Malory. Did you expect anything less?"

Don't miss the next installment of
the "irresistible" (*Booklist*)
Malory-Anderson Family series

THAT
PERFECT
SOMEONE

Available now from Pocket Books!

Keep reading for a sizzling sneak peek. . . .

one

IT MIGHT SEEM odd to consider Hyde Park your own backyard, but Julia Miller did. Growing up in London, she'd ridden there almost daily for as long as she could remember, from her very first pony when she was a child to the thoroughbred mares that followed. People waved at her whether they knew her or not, simply because they were so used to seeing her there. The *ton*, shop clerks cutting across the park on their way to work, gardeners, they all noticed Julia and treated her like one of their own.

Tall, blond-haired, and fashionably dressed, she always returned the smiles and waves. She was generally a friendly sort and people tended to respond to that in kind.

Even more odd than Julia's considering such a mammoth park her personal riding grounds were her circumstances. She'd grown up in the upper-crust end of town but her family wasn't upper-crust at all. She lived in one of the larger town houses in Berkeley Square, because it wasn't only the nobility who could afford those town houses. In fact, her family, who acquired their surname in the Middle Ages when a craftsman took on the name of his trade, had been among the first to buy and build in Berkeley Square back in the mid-1700s when the square was first laid out, so Millers had been living there for many generations now.

Julia was well-known and well liked in the neighborhood. Her closest friend, Carol Roberts, was a daughter of the nobility, and other young women of the *ton* who knew her through Carol, or from the private finishing school she'd attended, liked her as well and invited her to their parties. They weren't the least bit threatened by her pretty looks or deep pockets because she was already engaged to be married. She'd been engaged nearly since birth.

"Fancy meeting you here," a female voice said behind her. Carol Roberts rode up, and her mare fell into an easy trot beside Julia's.

Julia chuckled at her petite, black-haired friend. "That should have been my remark. You rarely ride anymore."

Carol sighed. "I know. Harry frowns on it, especially since we're trying to have our first child. He doesn't want me to take any chance of losing it before we even know it's been conceived."

Julia knew that horseback riding could indeed cause miscarriages. "Then why are you taking that risk?"

"Because a baby didn't get conceived this month," Carol said with a disappointed pursing of her lips.

Julia nodded sympathetically.

"Besides," Carol added, "I have so missed our rides together, I'm willing to defy Harry for these few days when I'm having my monthlies and we won't be trying to conceive."

"He wasn't home to find out, was he?" Julia guessed.

Carol laughed, her blue eyes sparkling mischievously. "No indeed and I'll be home before he is."

Julia didn't worry that her friend would get into trouble with her husband. Harold Roberts adored his wife. They'd known and liked each other before Carol's first season three years ago, so no one had been surprised when they got engaged within weeks of Carol's debut and married a few months later.

Carol and Julia had been neighbors their whole lives, both living in Berkeley Square, their respective town houses side by side with no more than a narrow alley separating them. Even their bedroom windows had been directly across from each other—they'd arranged that!—so even when they weren't in the same house together visiting, they could talk from their windows without raising their voices. It was no wonder they'd become the best of friends.

Julia sorely missed Carol. While they still visited often when Carol was in London, she no longer lived next door. When she married, she'd moved into her husband's house, many blocks away, and every few months she and Harold spent weeks at his family's ancestral estate in the country. He was hoping they'd stay there permanently. Carol was still resisting that idea. Fortunately, Harold wasn't the sort of overbearing husband who made all the decisions without considering his wife's wishes.

They continued to ride side by side for a few minutes, but Julia had already been in the park for a hour, so she suggested, "Want to stop by the teahouse for ices on the way home?"

"It's too early in the morning and not warm enough yet for ices. I am famished though and have truly missed Mrs. Cables's morning pastries. Do you still have a breakfast buffet laid out in the mornings?"

"Of course. Why would that change just because *you* got married?"

"Harold refuses to steal your cook, you know. I've nagged and nagged him to at least try."

Julia burst out laughing. "He knows he can't afford her.

Every time someone tries to hire her away, she comes to me and I raise her wages. She knows where her bread is buttered."

Julia had been making decisions of that sort because her father, Gerald, could no longer make them. Her mother had never made them when she was alive. Helene Miller had never taken control of anything in her life, not even the household. She had been a timid woman afraid of offending anyone, even the servants. Five years ago she'd died in the carriage accident that had rendered Gerald Miller an invalid.

"How is your father?" Carol asked.

"The same."

Carol always asked and Julia's reply was rarely any different. He's lucky to be alive, the doctors had told her after they had shocked her with their prognosis that Gerald would never again be himself. His head had suffered too much trauma in the accident. While his bones, seven of which had been broken that day, had mended, his mind would not recover. The doctors had been blunt. They'd given her no hope. Her father would sleep and wake up normally, he could even eat if hand-fed, but he would never speak anything other than gibberish again. Lucky to be alive? Julia had often cried herself to sleep recalling that phrase.

And yet Gerald had defied his doctors' predictions. One time that first year after the accident, and then every few months after that, he would know, however briefly, who he was, where he was, and what had happened to him. So much rage and anguish had filled him the first few times this had occurred that his lucidity couldn't really be called a blessing. And he remembered! Each time he regained lucidity he was able to remember his prior periods of mental clarity. For a few minutes, a few hours, he was himself again—but it never lasted for long. And he never remembered anything of the dead time in between.

His doctors couldn't explain it. They'd never expected him to have coherent thoughts again. They still wouldn't give Julia any hope that he might someday fully recover. They called his moments of clarity a fluke. Such an occurrence was undocumented, never known to happen before, and they warned Julia not to expect it to happen again. But it did.

It broke her heart the third time her father was himself, when he asked her, "Where's your mother?"

She'd been warned to keep him calm if he ever "woke" again, and that meant not telling him his wife had died in the accident. "She's gone shopping today. You—you know how she loves to shop."

He'd laughed. It was one of the few things her mother had been decisive about, buying things she didn't really need. But Julia had still been in mourning herself, and it had been one of the hardest things she'd ever done, to smile that day and keep her tears at bay until her father slipped away again into that gray realm of nothingness.

Of course she'd consulted different doctors. And every time one of them told her that her father was never going to recover, she'd dismiss him and find a new doctor. She stopped doing that after a while. She'd kept the last one, Dr. Andrew, because he'd been honest enough to admit that her father's case was unique.

A little while later in the Millers' breakfast room, Carol was carrying her filled plate *and* the large basket of pastries to the table when she stopped in her tracks, having finally noticed the new addition to the room.

"Oh, good Lord, when did you do that?" Carol exclaimed, turning around to stare wide-eyed at Julia.

Julia glanced at the ornate box on top of the china cabinet that had caught Carol's attention. It was lined in blue satin and edged in jewels, and behind its glass cover sat a lovely doll. Julia took her seat at the table and managed not to blush.

"A few weeks ago," she replied, and motioned Carol to take a seat at the table. "I came upon this fellow who'd just opened a shop near one of ours. He makes these beautiful boxes for items people want to preserve, and that doll is one thing I don't ever want to fall apart due to old age, so I commissioned that box for her. I just haven't decided yet where to place her, since my room is so cluttered. But I'm getting used to her being in here."

"I didn't know you still had that old doll I gave you," Carol said in wonder.

"Of course I do. She's still my prized possession."

It was true, not because Julia valued the doll so much, but because she valued the friendship it represented. Carol might not have given up the doll when they first met, but when she got a new one, instead of putting the old doll away in the attic, never to be seen again, she'd remembered that Julia had wanted it and had shyly offered it to her.

Carol blushed as they both remembered that day, but she finally chuckled. "You were such a little monster back then."

"I was never that bad," Julia snorted.

"You were! Screaming tantrums, bullying, demanding. You took offense at everything! You nearly punched me in the nose when we first met and would have, if I hadn't knocked you on your arse first."

"I was so impressed with that." Julia grinned. "You were the first person to tell me no."

"Well, I wasn't letting you have my favorite doll, not at our first meeting! You shouldn't even have asked for it. But really?" Carol said, surprised. "Never told no?"

"Yes, really. My mother was too weak and indecisive, well, you remember how she was. She always gave in to me. And my father was too kindhearted. He never said no to anyone, much less me. I even had a pony years before I was old enough to ride one, just because I asked for one."

"Aha! That's probably why you were such a little monster when we met. Spoiled beyond redemption."

"It wasn't that—well, maybe I was a little bit spoiled because my parents couldn't bring themselves to be firm with me, and my governess and the servants certainly weren't going to discipline me. But I didn't become a screaming, crying termagant until the day I met my fiancé. It was mutual hate at first sight. I didn't want to ever see him again. It was the first time my parents didn't let me have my way, so you could say I threw a tantrum about it that lasted for years! Until I met you, I didn't have any friends to point out to me how silly I was being. You helped me to forget about *him*, at least between the visits our parents forced on us."

"You changed quickly enough after we met. How old were we?"

"Six, but I didn't change that quickly, I just made sure you didn't witness any more of my tantrums—well, unless my fiancé came for a visit. Couldn't very well hide that animosity even if you were present, now could I?"

Carol laughed, but only because Julia was grinning over the remark. Julia knew her friend was aware that it hadn't been the least bit funny back then. Some of those fights with her fiancé had been quite violent. She'd almost bitten off his ear once! But it had been his fault. From their very first meeting when she was only five and had been so sure they would become the best of friends, he'd dashed those hopes with his rudeness and his resentment that she'd been handpicked for him. Every time they visited each other he would enrage her so that she'd want to fly at him and rip his eyes out. She didn't doubt that he'd instigated all those fights deliberately. The stupid boy somehow thought that *she* could end the engagement that neither of them wanted. She didn't doubt that he'd left England when he finally figured out that she had no more say in ending their betrothal than he did—and saved them both from a marriage made in hell. How odd to feel grateful to *him* for anything. But with him gone for good, she could see a little humor in what a terrible termagant she'd been—around him.

Julia nodded at their food, which was getting cold, but Carol shifted their conversation to a new subject. "I'm having a small dinner party this coming Saturday, Julie. You will come, won't you?"

The nickname had stuck since they were children, and even Julia's father had picked it up. She'd always thought it was silly to have a nickname that was just as long as her real name, but since it *was* one syllable shorter, she'd never minded.

She glanced at her friend over the scone she'd been about to bite into. "Have you forgotten that's the day of the Eden ball?"

"No, I just thought you might have come to your senses and begged off from that invitation," Carol said grouchily.

"And I was hoping you would have changed your mind and accepted the invitation."

"Not a chance."

"Oh, come on, Carol," Julia cajoled. "I hate dragging my wastrel cousin to these affairs, and he hates it, too. We no sooner step in the front door than he's already looking for the back door. He never sticks around. But you—"

"He doesn't need to stick around," Carol interrupted. "You'll know everyone there. You're never left alone for more'n a minute at parties. Besides, that marriage contract that the Earl of Manford keeps locked away means you don't even need a chaperone. A contract like that means you're as good as married already. Oh, good Lord, I didn't mean to bring that up again. I'm sorry!"

Julia managed a smile. "Don't be. You know you don't have to tiptoe around that distasteful subject with me. We were just laughing about it. Being that we hate each other, that fool I'm engaged to couldn't have done a nicer service for me than to fly the coop as he did."

"You felt that way before you reached the age to marry, but that was three years ago. You can't deny that being called an old maid doesn't infuriate you."

Julia burst out laughing. "Is that what you think? You forget I'm not an aristocrat like you, Carol. Labels like that are meaningless to me. What I find meaningful is having no one to answer to but myself. You can't imagine how wonderful that is. And it's official. The family wealth and holdings are all mine now—unless that bounder comes home."